Praise for
Kristen Heitzmann

"With a gifted pen, Kristen Heitzmann weaves a gripping tale of intense trials, and she peoples it with brave, ravaged souls who mold their limitations into blessings—and soar! Courageous. Remarkable. Insightful. *Indelible* is all that and more."
> —VICKI HINZE, award-winning author of *Deadly Ties*

"Kristen Heitzmann is a masterful storyteller. With compelling characters, lyrical prose, and spine-chilling suspense, she weaves another rich tapestry in *Indelible*."
> —COLLEEN COBLE, author of *Lonestar Angel*
> and the Rock Harbor series

"What she accordingly accomplishes here could be classified as rare and remarkable.... She creates scenes that are softly sensual and tension-filled, wrapped within a character-driven and ultimately uplifting mystery.... *Indivisible* is a strongly written work with a quirky and believable cast of characters and a plot that, though tightly woven, gives its protagonists room to breathe and grow. In fact, the people you will meet here are so memorable that you will want more of them, a prayer that hopefully will be answered in the near future."
> —BookReporter.com

"Heitzmann does a great job of weaving the back stories and too-present realities of each character into a unified tapestry of regret, hope, and redemption."
> —FictionAddict.com

INDELIBLE

KRISTEN HEITZMANN

author of *Indivisible*

INDELIBLE

A Novel

WATERBROOK
PRESS

INDELIBLE
PUBLISHED BY WATERBROOK PRESS
12265 Oracle Boulevard, Suite 200
Colorado Springs, Colorado 80921

Scripture quotations are taken from The Holy Bible, English Standard Version, copyright © 2001 by Crossway Bibles, a division of Good News Publishers. Used by permission. All rights reserved.

The characters and events in this book are fictional, and any resemblance to actual persons or events is coincidental.

Chapter epigraphs are taken from *Paradise Lost* by John Milton.

ISBN 978-1-4000-7310-8
ISBN 978-0-307-45923-7 (electronic)

Cover design by Kelly L. Howard

Published in the United States by WaterBrook Multnomah, an imprint of the Crown Publishing Group, a division of Random House Inc., New York.

WATERBROOK and its deer colophon are registered trademarks of Random House Inc.

The Cataloging-in-Publication Data is on file with the Library of Congress.

Printed in the United States of America
2011—First Edition

10 9 8 7 6 5 4 3 2 1

—

Dedicated to
Alfred Otto Heitzmann (1913–2011),
who enriched my life by his presence.

The unconquerable will,
And study of revenge, immortal hate,
And courage never to submit or yield.

nto his mind came thoughts. Sparks. Bright points of fire seared with blistering clarity. He touched the scars and found truth. Goodness and purity, like scales, fell away. He had cowered in shame and impotence, hating in silence. Now he walked to where the other lay, unsuspecting in sleep. His gaze slid from the slack face to his timid hands and what they held. All things wicked began in innocence.

One

A veined bolt of lightning sliced the ozone-scented sky as Trevor plunged down the craggy slope, dodging evergreen spires like slalom poles. Rocks and gravel spewed from his boots and caromed off the vertical pitch.

"Trevor." Whit skidded behind him. "We're not prepared for this."

No. But he hurled himself after the tawny streak. He was not losing that kid.

"He's suffocated," Whit shouted. "His neck's broken."

Trevor leaped past a man—probably the dad—gripping his snapped shinbone. Whit could help there. Digging his heels into the shifting pine needles, Trevor gave chase, outmatched and unwavering. His heart pumped hard as he neared the base of the gulch, jumping from a lichen-crusted stone to a fallen trunk. The cougar jumped the creek, lost its grip, and dropped the toddler. Yes.

He splashed into the icy flow, dispersing scattered leaves like startled goldfish. After driving his hand into the water, he gripped a stone and raised it. Not heavy, not nearly heavy enough.

Lowering its head over the helpless prey, the mountain lion snarled a spine-chilling warning. There was no contest, but the cat, an immature male, might not realize its advantage, might not know its fear of man was mere illusion. Thunder crackled. Trevor tasted blood where he'd bitten his tongue.

Advancing, he engaged the cat's eyes, taunting it to charge or run. The cat backed up, hissing. A yearling cub, able to snatch a tot from the trail, but unprepared for this fearless challenge. Too much adrenaline for fear. Too much blood on the ground.

With a shout, he heaved the rock. As the cat streaked up the mountainside, he charged across the creek to the victim. He'd steeled himself for carnage, but even so, the nearly severed arm, the battered, bloody feet...

His nose filled with the musky lion scent, the rusty smell of blood. He reached out. No pulse.

He dropped to his knees as Whit joined him from behind, on guard. He returned the boy's arm to the socket, and holding it there with one trembling hand, Trevor began CPR with his other. On a victim so small, it took hardly any force, his fingers alone performing the compressions. The lion had failed to trap the victim's face in its mouth. By grabbing the back of the head, neck, and shoulder, it had actually protected those vulnerable parts. But blood streamed over the toddler's face from a deep cut high on the scalp, and he still wasn't breathing.

Trevor bent to puff air into the tiny lungs, compressed again with his fingers, and puffed as lightly as he would to put out a match. *Come on.* He puffed and compressed while Whit watched for the cat's return. Predators fought for their kills—even startled ones.

A whine escaped the child's mouth. He jerked his legs, emitting a high-pitched moan. Trevor shucked his jacket and tugged his T-shirt off over his head. He tied the sleeves around the toddler's arm and shoulder, pulled the rest around, and swaddled the damaged feet—shoes and socks long gone.

Thunder reverberated. The first hard drops smacked his skin. Tenderly, he pulled the child into his chest and draped the jacket over as a different rumble chopped the air. They had started up the mountain to find two elderly hikers who'd been separated from their party. Whit must have radioed the helicopter. He looked up. This baby might live because two old guys had gotten lost.

———

In the melee at the trailhead, Natalie clutched her sister-in-law's hands, the horror of the ordeal still rocking them. As Aaron and little Cody were airlifted from the mountain, she breathed, "They're going to be all right."

"You don't know that." Face splotched and pale, Paige swung her head. Though her hair hung in wet blond strands, her makeup was weatherproof, her cologne still detectable. Even dazed, her brother's wife looked and smelled expensive.

"The lion's grip protected Cody's head and neck," one of the paramedics had told them. "It could have been so much worse."

Paige started to sob. "His poor arm. What if he loses his arm?"

"Don't go there." What good was there in thinking it?

"How will he do the stuff boys do? I thought he'd be like Aaron, the best kid on the team."

"He'll be the best kid no matter what."

"In the Special Olympics?"

Natalie recoiled at the droplets of spit that punctuated the bitter words. "He's alive, Paige. What were the odds those men from search and rescue would be right there with a helicopter already on standby?"

"We shouldn't have needed it." Paige clenched her teeth. "Aaron's supposed to be recovering. He would have been if you weren't such a freak."

"What?" She'd endured Paige's unsubtle resentment, but *"freak"*?

"Let me go." Paige jerked away, careening toward the SUV.

Natalie heard the engine roar, the gravel flung by the spinning tires, but all she saw was the hate in Paige's eyes, the pain twisting her brother's face as he held his fractured leg, little Cody in the lion's maw, the man leaping after…

She needed to clear the images, but it wouldn't happen here. Around her, press vans and emergency vehicles drained from the lot, leaving the scent of exhaust and tire scars in the rusty mud.

Paige had stranded her.

"Freak." Heart aching, she took a shaky step toward the road. It hadn't been that long a drive from the studio. A few miles. Maybe five. She hadn't really watched—because Aaron was watching for her.

Off the roster for a pulled oblique, he had seen an opportunity to finalize her venture and help her move, help her settle in, and see if she could do it. She'd been so thankful. How could any of them have known it would come to this?

———

Trevor's spent muscles shook with dumped adrenaline. He breathed the moist air in through his nose, willing his nerves to relax. Having gotten all they were going to get from him, most of the media had left the trailhead, following the story to the hospital. Unfortunately, Jaz remained.

She said, "You live for this, don't you?" Pulling her fiery red hair into a messy ponytail didn't disguise her incendiary nature or the smoldering coals reserved for him. He accepted the towel Whit handed him and wiped the rain from his head and neck, hoping she wouldn't see the shakes. The late-summer storm had lowered the temperature enough she might think he was shivering.

"Whose idea was it to chase?"

"It's not like you think about it. You just act."

Typing into her BlackBerry, she said, "Acted without thinking."

"Come on, Jaz." She couldn't still be on his case.

"Interesting your being in place for the dramatic rescue of a pro athlete's kid. Not enough limelight lately?"

"We were on another search."

She cocked her eyebrow. "You had no idea the victim's dad plays center field for the Rockies?"

"Yeah, I got his autograph on the way down." He squinted at the nearly empty parking lot. "Aren't you following the story?"

"What do you think this is?"

"You got the same as everyone. That's all I have to say."

"You told us what happened. I want the guts. How did it feel? What were you thinking?" She planted a hand on her hip. "Buy me a drink?"

He'd rather go claw to claw with another mountain lion. But considering the ways she could distort this, he relented. "The Summit?"

"I'd love to." She pocketed her BlackBerry and headed for her car.

Whit raised his brows at her retreat. "Still feeling reckless?"

"Sometimes it's better to take her head on."

"Like the cat?" Whit braced his hips.

"The cat was young, inexperienced."

"You didn't know that."

"There was a chance the child wasn't dead."

"What if it hadn't run?"

"If it attacked, you'd have been free to grab the kid."

"Nice for you, getting mauled."

"If it got ugly, I'd have shot it."

"Shot?"

He showed him the Magnum holstered against the small of his back.

Whit stared at him, stone-faced. "You had your gun and you used a rock?"

"I was pretty sure it would run."

"Pretty sure," Whit said. "So, what? It wouldn't be fair to use your weapon?"

It had been the cat against him on some primal level the gun hadn't entered into. He said, "I could have hit the boy, or the cat could have dropped him down the gulch. When it did let go, I realized its inexperience and knew we had a chance to scare it off. Department of Wildlife can decide its fate. I was after the child."

"Okay, fine." With a hard exhale, Whit rubbed his face. "This was bad."

Trevor nodded. Until today, the worst he'd seen over four years of rescues was a hiker welded to a tree by lightning and an ice climber's impalement on a jagged rock spear. There'd been no death today, but Whit looked sick. "You're a new dad. Seeing that little guy had to hit you right in the gut."

Whit canted his head.

"I'm just saying." Trevor stuffed his shaking hands into his jacket pockets. The storm passed, though the air still smelled of wet earth and rain. He drove Whit back, then went home to shower before meeting Jazmyn Dufoe at the Summit. Maybe he'd just start drinking now.

———

Arms aching, Natalie drove her hands into the clay. On the huge, square Corian table, two busts looked back at her: Aaron in pain, and Paige, her fairy-tale life rent by a primal terror that sprang without warning. She had pushed and drawn and formed the images locked in her mind, even though her hands burned with the strain.

No word had come from the Children's Hospital in Denver, where the police chief said they'd taken Cody, or from the hospital that had Aaron. Waiting to hear anything at all made a hollow in her stomach.

She heaved a new block of clay to the table, wedged and added it to the mound already softened. Just as she started to climb the stepstool, her phone rang. She plunged her hands into the water bucket and swabbed them with a towel, silently begging for good news. "Aaron?"

Not her brother, but a nurse calling. "Mr. Reeve asked me to let you know he came through surgery just fine. He's stable, and the prognosis is optimistic. He doesn't want you to worry."

Natalie pressed her palm to her chest with relief. "Did he say anything about Cody? Is there any news?"

"No, he didn't say. I'm sure he'll let you know as soon as he hears something."

"Of course. Thank you so much for calling."

Natalie climbed back onto the stool, weary but unable to stop. Normally, the face was enough, but this required more. She molded clay over stiff wire-mesh, drawing it up, up, proportionately taller than an average man, shoulders that bore the weight of other people's fear, one arm wielding a stone, the other enfolding the little one. The rescuer hadn't held both at once, but she combined the actions to release both images.

She had stared hard at his face for only a moment before he plunged over the ridge, yet retained every line and plane of it. Determination and fortitude in the cut of his mouth, selfless courage in the eyes. There'd been fear for Cody. And himself? Not of the situation, but something…

It came through her hands in the twist of his brow. A heroic face, aware of the danger, capable of failing, unwilling to hold back. Using fingers and tools, she moved the powerful images trapped by her eidetic memory through her hands to the clay, creating an exterior storage that freed her mind, and immortalizing him—whoever he was.

———

The Summit bar was packed and buzzing, the rescue already playing on televisions visible from every corner. With the whole crowd toasting and congratulating him, Jaz played nice—until he accepted her ride home and infuriated her all over again by not inviting her in.

He'd believed that dating women whose self-esteem reached egotistical meant parting ways wouldn't faze them. Jaz destroyed that theory. She was not only embittered but vindictive. After turning on the jets, Trevor sank into his spa, letting the water beat his lower- and mid-lumbar muscles. He pressed the remote to open the horizontal blinds and to look out through the loft windows.

Wincing, he reached in and rubbed the side of his knee. That plunge down the slope had cost him, but, given the outcome, he didn't consider it a judgment error. That honor went to putting himself once more at the top of Jaz's hate list. He maneuvered his knee into the pressure of a jet. When he got out, he'd ice it. If he got out.

He closed his eyes and pictured the battered toddler. The crowd's attention had kept the thoughts at bay, easy to talk about the cat, how mountain lions rarely attacked people, how he and Whit had scared it off, how DOW would euthanize if they caught it, how his only priority had been to get the child. He had segued into the business he and Whit had opened the previous spring, rock and ice climbing, land and water excursions, cross-country ski and snowshoe when the season turned.

That was his business, but rescuing was in his blood, had been since his dad made him the man of the house by not coming home one night or any thereafter. At first, the nightmares had been bad—all the things that could go wrong: fire, snakes, tarantulas, tornadoes. They had populated his dreams until he woke drenched in sweat, cursing his father for trusting him to do what a grown man couldn't.

The phone rang. He sloshed his arm up, dried his hand on the towel lying beside it, and answered. "Hey, Whit."

"You doing okay?"

"Knee hurts. You?"

"Oh sure. You know—"

"Hold on. There's someone at the door."

"Yeah. Me and Sara."

Trevor said, "Cute. Where's your key?"

"Forgot it."

Gingerly, he climbed over the side, then wrapped a towel around his hips, and let them in.

"You mind?" Whit frowned at the towel, although Sara hadn't batted an eye.

She came in and made herself at home. Whit carried their two-month-old asleep in his car seat to a resting place. Trevor threw on Under Armour shorts and a clean T-shirt, then rejoined them.

"So what's up?"

"Nice try, Trevor." Sara fixed him with a look. "I especially like the practiced nonchalance."

He grinned. "Hey, I've got it down."

"With Jaz, maybe. No claw marks?"

"Too public."

Whit rubbed his wife's shoulder. "We knew you'd worry this thing, so Sara brought the remedy."

She drew the Monopoly box out of her oversize bag with a grin that said she intended to win and would, wearing them down with her wheeling and dealing. *"I'll take that silly railroad off your hands. It's no good to you when I have the other three."*

He rubbed his hands, looking into her bold blue eyes. "Bring it."

The mindless activity and their chatter lightened his mood as Sara had intended. She knew him as well as Whit, maybe better. Each time he caught the concern, he reassured her with a smile. He'd be fine.

Whit played his get-out-of-jail card and freed his cannon. "Hear what's going in next door to us?"

"No."

"An art gallery."

"Yeah?" Trevor adjusted the ice pack on his knee.

"Place called Nature Waits."

"Waits for what?"

Whit shrugged. "Have to ask the lady sculptor."

"Won't exactly draw for our kind of customer."

"At least it won't compete." Sara rolled the dice and moved her pewter shoe. "Another outfitter could have gone in. I'll buy Park Place."

Both men mouthed, *"I'll buy Park Place."*

She shot them a smile.

Two hours later, she had bankrupted them with her thoughtful loans and exorbitant use of hotels on prime properties. He closed the door behind them, and it hit. He raised the toilet seat and threw up, then pressed his back to the wall and rested his head, breathing deeply.

The shaking returned, and this time he couldn't blame adrenaline. He had literally puffed the life back into that tiny body. If that child had died in his arms…

Midst came their mighty Paramount, and seemed
Alone th' antagonist of Heaven, nor less
Than Hell's dread Emperor, with pomp supreme,
And god-like imitated state.

Child snatched from lion's jaws. Two-year-old spared in deadly attack. Rescuer Trevor MacDaniel, champion of innocents, protector of life. Cameras rolling, flashes flashing, earnest newscasters recounted the tale. "On this mountain, a miracle. What could have been a tragedy became a triumph through the courage of this man who challenged a mountain lion to save a toddler attacked while hiking with his father, center-fielder..."

He consumed the story in drunken drafts. Eyes swimming, he gazed upon the noble face, the commanding figure on the TV screen. In that chest beat valiance. In those hands lay salvation. His heart made a slow drum in his ears. A spark ignited, purpose quickening.

Years he'd waited. He spread his own marred hands, instruments of instruction, of destruction. With slow deliberation, he closed them into fists. What use was darkness if not to try the light?

Two

Natalie draped a damp sheet over the statue and washed her hands. Daylight bathed the studio. Bringing her arms together, she stretched her back, fatigue finding every muscle with pinching fingers. She stepped outside, squinting in sunshine so bright and clear it mocked her fear and anxiety. She checked her phone. No missed calls.

Metallic doors closed to her left. Turning toward the van several yards away, she felt a shock run through her.

The man behind the vehicle said, "Are you okay?"

"Sorry. I was just..." She swallowed hard. "That was my nephew. The little boy you saved."

He cocked his head. "Really? How's he doing?"

"I'm waiting to hear. But he's alive. Thanks to you." She crossed the distance. "Everything was so crazy and awful out there. I didn't even get your name."

"Trevor MacDaniel. My partner's Paul Whitman." He nodded toward the store.

There'd been another man, but she hadn't even seen him. "You're the outfitters?"

"That's right."

Her business neighbors were the angels on the mountain. A shiver went up her back. "I'm Natalie Reeve." She crisscrossed her arms, collaring her neck with her hands. "I wish there was some way... Can I make you something?"

He raised his eyebrows. "Um..."

"That sounded weird. What I meant was, I'm an artist—a sculptor. When I've unpacked, come take a look. If you like my work, I'll do a special order. My thank-you."

"Oh. Look, uh...Natalie. Search and rescue is a service."

"You saved my nephew's life. I want to give something back." Anything to ease the burden.

"Well, the sheriff's department welcomes donations."

"I can't do anything in cash right now, but I could donate a sculpture." She didn't look into his face, but felt his scrutiny.

Hands on his hips, he said, "I'm taking a crew kayaking. We'll be on the water until three or so, assuming it's as swift as I hope from the rain. I'll have to stow equipment, but I can stop by after that."

"Perfect." She clasped her hands. "Thanks."

She watched him walk away. Trevor MacDaniel. Paul Whitman. She called Aaron's cell phone, praying Paige wouldn't answer. When no one picked up, she left both men's names on the message so her brother would know who saved Cody.

Trevor was every inch the avenger-protector she had fashioned out of clay from the image in her mind. If he saw it, he'd be stunned by the accuracy, but she didn't show anyone those sculptures. She knew better.

———

Trevor found Whit wielding a box cutter by a shelf near the front of the store. Flakes of cardboard and packing foam littered the floor, and cardboard dust scented the air. "Just met the sculptor next door."

Whit cocked a glance over his shoulder as he pulled aside the box flaps. "Yeah?"

"It was her nephew yesterday."

"No kidding." Whit settled on his haunches.

"I think I saw her in the parking lot when Jaz was hassling me, maybe on the trail—that part's a blur. But at the trailhead she looked lost."

"Shaken up, I'm sure."

"Yeah." But the woman had stumbled as though dazed. "She wants to thank us with art."

"How does that work?"

"I suggested a donation to the sheriff's department. I guess they can auction it or something."

"That's good." Whit reached in for the shipping ticket and checked it against the dehydrated food pouches in the box. "What's she like?"

"Hmm?"

"The sculptor."

"Oh," he said. "Grateful."

"Yeah, you covered that."

He frowned. "She's kind of…evasive."

"Shy?"

"Maybe." But that didn't feel right. "Anyway, I see the first of today's crew arriving." He watched a Jeep pull in, carrying a top-of-the-line kayak. These were die-hard sportsmen—correct that. The kayaker climbing out of the Jeep wore chin-length graying blond hair. He smiled, recognizing her. Die-hard, still fit.

Whit bobbed his chin. "Give 'em a good ride."

"You know it."

———

Natalie pressed her hands to her lower back. Sleep would have to wait, because the delivery truck would be arriving any moment. They'd compressed the time line to fit Aaron's scant availability, and she couldn't change it now.

After taking the tool chest from the back of her car, she went into the studio that occupied the riverside half of the building. Two-story windows revealed the breathtaking vista behind the gallery, dark pines framing a craggy rock face with spring water streaking and sparkling down.

She might have more foot traffic in Redford's Old Town or near the golf, ski, and gift shops at the Kicking Horse resort center. But she couldn't find better inspiration than what she saw outside these windows. And what she saw, or didn't, meant more than people knew.

The truck arrived, and the professional delivery men Aaron had hired unloaded and assembled her kiln. They positioned the platforms where she instructed and handled the larger sculptures—impressionistic clay and glass renderings of nature. Even she didn't know how the finished work would come out of the giant kiln with the glass melting into the glazed or sometimes unglazed clay, with the contrast of rough and smooth, of hues melding.

She ran her hand over a china blue and turquoise mountainscape with green bottle glass melted into the slopes. Her pieces had been accepted by a co-op in Santa Fe and a gallery in San Francisco. One had been shown in Manhattan and created a buzz. She had not lightly offered a gift to Trevor MacDaniel. But what he'd done for Cody was priceless.

Aaron had tried out there on the mountain, but she'd been worthless. She closed her eyes, then, at the sound of the door, blinked back the welling tears. In the light shafting through the windows, Trevor filled her doorway. Hints of copper tinged the brown hair that curled around his ears and neck, glinting on his suntanned arms. His image seared into her visual field, functioning like a blind spot when she looked away.

She stepped around the mountain sculpture. "You're here."

He said, "Too soon?"

"No, please. Look." In the edges of her vision, she watched him move through the gallery.

"I have to tell you, I didn't expect anything like this. I thought you meant a souvenir."

"That wouldn't be much of a donation."

He studied the fall of glistening glass flowing from an S-shaped cluster of boulders, then looked around. "Nothing's priced."

"Not yet."

"I won't know the value."

She said, "Whatever you choose, it won't equal my nephew's life."

He stopped at an elongated wolf forming the tunneled base of a cobalt and violet glass-coated mountain. "Does it have to be a special order?"

She had planned on opening with her current inventory, but told him no. He could take whatever he wanted.

Circling the piece, he bumped the shop sign waiting to be hung over the door. He steadied it and asked, "What *does* nature wait for?"

"The revealing of the sons of God. The touch of the Creator and care of its stewards."

"Aha." He nodded. "What would the ticket on the wolf be?"

"Eighteen hundred." In the New York gallery, it would get twice that.

"Then that's the donation I'll make."

"You'll make?"

"I want it."

She frowned. "Then you're paying for what you did. I meant—"

"I know. But everyone wins this way. The department gets reimbursed, you've expressed your gratitude, and I get the wolf."

He didn't want anything for what he'd done on the mountain. "I could sell it and earmark the profit for search and rescue."

"Then I wouldn't get my part."

Glancing into his eyes, she saw beneath the charismatic veneer to the tight control of something deeper, and that image joined the first, like looking twice at the sun and carrying the dots burned into the retinas. "Let me get a crate."

Together, they loaded the wolf mountain into his hybrid SUV. As he positioned it, she watched the water flowing behind their lots, dissipating the trapped glimpses of him. Kayaking that creek would not be a restful glide. It frothed up where boulders protruded. Trevor's tour had probably started higher up, where the water was white—and fast enough to suit him.

What other kind of man could have saved Cody?

Digging into her pocket for her ringing phone, she turned away from the vehicle. "Aaron?"

All day with no response to her calls had her half crazy.

Not Aaron, but her high-strung, angry sister-in-law. "You need to stop calling. We have enough to deal with." Her voice broke.

"What's wrong, Paige? Is it Cody?"

"They're taking off his arm—that's what."

"But I thought—"

"The surgery failed."

A sharp wind off the mountain chilled the back of her neck, but a deeper chill spread inside her. She'd been so sure…

"Just leave us alone. Aaron has nothing to say to you."

Her phone dangled from limp fingers as that statement sank in.

"Natalie?"

She couldn't turn, couldn't move. Cody was losing his arm. And Paige would keep her away.

"Hey." Cody's angel spoke.

"They can't save his arm."

"Oh…" His body slackened. "It looked bad, but I thought there was a chance."

In the shock of almost losing Cody, she'd been grateful for his life alone. Even now, she knew it a miracle that he'd been saved, but that didn't stop this hurt. Little Cody with only one arm. Paige and Aaron blaming her. Without thinking, she looked into Trevor's face. Eyes that had stared down a mountain lion now held a raw empathy. She looked away.

"You going to see him?"

"They don't want me there."

"Why not?"

She swallowed the lump filling her throat. "It's my fault."

"That's crazy. It was an animal attack."

"Aaron was using his injury leave to help me move in. Now his season, his future could be in jeopardy. And his son…"

"You want to go somewhere and regroup?"

Another gust of wind scudded ash-colored clouds across the sky. Her mind felt just as cloudy, a storm of tears held back by throbbing pressure.

"Come on." Trevor opened the passenger door and she climbed in.

———

Watching her take the call, he'd thought the rescue failed, that they lost the child after all. Not that bad, but bad enough. He said, "Think you could eat?"

She tilted her head. "It's…not dinnertime."

"It helps, though. Ask any cop." Carbohydrates were natural tranquilizers.

"Were you a cop?"

"My brother is."

She stared out the window. "Saving people runs in the family?"

"His work is mostly making people pay."

Thunder cracked as another afternoon storm moved in, sudden, sharp rain, driving into the windshield.

"Is it just the two of you?"

"Five—" He swallowed. "Four boys."

She didn't ask him to clarify.

He headed toward Old Town. "Are you all settled in?"

"We set up my studio before anything else." She rubbed the fingers of one hand with the thumb of the other. "Then Paige wanted to get the house unpacked, but Aaron suggested a hike. He told her I needed the big picture, to get outside so I didn't hyperfocus."

Not sure what she meant, he said, "You're set up at the gallery, but not at home?"

"I haven't been home since Cody..."

"Where'd you spend the night?"

"My studio."

He hoped she meant sleeping, but the bruised look of her eyes argued otherwise. He parked as close as he could get to the bakery bistro, turned off the engine, and eyed the rain. "You want to go in, or should I grab sandwiches to go?"

She blinked. "What?"

He said, "Sit tight. I'll be back in a minute." He left the low-key Ratatat CD on and locked the doors. He jogged beneath the awnings as much as possible, then ducked inside, bought each of them a turkey with Brie on sourdough ciabatta, and hustled back. Stashing the bag between them, he said, "Show me where you live."

She directed him to a dark red, single-story house overgrown with aspen, the sidewalk buckling from the interconnected roots. Her front room was stacked with boxes, a few pieces of furniture in place, others waiting to be assembled. In the kitchen, an open packing box had released only a single plate, glass, and mug. The only other thing on the counter was a Bible.

As he pulled another plate from the box, she filled two glasses with ice and water. Her visual avoidance was making him feel like a ghost she might sense but couldn't see.

He unwrapped the sandwiches, releasing a rich aroma as he put them on the plates, and said, "Where should we start?"

"Start?"

"Unpacking."

"No, don't." She pressed her hand to her eyes. "It's too risky."

"Risky?"

"Paige said all this happened because Aaron wanted to help. There must be some karmic—"

"You don't believe that. There's a Bible on your counter."

"She's pretty convinced."

"She's reacting." He nudged the plate, saying, "Try the sandwich. It has orange and fig chutney." He took a bite of his. She wasn't multitasking in her condition.

"I'm reeling. I won't pretend I'm not. But I'll get through."

"Not without eating."

She took a bite, chewed slowly, and swallowed. It occurred to him she'd been alone, dealing with this since the attack. No wonder she looked shell-shocked at the trailhead and acted strange when they met. Emotional shock had probably drained what energy she had, and today's news was another blow.

He couldn't stop seeing the little arm hanging by a thread.

Gripping the back of her neck, she said, "I thought it was going to be okay."

He'd hoped it would.

She took another bite. "I mean...you guys were there."

"Keep that in mind, okay? There's good here."

"I know." She nodded. "I do."

"So eat your sandwich and let's get to work." With his plate empty, he drained the water glass and brought them to the sink. She finished her food and thanked him with a quick glance aimed at his chin. She had yet to look at him directly.

He scanned her home. If the bedroom matched the rest, she didn't have anything to sleep on. "Let's get the furniture assembled." Bending one hand and then the other, he cracked his knuckles. "Rain canceled the bouldering I had scheduled, so I have plenty of time."

"Okay." Following him into the bedroom, she asked, "What's bouldering?"

"Climbing without equipment."

"No ropes?"

"You're only three to five meters off the ground. Over seven, you're free-soloing or you have a highball problem."

"Like an alcoholic."

Her deadpan made him laugh. Nice to see a sense of humor, but it was short-lived. Pain and worry crept back like the flu, draining the animation from her face.

Moving to the windowsill, she handed him the hardware for the bed
that leaned in parts against the wall and said, "Do you also climb with
ropes?"

"Of course. But bouldering's the best way to get a feel for the rock.
You should try it."

"Oh no."

"Fifteen feet max, and you'd have a crash pad and spotter." He positioned the side rail to the headboard, and she held it while he tightened the
bolt.

"You think you can catch me from fifteen feet up?"

"It's not catching. It's directing your fall."

"That's so much better."

He grinned. "We wouldn't start you higher than I could handle."

She shook her head. "I'm no monkey."

"Your hands are strong. They'd have to be for sculpting."

"Yes, but—"

He moved on to the other side rail and said, "I'll teach you to crimp
and flag and smear—what do you say, unpack today, boulder tomorrow?"
Distraction was the best way he knew to deal with stuff. And she had stuff.

She pulled a clip from her pocket and pinched it into her hair. "I'll
think about it."

With her hair up, she seemed like the little sister he never had. Or like
Sara. Yeah. Now he could fit what he was doing into a comfortable place.

They connected the footboard, placed the box spring and mattress,
and moved on.

———

The rain had stopped, the sunset burning the ragged remains of cloud
when she stopped and surveyed her home. "Wow. It's done."

"A few boxes to unload. But not bad." He checked his watch. "Uh-oh.
Whit's expecting me."

"Go." She motioned him toward the door, then said, "Wait."

He turned.

"Unless you want to pick me up in the morning, I need my car."

"Oh. Right. Let's go."

Whit was waiting in the narrow delivery lot behind their businesses with Sara wearing Braden in a sling. "Dude, where'd you go?"

"Gave Natalie a hand moving in." He turned to her. "Natalie, Paul Whitman."

"Whit," he said and shook her hand. "Only my granny calls me Paul."

"No, that's Paulie." Laughing, Sara said, "Nice to meet you, Natalie. I'm Sara. This is Braden."

The baby had one fist pressed into his cheek, the other under his chin. Natalie's tears welled up. "He's perfect."

He'd done a good job of distracting her, but he could see it rushing back in. "Her nephew lost his arm. They couldn't save it." He would gnaw that all night, wondering what more he could have done.

Whit and Sara offered sympathetic responses.

Looking at neither, Natalie said, "I should go. Thanks again."

"Bouldering tomorrow. Twelve o'clock."

She hurried toward her business. As soon as she'd gone inside, he told them, "Her brother and his wife think blaming her makes it better. They don't want her at the hospital, which is what she needs."

"That's messed up."

Sara shifted the baby. "How is it her fault?"

"They were here to help her move in."

"And?"

"And nothing. They took a hike and that lion changed their lives."

"That's cold," Whit said.

"Yeah. So I figured I could help her unpack the house."

"That was nice." Sara cocked her head.

"I'm a nice guy. Up for bouldering? It might take her mind off things." Sara's gaze intensified.

"She's in a rough spot."

"So it's a rescue."

He shrugged.

"I can read you like a book." She gave him her Sara smile, then made mommy eyes at her waking infant.

If thou beest he—but O how fallen! how changed
From him who, in the happy realms of light
Clothed with transcendent brightness, didst outshine
Myriads, though bright!

No strife exists but what pits good and evil, brothers of one cloth, one light, the other dark, seeking his opposite. Running fingers over the spiraled ridges and furrows of his flesh, he pictured the other face, unmarred, untested. Awe quickened. A purpose as old as time. Spurned and Chosen vying.

Was it fate that made one cursed, another blessed; that fickle hand sowing fertile ground and also barren stones? For two seeds fall and one grows strong, but the other is snatched by greedy beak, cracked open and devoured.

As water finds the path of least resistance, so misfortune finds the weak. But the feeble, broken, can be tempered, snapping chains of inhibition. The weak can become the strong.

Gathering what little he had—hoods and capes, tape, and, most importantly, the tome—he prepared himself as a warrior for battle. Everything had led to this, every dark and tortured moment, every fear, rage, and fury. The hunger. The need. He felt them all inside, coursing like blood through his veins.

He had not slept since the idea formed, had no need to slumber. Energy coursed through him, electrified, as he sought what he needed and there—lock freed—wires touched. Engine roars! Nimble fingers, crafty mind. Invincible.

He slipped inside the rusted shell—newer cars too complicated for a simple hot-wire, but not this. He revved the engine, a great silent laugh inside him. He felt himself an arrow drawn back to the taut, quivering point of release.

In the passenger seat, a duffel bag became his unspeaking companion. From its neck he took the book, set it between them, then fixed his gaze forward. Those behind heard nothing of his leaving. Those approached sensed nothing of his coming. Stealth and cunning bore him, as the breath of plague seeping over sleeping souls.

Three

Tapping her stick against the sun-warmed walls and sidewalk, Fleur moved down the street. The commotion had quieted since the rescue put Redford in the news, and she was glad for that. Not that she minded excitement, but lots of strangers and extra traffic complicated her routines.

With a clack, she found the metal plate at the base of the door and entered the bakery bistro. Scents surrounded her. Cinnamon, butter, and yeast. Fig, orange, and pine nuts. Also fontina cheese and capocollo. Rosemary—no, basil.

Voices chattered around her, the sounds of crockery and sipping, and then Piper said, "Hi, roomie."

Her posting for a roommate had hardly been on the coffeehouse board an hour before Piper had called, hoping to share the tiny two-bedroom house at the edge of Old Town. One conversation had clinched it for both of them.

"It smells like you have a lunch selection ready."

"Fontina, capocollo, and basil croissants."

Fleur smiled. "Yum."

"They're fresh out of the oven, so watch the heat."

"I'll take it to go, if you don't mind. I want to finish one last canvas to show the new gallery owner. I really hope she'll carry my work."

"She'd be crazy not to."

She loved Piper's optimism. With her own tendency toward melancholy, she collected positive people. After taking the warm bag in one hand and her stick in the other, she headed for the door, pausing when it opened. "Hello, Jonah."

He said, "I need you on the force, Fleur. You're the best detective in town."

It was hard to miss the chief of police—his woodsy scent, the wintergreen Tic Tacs he chewed, his confident, yet courteous stride. Remembering his rakish good looks, she mentally aged him fifteen years and still imagined greatness. "How's Tia?"

His fingernails scratched over his jaw.

"Uh-oh," she said.

"No, she's good. It's just… I guess people will know soon enough. Especially if the crying and vomiting keep up."

Behind Fleur, Piper squealed. "She's pregnant?"

"Yeah, well, I'm dead now that she didn't get to tell you."

Other congratulations came from around the room. Within minutes the town would know. Someone had probably Tweeted already.

Groaning, he said, "Seriously, Piper. Can you pretend you haven't a clue?"

"Of course I can." She made a zipping noise. "But I'm so happy! You're going to be a dad!"

Fleur reached a hand to his arm. "Congratulations."

Did she imagine the tightness of his tendons? With his childhood, the thought of fatherhood might be troubling at the least. One didn't suffer the former Chief Westfall and remain unscathed. Jonah thanked her—with more than a hint of trepidation.

———

Jonah held the door for Fleur's exit. He'd only been half kidding about death for telling Tia's best friend the news. They hadn't really decided to make it public, and fiery at the best of times, Tia had become a volcano. Since she'd spent nine years damming up her tears, he shouldn't be surprised they came out now that she felt vulnerable. Trouble was, crying made her furious.

The best defense he'd found was to grab on and hold her tight, as he had when the search last night left her exhausted and frustrated. She had found the elderly hikers when the original team got sidetracked by the mountain lion attack. Being tired afterward shouldn't have been traumatic.

"You have a little bit going on inside," he'd said.

"It's not like I'm hauling extra weight."

"Yet." No points for that one. He'd said, *"Be patient. Give yourself a chance to acclimate. You're going to do this as well as everything else you do."*

She had softened then, and he'd loved her gently and thoroughly, showing her she meant as much to him now as ever before. No small feat with their rocky history.

He smiled grimly at the luminous young blonde he considered the patron saint of his marriage. She'd curbed her crush when she realized he and Tia were locked in a death grip of regret and desire. Without Piper's interference, Tia might still be the thorn in his side instead of his wife, or...both.

"Don't worry," she soothed. "I won't give you away." She handed him an almond bear claw, his favorite since Sarge opened the place years ago.

He said, "One for Sarge too."

"How's he feeling?" Piper's compassion for her crusty former boss and current benefactor came through.

Jonah shrugged. Though no relation, the old man lived with him now, almost incapacitated with arthritic scoliosis. "I need to check in on him before I go spend eternity in county court."

"That's why you look so nice."

He looked down at the full uniform, in place of the jeans and uniform shirt or simply the bomber jacket with the department emblem he usually wore. He could do a suit for court, but might be taken for a lawyer. He said, "Thanks. And get Tia to spill before I blow it again."

"You know I will."

He went out with a heavier step. Saying it out loud made Tia's pregnancy real. Policing Redford used to be a mellower job. The influx of rich residents brought different levels of crime. He'd testify on three separate cases this afternoon alone.

He pressed his remote and got into his Bronco. No point having a job you didn't put everything into. How much of that would change when the baby came? He pressed the bullet scar in his side. Could he be effective with so much more to lose?

Dressed in loose-fitting cargo pants, a fitted navy T-shirt, and an unzipped Windbreaker, Natalie entered High Country Outfitters where Trevor stood like a Titan at the base of the climbing wall. His arms moved the rope through a clip on his belt in a hand-over-hand motion for the person near the ceiling. Maybe he'd get it out of his system right here.

"Now what?" The gangling adolescent shouted in a breaking falsetto.

Trevor said, "Lean into the rope and walk off the way I showed you."

Natalie commiserated as the youth descended with less grace than haste. No disguising his apprehension.

"Sweet, huh?" Trevor untethered him.

"Yeah. Sweet." The kid shoved his hands into his pockets and ambled off as Trevor hung the harness on the wall.

She said, "I'll understand if you're too busy."

His smile spread. "Nice try."

"Well"—she gripped the edge of her shirt—"I wasn't sure…"

"You're fine. We'll get you some climbing shoes, though." He moved into the gear area. "You're a seven—"

"Eight."

At five-eight, it took someone like Trevor to make her feel short. He had to be four or five inches over six feet with no surrender at all in the muscled shoulders she remembered forming in the clay. When he came back out with a shoe box, she said, "That's seven and a half."

"You want them tight."

"I'm not big on curled toes."

He extended the box. "Let's try them."

She sat on the bench and pulled the narrow square-toed shoes on.

"How's that feel?" Trevor squatted down.

"Between stuffed and squashed."

"Hurt?"

"Not exactly. But why can't they fit?"

"Don't want slipping inside the shoe." He felt the toes. His long, square-nailed fingers gripped her feet as he felt the width and insteps. A raised, V-shaped scar cut across the first joint of his index finger. Another ran faintly up the side of his wrist where the bone made a white mound beneath his coppery skin—all of it now impressed on her mind.

"I think these are good." Trevor's voice brought her back.

"Okay," she breathed. Three days ago they'd occupied this world without knowing the other existed. Now they'd been entwined by one event and its aftermath. It felt strange but…right.

Sara came in, blond hair in a tight ponytail, the baby wrapped against her in a sling. Her wide blue eyes had flecks of tan around the pupils, the lashes making starbursts all the way around. A sprinkle of freckles formed a faint raccoon mask.

Natalie looked down before more details got trapped, watching obliquely as Whit came up from behind, encircled mom and baby, and said, "Everyone ready?"

Trevor tapped her foot and rose. "Wear your boots and save the climbing soles for the stone."

She switched footwear, wondering if he'd ever used a plural pronoun when he talked her into this. She hadn't expected an audience, didn't do great in crowds.

Whit called, "Ryan, you've got the store."

The young man with greenish blond hair and gauged holes in his earlobes spread thumb and pinkie in a hang-loose gesture. In the front of Whit's SUV, the men talked over the music. She and Sara sat on either side of the infant car seat that faced backward. Even though the image would be trapped, she couldn't look away from Braden's sleeping face. Could anything compare to that sweetness?

She said, "How old is he?"

"Two months. I can't tell yet who he takes after."

She could tell her that the infant's bone structure mirrored his mother's, but she would let that realization arrive on its own. She looked out the window. By sending her gaze long and wide, she managed to dissipate the trapped images of Sara and the baby and felt the strain in her temples ease.

"This is your first time climbing?"

Her gaze scanned the craggy peaks. "It never entered my mind before."

"That's Trevor." Sara laughed. "The man casts a long shadow."

Long indeed. Seeing him emerge from her hands in the clay had stripped away the surface where most relationships began. She was still raw from it.

The unfiltered sunlight felt sharp when Natalie climbed out. Just as she was thinking she should have used sunscreen, Sara produced it from the baby's pack.

"Want some?"

"Thanks." She lubed her cheeks and nose.

Trevor came around the SUV, full of energy. He rubbed his hands. "Ready?"

"I don't know about ready, but I'm willing."

While Whit and Sara extracted and repackaged Braden, Trevor grabbed the rolled-up pad from the back and led her to the rust and white rock protruding from the pale pink granite.

"As I said, no ropes for bouldering. You can chalk your hands, and your shoes have a hard rubber sole for traction. Beyond that, it's just fitting yourself to the rock, finding holds, and working your way up."

She eyed the boulder looming before her.

"This rock has multiple problems—routes—some fairly complex, others not so much. We sometimes restrict holds to make it harder."

"Joy."

His expression warmed. "First-timers can use anything."

"Great." She changed shoes and clipped on the chalk bag.

"Once you're on the rock, you won't see the surface as completely as now, so—"

She said, "I will."

"I mean, the angles are such that what you saw from down here won't be visible."

"I know what you're saying. But it will for me. I have the boulder memorized."

He looked at her.

"Eidetic memory. I retain what I see."

He squinted. "So, right now, looking at me, you have the layout of that boulder in your head."

"The problem will be getting it out."

"Everything you look at?"

"Long enough. Directly enough." With enough trepidation.

"Huh."

She used to try to hide it, but inevitably gave herself away, so her current policy was to get it out there and let things fall where they may.

He spread the mat at the base of the rock and said, "This is your crash pad. Softens the landing if you slip."

"And you'll direct my fall."

"Right. This boulder has a pretty good slant so you won't be negotiating any acute angles or overhangs."

"Small mercies."

He pulled a sideways grin. "Chalk your hands for grip."

"Should we give her a demo route?" Whit said, eyeing the boulder.

"I know which way I'm going." She clapped off the excess chalk.

Whit looked at her, then him.

Trevor tapped his temple. "She memorized the rock."

Sara said, "You have photographic memory?"

"Sort of."

Trevor patted the rock. "Which way you go is only half of it. The rest is listening to your body, feeling your limitations, your strengths."

Right now her limitations felt insurmountable, but if she imagined the rock a mound of clay, her mind would direct her hands as though she were shaping it. She hoped.

"Let me show you a couple things." He took her hand and put it against the rock, fitting her fingers into a diagonal crack. "This is a crimp, when only your fingertips fit. You can close it like this with your thumb over the index finger. That adds strength but puts more stress on your hand than an open crimp."

He wore cologne not found at a drugstore counter, she guessed, and she made herself breathe normally.

He rotated her hand. "When you're thumb down like this, it's a left-hand Gaston." He moved her right hand over, also thumb down over the same grip. "This is a right-hand side pull. If you get stuck and I can see one of these working for you, I'll call it up."

Grabbing a hold on the rock at about her waist level, he squatted down and demonstrated, "This move is a mantle. You pull first to propel yourself up, then push down as you pass it. If I say you can mantle that hold to your right, now you know what I mean."

And that, of course, meant she could do it.

"If there's no foothold, you can smear, which means pushing off with the ball of your foot on the face. At the crux of this rock, you might need to."

"It's a lot of terms." She was not an auditory learner, and his proximity didn't help.

"They're labeled for instruction and grading."

"I'm going to be graded?"

He laughed. "The problems are graded. You're just learning to climb."

Was she? Yesterday it had seemed like something else.

Whit clapped his hands together. "Let's do it."

She took hold of the rock and started her ascent, moving awkwardly, but she knew what was coming and stuck to the line she had planned. Between her arm and the rock, she saw Whit murmur, "Freaky."

If this wasn't so scary, maybe she'd fumble around, but she kept reaching and stepping where she knew she should. Sara bounced a waking Braden beside Trevor squinting up, ready to direct her fall if she broke loose.

A sudden, hot pain gripped her right hand.

"You okay?"

"It's a cramp," she said.

"Drop if you have to."

No way was she letting go. "I get this when I'm sculpting. It'll pass." She reached for a pinch hold and pushed with her left foot. It might be about balance and creativity, but it was also hard work. She pressed the toe of one shoe into a crack and propelled herself to a grip just below the top, then bellied up and over, relief and wonder rushing in. She made it! Who'd have thought?

Looking down, she caught Trevor squarely looking up. A jolt passed through that had nothing to do with rock climbing. His jaw slackened.

Heart rushing, she swallowed. "Please tell me I don't have to climb down."

Whit pointed. "There's a walk-off in the back."

Natalie turned, shaky as she descended the crevice where the rock met the land behind it. Reaching them, she said, "Wow. That was hard."

Trevor bent to fold up the mat.

"It's a good training rock," Sara said. "Lots of choices."

"Yeah." Whit removed the chalk bag. "But flashing your first free ascent without bailing is good stuff."

"If I flashed anything, it wasn't intentional."

He laughed. "It means you made your climb the first time without falling."

"I was too scared to fall."

Trevor put his hands together. "You guys hungry?"

The others seemed surprised by his lack of enthusiasm. She wasn't. That shock of connection required a response. His was obviously to withdraw. He might not know why, but she did. In her exuberance, she'd shown herself. It was one thing to memorize a rock, another altogether to capture him as she had, yet again. His face filled her vision and wouldn't go away until she exorcized the image.

She thanked Sara for the boxed lunch. The roast beef on rye with horseradish tasted good with potato salad and strawberries, but she ate only half and wrapped the rest. Braden cried, and Sara nursed him while the guys talked schedules and business. She maneuvered the baby upright and coaxed a burp, then praised him. That would change right about the time he turned ten.

A noisy squirrel ran the length of a nearby branch, leaping into the next tree where a big black crow protested. Natalie took in the jagged rocky promontories forming the aged faces of Native American chiefs, proud horses, and even a dragon—all blocked straight on by Trevor's stunned expression. The need to release it throbbed in her temples.

The splendor and beauty of nature had eased the condition when she was small. If her parents had let the overload continue before she developed coping skills, she might have permanently shut out the world. Now she protected herself by rarely looking directly and constantly changing focus. It made her seem shifty to people who didn't know, but when she did look, they called it spooky.

"Don't look at me like that."

"What's wrong with your eyes? They're putting holes in me."

She understood Trevor's recoil, even as disappointment stung. Her attraction would pass. It wasn't for the flesh-and-bone man anyway, but her idealized version. Not fair to expect him to live up to that. His shadow announced his approach. She glanced up to the hands hanging casually on his hips and said, "Are we done?"

"If you are."

"Sure." The others must have come only to spot her. That beginning rock she'd conquered would be child's play to them. Sara could probably do it blindfolded, clutching Braden in one hand. She silently laughed at the thought as they got back into the car. So she wouldn't be ice climbing Mount Everest. Or seeing Trevor MacDaniel. She could live with that.

Back at the gallery, she thanked them all again, then went inside and mapped the boulder in clay, every crack and bulge, the ones she had used, the ones rejected, the problem she had solved, too easily maybe, not with her body, but with her eyes. From the landscape of the boulder emerged Trevor's face. Her hands remembered his positioning hers on the rock, the warmth and scent of him. She stepped back, studied her creation, then shoved it all into the sludge bucket.

Round he throws his baleful eyes,
That witnessed huge affliction and dismay,
Mixed with obdurate pride and steadfast hate.

Though he burned for the encounter, it could not be rushed. There was a purpose larger than he, a reason for his existence that could not be put aside. He must allow for both. The journey serving the end. But how?

He rubbed his chin, pondering. And then it came—prepare the way. Yes! What before was done in secret, he would document and demonstrate, and when the time came, they, each, would know the other. By their deeds, they'd be known. They'd be judged.

He had no newscasters, no TV cameras. His message would be subtle, a whisper, not a shout, a dim reflection of the other's glow, a moon to his sun, a shadow in his mind.

It required preparation, one thing he lacked especially. Not an obstacle—thieving was as simple as breathing when people left doors and cars unlocked, and even locked he found ways—not greedy, needy. No remorse for the wealthy ones whose insurance bought newer, better. One small loss against his myriad.

That would wait for dark. Until then, his mission called. Silent cries of desperation. They were everywhere, the broken, neglected, hidden among the fortunate. Seeing the one playing alone, he approached. The face tipped up had not yet turned to stone, not abandoned hope. He held out his hand, and it was taken.

Where were the forces arrayed, the avengers, the guardians? He gnashed his teeth. At some point they would wonder. But would it be too late?

Four

After tucking her stick under her arm, Fleur reached for the door, but heard it swing open before she turned the handle. "Ms. Reeve?"

"Natalie, please." Her voice was warm and young.

"I'm Fleur Destry. We have an appointment?" She indicated the portfolio under her arm that held one loose canvas and photos of the rest.

"You're the painter."

"Yes."

An understandable pause, then, "Thanks for postponing yesterday's appointment."

"Sure." The door swung wider, releasing tones of hammered dulcimer and flute.

"Come in, please."

Tap. Tap. Stone or ceramic tiles on the floor. The air was freshened with a hint of apple underlaid by juniper. Fresh potpourri, she guessed, although imitation fragrances were hardly discernable from the real thing anymore.

"Bring your portfolio to the table here. The light is good and we can spread out."

Though covering well, her surprise was still apparent. "You didn't expect me to be blind."

"I haven't known any blind artists."

"I didn't tell you on the phone because I want you to see paintings, not a blind person's paintings."

"I will, then."

"I lost my sight when I was fourteen. I see now with my mind's eye." She tapped the table leg and reached out to the surface. She laid the portfolio down and opened it. "I set up my palette in a certain order, so I know which colors I'm putting where. It isn't random."

"No, I see that. The structure is dynamic."

"Thank you." She'd been hoping for something like that. "The other canvases are much larger, but I'm told the color in the photos is accurate."

"Fleur, these are wonderful. I'd love to represent you in the gallery."

"Really?" The music changed to a lively jig of tin flute and Celtic fiddle.

"I've been overwhelmed with landscape artists, and while some were quite well done, that isn't what I'm looking for. These will be a striking complement to my sculptures."

"Would you mind if I examined one?"

"Not at all. Come this way." After several steps, Natalie stopped her. "The platform is waist high. The sculpture is an arm's length in front of you."

Carefully, she reached out and found the cool, smooth, and rough shape. She ran sensitive fingers over it. "What are the colors?"

Natalie described the hues as Fleur's fingers traveled it once again. "Is it a waterfall with a coil here at the top?"

"Yes. The coil is just whimsy."

"I like that."

"Want to see another?" Natalie brought her to one piece after another.

Laughter welled up as she felt the clever renderings, nothing just the way it would be in life. "They're delightful."

"You agree your work fits?"

"I do."

"So let me explain the terms." Natalie read her simple contract. "I'd have you sign—"

"I can sign. Just place the pen on the line." By the scratch of the tip, it was a liquid ink pen.

"How did you keep it so straight?"

"The tilt of the paper."

"You're amazing."

"The chief of police wants to make me a detective."

"You should take him up on it."

Fleur laughed. "I'd rather paint."

Natalie watched Fleur Destry leave, once again aware of God's hand, in that a sightless and a hypersighted artist formed a perfect blend before ever encountering each other's work. It was there always, if she looked, the presence that said, *See, I told you. All things working together for good.*

Cody's disability broke her heart, but if a blind woman could paint, who was to say he couldn't do anything he put his little mind to? She closed her eyes, seeing Fleur as though she stood before her, the long nearly black hair, her soulful, sightless eyes, thin, waiflike features. Another angel in this place of miracles.

She went into her studio. With thumbs and palms and fingers, she transferred Fleur's face to the clay, a less painful process than the last one. Part of her wished she hadn't consigned Trevor's face to the sludge, because the climbing three days ago was the last she'd seen of him. But she'd have been tempted to revisit that stunned moment of connection, and what good would that do?

She gently draped Fleur's face with a damp cloth and slid the board that held the bust into one of the deep shelves lining the walls. It wouldn't go into the kiln, but she wasn't ready to part with it. She hadn't parted with Trevor's heroic rescue either. Far too large for a shelf, it stood, likewise draped, in one corner. She left him standing there and went out.

———

Jonah came up from behind and circled his wife in his arms. "What's that?" He looked over her shoulder.

"An invitation to the Nature Waits art gallery opening."

"And we're invited why?"

"I'm guessing all the city notables received one—Chief."

"What do I know about art?"

"You don't have to know anything. But here's something neat. Fleur's paintings will be displayed."

"Fleur's?"

"Don't tell me you didn't know she paints."

"I didn't know she paints." He nuzzled her collarbone. "How does she paint?"

"How does she do anything she does?" She turned and circled his neck with her arms and kissed him.

"I love coming home."

"I love you coming home."

"But I have to go out. I'm addressing the parents at back-to-school night. Want to come?"

"If I never set foot in that school again, it will be too soon."

"You shouldn't have been such a rebel." She opened her mouth to respond, but he kissed it. "Kidding." He brushed her cheek with his fingers. "You were the star they missed."

She shrugged a single shoulder. "Good thing I don't care."

"Uh-huh. They could use you over there. A hard-nosed counselor—"

She put a finger to his lips. "Don't even breathe it. Besides, I'm still getting certified, I have Sarge to look after, a pair of half-breed coyotes, and a baby on the way."

"How are you feeling?"

"Better. As long as I don't eat, smell, or think about food."

"You need to eat."

"Closing my eyes and plugging my nose, I managed some cereal. Now I don't want to talk about it."

He rubbed her back. "How long does this last?"

"Do you think my mother told me these things?"

Not a chance. Stella was a wretched parent, punishing Tia for her own guilt—something they hadn't known until Sarge illuminated them.

"Or even my sis—half sister." Her brow puckered.

He felt the worst about that. Tia and Reba had been close, so close. This baby coming should be something happy they could share.

"Are we informing her?"

"She doesn't want to know." She raised her eyes to his. "She'd just imagine…"

Having a child with him. As once they'd planned. "I really wrecked things."

She pulled a crooked smile. "You don't get that much credit. They were pretty wrecked already."

He stroked her face, her skin warming in his hands, the misery melting away. Her crazy mahogany hair fell all over his fingers, her nearly black eyes and arching brows an exotic contrast. He'd loved this woman since he first saw her on the playground when he was nine and she was only five. A fierce warrior child as needing of hope and affection as he was himself.

He slid his arm around her shoulders and pulled her close. She wrapped his waist and pressed the side of her head to his chest. She stirred when Sarge rolled slowly from his room toward the kitchen where they stood, but Jonah held her fast, then squeezed and let go. "Ready for dinner, Sarge?"

He craned his head up from a spine curling over on itself. "What's on the menu?"

"Wait, don't say it." Tia stepped back. "I'll take the dogs for a run while you cook. Please open the windows." She went out with the coydog Enola—half coyote, half German shepherd—who had come to him last summer. Her yearling pup, Scout, bounded after.

"That woman is starving herself," Sarge growled. "She have one of those eating disorders?"

"Yes. Morning sickness."

Sarge's mouth sagged open. "*That's* what you've been doing?"

"A good job of it too."

Sarge barked a laugh.

"Feel like steak?"

"Anyone ever say no?"

"Besides Tia?"

Sarge rested his hands in his lap and looked at the door she'd gone through. "She's a good girl."

"The best."

"I never knew."

"Her mother sullied the waters. I can't blame you for listening, but why couldn't you see through Stella the way you saw the truth about my dad?"

"Your damage was in the flesh, clear to anyone with an eye. The things Stella said about her girl, well, you wouldn't think a mother could make that up. Such a pretty woman, but she had a streak." He shook his head.

"Tia's the best of them."

Sarge shot him a look. "What got into you, proposing to her sister?"

"Hormones."

Sarge nodded. "Hormones got you out of it too."

"It wasn't hormones with Tia, Sarge. It was soul-starved need."

"Paid a price for the error."

"Nine years."

"And now she's having your baby."

He breathed, "Yeah," and wondered if Sarge saw his terror. Like every good soldier, if he did, he kept it to himself.

———

A string quartet played Vivaldi in the lower level of the gallery as her guests mingled among the art. In a scoop-back Donna Karan dress, onyx choker, and heels, Natalie drew a trembling breath. It was real. It was wonderful. She could do this.

She moved through the room, greeting and thanking people for coming. She had developed the appearance of eye contact without actually focusing, the closest she'd get to looking normal. It helped that the focal point at a gallery was the art.

Besides her sculptures, she was showcasing two bronze abstracts from an artist she'd met through a Santa Fe co-op, five of Fleur's paintings, and three paintings each from two New York artists. Quality work from them all. The electrician had fixed a glitch in the lighting, and the display floors on both levels shone with an elegant ambience. The only thing missing was Aaron, who, more than anyone else, had made this happen.

Two weeks since the attack, and he still hadn't called. That was Paige's fault—she hoped—and, truly, Aaron had done more than enough, buying her home and business. It was up to her to shape her future now, in the same way she took the raw images from nature and made them her own creations.

She turned as Paul Whitman and Sara entered, then Trevor with a platinum blonde who could rock a cover of *Elle*. Almost his height in four-inch stilettos, one snap of the single rhinestone strap and her electric blue sheath would slide to the floor with hardly a ripple. Nothing like making a statement.

Chic and elegant, Trevor's gray suit must have been tailored to him in a lightweight fabric that formed as he moved. An eye-catching couple, even among the notable others.

"I know you need to mingle, dear," the elderly Mary Carson said, patting her arm. "Go spread your charm."

Before she got far, a heavyset photographer in rolled shirt sleeves and leather vest shot her at two quick angles. "My reporter would like a word when you get the chance." He pointed to a striking redhead in a shimmery white halter dress with a traffic-stopping leg split.

"Okay. Thanks." She started in that direction, passing Trevor's group closely enough that she heard his companion.

"Thank Gawd. Champagne. I'll need it to fawn over nature statues."

Natalie glanced away but not quickly enough, as Trevor, frowning, murmured in his girlfriend's ear. He might have worked that little detail into the conversation before they'd gone climbing and saved them both the awkwardness. She sighed. At least she could hope this explained his reaction, not her oddness, after all. She'd read more into his helpfulness than it deserved.

"Ah, the lovely wonder who's brought sophistication to our slopes," said a white-haired gentleman with a liver spot shaped like an oak leaf hugging his jaw. "Sim Lemmons."

She had to smile when he kissed her hand, a sweet, elegant gesture.

"I can't tell you how delighted I am with your work. I believe you'll find me a patron."

"Thank you so much." Patrons were an artist's dream.

"I understand one of your painters is blind."

"Fleur Destry." Natalie nodded toward her standing by the wall. "In the green dress."

"I must congratulate her as well."

"She'll be delighted."

Approaching with Sara, Whit did an impression of discomfort with his shoulders. "I feel like the riffraff next door."

Natalie laughed. "I'll send them all over to kayak in the morning." She turned to Sara. "You look beautiful." Her navy and cream dress criss-crossed in front, where for once no baby nestled.

Sara ran her hands down the skirt. "I barely fit back into it. The waist isn't so bad but breast-feeding gives me what I never had before."

"It's a flattering style. I hope you'll enjoy your evening out." Before she could move on, Trevor joined them.

"Natalie, this is Kirstin."

"Oh good, you found the champagne." Natalie squeezed her elbow and tried to escape, but the reporter chose that moment to approach. Except the woman's gaze wasn't on her.

"Trevor MacDaniel at a gallery gala." Her acerbic tone set Natalie's teeth on edge.

"Jaz." His mouth formed a wry twist.

"In a suit. A tailored suit." She circled him. "Very chic. Did you steal it off a truck?"

"You might want to pass on the next tray of champagne."

Her eyes chilled. Before Jaz bit back, Kirstin tugged his sleeve.

"Jazmyn Dufoe, my date, Kirstin Bach."

"Aren't you stunning? Do you charge by the hour?"

The photographer hooked Jazmyn's arm and towed her away, sending a plea over his shoulder.

Nodding to the group, Natalie said, "Excuse me," and followed them. The photographer hadn't given his name, but they shared a desire to save the degrading situation.

He said, "This is Natalie Reeve, Jaz."

Her eyes still shot ice-blue flames.

"The gallery owner." He turned. "Ms. Reeve, tell us about your art."

With this level of emotional tension, she couldn't even fake eye contact. "What would you like to know?"

Jaz hissed, "Why on earth would you invite Trevor MacDaniel?"

———

Trevor turned his back on Jaz and effectively on Natalie also. He could hardly have made a worse appearance at this event Whit insisted he attend.

"She's our neighbor. You took her climbing. You can't blow off her opening. You're the one with experience at these things."

Whit was right, he had to come. But the last thing he'd wanted was to draw attention. Natalie deserved this night. And he hadn't handled their last interaction with the greatest finesse.

"You're kidding, right?" Kirstin looked down her nose at Jaz. "You dated her?"

"Briefly."

"Do you do it any other way?"

He shrugged, hands loose in his pants pockets.

She pouted her lower lip. "How long do we have to stay?" She'd exhausted her attention span.

"Long enough to see the exhibit. And buy something." He'd noticed several SOLD tags already.

"For me?"

"You don't like art."

"I like art."

He didn't argue the point, but neither did she. She grabbed another flute of champagne. He felt like swilling from the bottle.

A petite woman stepped around her companion and called, "Trevor."

He did a double take. "Tia?"

She laughed, touching the deep auburn twist of hair. "Not my normal style."

How had she even gotten her lion's mane in there?

Her husband, the chief of police, turned. As they shook hands, Trevor could tell the hawkish eyes caught everything, including the look he'd given Tia, though that couldn't be unusual. She had a dusky allure.

"Quite an event," the chief said.

"Culture comes to Redford."

"I'm Tia." She reached a hand to Kirstin.

"I'm sorry." Trevor turned. "This is Kirstin Bach. Jonah is chief of police, and Tia works search and rescue."

"Really?" Kirstin could not have sounded less interested.

What had he been thinking? "Nice to see you both." With a grip on Kirstin's elbow, he mounted the stairs to the loft.

Kirstin helped herself to another flute from the tray on a stand. He lifted and drained one himself. With the bubbles climbing up his sinuses and watering his eyes, he perused the offerings. One painting that was deep tones of blue shifting across the canvas caught and held his eye. The hues matched the wolf sculpture he'd purchased, but it had a power of its own.

"Trevor, I'm bored."

"Okay." He leaned in and got the ID number from the card beside the painting. Artist: Fleur Destry. Wasn't she the blind woman he saw around?

He went downstairs, Kirstin descending on her stilettos like the runway model she was. Behind a discreet podium, a proper-looking woman quietly tallied purchases. Trevor approached and gave her the number on the painting. It would be delivered tomorrow or the next day. Unless he needed it shipped.

"I'm local. Pine Crest."

"Oh, very good, Mr. MacDaniel. We'll look forward to future visits."

He didn't tell her he owned the business next door, just slid his wallet back into his coat and thanked her. She thanked him back. Kirstin gave his arm a tug. Maybe she thought this their lucky night. No one believed he wouldn't take the opportunities offered. Especially Jaz, who had taken it personally.

He stopped behind Whit and told him they were leaving. Jaz stood head to head with her photographer, checking his shots on the digital camera. Natalie stood near the door, speaking with a man wearing a pale blue jacket and black turban. He ought to congratulate her, but he'd done enough damage for one night.

———

Dazed and exhausted, Natalie leaned against the door between Fleur and Lena, the manager she'd hired on sight when the sophisticated, strong-featured woman interviewed. She could hardly believe their success, not simply in sales, but also community goodwill. People were delighted to have a gallery of this caliber.

"What a night." Lena spoke for all of them, her eyes alight.

Fleur laughed. "When that reporter went off on—wasn't it the search-and-rescue hero? Trevor MacDaniel?"

"It was." Natalie sighed. Not her favorite part of the night.

"Obvious history." Lena raised an eyebrow.

For a second Natalie thought she meant her brief fantasy relationship, then realized she meant Jazmyn Dufoe.

"And the date he brought... *Really?*"

Given her experience with Aaron and Paige, she wasn't at all surprised someone who looked like Kirstin appealed to him—and he to her. Strength and beauty. Natural draws. Aaron hadn't chosen a trophy wife— she'd chosen him. Where he imagined substance, there was only froth, but for his sake, they all kept looking.

Lena turned to Fleur. "Can't complain, though. He bought *Musings in Blue.*"

"He did?" Natalie and Fleur said together.

"Wow." Fleur brought her hands together, beatific. "My first sale at gallery prices."

"You're worth every dollar."

"Now see, I would have said penny."

They laughed.

Natalie yawned. "Ladies, I'm too tired for any more tonight. Thank you so much for being here and doing this. You were quite a hit, Fleur. I won't be surprised if you're all over the Internet tomorrow."

"Not because I'm blind, I hope."

"Being blind is part of your gift. Lena, I think you came straight from heaven."

The older woman laughed. "Where's my raise?"

"I hope for enough success to do well by everyone." She saw them out, but didn't leave. In the studio she pulled a smock over her dress, dragged a block of clay from the shelf, and beat it into a mound. Her whole body shook, the dizzying images making her ill. She started to work and kept on through the entire night, forming face after face. All were smiling but Kirstin, Trevor, and Jaz, and the force of those expressions overwhelmed the rest.

In every face she saw too much. Joy, excitement, pleasure. Envy, disdain, rage. It was like reading minds, seeing the shifting expressions, trapping and holding them without release. Crowds took a devastating toll.

She slumped down and closed her eyes. Aaron would have understood. But even though he knew this was the night, there'd been no word.

Th' infernal Serpent; he it was whose guile,
Stirred up with envy and revenge, deceived
The mother of mankind.

Act One. The first. He felt almost shy, certainly nervous, introducing himself, as it were. Not in person, but in deed.

The setting, a steamy wetland of sycamores spectral with Spanish moss, homes engulfed in kudzu, gnawed by termites. The air throbbed. Biting gnats. Dark mysteries moving through dark waters.

He'd chosen his subject well and carefully, the unruly child, the apathetic mother resenting an offspring she despaired of. Disobedient weanling, incapable guardian.

Disregarding his bellowed demands, the woman slammed the door, separating herself from the discharge of her womb. Enraged, the monster she'd created beckoned a monster she'd never imagined.

He set the toy on the muddy ground and, with the radio control, set the playful messenger in motion. Seen! Desired! As the all-terrain truck wheeled around, it drew on chubby legs, the curious brat. Out of reach— only just—until a greedy dive landed the boy on his prize, and with the swipe of an arm, the clamp of a hand, he lifted and carried the squirming quarry.

Five

With Lena managing the gallery, Natalie had spent the morning packaging last night's sales, arranging for two shipments and preparing five deliveries. UPS would handle the shipments, but she wanted to make the local deliveries as a show of gratitude. After leaning the two-thousand dollar, bubble-wrapped, and crated eagle mountain sculpture onto the dolly, she backed against the exit door.

Sunlight cast her shadow into the studio as she pushed through the door. Another shadow loomed to her left. She jumped, banging the dolly still caught in the door.

"Sorry." Trevor steadied the sculpture. "You shouldn't come out without looking."

She pressed a hand to her heart. Two weeks with neither an accidental nor intentional encounter, now twice in twenty-four hours? "What are you doing here?"

"The manager said you'd be delivering local sales. I thought I'd pick up my painting, save you the trip."

"Oh." She brought the dolly around. "It's inside. I'll get it in a minute. And thank you, Trevor. That sale meant the world to Fleur."

"Her painting made the sale. Can I give you a hand?"

"I can manage." She pushed the dolly toward her vehicle.

"We could use the company van. Take everything at once. It's not glamorous, but it can haul."

"I don't need help."

"You'll be surprised how inaccessible Pine Crest properties can be."

"How do you know I'm delivering to Pine Crest?"

His spread hands explained the obvious. That's where the money was. She gripped the nape of her neck. "I really don't—"

"Need help. I know. But an extra pair of hands…"

"I have the dolly."

"Trust me. That dolly won't go everywhere."

So he was offering assistance once again, which might be the way he liked things.

He said, "I have a sculpture and painting I want to coordinate, but I'm not sure where to put them. You have the eye for it, so after we deliver the rest, can you take a look?"

"You mean go to your house and arrange things?"

He shrugged. "We did yours. And seriously, Nattie—Natalie—"

"Nattie's fine." She was that to family and old, close friends, and for some reason she liked it from him.

"There's no way you're getting these crates delivered alone."

With no excuse to refuse except her own tender feelings, she let him into the studio where her private sculptures were draped and out of sight. They set out with a full van, and on the very first delivery, Trevor proved invaluable. The quarried stone steps rose at a heart-pumping pitch. She hated to think how embarrassing it would have been to ask Sim Lemmons to help haul his purchase.

With the last item delivered, she told Trevor, "Sorry to drag you through that."

"Do you see drag marks?"

"Nothing bloody," she admitted, staring out the window as he drove to a swank new condominium complex in Pine Crest. He scanned an ID key that allowed the van through the gate. He might be more the guy in the suit than she'd thought. On the top floor, he swiped and opened the door.

"I don't know why I expected a climbing wall and tent."

His smile warmed her as she studied the loft's interior. Her sculpture fit his minimal clean-line furniture. It sat on the hammered copper, C-shaped table between his couch and fireplace. "How committed are you to the furniture arrangement?"

"Not."

They shuffled his room around, lamps, tables, even the art on his walls. The wolf mountain ended up beneath a recessed ceiling spot on a black rectangular pillar that had previously held a lamp. Fleur's painting made a dramatic complement.

"You should offer this service to your customers, or is it just guys like me who need it?"

"Guys like you?"

"You know, tent dwellers."

She shrugged. "Seriously. You're Mr. Extreme Sports, but no trophy heads."

"I don't hunt."

"No canoe paddles, snowshoes, or barn wood."

He laughed. "I wasn't going for rustic."

She glanced over her shoulder. "This is sophisticated."

"What I do isn't all I am. Any more than what you do is you."

She'd have to disagree there, but kept it to herself.

"Would you like a glass of wine?"

His offer brought a clear memory of Kirstin with her champagne. "I should apologize for my catty remark to your girlfriend last night. I certainly don't expect everyone to love my work."

He expelled a breath. "Kirstin doesn't reflect my views and opinions."

"I hope she wasn't too bored."

"No, she was."

Refreshing honesty.

"Kirstin likes to be seen. She got bored because it wasn't the sort of crowd to be distracted by her." He dug in a drawer and produced a corkscrew. "And she's not my girlfriend."

Natalie moved to a photograph on a shelf that broke up his open space. A woman and five boys. He'd said four. "Your family?"

"Yeah."

"The oldest looks like you."

"Yep."

She leaned in. "Which one is the cop?"

"Second tallest, to my left. White or red?"

"White." If he was determined to pursue it, why not? But it might be these mixed signals that frustrated the reporter. "What's the story with Jazmyn Dufoe?"

"I'd rather not go into that."

"Okay."

"No prying or wheedling?" He poured the wine and brought her a goblet. "With Jaz, even the hint of something unsaid brought an assault."

"She's a reporter. You ought to expect that."

"I guess there's an element of buyer beware." He clinked her glass with his.

"Unless she failed to inform you, I have to say there is."

"Oh, I knew. Our first conversation was an interview."

"Forewarned is forearmed." She took a sip, perfectly chilled and smooth with just enough bite to keep it interesting.

"You'd think." He smiled. "So tell me about this eidetic memory."

"I wish I hadn't brought it up."

"Are you saying don't ask?"

"I'm just the weird one who remembers what I see. Especially faces."

"Why faces?"

"In the words of Ralph Waldo Emerson, 'A man finds room in the few square inches of the face for the traits of all his ancestors; for the expression of all his history, and his wants.'"

"A heavy thought." Trevor's eyes narrowed. "It isn't really remembering with you, though. Don't eidetics continue to see the image as though it's visible?"

She looked at him, surprised.

"I Googled it."

"I… Yes, that's right."

He sat against the back of his sofa. "I'm not sensing a deficit IQ."

"No." She stared at the floor.

"You think I prefer airheads."

"I didn't say that."

"Kirstin's not actually stupid. Just her own universe. Which works well for me."

"I see." Though she didn't see how that element could attract an altruistic man like Trevor. She took another sip of wine. "I like it."

"2008 Wind Gap Pinot Gris."

"I'll have to remember that."

"You can take the bottle. That's the first glass I've poured."

If she wasn't careful, she'd start crushing on him again.

"Have you heard from your brother?"

She sighed. "A text this morning that said, 'Sorry.'"

"Sorry?"

"Maybe that he missed the opening, or that he hasn't called. I think it's because of Paige. He's right to focus on her and Cody."

"And you're cut out?"

"I've been calling the hospital. The nurses know I'm family."

"And Cody?"

"They induced a coma to keep him still and to fight a systemic infection. They won't say it, but I know they're worried. I mean, two weeks is long, right?" Her voice caught.

"His injuries were severe, and carnivore attacks are rife with infection."

She fought back tears. "They're hitting it with the big guns—whatever that means."

Trevor nodded, sipped, then said, "How did they discover your ability?"

Grateful for the change in subject, she said, "Something in my development was different enough from Aaron's to make them wonder. Eidetic memory is very rare, even controversial, and never the same from one person to the next. The autistic painter Stephen Wiltshire can draw an entire city skyline after a single helicopter ride over it. That broad a vista leaves no residual image for me."

"Only people?"

"Mostly. Now."

"One article said many small children have it to some degree."

"That's true. Mine was extreme and didn't fade. I had to develop methods of controlling it."

"Art therapy?"

Again she looked surprised.

"You're a sculptor."

He'd put time and thought into it. "When I form images in clay, it processes them to a part of the brain that can let go."

"Until then it just sticks?"

She shrugged.

"And you were born with it."

"At one, they showed me books, then replaced them with blank-page versions. They'd ask, 'Where is the bunny?' and I'd touch it on the blank white page."

"Cool."

"At two, I colored complicated images I was shown onto a blank easel. The easel was only blank to them. By three, the overload of images demanded management, but because I wasn't able to distinguish essential and nonessential, the ones with the highest emotional impact stayed front and center."

A flicked glance revealed him fully engaged.

"I suffered night terrors and withdrew—severely. My parents removed me from preschool and ceased all testing and experiments. I was reading at a third-grade level, but refused to open a book, watch a movie, or interact with anyone. They put the TV in the closet and spent most of the next two years outdoors where the vista broadened to a degree I processed less traumatically."

"Wow."

Thinking back always made her realize her family's sacrifice. "The high points of my life were Aaron's Little League games, partly because the focus was away from me and my weird abilities. And I adored Aaron."

She wandered over to another series of photographs. "I guess you like to ski."

"I can't compete anymore."

Compete. She noticed the sports magazine covers on the next higher shelf and pointed to one. "Is that an Olympic banner?"

"The year I tore up my ligaments and shattered my kneecap."

"Ouch." He'd been a professional, a consummate athlete, and she knew from Aaron what effort that took.

"Speaking of which, do you care if I use the Jacuzzi?" He raised his foot to the back of the couch and rubbed his knee. "That last set of stairs…"

"I knew you shouldn't—"

"Hey." He lowered his foot. "It does this. I'll just give it heat and jets, unless... You want to get in?"

"Your Jacuzzi?"

"Sara keeps suits here."

He hot-tubbed with Whit's wife?

"They're over here all the time. The spa seats four."

"Oh."

"It's therapy for me, but you don't have to hurt to get in."

She brushed a strand of hair behind her ear and risked a quick glance up. "I'll just sit, if that's okay."

"You might change your mind." He led the way to a sparkling, clear spa built into a spacious balcony with a dressing room and towel closet. "If you do, suits are in there."

He went into an adjoining room and closed the door. She settled onto a cushion on the deck beside the spa, resisting the water's allure. With today's hauling, some residual strain from climbing, and all the stress, she imagined how great it would feel—and how disconcerting.

Trevor must have exited the room a different way, because he came back with the wine bottles and set them on the low table.

She sent her glance around the enclosed balcony. "This is really nice."

Wearing dark green swim trunks, he eased into the water. "This is nicer." He positioned the damaged knee in a jet.

She dipped her fingers into the frothy water. "You keep it hot."

"Effectively." He used a remote to open horizontal panes on the windows, letting in the mountain air. "Tell me if you get chilly. Or you really could get in. I'm not coming on to you."

"I didn't imagine you were." Not with women like Kirstin at his call.

"You're actually the only person besides Whit and Sara I've invited."

"Why me?" She pulled her feet in under her.

"I was just wondering that." He set down his glass and adjusted his leg. His knee must really hurt, the way he braced it.

"Are you okay?"

"I will be."

"I don't see how you climb and do all you do if it's that sensitive."

"It's not." He spread his arms across the back. "I jacked it chasing the cougar."

"Should you have it looked at?"

"No, believe me, there's nothing more they can do."

"But you might have reinjured it."

"I'd know."

Rescuing Cody had cost him more than she'd realized. His gaze landed on her, but she didn't return it, not directly.

"So what's it like having perfect recall?"

"I don't, really. Not like eidetic savants."

"Savants like Kim Peek?"

He'd researched thoroughly. "What did you learn?"

"Peek was missing a part that connects the two sides of the brain. Each of his eyes relayed independent information, so he read the left and right pages of a book simultaneously—and recalled over ninety-eight percent of the twelve thousand books he read." He extended his pointer. "And Dustin Hoffman played him in *Rain Man*."

"He was profoundly developmentally challenged."

"Your brain is obviously connected."

"Hyperconnected." She crossed her arms to hide a shiver. In that heat he'd need the cool air. "An MRI resonance showed extraneous activity when I was flashed face cards. That excluded the autism spectrum, since autistics don't recognize or interpret expressions until they're taught to. But they had no likely alternative."

"So what you have is a fluke?"

She considered how to answer that. "Every brain is different. Most share functional characteristics, but there are more anomalies than people think. Some cause disorders, others are considered gifts. Some brains are prodigious. And then there are the savants and super savants."

"Where are you?"

"If I believed in labels, it would be prodigy."

He sipped his wine. She watched the rim reach his lips, but looked no farther up his face.

"Sounds pretty cool."

"You haven't seen me self-destruct." She frowned. "Last night, all those faces made me physically ill. I couldn't get them out fast enough."

"How did you?"

"I sculpted a face mountain. Everyone who made an appearance."

"Really?" His reflection formed on the stilled surface as the jets turned off. "Can I see it?"

"No."

"Why not?"

She pressed her hands to her eyes. He'd caught her off guard to even mention it.

"You do that a lot."

"What?"

"Put up a shield."

He had no concept of the shields she put up.

"Look at me."

Resigned, she lowered her hands.

———

There it was again, the stare that in medieval superstition might have identified a seer. He'd wondered about her idiosyncrasies, never really looking at people, always shifting her view. Now he got it. Her prodigious brain held more than she wanted to retain. Given the difficulties she'd described, it took courage to interact at all.

It was also, he hated to admit, uncomfortable to sit there in her view and wonder what she saw. "Knee's good now. Thanks for letting me soak." He closed the windows with the remote, stood, and dried off with a towel, then gave her a hand standing up, surprised that she seemed a little unsteady. Must be a lightweight. Her wineglass still held half an inch.

"I'll be right out." He changed in his bedroom and met her in the hall. She had unclipped the hair that fell like brown gossamer strands over her collarbones, wreaking havoc with his convictions.

They drove in silence, but he didn't feel compelled to fill it. Neither, it seemed, did she. Jaz would have fit another thousand words in, prodding and provoking. Kirstin would have felt ignored. Of course, with her face turned away, he couldn't really tell what Natalie thought or felt.

He parked behind her studio and placed his hand on her headrest. "I'll only ask once again, but I'd like to see what came out of last night."

Staring at her hands, she blew out a slow breath. "Okay." She let him in through the back, worry creasing her brow as she slid the cloth off a cone-shaped mound on the huge Corian table. A mountain clogged with faces.

He stared. It was like seeing the event again, even the smallest faces reflecting the vibrant evening. Then he realized the most prominently represented were Jaz, Kirstin, and he, the expressions anything but vibrant.

He circled the piece. "There's Whit and Sara, Tia, the chief, the mayor." He shook his head. "They were all in there, clamoring to get out?"

"A silent cacophony."

It was like seeing her soul. "Your wolves and waterfalls are great. But this is…something else altogether." Prodigious. He returned to his aspect. "Is that how you see me?"

"It was last night."

"I didn't mean to be so hard."

"It was one night."

He looked at the cloth-covered pieces on the deep wooden shelves. "More?"

She nodded.

"Can I?" He removed the cover from a stunning bust of Sara holding Braden. A present-day Madonna. "These are not only accurate, they're insightful. Like you see inside."

"It's microexpressions."

He nodded toward a man-sized statue in the corner. "And that one?"

She hesitated, then walked over to it. "It's the first one I did here. The night Cody was attacked." She removed the cover.

He could hardly move.

———

Natalie felt the shaking begin as Trevor stared at the unfired statue.

His body stiffened. "You only saw me once."

"The image you left was very strong." Hands pressed to her back, she paced in short quick steps. "If what I capture is emotionally static, it fades. If not, it leaves an indelible imprint—until I transfer it to the clay."

"That makes you forget?"

"I don't see it anymore."

He frowned. "Show me tonight."

She startled. "You mean you?"

"Show me what you saw. In the spa." When she shook her head, he took her hand. "I saw you do it—the capture thing. Don't you need to get it out?"

She lied with another shake of her head.

"Yes, you do."

Closing her eyes, she jerked her hand free, pulled a mound of clay from the slop bucket onto the wedging surface, then pressed and rolled in a triangular motion until the excess moisture and air bubbles had been expelled. Taking a moment to calm herself, she started in. The aspect formed on the clay, an intense, sensual, haunted man.

She didn't know why or what she'd seen. She only copied what showed in his face. Finally, chin to her chest, she stepped back.

He rasped, "It's all there."

"I'm sorry."

He stared at the sculpture again, then walked out.

Trembling, Natalie covered it. She'd tried to tell him, but he had forced entrance to the freak show. She washed up, locked the gallery, and went home.

His pride
Had cast him out from Heaven, with all his host
Of rebel Angels, by whose aid, aspiring
To set himself in glory above his peers,
He trusted to have equaled the Most High.

The sign said OPEN TWENTY-FOUR HOURS, in recognition of people
for whom day and night were indistinguishable. He went inside,
aware that the bulbous mirrors in the corners were in fact surveil-
lance cameras. He had no intention of robbing the store. He would
not plunder, not even pilfer.

The woman at the register dug something out from under a nail,
too bored to notice him unless he brought something to be paid for.
He wouldn't. He moved to the end where the photo printing machines
explained their operation. He read every step, removed the part from the
camera that went into the machine, pressed the correct buttons on the
screen, inserted the credit card, and waited.

A sigh of relief. The card had not yet been missed, one among so
many, and of a lesser pedigree than those he'd left in the wallet, replaced
exactly as he'd found it. Having been instructed and duly paid, the machine disgorged the photograph, taken at the moment Leviathan surfaced,
inspiring maximum decibels from the star of the first act.

A tremor ran through him as he beheld his opening tableau, feeling,
for the first time, something more than invisible.

Six

Five days after the opening, Fleur led Piper and her quirky giant, Miles, into the gallery. The event itself would have meant too many people, too many germs for Miles to bear gracefully, but they entered now with anticipation she could feel.

"Oh, look!" Piper exclaimed—to Miles, obviously. "What fun!"

"Yes, fun, very fun. Who could imagine such fun?"

Fleur pressed her fingers to the smile pulling at her lips, in case they were looking. She suspected at least part of what Miles said poked fun at himself and the world he had such a hard time in.

"Fleur, your paintings look fantastic here. Don't they look fantastic, Miles?"

"Quite fantastic."

"Hello." Natalie joined them, but her greeting seemed uncharacteristically flat. Concerned, Fleur stayed behind while Piper and Miles moved through the display floor. "Has something happened, Natalie? Is it your nephew?"

Natalie released a slow breath. "Cody's still fighting infection. I guess animal attacks are bad that way, but it's going in the right direction, thank God."

"Your brother?"

"He's all right, I think."

"Then…" She tipped her head, waiting.

Natalie sighed. "I did something stupid, and now, days later, I can't stop thinking about it."

"What did you do?"

"I showed Trevor something I shouldn't have."

"Trevor MacDaniel?"

"I knew better and let him talk me into it anyway."

"That sounds…a little hinky."

"No." Natalie groaned. "Nothing like that." She took her arm. "Come with me."

Fleur went with her into the studio at the back of the gallery. She heard the soft plop of a moist cloth, and a moment later Natalie directed her hands to cold, damp clay. Not a lump. A head. A face. Familiar. "Is this me?"

"I hope you don't mind. Faces get stuck in my head. It's called eidetic memory, to keep seeing something as though it's still there. This is how I make it go away."

Fleur fingered the hair, the brow, the bridge of her own nose. "You showed Trevor my face?"

"Not yours. His."

"So what's the problem?"

"Faces are like maps, showing where they've been and what happened along the way. Not specifics, of course. But joy and pain and goodness… and not."

"You saw something bad in Trevor?"

"Not bad. No. But not what he wanted me to see."

Fleur rested her hands on the smooth work surface. "Show me."

"I can't. It's his." Another sigh. "He wanted me to make it, practically forced me to, but when he saw it, he walked out."

"I didn't realize you were friends."

"I don't know what we are. I hardly know him, and yet…" Her voice trailed off as she bent down for something, opened a cabinet and closed it. "It's just without Aaron, this is harder than I imagined."

"Is he your only family?"

"My parents head a relief team. For the last two years, they've gone from one disaster area in the world to another. That was their dream and they're finally doing it."

Warmth and esteem came through in her voice.

"They check in when they can, but it isn't often. Anyway, I'm twenty-five. I'd be fine on my own, if I could stop *seeing* people."

"Careful what you wish for." Fleur heard the cloth covering the model. "Natalie, if you fire and display that, I won't mind. It should be enjoyed like the rest of your work."

"I don't show the faces. I only thought, if anyone could, you'd understand my making them."

"I do understand that. But not your hiding them. Gifts are given for a reason, you know."

"I'm using my gifts and my blessings. But this part sometimes feels more like a curse."

"All right." Fleur reached and found Natalie's hand. "Come on, then, let's get Piper and Miles. We're going out for dinner, and you're coming with us."

———

The Tarleton Hotel in the heart of Old Town hearkened back to genteel times with spoked gingerbread trim in the archways; sheer-draped, leaded-glass windows; and beveled mirrors in carved frames. Sitting at the table with Fleur and her friends, Natalie felt the pressure inside her easing. These people were genuine and funny.

She listened with dismay and amusement as Fleur's roommate, Piper, told about her first experience in the grand old dining room. "My date drugged my wine and it turned blue, but did I notice? I'd have chugged squid ink to kill Bob Betters's droning on and on and on."

"Some men have that effect," Fleur agreed.

"Bob should drink squid ink," Miles mumbled. "Every day. A complete diet of squid ink."

"What happened?" Natalie leaned in.

"Chief Westfall saw the whole thing and arrested him on the spot. I wish I could remember Bob Betters getting perp-walked through the restaurant he thought would impress my socks off."

"You're better off with socks on," Miles quipped. "And Bob can't eat here anymore. He has to eat squid ink."

Piper giggled. "Well, it's true he can't eat here. The owner banned him."

Fleur said, "Why did you even go out with him?"

"Coercion."

Miles looked grieved. "I should drink squid ink. Squid ink for me."

"Stop it, Miles. Don't even say it."

A towering, slope-shouldered man with a mild face and goofy haircut, Miles looked less like the genius geek Piper claimed he was, than a melancholy circus clown who might slip into a slow soft-shoe. His sizeable frame was not athletic like Trevor's, but ungainly, as though it still took him by surprise.

"Bob's a bully," Piper said. "Feeling bad lets him win."

"We'll drop the squid ink." Miles squirted his hands with disinfectant as though washing the slate clean. "Squid ink's run its course."

"Sure has." She laughed. "Remind me not to fuel your fire."

"Squid ink. Fuel of the future."

"Oh my gosh." Piper clapped her hands to her head. "If anyone could do that, it's you. But if you say it once more, I will tickle you."

Miles drew a straight face and refrained from speaking.

Piper crumpled. "You know I won't, right?"

He gave a solemn nod, but still looked peaked.

"Well, okay then."

Barbie-doll tall and blond, Piper seemed truly fond of the big guy, whose idiosyncrasies didn't hide his keen intelligence and dry wit. Natalie warmed. They might be the only misfits in town, but with them she wasn't a pariah. She just had to avoid people who thought she was. She excused herself when her phone vibrated, hoping fiercely it was Aaron, but she didn't recognize the number and let it go.

"Bob Betters wasn't your worst nightmare," Fleur told Piper.

"Isn't that the truth?" Sobering, Piper took a swallow of her lemonade, and then told her what happened last fall in their sweet mountain community.

Natalie shook her head. "The woman kidnapped you to save her sister?"

"In her own special world."

Miles muttered something low.

"As awful as it was for you"—Fleur touched Piper's hand—"I've never heard of anything so sad as that poor woman."

Piper shuddered. "Good thing lightning never strikes twice. Redford's had its monster."

"You're staring." Sue elbowed him.

At a table near Piper's, Jonah grunted. He had gathered his off-duty officers at Redford's nicest restaurant to celebrate Sue's birthday, since her husband had been killed last year and between the job and two little ones, she hardly ever got out. That elbow might be a contributing factor. "I was remembering."

She leaned her chin on her fist. "Collaring Bob Betters for drugging Piper? Or how wrong you were about Miles?"

"You're feeling it tonight, aren't you, Officer Donnelly?"

Her dimples peeked out. "Or did you enjoy Piper's recounting your rescuing her from a strange and gruesome fate?"

"As you recall, that was Tia and Miles."

"You brought the cavalry."

He looked across at the party of four. That business last year had driven home his need for a stronger force—and he was still waiting. Thank you, Mr. Mayor, city manager, and council. "I like Piper's optimism, but I'm not sure it's all sunny skies and rainbows for this town."

"Well, of course not, Chief. We live in the real world."

"That we do." He nodded as the cell phone vibrated in his pocket, knowing before he checked that it was dispatch. He could send any one of them to back up the officer on duty, but instead he wished Sue a happy birthday and headed out himself.

———

Natalie demurred, but Miles insisted on paying for dinner, using the credit card Piper had convinced him was even better than uncirculated bills.

"He resisted at first, because fingerprints show on plastic," Piper said.

"Germs on fingerprints," Miles said. "Germs on everyone, everywhere."

"But"—Piper pointed when the server returned the card—"now he simply sanitizes."

Miles gave the card a good cleaning with a disinfecting wipe.

Feeling lighter than she had since arriving, Natalie headed back to the studio to model Piper and especially Miles. His face had told her so much, lots of it sad and strained, but also joyful. There was even a playful streak. The release of their images wasn't urgent, a quick study would do.

She had just covered the clay and washed her hands and arms when the knocking came at her back door. She had not set the alarm and looked quickly for a protective weapon. Not finding anything of use, she went to the door and said, "Who is it?"

"Trevor."

She dropped her forehead to the wall.

"Natalie?"

Groaning silently, she opened the door but kept her gaze lowered.

He cleared his throat. "Can we talk?"

She weighed the "No, thanks" option, then with a sigh, pulled her jacket on, locked up, and stepped outside. He seemed surprised but must have understood her reluctance to invite him into her private space again.

He said, "It's dark out."

"Dark is good." She could see him by the single security light, if she wanted to—but she didn't.

"It's cold."

The first week in September had that tendency at eight thousand feet. She folded her arms and waited.

"Okay, so…" He expelled a breath. "I ended the other night badly."

The climbing, the opening, the studio. She wasn't vindictive, but recognized a pattern.

He shoved his hands into his pockets. "I can imagine what you thought."

"Oh, it was pretty clear."

He popped the vertebrae in his neck with a twist. "Can we at least get in my car?"

"You saved my nephew, Trevor. I'm forever grateful."

"But…"

She blinked her own car lights with the remote. "Let's just leave it."

"You saw something I don't show people."

"You showed me. And you made me show you."

"I realize that." He leaned his arm on the outer wall. "I just didn't expect it."

He should have. She'd revealed more of herself to him since they'd met than most people saw in her whole life. She shivered. He started to take off his coat.

"No." It came out sharply. "We can get in the car."

"Mine's still warm."

His engine started with a heat blast that felt good but didn't take away the chill. The dome light faded and died, leaving blue console lights illuminating words with no meaning in this moment, fuel, speed, and music settings. The stars outside were brilliant, cold white sparks, together but untouching in a blackened sky where she fixed her eyes to avoid the ghostly planes of his face.

"I tried to call."

"I didn't recognize the number."

"I went by the house, but you weren't there, so I came here."

The corner of a receipt was pinched in the glove compartment flap, out of place in the otherwise orderly vehicle. "You went to a lot of trouble to say something you still haven't said."

He rested his forearms on the wheel. "Watching you sculpt me was like seeing my life there in the clay."

"I don't know anything, Trevor. You have the context. I just saw the effect."

"I know. There's just stuff I don't talk about, stuff that's not part of now."

"Everything is part of now."

"I don't let it be."

"Then what are we doing?"

He tucked his chin and sat there. She reached for the door.

"No, wait. Just listen a minute, okay?"

She settled back, feeling the stitches of the leather seat with one hand.

"I like you, Nattie. You're different."

"Big surprise."

"That's not criticism. You think what you have is a problem for us, and, yeah, it looked that way the other night."

"Looked that way?"

He expelled a breath. "The issue isn't you. I felt…exposed."

"I can't stop seeing the way I see, but I don't show the models, and I don't know anything. It's expressions, not voodoo. If you think—"

"I don't. But I've been in the spotlight, had my life open to paparazzi, media, reporters like Jaz who keep digging and digging. I thought I'd learned to hide what I didn't want to show, then you shattered that belief."

"You just spent days in the news."

"For something I did. Not who I am."

"That's who you are. Why do you keep—"

"It's not the whole story."

She flicked a glance.

"If you give me some time..."

She shook her head. "You don't owe me an explanation. You of all people."

"Inviting you into my hot tub was a bigger deal than I realized." The timbre of his voice paled with that admission. "It's where I let down my guard." He swallowed. "In the heat and the jets, I admit my body hurts, and more than my body."

"Then why were you surprised by what I saw?"

He smiled grimly. "I thought I had it under control."

Of course he did. This man had snatched Cody from the lion's jaws. He had assembled her furniture and unpacked her things, stepping in again with the deliveries. He had taken her climbing, then shut her out. Made her see him, then walked away.

"Trevor, what you did for Cody had a strong impact on both of us. If that hadn't happened, you wouldn't be here."

"So? Everyone meets somehow."

"He needed saving. I don't."

"You think I'm saving you?"

"I think it's what you do."

He didn't argue.

"You challenged a mountain lion for a child you'd never seen. I can't imagine what it takes. You know how grateful I am, but I have to wonder what could drive you to face danger like that."

"In search and rescue—"

"Whit would have stopped. You didn't. Either the danger didn't matter or you thrive on it." A slinky coyote trotted past their doors, cast them a glow-eyed stare, and disappeared along the creek.

He said, "It isn't that."

"Then what?"

He spread his hands. "Things aren't dangerous if you know what you're doing."

"Like the cougar?"

"I was armed."

"What?"

"I had a gun. I'd have used it."

She looked up, confused. "But you didn't."

"I was after your nephew, not the cat."

"You threw a rock instead of drawing the weapon."

"The rock was a threat it could see. Animals can't comprehend a bullet."

If he'd killed the cougar, would they have saved Cody's arm?

"With the speed and terrain of the chase, I might have hit Cody. Even with a clean shot, the cat could have fallen on him."

She held back the desire to scream, "Why didn't you try!" even though what he said made sense. "So you were calculating everything."

"I wouldn't have reached the top of my sport if I couldn't plot my line."

"Skiing is hardly the same."

"Well, one accident can end it all."

A bad thought, given Aaron's injury. She pressed her palms to her eyes. "Do you ever just watch a movie?"

"I play Monopoly with Whit and Sara."

That caught a laugh from her. "People still play that?"

"Sara wasn't allowed video games. She has every board game ever made."

"Do you win?"

"Sara, inevitably."

"Do you let her?"

He cocked his head. "Why would you think that?"

"Just curious about the dynamics." How aggressive was he with his friends? Did he ever let down?

"The dynamic is Sara wins and Whit and I act like we care. She's a blond Hermione Granger, always right, always better, but true blue and pretty handy to have around."

"You've read Harry Potter?"

"And seen the movies. Younger brothers, you remember."

"Are you Harry or Ron?" Though she knew the answer.

"The analogy ends with Sara." He shifted uncomfortably.

There it was again, his wall. What was so hard about admitting what everyone else saw? "You're Harry. The besieged hero, standing between evil and innocence."

"If you're talking about Cody, I was only doing my job."

His dogged insistence wore thin.

"Look, I just meant to apologize and make sure you're okay." His tone shut the door on that subject.

Fine. He could keep his secrets. She'd already told him that much. "I'm okay. Thanks." She opened the door and climbed out.

———

Trevor clenched his teeth in frustration as Natalie got into her car and drove off. At least she didn't go inside to purge him from her sight, probably because she hadn't once looked at him directly. His hands gripped the steering wheel.

It was not how he meant to end this. He'd wanted to ask her out, have a nice time together, good conversation, food, wine, whatever she liked— if she would just stop pushing the hero thing. But she wouldn't. She had to know what drove him. Shaking his head, he put the car in gear.

He didn't need this hassle. He'd gotten his life right where he wanted it. A thriving business with his closest friends, the opportunity to use his skills—not the ones he really wanted to, but close enough. A great place to live and the sense to appreciate it. He was satisfied with that. No matter what Natalie saw in unguarded moments.

Besieged hero? All he was trying to do was help where he could. If

Natalie didn't want it, fine. But she needed what else he'd planned, whether she'd admit it or not.

His phone bleeped a low battery warning. Having forgotten to plug it in last night, he'd brought the charger to the office and still forgot to charge up—an indication things were getting complicated. He killed the engine.

After unlocking and opening the office door, he saw something on the all-terrain carpet. He flicked on the light and picked up the envelope addressed to the store, tossed it on his desk, and plugged in his phone. No sense going home. Might as well handle loose ends.

He slit open the envelope and took out a photo.

A boy, five or six years old. Dark hair, heavyset. His face contorted, mouth so wide the sound coming out must be caterwauling. Understandable, in that he sat in a splintery skiff sitting low in swampy water with ominous, sequential bumps and jagged teeth protruding.

Trevor frowned. He knew people found this kind of gag photo comical, but it wasn't. He flipped it over. No note. He tossed it in the trash, unplugged his charger, and decided to go home after all.

"Is this the region, this the soil, the clime,"
Said then the lost Archangel, "this the seat
That we must change for Heaven?—this mournful gloom
For that celestial light?"

He had not prepared Act Two, neither setting nor subject. It came to him—like cancer.

The baby-sitter, cell phone still caught between rapidly texting thumbs, had finally realized the giant, red plastic car-shaped shopping cart held animal crackers, milk, Oreos, and a squeezable bath toy, but no dimpled, drooling tot. Panic catching her like an electric current, she bolted around the end cap, scanning one aisle and the next, then ran for the doors and for the vested employee who might have—must have—seen her charge.

"Have you seen a two-year-old? He's blond... A...a red hoodie, blue jeans. Please, I can't find him." Spinning, staring back inside the store. "He was in that cart." In plain view of the doors.

The employee alerted another to start looking at the far end. A manager, sensing a shift in the normal commerce, turned her attention outward, over the parking lot with scattered vehicles clustered more densely near the entrance, to the street, to the screech of brakes.

Hands pressed to his ears could not block the screeching, screeching in his head. He cried and beat his chest, the pain, exquisite, excruciating. Their failure a knife edge of despair. Past and present merged. He writhed.

No light. No air. Hungry. Scared. A shudder rippled through him. He despised the hushed and weeping crowd. How could they be so blind? self-absorbed? dull-hearted? Fools. Beasts! Bathed in blue and blood-red lights, he left them, bearing witness in the camera he clutched.

Seven

Fleur stood beside Natalie, her fingers once again tracing the artist's model of her face. She had no illusions of creating anything so fine and perfect, but Natalie had suggested she try sculpting a self-portrait, so here she was. She puffed out her lips with a breath.

People might think that, since she was blind, she didn't care how she looked, but it wasn't true. Her retinas were useless, but once the infection had passed, her eyes looked like everyone else's. To keep the muscles functional she tracked toward sounds, especially voices, to act as much like a sighted person as she used to.

She took care with her appearance. Her naturally thick, dark lashes required no mascara, but she moisturized and applied a soft blush and lip glosses of various colors. Her hair was always clean and brushed. She dressed with care, trusting companions to choose items that fit her style when they took her shopping. Piper was especially wonderful for that.

Outwardly, she was chic and composed and capable, and people marveled at her amazing adjustment, her healthy acceptance. They didn't recognize her need to be what she'd been, what they were, didn't know the terror that seized her sometimes when she was alone. Helplessness that paralyzed.

Natalie gently positioned her hands on a fresh mound of clay, the earthy scent of it ripe and elemental. "I've wedged the air out. It's all ready."

"But am I?"

"Only if you want to."

Fleur felt the clay. Natalie had already formed the rudimentary shape of a head, neck, and shoulders. All she needed to do was make her face. How hard could that be? She drew a breath and nodded. "Here goes nothing."

"I'll be out front if you need anything."

"Okay." Hearing the door close, Fleur pressed the clay to test resistance. She'd never excelled in three dimensions, had not worked in it very much at all. Awkwardly, she started, working the far side of the sphere as she would touch her real face. The cold clay made a deathly flesh, but it warmed with friction and her body heat.

———

Through the gallery windows, Natalie watched Trevor return with his group, boisterous after their experience. They'd been in capable hands. Maybe someone who cared so well for so many couldn't limit himself to a single relationship. Even his friendship with Whit had the duality of Sara.

He was the go-to guy in a crisis—no contest. Her gratitude and amazement welled up afresh. He didn't pretend to be anything he wasn't, and he didn't have to. But then, neither did she.

She had joked with Whit about the difference in their clientele. You could see it in the way they approached one door or the other. Art aficionados strolled, while the adventure seekers charged in, especially in these last warm days as fall encroached. Just one more experience before the gear changed from life vests to snowshoes.

But art was timeless. It was sipped, not gulped. Art didn't plunge down mountains or dodge boulders in white rushing water. It might challenge, even unnerve, but always invited contemplation, appreciation.

Art soothed and intrigued and unfolded layer by layer, revealing more and more with every glimpse. Turning away from the window, she took in the citadel she'd created—with Aaron's funds and God's grace—a place of beauty, serenity, and on occasion commerce. How had she imagined traffic between two such worlds?

Better to thrive on her own terra firma. She looked over when someone entered, felt herself light up. She couldn't have chosen a more perfect example. "Mr. Lemmons."

"Now we've covered that." He wagged a finger.

She smiled as her patron approached. "Sim."

"Mademoiselle." Again he kissed her hand, half jester, half prince— she'd seen his castle. "Would you have some moments to spare?"

For the better part of the next hour, she walked him through the exhibit in a private tour, describing the subjects, and the impressionistic treatments that had developed from the original settings. Already the owner of her eagle mountain, he settled on his next purchase, *Crystal Lake*. Lena handled the sale. Her manager had insisted the artist should not double as the money-changer. Except on Lena's days off, of course.

As she was thanking him, a cry came from the studio. Natalie rushed back and found Fleur, bent over the worktable. "What is it? Are you all right?" She looked at the clay, thinking Fleur had been too frustrated to try, then realized the other side bore the features.

Moving around, she saw the shape of Fleur's face, a good replica of the narrow jaw and pointed chin, unsmiling lips, and delicate nose. But what drew and held her gaze were the eye sockets. Fleur had bored her fingers in, creating hollows that must have wrenched the cry from her.

She hadn't imagined this would be painful, but the agony in that clay face rivaled anything she'd created. She wrapped an arm around Fleur's shoulders. "I'm sorry. I'm so sorry."

Fleur groaned. "It's not you."

Natalie pressed the side of her head to her friend's. "Sometimes the clay pulls things out from somewhere deep inside." She just hadn't realized it would be that way for anyone else. "I mean, think about it. God made everything else with words, but it took clay to make a soul."

Fleur sighed. "I ruined it."

"No." Natalie stroked her arm. "You gave the clay your wound."

Fleur straightened. "Will you keep it? For a little while?"

"If you want me to."

"I might, at some point, be able to make eyes."

She tried to hide the ache from her voice. "It will be here."

"Do you mind if I go now?"

"Of course not." She squeezed Fleur's shoulder. "If you're all right."

Fleur shook the hair back from her face. "I am, just... Show me the sink?"

Natalie helped her wash up, then pushed open the door dividing the studio from the gallery. Since Mr. Lemmons had gone, she asked Lena to take Fleur home.

"I've just finished up here." Lena moved the glasses from her eyes to the crown of her head. "You all right, honey?" she asked Fleur.

"Yes. Thank you."

Natalie squeezed Fleur's hand. "I'll see you tomorrow." She went into the studio and, without looking at it again, gently draped Fleur's model. Trevor was right about the nakedness.

After turning off the display lights in the loft, she came down to find him, wearing chinos and a sports jacket. Her stomach tightened.

"Hey." He slid his hands into the pockets.

"Hey." She moved to the bank of light switches behind the podium.

"How're you doing?"

"I'm in no imminent danger." Peripherally, she saw the corner of his mouth pull.

"I was hoping to catch you before you left."

"And so you did."

He shifted the weight on one leg, probably easing a newly strained knee doing whatever he'd done with the group earlier. "I'd like to take you somewhere."

They obviously had different impressions of their last conversation. She felt pretty certain she'd closed that door.

"You'll be glad you came."

She cupped her hands over the keys on the podium. "I'm listening."

"I'd rather surprise you."

"Trevor." She couldn't help it. The whole thing made her laugh.

"What?"

"Is there any reason a famous professional athlete—"

"Formerly famous, former professional athlete."

"—needs to spend time with me? Come on."

He gripped his hips. "Okay, wow. You have a serious misperception. I'm a guy asking you out. Nothing else. No hidden agenda."

Only a ride on a roller coaster she never bought a ticket for. She fiddled with her keys. If she went, it would be with eyes wide open—just not on him. "I'm not dressed for anything rugged."

He perused her oyster silk blouse and gray skirt. "That's perfect."

The kind of roller coaster that screeched to a stop, then did it all again in reverse. "Let me set the alarm." She pulled on a matching wool suit jacket and went out behind him, securing the door. To her surprise, he didn't drive toward town or toward the Kicking Horse center, but merged onto the highway. "So this place isn't local."

"Did my face tell you?" He cracked a smile that infiltrated her defenses like tree roots through rocky fissures.

"Fine, joke about it."

"Just calming your nerves."

"My nerves?"

"Or whatever." He smiled again, the creep.

She crossed her arms. "I have nerves of steel."

"I saw that bouldering."

"And just now got around to saying so?"

He gave a long sigh.

The scenery made driving in silence acceptable. But after a while, the crags and slopes and Trevor's presence brought back Cody's attack and the familiar ache inside. He could keep their destination secret, but she had a lot to learn about this guy who kept showing up at her door. "How long have you done search and rescue?"

"Almost five years."

"How did you start?"

"Got a call for an expert climber to help search some gnarly terrain in Utah. A solo backpacker missing twenty-four hours. They'd exhausted a surface search and suspected a fall in one of the cliff areas. I grabbed Whit and they flew us in by helicopter, but from the start it was a bad situation, poor access and bitter weather moving in. By the time we mobilized, visibility had degraded."

"You still went in?"

"We hoped for enough of a window, and with the temperature plunging…" He reached down and adjusted the heat dial as though reliving the cold. "We'd have gone right past if the team leader hadn't glimpsed the victim through the blizzard."

"What did you do?"

"I had to get down there and check for life before we risked more in those conditions. The wind kept blowing me off the rock and dashing me back into it."

Of course he'd been the one to go down. "Was he alive?"

"She was. Marin Bircher, forty-five, survival trained and skilled. As far as we could guess, she got disoriented and stepped over the edge."

Natalie shuddered. "What a horrible feeling that would be. Not to see it coming."

"She doesn't remember."

"Anything?"

"Just waking up in the hospital."

"You talked to her?"

"She wanted to thank me. We touch base now and then."

Natalie flicked him a glance. Still caught in it herself, she understood the woman's gratitude. "You must have a lot of stories."

"They're not all good."

"How do you deal with the bad ones?"

"That depends. If there was nothing we could do, as in the trauma killed them, then it's not so bad. But when they could have lived if we'd found them sooner, or got them out faster... Those are the ones that come back in the dark."

She imagined that awful blizzard, the rugged terrain, the sheer difficulty of what they did. "Do you ever work with dogs?"

"Not directly, but with their trainers. Especially when there's a lower chance of survival. A dog knows if someone has slipped into an ice or stone crevice where we'll never reach them."

"Do you keep looking for remains?"

"Of course. People need closure."

"So you keep on, even when you're certain they're dead."

"There's always the balance between finding the lost and risking the rescuers. As the chance of survival decreases, more weight goes to the team."

"Have you ever stopped too soon?"

"Every time there's no answer at the end."

"That must be a difficult call to make."

"Sometimes it's clear, storm or geography making progress impossible. No one ever wants to stop. But the wilderness has a brutal power you ignore at your peril."

He told her about rescues where they'd been overwhelmed, driven back again and again. The conversation occupied her so completely she didn't realize where they were until he parked.

"Oh, Trevor."

"I'd have come sooner if it hadn't been complicated for you."

"Will they let you in?"

He opened his door and turned. "They'll let us in."

Riding the hospital elevator, she was not as confident. Her feet grew heavy. Could she face them?

"I kept hoping your brother would relent, and we could come with his blessing."

"It's not Aaron." In the three weeks since the attack, she'd been offered no opportunity, but she knew whose choice that was. She hoped she knew. What if she saw something else in her brother's face?

No longer in ICU, when the infection abated at last, Cody had been moved to the amputee clinic. Just the name broke her heart, but when she walked in, his sweet voice cried, "Auntie Nattie!"

Tears streamed down her face as Cody's arm came up.

In a wheelchair, leg extended, Aaron turned, the love in his eyes unmistakable. "Nat."

She squeezed her nephew until he squirmed, then turned to her brother. "Where's Paige?"

"She went home to clean up and rest."

God was good. "This is Trevor MacDaniel."

Aaron held out his hand. "You're my hero, man."

How many people had used those words to her brother for simply playing a game?

Aaron's throat choked with emotion. "Anything I can do for you, ever, you just say it."

"Just glad he made it."

As the guys talked, she sat on the bed and drank Cody in. "How're you doing, honey?"

"My arm fell off." His straightforward delivery squeezed her heart. "Dat lion made it."

"I'm so sorry."

"Dey make a new one."

"That's wonderful."

"A wobot one."

"Wow." She didn't have to fake her awe. Blinking back her tears, she turned to her big brother, who nodded. Amazing.

"How's your leg?"

"I don't get a robot one."

"Those are saved for the best boys in the world." She hugged Cody again and stood up.

Aaron said, "The team sent in their orthopedic squad to consult. I'm healing well. But Cody's the star here." Pain and courage marked his face, looking at his little boy.

She couldn't begin to know how hard it was. She hugged his neck and kissed him. "I've been so worried."

He kissed her too. "I know. I'm sorry. Paige is out of her head. This... It's so much to deal with. Just keeps coming at us like a wicked screwball."

"Is there anything I can do? I want to help."

"I know." He glanced over his shoulder at Cody and Trevor. "You know better than all of us what it takes to live different. I hope—"

"What's she doing here?"

Natalie spun out of his arms.

"You must be Paige." Trevor rose and extended his arm to shake her hand, it seemed, but also coming between them. "I'm Trevor MacDaniel."

Paige ignored him. "Why is she here? I told you to leave us alone."

"Paige." Aaron's voice broke.

She turned on her husband. "Get her out of here."

"I'm going." Natalie sent Cody a last lingering look, his bewilderment piercing her heart. With a quick, stricken glance at Aaron, she shot past Paige to the hall, her legs moving with involuntary volition.

Trevor caught her arm and turned her around the other way. They moved in silence to the elevator and down. Eyes closed, she felt the cab land. He walked her to the Lexus.

"Are you all right?"

"I can't see."

He turned her toward him. How could she explain that images of Cody's fear and confusion, Aaron's despair, overlapped by Paige's rage and hatred all but blocked what was right in front of her?

"Do you need your studio?"

She nodded. In the passenger seat, she held her hands over her face as the miles passed. It didn't hide the images behind her eyelids, but kept her from trying to see like a normal person. "I'm sorry."

"Hey." He squeezed her knee. "I shouldn't have forced it."

"You didn't force anything."

"I could have told you what it was."

"I'd have chosen to go. You saved me the angst of worrying the whole way." She looked, and his face came over the others, surprisingly dulling Paige just a little. "Now I know Aaron doesn't blame me. He's trying to hold his family together. And I got to hug Cody."

"He seemed fine until his mom arrived."

"Paige has nothing to help her through this. No faith, no fortitude. She's never fought for anything in her life. I don't know if she can."

"So everyone gives in?"

"That's her baby in the bed, her husband in a cast. If she doesn't want my comfort, who am I to force it?"

He rested his wrist on the wheel and said nothing. He didn't know what a strain she had put on her own family with her limitations. Aaron loved her, she didn't doubt that now, but he had spent enough years helping her. He had to set his priorities, and he'd done it right.

"I'm sorry we had to rush back," she said as they entered the studio.

"That's all right." He sounded sincere. If anyone understood duress, it was this man.

"You can go now. I'll be fine."

"I'm not really comfortable with that."

"Why not?"

"You were wandering like a punch-drunk fighter."

Great image for him to have of her. "I'm here now. I just need to work it out."

"If it's all right with you, I'll camp on that stool until I know you can see."

He sat with his forearms resting on his thighs, his posture pensive, while she worked. The clay felt like mud in her hands. Too wet. Too soft. It wouldn't hold the shape. She worked it so long and hard her arms ached by the time the clay stiffened enough to model.

A great surge of love and sorrow flooded her as she shaped Paige's misery. Next she formed Aaron, his loyalty torn between them. She didn't want that. He needed to be whole. And finally Cody, who would receive a "wobot" arm. She molded the precious features just as she had braced his soft, warm face and kissed the curve of his head.

Finished, she staggered back, arms and heart aching, into Trevor. She felt wrung out—and hated that he saw. Now he wouldn't believe she could handle anything.

He steadied her. "Mind if I look?"

She sagged. "You saw the real thing."

He let go and studied her sculpture. "You were kinder than I'd have been. Especially on Aaron. He should have stood up for you."

"I know it seems that way, but you're not married, Trevor. Aaron's heart is in the right place."

He turned. "Can you see me?"

"Yes."

"Then can we get some food? I'm starved."

She swallowed the tightening in her throat. "You're not getting out of here as fast as you can?"

"I played that scene—not a great performance. The Summit's open, but Jaz hangs out there. The other spots stop serving at nine."

"Take me home and I'll make us something."

He scratched the back of his neck. "Some date, huh?"

"I'm not much of a dater."

"I'm usually a rock star."

She laughed. "Well, I've thought Titan and hero and archangel, but—"

"Archangel?"

"The first sculpture."

He shook his head. "Nattie..."

"I have some roasted chicken and asparagus."

"Now you're the rock star."

"I might be too tired to warm it."

He beamed. "Cold chicken is my favorite."

Before they reached his car, Trevor checked his phone. "Hold on, I need to call Whit back."

"This late? With a baby?"

"He tried six times, but I turned my phone off for our trip." He held up a finger. "Yeah, Whit. What is it?" A pause, then, "Now?" He glanced at her. "Okay, I'm coming."

"Change of plans?"

"We need to swing by their place."

"Is something wrong?"

"Something weird, I guess. Whit wouldn't say."

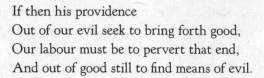

If then his providence
Out of our evil seek to bring forth good,
Our labour must be to pervert that end,
And out of good still to find means of evil.

Miles and miles by car had not dulled the throbbing wound of senseless death. It abscessed and putrefied, filled him with silent keening as he perused this fallen world, his domain. After leaving one gasless vehicle, he searched for another and heard, like a whistle to canine ears, an infant wailing.

From a frame house begging drafts through dingy window screens came wail upon wail. How could no one hear?

Drawing close, he saw. Their ears were not deaf, rather blocked by carnal desires consuming them. Selfish passion sated; helpless need unheeded.

Deftly, he slipped through the farther window, lifted the bawling babe from his bed as their lusty coupling covered the sound of his retreat. With a mouth like a bird's, the young one's cries sought sustenance. A nest, then. A lofty perch for this featherless fledgling. Act Three.

Eight

Whit and Sara's two-story cabin stood in tall pines with ruts for a driveway. At almost midnight, the other houses around them were dark and quiet. A herd of elk bedded down on the side lawn, their coats silvery gray in the moonlight. They lifted their heads as she and Trevor passed by.

He knocked once and walked in. "Whit?"

Whit came toward them, surprised, not to see Trevor in his house, but that he'd brought her.

Sara hurried behind, then halted. "Natalie."

Even by glimpses, she could see them shifting course. Whatever was happening, she was out of place in it.

Whit said, "Where were you?"

"Denver. Nattie's nephew is getting a robot arm."

"Yeah?" He looked intrigued.

"It'll connect to his nerves at the shoulder, move when he thinks, and even send touch sensations back to his brain."

Natalie turned. "How do you know that?"

"Your brother told me while you were hugging the little guy."

That one-armed squeeze tugged her heart, but there might have been no hug at all and a funeral instead. "It keeps hitting me that Cody's alive because of you two."

"Oh yes," Sara said. "They're superheroes in disguise."

"I'm in disguise," Whit said. "Trevor doesn't bother."

Trevor gripped Sara's shoulders. "Got food?"

Rolling her eyes, she slid her arm through his and pulled him to the kitchen.

Natalie chewed her lip, her disconnected feeling growing. "That's a good friend. I hope she knows he's starving."

Whit shrugged. "She's used to it."

"You've all been friends awhile?"

"Big T and I have. Sara was more of a nuisance." He rubbed a hand over his short-cropped hair. "She never lets me forget I told Trevor to ditch her."

"He didn't?"

"Not having sisters, unlike *moi*, he let her tag along—which, as I could have told him, only lasted until she took charge."

"And then you married her."

"There's a lot of story in between." Whit's eyes crinkled, the stubby black lashes dipping over coffee brown irises. A small scar rode high on one cheekbone, and a slight cleft made a shadow on his chin. "It's better when Sara tells it."

Natalie doubted it. Whit was pretty amusing, while Sara… There'd been near hostility in her greeting. She wished Trevor could have waited to eat. He was like Pavlov's dog thinking food when he glimpsed Sara's kitchen.

"I like your house." She glanced around. The walls had a faux treatment that made them look marbled, cream and tan in the living room, shades of gray blue in the dining room. In the teakwood mirror over the matching buffet, she caught a reflection of Sara and Trevor in the kitchen.

"What?" Trevor spread his hands.

"You know what."

"Enlighten me anyway."

"If you're never going to commit, you shouldn't lead someone on, especially—"

"So." Whit led the way in before it got really embarrassing.

Natalie tried for a light tone. "I love your walls. I was going to paint before I unpacked, but it didn't happen."

"Must not have told Trevor." With yellow-flowered mitts, Sara pulled two plates from the microwave and set them on the table. "Leftover veggie lasagna."

Feeling like a new stray tagging along, Natalie squirmed. "Sorry to trouble you."

"Oh, please." Sara laid out forks and knives. "Trevor has no qualms."

"Su casa es mi casa," he agreed.

"Well, if my house is yours, you can do the dishes."

"You know it." He took a gooey bite of lasagna. "This is excellent."

Better than cold chicken and asparagus. "A family recipe?"

"The Internet." Sara leaned back against the counter, arms folded.

Whit got himself a can of root beer and offered the same. Trevor accepted. Natalie just wanted to see what they'd come for and go home. Before that happened, Braden's cries came through the baby monitor on the counter.

An almost frantic look passed over Sara's face. Clamping her jaw, she threw down her hands. "Guess I'm the food source for everyone tonight."

Trevor watched her go out, then turned to Whit. "Is she upset?"

He was only now noticing?

Something moved through Whit's eyes. "Finish eating."

Natalie focused on her food, trying to force the expressions to fade. If she stopped looking, she might get away without needing to sculpt them.

Trevor gulped his down, gathered their plates and forks and slid them into the dishwasher. "So what's up?"

"Have a seat."

Puzzled, Trevor got back into his chair. Whit set an envelope on the table.

That was it? Mail that couldn't wait until morning?

But Trevor sobered. "Where'd you get this?"

"It came to the store. Sara opened it before she saw it was addressed to you personally."

Trevor slid two snapshots out. Glimpsing the first across the table, Natalie frowned. It looked like a toddler in the middle of a street. Sliding that to see the next, Trevor went horribly still.

"What is it?" She leaned forward.

"Don't." He put his hand over the pictures.

"Is that child in the street? Is it someone you know?"

The skin of his neck had lost two shades. His veins bulged. "I don't know who it is." He turned to Whit. "Did Sara see?"

Whit nodded grimly.

"Trevor," Natalie probed. "What is it?"

He shoved the photos into the envelope and stood. "Let's go." To Whit, "Tell Sara thanks and…sorry." With a hand gripping her elbow, he walked her back through the sleeping elk to the car. He started the engine. "Do you need the studio?"

She couldn't believe it entered his mind. "No." She'd manage without that if it choked her.

Outside her house, he parked and got out. He didn't have to walk her to the door, but he did. "Sure you're okay?"

"Are you?"

He dropped his chin.

"Maybe that child's lost, and they want you—"

"He's not lost, Nattie." His voice rasped.

Her chest stilled as she realized what the second photo must have shown. "My God." That toddler was close to Cody's age. Where was his angel?

Trevor leaned on the door frame. "Are you okay?"

Of course not. How much worse for him? She looked up, but he angled his face away.

"Please don't." He turned her toward the door and gave a gentle push. "Go inside."

"Trevor."

"Please."

The ragged request left her no choice.

———

Eyes burning, Trevor drove back to the office and searched through the recycle bin for the first photo. He hadn't believed it anything but a postcard in poor taste. Now he realized it was real.

Laying it and its envelope with the new mail, he fought the blackness seeping in. Two little boys in danger. One of them—

The shaking possessed him like an evil spirit. Who knew the private hell those photos pierced? Who would exploit it?

He pressed his hands to his face. Both mailings had come to the store, but the second had his name on it. He wished to God that Sara had noticed. She'd been sharp as sour milk tonight and no wonder. He swallowed the knot in his throat. Nothing he could do about that now.

He gathered it all up and drove home. As soon as morning came, he hit the shower, then picked up the phone. His sister-in-law answered.

"Hey, Suzie." They shared some small talk, then, "Is Conner there?"

"Let me see if he's up."

If he was in process, he'd be taking a five-minute power shower, donning his uniform, and grabbing a travel mug to tide him over to the drive-through breakfast he'd eat on the way in. He had a long drive through Beltway traffic.

"Big bro." Conner came on.

"Sorry to interrupt your routine."

"No problem. Talked to Mom lately?"

"Last week."

"So you know she got tenure."

"It's excellent."

"But you didn't call for that."

"I need to run something by you." He took out the photos. "Can you receive a fax?"

"Not without hanging up. But go ahead and I'll call back from my cell when it's through."

"Okay, but don't let Suzie or the kids see what I send."

"If it needs a bra, don't send it. The guys got me in trouble on my birthday, and Suz withheld my present. Ouch. They can't hear me in here. Okay, I'm in the office so hang up and send it."

Trevor laid the three photos on the scanner and pressed the buttons. He closed his eyes and waited. When his phone rang, he said, "Sorry to ruin your day."

"What is this?"

"Someone sent them in the mail. To me. No explanation."

"These are on-scene photos." His throat made a sound of disgust. Conner's reaction mirrored his own—as it should, since they shared the pain.

"There's a street sign in one of them. Can you plug it into an accident database or something?"

"We ought to search YouTube. Stinking voyeurs."

"Reel it in, little brother."

"I have a friend with the feds. I'll see if he'll run it. Was there a post-mark on the envelope?"

"No return address on either, but let me check postmarks." He lifted the first from his desk and sounded out a city in Mississippi.

"Know anyone in Mississippi?"

"I can label it on a map. The other's from Arkansas. Not even the same state. What's that about?"

"Huh." Conner pondered. "Have you offended some activist group?"

"What, the anti-rock-climbing federation?"

"How about personally? Torqued anyone off?"

The only recent altercations were with Jaz. "There's a journalist on my case."

"She wanted you, huh?"

"How do you know it's a female?"

"That *je ne sais quoi* in your voice."

"Enough with the French. Besides, she's here in town, not in two Southern states."

"Sure about that?"

Trevor turned and paced. "Well, I haven't tracked her."

"So she could be messing with you."

He frowned at the photos. "That would be psychotic. Even for Jaz."

"Wouldn't hurt to have a conversation."

"Yes, it would."

Conner sighed. "All right. Send me the originals and the envelopes they came in. I'll have my guy run it all through the system."

"Thanks, Conner. Kiss Suzie." He set his phone down and rubbed his neck. He considered calling Jonah, but he'd see what Conner came back with first. He yawned. He had a climbing course in two hours, but he might get a power nap—if he dared close his eyes.

———

Jonah paused his walking patrol of Old Town to study the guy approaching him. It wasn't that Jay never entered the quaint shopping district, though if he did, it was rare. It might be that it was midmorning, and he knew for a fact Jay wasn't happy with his current construction foreman and would ordinarily be watching the crew like a hawk. But actually, it was something he couldn't put his finger on.

With a ball cap over his raven black hair, and a searching look in his bicolored eyes, Jay came to a stop and studied him back.

Jonah said, "Okay, I'm curious."

"Something in the air… Can you feel it?"

Jonah looked up and around. The day was actually quite seasonable and so far peaceable. "What am I missing?"

"I was hoping you'd tell me."

Though Jay had a wry sense of humor, Jonah could tell it didn't apply here. "It's all quiet. No calls, though Moser had a profitable time with speeders last night. I backed him up on a drunk and disorderly."

Jay's eyes narrowed. "Something wicked this way comes."

Icy breath found the nape of his neck. "Um…"

"Macbeth."

"Right. Please tell me it doesn't apply."

Jay shrugged. "Just came to mind."

Jonah rubbed the back of his neck. He loved Jay better than a brother, owed him his life, and trusted him completely. Right now, he really wished he didn't.

For this infernal pit shall never hold
Celestial Spirits in bondage, not th' Abyss
Long under darkness cover.

Through narrowed eyes, he identified the evil as like to others of its kind, as if spewed from the same putrid breath, spawned from the same fetid seed. Through chain link, this one observed the carefree play and scuffling of its subjects, the practiced nonchalance a poor disguise to one who recognized the twisted soul. *I know you,* he breathed. Their paths never crossing, still he knew.

Maybe sensing itself observed, it moved from the fence. Following, he made himself a ghost. A shade. Personless. A shadow moving through the monster's mind, leaving gray insipid prints in the ash of its conscience. The hunter hunted to its den.

Denied, it drenched its hunger in booze. He waited, silent as death in afternoon's heat, for sleep to come, then entered. Carelessly displayed material confirmed his guess. His course was clear, but first he must be sure no others breathed the tainted air expelled by drunken lungs. From one end to the other of the corrugated home, into closets, cabinets, makeshift crawlspace, he peered and found no fearful trembling, no pleading eyes staring.

Back to the ratty kitchen, behind the stove, one twist, two. The odor sent tentacles through his sinuses into the recesses of his mind. Fire-scourged fingers ached for a spark, a single spark in gas-soaked air. But having found no cowering captive, he slipped away, leaving fate to decide.

Nine

t had been almost impossible to keep his focus, teaching people to climb when somewhere a little boy—Trevor shoved the ropes onto the shelf. Whit came and stood in the storage-room doorway. He knew the corrosion that had surfaced with those photos.

"Sara wants you to come over."

Trevor hung the belts, clanking with carabiners, on the wall.

"She wants to apologize."

"For what?" He heaved a crash pad into its spot against the wall. "Being less than perfect last night?"

"You know how she is."

"Tell her everything's fine."

"Is it?"

Trevor lowered his arms and canted Whit a look. "She knows she can say what's on her mind."

"She says what's on her heart."

"Okay."

Whit braced his hips. "It wouldn't hurt to come by. Nothing went the way she expected."

"What do you mean?"

"She remembers too, Trevor."

His shoulders slumped. She'd wanted to work through it with him. But he brought Natalie, who didn't know the half of it.

"Come for dinner. Bring wine."

"I thought she wasn't drinking with Braden—"

"I am."

Trevor cocked his head.

"What, I can't covet your wine budget, Mr. Endorsement?"

"Long time ago, dude."

"Still paying off."

He narrowed his eyes. "I invested."

"That Midas touch."

Trevor raised his hands. "Okay. I'll be there, bearing wine."

———

The Bordeaux he brought was a 2008 Beychevelle. Sara took it wistfully. "I'm glad you could come." She looked glad, but also anxious.

He closed his eyes and sniffed long and slow. "Tell me that's roast beef."

"Prime rib in burgundy sauce with roasted potatoes and shallots."

"You're killin' me."

The sparkle found her eyes again as she pulled his head down to kiss his cheek.

Whit came down the hall with Braden in his arms.

"Hey, buddy." Trevor reached.

Whit handed the baby over. "Fed and changed, just the way you like him."

"They come that way now?"

"Sure." Sara snorted. "And they stay that way right until they feed themselves and use the toilet."

He pressed his face to the baby's. "You're a biological marvel."

"So," Whit said. "What'd you do with the pictures?"

"I faxed them to Conner. He's got a Fed running them through a database that might identify the incidents. I haven't heard back." He turned to Sara. "I'm sorry you saw that."

"I just can't believe someone would do that to you."

"I can't believe someone did it to him." Hurting all over again, he slipped his free arm around her. "Are you okay?"

She shook her head, tears welling.

"She had nightmares last night. Braden's baby seat in the street. Cars coming."

He looked into the baby's face, felt his arm tighten reflexively. "Don't open anything else that comes to me."

She sniffed. "You think it'll happen again?"

"This wasn't the first. I got one the other night."

She looked at Whit, who shrugged.

"I didn't think it was real, just a stupid gag photo."

Sara stared. "Another child?"

"Just the setup. No outcome. Maybe he's fine."

"What is wrong with people!"

He shook his head. "Let's have wine. One glass won't hurt."

"Maybe half a glass." She took the bottle to the kitchen to decant.

Trevor swayed side to side with the baby, a motion that happened automatically as though Braden transmitted a signal.

Sara handed Whit, then him, a goblet of the dark ruby-colored wine. Her own glass held a fraction of theirs. Mother's sacrifice. His mom had splintered five ways when his dad walked out, trying to meet all their needs. It took no thought at all to step in and fill what gaps he could.

His chest squeezed hard. He didn't want to remember how he'd failed. But he'd had his own nightmares last night.

Sara rubbed his arm. "I was worried about you."

"I know. I'm sorry."

"After Ellis—"

"Sara. Don't." With the baby crooked in one arm, he took a sip, hardly tasting it.

She slid an arm around his waist and squeezed. "I'll check the roast."

Glancing, he caught Whit's crossed arms and complex expression. If he'd tried the wine he asked for, he made no comment. His glass sat on the curio cabinet beside him.

Trevor handed the baby over. "Are we okay?"

"You have to admit it's weird."

"What's weird?"

"Me, Sara, you."

After all these years it was weird?

"Forget it."

"Whit, if there's an issue…"

"There's not."

"You want some space? If you and Sara want to get away, I can manage the store."

"Yeah, maybe. Might be good for the three of us to take off for a bit." He snuggled his son.

"Plan it. I've got you covered." If what he saw indicated more, Whit needed a break. This crazy mail didn't involve them or anyone else. It had come to him personally.

———

Natalie slid both hands into her hair, surprised and not, to have Trevor at her house again. "Hi."

"Hi." He leaned on the door frame. "Are you busy?"

His arm was powerfully built, muscles and tendons like a Da Vinci masterpiece, lean and defined—just the way she'd sculpted them. He no longer seemed immortal, but very much flesh and bone, even vulnerable. What was he doing with rolled shirt sleeves and no coat in the dark at eight thousand feet?

"Aren't you cold?"

"Forgot my coat at Whit's."

"Well, come in." The story she was reading would wait.

He nodded over his shoulder. "You want to go out? There's dancing at Fuego."

She'd heard the crowds at the new club were stretching occupancy limits. "I'm not sure I'm up for that."

"You could sculpt a face volcano."

She laughed, pyrotechnics behind the bar being part of the draw. "If it's fire you want…" She motioned him in, but headed through the house, grabbing a big, down-filled throw off the couch. "Wrap this around you."

He wrinkled his brow, perplexed.

"I don't have a coat that'll fit." She pulled on her own, and pushed open the back door to her small flagstone patio and an abundance of stars.

He cocked his head in the doorway. "You have a thing for the dark?"

"It's not dark." The gibbous moon made a lopsided spotlight that revealed shrubbery and a low fence. She crossed the flagstone to the covered wrought-iron fire pit, a serendipitous castoff from the previous owners.

He pulled the comforter around his shoulders. "So…" He cleared his throat. "You heard, last night—what Sara said?"

Using a lighter on the tinder in the fire pit, she got a flame going all around. "She's not subtle."

"But she's wrong. I'm not leading you on. I'd have cleared that up right away, but then that mail…"

"It's okay." She added fresh fuel as the fire demanded.

"I'm honest with people I date. They know that's all it is."

With tongs she closed the diamond mesh door. "Good thing we're not dating."

"What do you mean?"

She straightened. "All it is? You have to know when you spend time with someone in the cultural method of choosing mates, certain expectations will develop." A glimpse of his face showed amusement. "What?"

"Nothing."

"What's funny?"

"I just—you don't usually flash your smarts."

Heat found her face. "That's not what I'm doing."

He raised his hands. "Don't misunderstand. I'm not threatened by intelligence. I worship from afar."

"You're just a dumb jock?"

"I'm smart enough, but my diploma's from the school of hard knocks."

"Hard knocks and celebrity." She laid the poker on the ground. "Want to sit?"

"Will it be culturally misunderstood?"

"That depends on your intentions."

"They're a little confused right now."

"Confused is okay." She settled onto the wrought-iron love seat, near enough to the fire for the pine-scented smoke to sting her eyes and the flames to flood her with golden warmth. "You're making it too hard."

"Wouldn't be the first time." He sat down beside her.

"Forget dating. This is better."

"What's this?"

"Being."

His fire-gilded features revealed another pull of amusement. "Maybe that's it," he said, half to himself.

They sat in the quiet crackling of the fire, the night stars flickering in the smoke. Aspen leaves whispered in the language of their pivotal stems. He reached over and twined her fingers with his, resting their hands on his thigh. "Do you mind?"

"No." Her heart skipped.

"I don't know what it means culturally, but I'm different with you."

"That's what Sara saw."

"I guess." He frowned at the flames. "And I guess it matters, although it shouldn't. She loves Whit."

"It's not that simple, though, is it?"

"Apparently not. I told them to take off for a while. Go be together with Braden."

She nodded. "That's good."

His chin brushed the top of her head. "You smell nice."

"I don't know how you can tell over the smoke."

"I have a finely tuned olfactory system, but I don't recognize the fragrance."

"It's an essential oil from a shop in town. Tia Westfall makes the scents."

"Tia." He smiled.

"That's right, you know her from search and rescue. She used to have a candle store. Now she's a counselor."

"I heard."

"You should ask her what kind of person would send those photos."

He tensed. "She's no profiler."

"No, but she and the chief dealt with a bizarre situation last fall. Fleur's roommate told me."

He brought his heel up against the edge of the seat. "I have my brother working on it."

"The cop?"

"He has a contact with the FBI."

"I guess that covers it." She shuddered, thinking once more of that little child.

"Cold?"

She shook her head. "But I can put more wood on the fire."

"No." Adjusting the comforter, he slid his arm over her shoulders. "That's better."

Calming her quickened breath, she said, "What are you doing?"

He tipped his face to the stars. "Being."

Here we may reign secure; and in my choice
To reign is worth ambition, though in Hell:
Better to reign in Hell than serve in Heaven.

S centing the coming storm, he sat, hooded, his visage shadowed as
people passed, thinking him unfortunate, unwashed, reviled. None
saw the power he held in check, the will that stayed his hand. No
harm came through him, but through their carelessness.

Thunder rumbled. The setting for Act Four, but where was the
subject? Still far, lightning flashed. It seemed God himself would play a
part.

The park was beginning to clear. He slid his hand beneath the cloak,
pulled out the quivering rabbit and stroked between its ears. The pet had
come with him from the home he slept in, its food running low and
water dry. Perhaps someone had been asked to feed it in their absence,
but the care was insufficient, callous.

He stroked and smoothed the fur, waiting until the sight of it drew
them, all wanting to touch, to hold, to manhandle the quaking creature.
Only one held back, scratch marks on thin, sweaty arms. A lip chewed
raw.

Misfortune had a scent. Its memory filled his nostrils. Casting his
eyes to the bulbous water tower, he decided. Into those hands he placed
the bunny. "Come."

Ten

Natalie screamed as the cougar charged, its bloody maw flashing saber teeth, leaping, snatching Cody, his eyes drenched in terror as the crowd snapped pictures. Somewhere a carnival barker called out, *"Come one, come all."* The scent of popcorn cloyed.

She shoved against the bodies. "Cody!" She clawed and pounded as they pushed closer and tighter, reveling. "Trevor!" He wasn't there. She had to save her nephew, but her feet were frozen and her eyes filled with other people's faces.

Heart hammering, she jolted awake in the darkness, sucking deep, hard breaths. "Cody." Her voice rasped. Why hadn't she dreamed the rescue, Trevor's strong back and powerful legs as he hurtled down the slope? Even terrified out there, some part of her had known he'd succeed. But this...

Her hands felt clammy where they gripped her arms. The ghoulish glee in the faces, the cameras flashing—the horrible reality of Trevor's mail sank in. A cold sweat soaked into her shirt, fear and sorrow, but not... not for Cody.

She closed her eyes and groaned. *Whatever it is, whoever's in need, please send an angel.*

———

Holding her telescoped pole beneath her arm, Fleur walked beside Natalie in their neighborhood of small, older houses. Sometimes they talked about art and life, but today she tipped her face up and said, "Tell me what I'm missing."

"Well." Natalie drew a deep breath. "In the valley, there's a pearly gray bank of clouds, all lit up with opalescent lavender, and above that a vast cerulean dome."

The sky came alive in her memory.

"The mountain cuts a dark, teal swath across the firs to the sun line, where they burst goldy moss—except for the beetle rust patches. The aspen are still kelly green but tingeing yellow up the slopes, their trunks stark white in the morning light with their black bands like staring eyes."

"You could be a poet."

Natalie laughed. "Just saying what I see."

Fleur cocked her ear. "I hear something on the right."

"The neighbor's old gray tom. His bent tail looks like a periscope above the ferns he's slinking through. The brown-tinged fronds are spoiling his stealth, though he's pretending not to notice."

"Do you read cats' faces too?"

Her friend laughed. "If one would look at me long enough. The house on the corner, with the green shutters and tan siding is for rent. Looks like they've already moved out. The lawn is going to sandy gray hay."

A bird sang, and Fleur said, "Tufted titmouse. In the old oak."

"Show-off." Natalie elbowed her. "What do you need me for?"

So much more than she knew.

Fleur recognized the wheezing battle a canine waged against his leash as William Farris approached with his indomitable pug. Reaching down, she waited for the imperious nose to butt her fingers, then petted the spongy head. The animal smelled of the canned sardines his master let him dance for.

Circling toward town, Fleur felt more grounded, once again part of the world that had been turned off for her. But after a while she realized they'd fallen silent. "Natalie?"

"Sorry, I was… Do you think dreams mean something?"

"Dreams like hopes, or sleeping ones?"

"I had a nightmare last night, and I can't shake the bad feeling."

Fleur paused. "Being without one sense has strengthened my other four. But I'm not sure they're all we have. Maybe God's talking to you."

"It was Cody, and the cougar, of course. But when I woke it felt like someone else, someone I couldn't see, couldn't reach."

"Someone specific?"

"I don't know." She sighed again. "I wish I could shake the foreboding."

"I dreamed once that I was in a lake, sinking, sinking through the blue, blue water."

"Were you terrified?"

"Not in the dream. But when I woke, I was too afraid to leave the house. So I took out paints I hadn't used for years and painted my studies in blue."

Natalie's voice thickened. "Sometimes it shocks me how alike we are."

"You sculpt what you can't stop seeing; I paint what I long to see."

Their hands came together in a tight clasp.

"I'm so happy to know you, Natalie."

Her voice thickened. "I've waited a long time for you."

———

Before she'd finished basking, Natalie looked up and saw Trevor, holding the bakery door. Unfiltered sunlight gilded his shaggy lashes, cutting sharp shadows around his nose, lips, and chin—and now that image blocked the upper-left quadrant of her vision. She didn't care. The day that started in nightmare sweat had surely come full circle.

"Ladies." He waved them in, clueing Fleur to his presence if not his identity. They'd talked about him, but as far as she knew, Fleur had never spoken to him.

"Fleur, this is Trevor, the one who rescued Cody."

"Oh." Fleur turned, uncannily aware of where he stood. "You have my *Musings in Blue.*"

"I love it."

Natalie felt his hand on her back as she passed through the door, a brief, intentional gesture.

"Good morning!" Piper's greeting drew them to the counter. "I have your order ready, Trevor."

"Great. We'll grab breakfast first. My treat, Natalie, Fleur."

Fleur looked surprised, but she would see how he worked.

With a little shrug, she said, "I'm splurging on maple huckleberry coffeecake."

"It's the best thing I make." Piper slid the platter from the case to the counter. "Miles found a source for wild huckleberries that are so much nicer than blueberries. Look how they burst and bleed this beautiful deep violet. Sweet, tart, and flowery. And the crystallized maple sugar? Yum."

Natalie pressed a hand to her stomach. "I've gained ten pounds, just listening."

"You don't need to worry." Trevor's thumb brushed her elbow.

That from the man who dated curvy sheets of paper?

"Make it three." He laid down his credit card. After signing, he picked up the serving tray. "Mind if I join you?"

They could hardly say no, not that she wanted to. A smile pulled at her lips.

Fleur tapped her stick to find the chair he pulled out as he guided her down by the elbow. She thanked him, and then asked his plans for the day with sugar melting in her mouth. Natalie nudged her foot under the table. The time she'd spent with him last night was like a pearl inside the oyster shell. She didn't want it exposed.

He took his seat and removed the lid from his cup. "One final kayak expedition."

"You can't be serious." Natalie shivered. "The river is frigid."

"That's what wet suits are for."

"Still…"

"It's hard-core," he admitted, "but when you're working a wake or fighting the current, there's serious muscle burn. Trust me, you don't feel the cold."

The warmth of his voice brought her back to last night when the embers burned low and they leaned together talking books and movies and leaving the crazy parts of their lives somewhere else for a while. Not dating him felt pretty nice.

Fleur sighed. "This coffeecake is heavenly."

As close as they'd get on earth. Piper hadn't exaggerated.

Through her lashes, Natalie saw Trevor studying the blind woman, maybe wondering what she might need and if he could help. He tucked his last bite in and drained his cup. "Sorry to run, but I have to go pack up."

"Thanks for breakfast," they said in unison, then laughed.

"My pleasure."

And it was. He gave easily, but she wasn't sure yet whether anyone could give back. He picked up his order, probably lunch for the kayakers, and went out. A little part of her felt bereaved.

Fleur fanned herself, and Natalie nudged her again. "Stop."

"Don't need to see sparks. It felt like the Fourth of July."

"It's not like that."

Fingering her plate, Fleur broke off a bite of coffeecake and popped it in her mouth. "You want to know what's brewing, ask the blind woman."

Natalie laughed. "You're impossible."

"But right."

"We spent time together…"

"Amazing."

It had been.

"But, Natalie"—Fleur leaned in—"how much do you know about him?"

She mused. "Just what I've seen."

"Because…he had a reputation."

"Oh?"

"As a hot-dogger and, well, he didn't like to lose."

"So, what—he cheated? Hurt people, hired Guido to take out the competition?"

Fleur's laugh burst out. "Of course not. But he's fearless and aggressive. Mad Dog MacDaniel."

Mad Dog? Natalie dabbed her finger on the fragments of maple sugar. "My brother's a professional athlete. I know what it takes to be at the top. To get there and stay."

"Well"—Fleur nodded—"Trevor knew he was the best and acted like it."

"Was he?"

"Three gold medals in his first Olympic games? He was only nineteen."

"I didn't realize he competed so young."

"Didn't you ever watch him race? His form was so fluid, as though it took no effort at all." Her voice softened. "By his second Olympics, I couldn't watch, but I listened. You won't believe me, but I could hear the difference. His line was so clean, no flapping skis, no awkward skids…no warning before the gasps and cries of the crowd, the hushed tones of the announcers."

"What happened?"

"A banner tore loose and blew onto the course."

"Oh no." Had he realized even seconds before that something so random would change his life?

"There was an investigation. The press went wild with conspiracies."

"Someone did it on purpose?"

Fleur shrugged. "You know how political the games are."

"I never really watched."

"Nothing was proven. It was just one of those things." Fleur's voice carried the knowledge of something lost that would never return.

"I can't believe you listened to the Olympics."

"I'm a mountain girl. I loved skiing."

"You must miss it." Natalie squeezed her hand.

The sigh came from deep inside. "I miss a lot of things."

———

Angling the bow of the kayak with hard strokes of the paddle into the frothy crevice between rocks, Trevor thought about Natalie. He'd love to get her on the water, see what she could do. Broaching a wave, he found the swift current of the chute. Seconds later he made a Duffek turn to enter the eddy behind a large rock. It was always fun, but having her there would be better.

He played the eddy as the forty-eight-year-old woman shot past. Built like an action figure, Gwen commanded the kayak as though she never left it. The next three men were about her age and impressive enough, but for the first time, it bored him doing this with practical strangers. He angled his bow into the current and followed.

He got the feeling Natalie hadn't experienced many sports besides Aaron's baseball games, but he'd change that.

Whoa.

His head spun. What was he thinking? Women wanted love, relationship. They wanted men who didn't leave them with five kids under twelve, whose carelessness didn't cost lives.

Who did he think he was, holding Natalie last night, acting like a couple this morning? Who was he to make plans for next year, next month, tomorrow? Her ego—if she had one—would not get her through a breakup. He'd been fooling himself that any of theirs would.

He finished the trip on autopilot, saw the people off, and stashed the equipment.

Sara joined him, bright eyed, wearing the baby in a sling. "Phew," she said. "No more water events until June."

He groaned at the thought of June, at the thought of tomorrow. He felt fractious, and it surely showed. So much wrong with this whole situation.

Sara frowned. "You haven't heard a word I said."

"No more water events until June."

"What about everything I said when you went into your funk?"

He braced his hips. "Zoning out of a conversation isn't a crime."

"Everything okay?" Whit pressed into the storeroom, but they ignored him.

"When friends have conversations, it's customary to listen. It's called courtesy."

Trevor hooked his hands behind his neck. "Sometimes, Sara, I don't hang on your every word. I'm not required to."

She huffed, face reddening.

Whit rubbed her arm. "He didn't mean to hurt your feelings."

He hadn't even done anything—proof he had no clue what women wanted from him.

"This isn't about my feelings." Sara's eyes sparkled dangerously. "It's not asking that much to treat people with respect, even if you've known them so long they're like furniture to you."

"You're not furniture. You and Whit are my family here." So why did he feel so alone?

Her eyes brimmed.

"Hey." Whit reached around and held her. "It's all good."

Except it wasn't. "I'm sorry, Sara. Please, just let me finish here."

"Oh sure. Wouldn't want to get in your way."

"You're not—" What was the point? Maybe he was tired of bumping his shins.

He went into the cramped office, bent down, and picked up the mail dropped through the slot. He leafed through it and froze. Another envelope addressed to him, no return address, postmarked in Missouri.

Throat dry, he took out his phone and called Conner. "Officer MacDaniel?"

"Bro."

"Anything on the photos?"

"I left you a voice mail."

"I was on the water."

"Got a match on the vehicular homicide. It wasn't a hit and run. The working theory is that the boy was taken from a shopping cart in a Mississippi supermarket and dropped in the street."

Feeling like he'd been punched in the gut, he rasped, "Why?"

"Maybe the abductor thought he'd been seen."

"Did they get the guy?"

"No, and witnesses were sketchy. Some thought the kid walked out there by himself. Others said they saw a weird guy hanging around."

"Weird how?"

"No one could really say. Baby-sitter was texting twenty-seven minutes straight. No clue the kid was gone from the cart."

He pressed a hand to his eyes. "Is there anything at all that would connect it to me?"

"I can't imagine."

"Well, start imagining. I'm holding another envelope."

The silence on the line reflected his own disquiet.

"What's going on, Trevor?"

"I don't know." With his pocketknife he slit the envelope. Maybe this time there'd be an explanation. But once again it held a single photo. Bracing himself, he removed the picture and took in the six- or seven-year-old boy, clutching something in one hand, clinging with the other to a rung near the top of a silver water tower. The most striking feature in the photo was the lightning flashing.

His throat constricted.

"Trevor?"

He described it to his brother.

"Is he tied or manacled?"

"Not that I can tell."

"So he could have climbed there himself."

He frowned. "Why would he?"

"What's in his hand?"

"I can't tell. It's way too far. You guys have enhancement tools, right?"

"Oh sure, just like CSI. Can you read anything on the tower?"

"No. But the envelope's postmarked West Plains, Missouri."

"Three states. Either it's a group or someone's moving around."

"The photo's dated a few days ago."

"By hand?"

"No, digitally."

"Well, three states is federal. No offense, but I can't do anything with it. I'm just a rookie detective."

"What? You got detective?" Trevor grinned. "Do I hear buttons popping?"

"Suzie's calling me Holmes."

"No living with you now." Another pang of loneliness. "Where should I send this?"

Conner gave him his contact's name. "He's based here in DC, but he'll contact the appropriate field agents."

Trevor shook his head. "Three little boys in danger. How are they connected to me?"

Conner's voice thickened. "You don't see it?"

His chest chilled. "Ellis?" Waves of grief and guilt moved through like a tide. "Who knows about that?"

"Everyone who went through it with us."

Trevor jammed his fingers into his hair. "That was thirteen years ago and…"

"You mentioned a reporter."

"No way. I never told her that."

"You think she can't find out?"

He tipped his head back. "Then what? She goes all sweet Baby Jane and tortures me with similar tragedies?"

"You tell me, bro."

Jaz wasn't that far off a Bette Davis horror flick. "Fine, I'll talk to her." He disconnected Conner and keyed the number, got Jaz's voice mail, and hung up.

A moment later, she called back. "Trevor?"

"Exactly how much do you hate me?"

She expelled her breath. "A tiny bit less than yesterday. Why?"

He swallowed. "Is it you?"

"Is what me?"

"Sending things in the mail?"

He could almost hear the antennas rising from her skull. "What are you getting, body parts?" She was going for shock value, but it hit pretty close.

"Never mind."

"If you hang up, I'll camp out on your doorstep."

"It's just rude mail, Jaz. I thought it might be an expression of your love."

She told him to do something crude, and hung up.

He pressed his shaking hands to his temples. In both the swamp and now this storm, there'd been no conclusion photos. Both kids might be fine. Both might be dead. Who knew, except the one who'd taken the picture. And sent it to him.

That glory never shall his wrath or might
Extort from me. To bow and sue for grace
With suppliant knee.

The polyurethane sheen of the table had been dulled by hundreds of
identities, unique oily ridge patterns that distinguished every
individual, left as proof of their passing. Turning his hands over, he
stared at scar-smoothed flesh. His presence there would not be recorded.

He spread the creased and softened account of Trevor MacDaniel.
By luck he'd found it, an article not of news but personal profile. Each
word of it was his already—devoured, digested, but like a cow regurgi-
tating his cud, he read again. "The better to know you," he murmured.

Reckless courage. Rash determination. Prodigal confidence. It was not
the story of the rescue, but of the man, and in its telling, he found also
the heart of the teller. Here was not the fawning glow, but biting rhetoric.
His gaze slid to the byline. Jazmyn Dufoe. Seer. Skeptic. Instrument?

The copier had reproduced the creases, but with a pen he drew over
every imperfection, then added details no one but he could see. In the
same way he cloaked his dark power, this one masked his majesty. With
her disdain scarcely beneath the surface, the writer saw none of it, or else,
perchance, she saw and still disdained?

What strength she must possess, this Jazmyn Dufoe—or utter
sightlessness. If the latter, this missive would open her eyes. If the first, he
might discern her secret. For he feared—yes!—the paralyzing beauty of
his foe, his brother, his other. Feared and yearned.

Eleven

Natalie knocked on Trevor's office door. She'd seen him return and wanted— The door almost hit her in opening. "What?" His bark startled her, his dark look a force field.

She stepped back, hurt. "I— Do you have duct tape?"

He stared as though he didn't recognize her, then went back in. Just as the door had almost clicked shut, he pushed it open again and held out a roll. "You can keep it. We have more."

"Okay." She wanted to ask who'd body-snatched him. "Thanks."

After returning to her studio, she set the duct tape on the shelf and went for clay instead. She could do a series. *The Many Moods of Mad Dog MacDaniel.* Had Fleur's warning been prescient? Just when they'd found some equilibrium… She drove her thumb into the clay and drew it into a scowling mouth.

An hour and a half later, she'd washed up from sculpting, used the duct tape, and was preparing to leave when Trevor spoke through the thick door.

"Natalie? I know you don't want to let me in." He cleared his throat. "But if you'll hear me out…"

She opened the door and stared at the flowers he held, a troubled mix of tight button mums, alstroemeria, and daisies dyed pink. The cool air was either reviving or extinguishing them.

"Do you know how hard it is to find flowers after Bless Your Heart closes?"

The family-owned floral gift shop did great business in its few hours of operation. Outside of that, it was touch and go. "Where did you?"

"The supermarket. They've been picked over and maltreated."

She touched a daisy petal. "There's life in these. A fresh cut and some lightly bleached water… They'll make it home."

"The next ones will be better."

Her heart fluttered. "Why are you giving me flowers, Trevor?"

"How about I was a jerk?"

She looked at the bewildered blooms. "You'd have to work harder than that."

"I'm capable, believe me. I've got references."

Glancing up, she risked a glimpse to see if he was better now. "Want to tell me what happened?"

He rubbed his cheeks and jaw with one long-fingered hand. "No, but I do need to tell you something."

"Okay." She pulled the door closed behind her until the lock clicked, engaging the alarm. The evening sun shafted through the valleys, layering the mountain range. She walked to the creek bank and settled on a large flat boulder. Laying the flowers beside her, she drew up her knees and clasped them.

He stood before her, downslope, his back to the water. Moments ticked as he decided what to say. "First, I'm sorry about before."

"The flowers told me that."

"I got into it with Sara and Jaz and—"

"Nattie makes three?"

He crooked the corner of his mouth. "You're aware of my wretched track record."

"Only by reputation."

"I never cared. Jaz and the rest of them could take me where I was or not at all."

She rested her chin on her knees. The air carried a scent of wood smoke she might always connect to him.

The muscles of his throat worked. "It's not that way with you. But if we're going to do this, you need to know where I'm coming from."

She shrugged. "I missed your Mad Dog shock and awe."

He stared slack-jawed, then shook his head. "Please. Don't say that again." His vehemence surprised her. "It's part of…something else, okay?"

"I didn't mean to offend you."

"You didn't." He braced his hips. "It's just, I wasn't referring to my former *greatness*."

"What then?"

"Things that happened before all that."

A scolding squirrel bounced from branch to branch of a blue spruce, sending a thin, papery cone on a crash course to the ground.

Trevor paced two steps and turned. "Two months before my twelfth birthday, my dad took off."

She tipped her gaze up, but he wasn't looking at her.

"A wife and five sons"—he blew out a breath—"weren't enough for him."

She heard bewilderment and disgust, the confusion of a child betrayed by a trusted adult, still trying to make sense of it. "I'm sorry."

"The night he left, he took me to a pub for pizza and beer."

"You were eleven."

"He knew the proprietor."

"Still."

"I think it helped him to treat me like a man." He shoved his hands into his pockets. "Since he expected me to be one—in his place."

"That's just not right."

He pulled a grim smile. "Think that mattered?"

She shook her head.

"I was the oldest, and my brothers Conner, Trey, and Matt followed pretty close behind. The youngest, Ellis, was only eight months old. My mother worked, and I kept the boys in line, kept them safe."

Of course. Her heart fluttered.

He hooked his hands behind his head, tensing. "When Ellis turned five, I gave him this kitten, a scrawny little thing I'd found outside the ski store where I worked after school. He loved that kitten. I'd always see him snuggling it up under his chin. And you wouldn't think it of a cat, but it loved him. It pined when he wasn't there."

"What happened?"

"It got out. Ellis went after it." His voice got raw. "He fell over an embankment and died while I was playing basketball with my friends."

"Oh, Trevor." The loss and condemnation in his face pulled her into his pain. He couldn't believe it was his fault, but a passing glance at his face said he thought nothing less. "Could you have stopped it?"

"I could have caught the kitten, or kept it from getting out. Maybe I'd have caught him. If I'd been there." He stared across the river to the crags. "I did what I wanted instead of…" He lowered his chin and stared at the ground. "I have a lot of my dad in me."

"Not that, Trevor."

He cocked his jaw, fighting the emotions.

"You're not him." She stood up and looked him in the face. "Nothing you did made your dad leave, and nothing you could have done would make him stay. I'm so sorry your little brother died. But you've used that tragedy to help so many others. You are not your dad."

———

The look only lasted a moment, but he knew she'd locked him in. He felt her assurance like epoxy shoring up his cracks and fissures. Other people had said it. His own mother said it. But not like this.

"You matter to me, Nattie. But I'm skiing cruddy snow with a bum knee. It could fail at any time." A pale moth fluttered by. Soon the bats would come out to feed.

"Well." She blinked at a spot beneath his chin. "You have the spa— for rehab."

The place he'd let her in. Did she believe they could repair all the damage he might do? "Out on the water, I was wishing you were there, and then I thought how many other things I want you to be part of." He opened and fisted his hands.

"Do they all require equipment?"

He loved her sense of humor. "I hope not." He brushed a strand of hair behind her ear. "I'm going to be gone and out of touch for the next week."

She raised her brows.

"Wilderness survival course for the high school seniors."

"Sounds serious."

"It is. Long-distance trekking, climbing, first aid, endurance training, orienteering, and shelter construction. The school adjusts their course load around it."

"Mountain community." She smiled.

"Saves me rescuing them later."

Setting out, he might know their names, but before the end he'd be familiar with the limitations and excesses in each individual. He would break through the first and curb the second. Life was too precarious to live it halfway, too fragile to leave anything to chance.

She angled her gaze up without quite meeting his eyes. "I'll miss you."

A lump formed in his throat at her unexpected and sincere response. After clearing it, he managed, "Gives you time to consider what I told you. It had an impact. It still does."

"I know who you are."

"You think you do." He cradled the curve of her neck, brushing her cheek with his thumb. "Just give it to me straight if you change your mind while I'm gone."

"I won't."

"I'll walk you back in."

"It's okay."

He tapped her head with a finger. "I know I'm stuck in there. Go work it out."

She sent her smile to the ground. "That's a little unnerving, you knowing what I need."

"It's what I do, Nat. And believe me, you do it too." Pausing at the door, he thought hard about kissing her. He'd give her time, let it sink in, let her decide. It was going to be a long week.

———

With the mountain scenery giving the illusion of perfect peace, Jonah dangled a line into the water beside Jay's. The half-Danish Cherokee had not repeated or elaborated on his prophecy of doom, but it hung like the predawn mist rising from the water.

Something evil this way comes.

"What," Jay said, though neither one had spoken.

Jonah tucked his Tic Tac into his cheek. "Tia's pregnant."

Jay showed only a slight pull at the corners of his lips.

Jonah gave his line a flick with his wrist. "As you know, my training came at the edge of a belt and the mouth of a whiskey bottle." Jay did know, having saved him from that same bottle. Seven years sober, something the old man never even attempted.

"One of the mysteries of the universe is that trees grow out of decay. The more rotten the decay, the stronger they grow."

Jonah stared at the clear water running through the gold-flecked bed, carrying the trout like ghosts beneath the leaf-strewn surface. "Sometimes they grow bent and twisted."

"Sometimes."

He'd followed his dad into law enforcement, but it ended there. No child of his would shudder at the sound of his voice, dread his steps coming closer. This baby...

"You've got it bad," Jay stated the obvious.

It practically consumed him, his thoughts going there every day all day. It was bigger than marrying the love of his life, bigger than his job, his town. That one life had taken over. "When I put my hand on Tia's belly, I swear I feel someone there." Too soon for anything tangible like kicking, it was no more than a profound awareness.

Jay stared into the woods in the waxing light, for once not sharing a quip or piece of lore. They sat in silence, Enola and Scout trotting the creek side watching for trout. The evening had a brittle quality that made the trees suck in their sap and prepare to shine. Any week now, the brilliant yellow leaves would burst into glory.

"The thought of that innocence terrifies me. I know what's possible. I can only do so much." He watched the water ripple around his line, something curious beneath. "I used to think I could tell evil by looking. Now I'm not sure I can. What if I miss something crucial, something right in front of me?" As he'd missed the signs with Liz, never guessing the nightmare inside that troubled woman.

"None of us saw it. She was broken."

Did that make it better? Evil had a form, a force that twisted the minds and character of weak and damaged individuals—or just plain mean ones.

A tug on his line brought him around. Curiosity had snared the unsuspecting quarry. Jay held a hand over the struggle in the water, thanking the fish for its sacrifice, partly tongue in cheek, partly dead serious.

His hair, pulled into a stubby black ponytail, revealed the sharp Scandinavian bone structure, his Cherokee complexion a stark contrast with the startling eyes. His looks intrigued and discomfited people, creating a mystique Jay fostered. But it went deeper than looks, much deeper. They'd been closer than brothers for seven years, and Jonah still hadn't seen anything Jay didn't want to show.

Jonah landed the trout, thinking maybe Tia could eat, then groaned when his radio burbled. But it wasn't the job intruding on this rare day off. His mother was having a second cardiac event. He closed his eyes.

After a while, Jay gripped his shoulder. "Let's clean these fish."

———

Waving a mechanical lobster claw, Cody wobbled on a tightrope across a cavernous fissure.

"Cody!" Natalie cried.

He moved one sneakered foot back, then the other, canting and jerking.

"Don't move. You'll fall!"

"Where are you, Auntie Nattie?" His little body shook.

"I'm here. I'm here!" Gripping the rope, she tried to pull him in, but it unraveled in her hands, becoming dust.

"Cody!"

His robot claw snapped open and shut, open and shut, grabbing nothing but darkness rising up like thick, choking smoke. Heat blistered her face as something formed in the darkness. A giant mouth, laughing. Eyes like bloody flames.

With a cry, Cody toppled, spiraling down, down.

She screamed and woke.

Tears coursing her cheeks, she threw back the covers and slid her bare feet to the wooden floor. In the cramped bathroom, she ran the hot water, filled her cupped hands and pressed them to her face, feeling useless and disconnected.

Back at the bedside, she took her phone and texted her brother. "Tell me Cody's safe." Every second accelerated her heart rate until the phone vibrated in her hand. She fumbled her thumb over to press View.

"Cody's safe. Are you okay?"

She held the phone to her chest, quaking, then remembered he'd be waiting for an answer. "Fine. Sorry."

A moment later. "Love you, Nat."

"I love you too," she said. Paige had issues with their closeness, jealousy maybe. She forgave this latest rejection, but in the dream Cody called to her, and she would do everything in her power to be there for him, as Trevor had.

Swallowing her tears, she wished Trevor was with her now, wished she could text him as she had Aaron, get a response that would make the dread go away. He told her to consider whether she wanted this relationship, but she wanted it more every hour he was gone.

He'd been raw, sharing his loss, and that released a tenderness she reserved for those closest to her. She didn't need time. The two days he'd been gone had lost their sheen. She fully expected the five still to go would be as dull as old wool. And right now with her nerves all pinchy and reactive, she'd feel so much better knowing he was near.

After spooning the bag out of the tea, she warmed her icy hands with the mug. It was going to be all right. The awful dream images were fading. Thank God they didn't stick like real vision. She shuddered, thinking of that face in the smoke, waiting to gobble Cody like the mountain lion, only evil.

Lord, whatever it is…

She set down the mug, reached for her Bible, and looked for something inspired to chase the smoke away. *My flesh and my heart may fail, but God is the strength of my heart…* Some might call it superstition, but she felt the peace descend.

Soothed by the ancient, timeless words, Natalie showered, dressed, and headed over to Fleur's. She raised her brows in surprise when her friend didn't come out to walk, but invited her in with a finger to her lips.

"Something important's happening. Be my eyes."

Natalie followed her to the kitchen. Hovering at the doorway, she glimpsed Piper and Miles standing on either side of a wooden stool in the sun porch where Fleur painted.

"Ready?" Piper held a comb and scissors.

Miles nodded, but his Adam's apple rose and plunged.

"You'll have to sit."

He went down as though his knees gave out.

"Don't panic, or I might cut you, okay?"

He nodded mutely.

Fleur whispered, "How's Miles?"

"A few shades off antique white. He winces every time Piper slides the comb through the hair he wears like a helmet." Her brow pinched. "Talk about a tender-head."

He sucked a sharp breath as Piper snipped a strand and said, "I took cosmetology courses in high school." *Trust me,* her face pleaded. "You need some shortening here at the back and texturizing on top." *Tenderness and understanding.*

"Miles doesn't like being touched," Fleur murmured. "He panics."

So that was it. She knew his problem with germs, but hadn't connected an aversion to touch. She felt for him, being so limited. And then she laughed to herself. Look at them all—except for Piper, blessed with normalcy. No, that wasn't true. Piper was extraordinary, a sweet benison of acceptance.

Miles wore an exquisite, martyrlike expression of ecstasy and torment. He might be dying a thousand deaths, but he didn't tell Piper to stop. His courage had texture and depth. People conquered obstacles every day. Miracles happened. But, oh, the price.

Too late she looked away.

At last, Piper put down the scissors and exclaimed, "My teddy is handsome!"

"He is," Natalie told Fleur, "but Piper will have to tell you. I need to go." She made her way to the door, everything else almost completely blocked by the resonance of his ordeal. Had the poor man never been touched?

She needed clay. It was almost never this intense, but his emotional tension had seared him behind her eyes. *Oh Lord, for a shred of normalcy!*

Fleur said, "The gallery, Miles. She needs to sculpt."

And they thought Miles could help?

"I can drive you." He loomed over her. "If you let me, I can drive you."

"I have my car at home." And a little peripheral vision to see by.

"He doesn't mind driving you," Piper said. "He'd like to."

He was in her head, so intensely vulnerable, but he didn't realize that, and she wouldn't tell him. "Okay." Safer for all this way. She got into the passenger seat of his BMW. How could being driven by an OCD man with an aversion to touch, who had just undergone a harrowing experience, feel so right?

Because angels came in all shapes and sizes, strengths and weaknesses.

He started the engine. "Different is hard. It's hard being different."

She pressed her palms to her eyes. "You can do something about your difference, Miles. You just did."

The car eased backward, swinging onto the street.

"I love Piper. I love her so much it makes a hole in me. But my head feels like a million red ants because the person I love touched me. All I want is to wash it off, to wash her touch away, down a drain where it can't hurt. To wash Piper away."

She swallowed the lump in her throat. "I'm sorry."

"Don't touch. People don't touch. That's what happens in my head, but I *want* to touch. I want to touch her."

"Keep trying, Miles. Find something like the clay is for me, a way to process it out of the part that can't handle it into a part that can."

He parked and let her into the studio. She felt the keypad and pressed the alarm code.

Miles said, "Are you all right?"

"I will be." She turned to face him. "And so will you. Find the way."

With deep compassion, she sculpted the man who couldn't be touched getting his first real haircut. She had described it to a woman who listened to a sport she used to love and would never watch or do again. These people didn't simply survive, they overcame. And while Trevor might look like the most perfect, powerful, and put-together person, he'd overcome injury and loss and become heroic to everyone who depended on him when life hung by a thread.

She strode to the unfinished statue in the corner and removed the drape. It had been raw clay long enough.

For who can yet believe, though after loss,
That all these puissant legions whose exile
Hath emptied Heaven, shall fail to re-ascend,
Self-raised, and repossess their native seat?

With every mile, anticipation; with every change of scene, inspiration. What heights he ascended. What glory. He soared. He swooned. This was heaven itself he entered, and yet mere humans dwelled in mansions, shoulder to shoulder with lowly domiciles, equality bestowed by an overarching grandeur.

In this pristine village, the main street bore charming shops, a coffeehouse, a bakery, no fast food, no pawnshops. No children wandering the streets, no stink and squalor. They played in yards, at a small enclosed park with parents in careful attendance, at a day care closely monitored. Privileged. Protected. Opposing emotions strove inside him as he slowly cruised through the town.

From that road, he accessed intersecting streets with older wood and stone and log houses, seeing not one lost and wandering, hurt or hungering urchin. Through the car's cracked window, he craned. His mouth and eyes felt dry. No moist and mild clime here, but piercing through, the sun shone bright.

Near euphoric, his thoughts flew at lightning speed. He had sent his missives, and now he must learn what he could of his adversary, beyond what he knew from the news, from the article still tucked inside his cloak. He would prepare to meet him face to face. Soon, soon! A rhapsody of possibilities. He clutched himself in a tight embrace.

Twelve

C hief." Mayor Buckley spread his perfect, cap-tooth smile. Not a person Jonah expected to meet outside his mother's hospital room.

"Mayor." He felt Tia stiffen. "I don't know if you've met my wife, Tia."

"I don't think so. But I know who you are. Candles, isn't it?" He held out his hand.

"It was." She gave it a brief shake.

"Ran your mother's shop."

"It started that way." The edge in her voice could etch glass. But she hadn't planned to come face to face with her alleged father.

Buckley's silver hair glistened in the fluorescent hospital light, and for the first time, Jonah noticed similarities in the features of Buckley's face and Tia's.

Sarge gave up the secret, thinking Tia knew about her mother's affair and the resulting pregnancy. He had no doubt Stella told him the truth, even though she never filled her daughter in. Not even to explain why she loathed her.

"You're here for Laraine?"

"My mother, yes." In the parental department, he and Tia had both drawn chaff.

"The doctors don't want her upset."

Jonah crooked a brow. "That's usually the case with heart attacks."

Buckley's smile patronized. "Sure, sure. But you know, Jonah—"

"Nice seeing you, Owen." He took Tia's icy hand and eased past the man with whom his dad had schemed and scammed to solidify their power. He hadn't realized Buckley and his mother maintained a relationship, and didn't really care. He pushed the door wider and entered her room.

Her gray blond hair spilled over the pillow, her puffy face showing a beauty that could have been amazing. Everything about her had diminished—her hatred had not.

Blue eyes burning from him to Tia, her nostrils distended. "This is what you married?"

Since the wedding happened in his hospital room after being shot, guests had been few, his mother not among them. Nor had she made any effort in the year since. Tia made him stop going to her house to avoid verbal and emotional abuse. But even she agreed a second heart attack required a visit.

"I'm Tia." She didn't offer a hand or a hug.

"You're pregnant."

As trim as Tia was, the beginning bulge of their baby showed through her India cotton dress. "Four months."

His mother's eyes narrowed on his like an adder's. "I hope that spawn is as sharp a knife in your heart as you are in mine."

"Kids are what you make them."

Tia turned to him. "No, Jonah. Some people turn out truly fine, in spite of their parents." Then, to his mother. "I'm sorry for your illness."

"I'll just bet you are."

"And I'm sorry for you."

"Get out." Her monitor started beeping.

Jonah motioned for Tia to go, then turned to his mother. "I don't care how you treat me, but I draw the line with Tia. And my children."

"Aren't you the big man?"

His father's taunt from her mouth twisted the knife. "I'm sorry for you too."

"I don't want your pity," she spat.

"Well, that's all there is." To the nurse that came in, he said, "Don't worry. We're through here."

In the hall, he slid his arm around Tia's waist.

"Wow." She walked beside him. "Is this as twisted as it seems?"

"Pretty much. Your dad's looking good." He stuck his tongue between his side teeth.

Groaning, she elbowed his ribs. "Is it wrong that I wanted to wipe off that politician's grin by calling him Dad?"

"Not at all. It was admirable restraint." He rubbed the back of her neck. "Can't store it, though."

She sighed. "What was he doing here?"

"He and the former chief were cronies. I guess he's still friends with my mother."

"Doesn't he mind being connected to that scandal?"

Jonah shrugged. "Maybe he's afraid she'll mumble something damaging. He's up for reelection."

"You think there are things she could mumble?"

"Not as putrid as my dad's maybe, but you'd better believe there are corpses in his closet."

She slid her fingers through his belt loop and whispered, "Like me."

"I'm not sure he knows, Ti. I'd bet against it."

"Why?"

"Because he looked at you and saw your mother."

"What do you mean?"

"He found you attractive."

She jerked to a stop.

"You're very close to Stella physically. If he even suspected he provided the rest of your DNA, he wouldn't have had that glint in his eye."

"If he didn't know, she had no reason to blame me for losing him."

"People don't need reasons to blame." Though it was true his dad would not have shotgunned his own head if Jonah hadn't held him accountable for the teenage girl he'd raped and killed. His mother knew the score and still wanted her man—for better or worse.

Tia pushed the elevator's down arrow. "I guess it's better he didn't know."

"Are you going to leave it that way?"

She shrugged. "Shaking his hand was weird."

"I bet." They got into the elevator.

"He knew about the candles, but not what I do now, so his only interest was in connection to my mother's store."

"Think he carries a torch?"

"I can't imagine it."

"I can. You Manning women are hard to get over."

She gave him a dusky look.

As the doors closed them in, he pulled her up against him. "Thanks for speaking up to my mom."

"Our families turned coal into diamonds."

"You'd dull the Hope itself." He lowered his face to hers.

The cab settled. The doors opened. A man said, "Good morning, Chief," and came in.

Jonah broke the kiss and said, "Morning, Russ."

The district attorney nodded to Tia. "Mrs. Westfall."

"Visiting someone?" Jonah asked.

"Getting a statement. The Axley case."

They reached the lobby and stopped once more. DA Cutler gave them a wave. "Nice to see you both."

"That was awkward," Tia murmured.

"Nah." She was as beautiful and mysterious and consuming as the first time he'd seen her on the playground.

"I know that look." She nudged him with an elbow. "Don't start something you can't finish."

"I have—"

"An appointment with Dave Wolton, city manager."

He checked his watch and sighed.

———

Natalie picked up the package outside her studio door and realized it was for High Country Outfitters. Buffeted by a chilly wind that smelled of fresh-mowed grass—fire prevention along the highway—she headed next door.

She didn't notice Whit until he greeted her from a rack of trail books. "I thought you went with Trevor."

"No, he runs off. I run the business." He pulled a comically pained face.

"I see. Well, this came to me by mistake." She held out the package.

He took it, checked the label with a disquieting expression, then relaxed.

She tipped her head. "Did you expect something else?"

"Just checking the source." He patted the box. "Water purification tablets."

"Whit. Has there been more mail?" He knew what kind she meant.

"Just the three envelopes, so packages are probably—"

"Three." Trevor hadn't mentioned any but the one she'd seen him open. "With photos?" One could be a prank, an insult. Three was a campaign.

Before he could answer, Jaz charged through the door. "Where is he?"

Whit planted his hands on his hips. "Can I help you, Jaz?"

"I need to see Trevor."

"That'll be difficult. He's out with the wilderness class. Three more days."

She arched a brow. "That's why he's not returning my calls?"

Whit spread his hands. "Nothing personal, I'm sure."

She glared. "This came to the magazine that carried my article." From an envelope she removed a copy of the magazine photo—modified.

Natalie stared. It was Trevor, but with huge arching wings and a fiery sword, so much like she'd imagined him, it took her breath away. "What is this?"

Jaz seemed only now to notice her. "A joke?"

Whit shifted his weight, surprised and uncomfortable.

"Is this what he thought I sent him?"

"What are you talking about?" Whit frowned.

"The hate mail he got."

"You know—"

"Trust me, if I drew him, it would have horns and a tail." At their confusion she narrowed her eyes. "It's not what he got, is it?"

Whit cleared his throat. "Why don't you two talk when he gets back?"

"Oh, I intend to." She stuffed the picture into the envelope and stalked out.

"Well." Natalie shivered. "That was weird."

Whit pulled a pad from his pocket. "Do you mind?"

She looked from the pad to him, then took the pen he offered next. In moments, she had recreated the picture, including the parts someone added by hand.

"Thanks. He'll want to see it."

"What's this about, Whit?"

He shrugged. "It might not be connected."

"What are the chances of that?"

"The photos have all come here, but that went to Jaz." He studied the drawing and frowned. "It seems weirdly more sinister."

"It proves it's personal. Someone knows who he is and what he does."

"That's not hard. He's been in the spotlight."

Spotlight. Celebrity. "Blackmail?"

Whit shifted his stance. "He has no connection to those kids."

"Can he prove that?"

Whit's brow lowered. "You have a dark side, Natalie."

"Are you kidding? An insinuating Tweet is as good as accusation any-more. Whoever it is involved Jaz, a reporter whose animosity toward Trevor is no secret."

"But this person thinks Trevor's an angel." He flicked the drawing.

Or they meant it ironically, but following Whit's lead, "Could he have a stalker?"

"How does that fit the photos?"

"He's a rescuer. Maybe she's…calling him." A frisson ran up her spine. "Using these incidents as bait."

"You think it's a woman?"

"Only guessing, if someone's stalking him. Isn't emotional or physical attraction a component?"

"I hadn't thought in those terms, but it could be."

She frowned. "In the pictures I didn't see, did the children die?"

"They were all in dangerous situations, but none of the pictures except the one showed what happened. They might not even be crimes but…mishaps."

She looked up. "Maybe she has access to a database."

"Like a reporter?"

They landed on the same branch. "If it's Jaz," Whit said, "why come here with that drawing?"

"To force a confrontation? If Trevor thought she sent the photos, maybe he knows more than he's saying."

Whit frowned. "It has a sick sort of poetry. He really didn't handle that one well. And Jaz takes vindictive to the max."

But was she capable of subtlety? "When he gets back, you need to warn him, before Jaz confronts him with it."

Whit nodded. "Or you, if you see him first." By his tone, he considered that likely and didn't seem distressed. Sara might be another story.

As she started for the door, he said, "Natalie. Be careful of anything that's delivered, okay?"

Three sets of photos and the drawing. Someone was determined. But to what?

Lena raised warning brows as Natalie entered through the front door of her gallery. She wasn't surprised Jaz had marched straight over. She'd expected it.

"Seriously?" The intrepid reporter stood before the statue of Trevor.

Finished and fired, it stood near the front windows. He was a local hero, and she'd captured the depth of his gift to her, to Cody and his family. People deserved to see. He deserved to have it seen.

"You've memorialized him?" Jaz's lip curled.

"It's for Cody. I want him to remember the man who saved his life."

Jaz wrapped one arm across her waist, crooking the opposite hand beneath her chin. "You knew about that drawing."

"No, I didn't."

"I saw recognition in your eyes."

"That wasn't recognition." Though she supposed it could look that way.

"What then?"

"I'm an artist. I was interested."

With a snarky tone, Jaz said, "Do the mustaches and spectacles people draw on faces fascinate you too?"

"I have a photographic memory. The drawing stuck, that's all."

Jaz arched a brow. "Prove it."

Reluctantly, Natalie crossed to the podium, drew out a sheet of printing paper and reproduced the angel with Lena's pen. Jaz carried the drawing over to the statue, obviously intrigued, just as obviously embittered. "All you missed were his wings."

"Actually, I saw him as an angel that day, a great avenging guardian, saving my nephew."

A little of the stiffness left her. "Who did you tell?"

"No one. Well, Trevor."

"Bet he loved that."

"No, actually not."

Jaz shook her head. "He has you so snowed."

"That's really hard to do. The way my brain processes facial expressions, I get a pretty good picture of reality."

"That's why you won't look at people?" To put it bluntly, as only Jaz could.

"I need to be careful. Once an image sticks, I have to sculpt it."

"So the statue of Trevor…"

Natalie glanced over her shoulder. "He didn't pose, if that's what you mean."

"Right now you could make my face?"

Natalie swallowed. "I already have. After the gallery opening I had to get everyone out of my head."

Jaz planted her hands on her hips. "Let me see."

It was probably a mistake, but she took her into the studio and uncovered the face mountain.

Jaz stared. "All this came out of your head that night?"

"I see every image on the clay. It's just fleshing it out."

Jaz circled around and found herself. "Ouch."

"That's why I don't display these."

Grimly, Jaz stared at her image, then at Trevor's and a brief flick at Kirstin. "I was a mess."

"You were reacting."

Pressing her hands to her cheeks, she gave her head a slow shake. "I'm so tired of reacting to that man." Seeing herself was having an impact—and it wasn't feigned.

Jaz turned. "I would tell you to run hard and fast, but it's too late, isn't it?"

Natalie chewed her nail.

Jaz shook her head. "If you didn't send the angel, then someone else sees him that way."

Why was that such a terrifying thought?

———

Trevor crouched beside the young man shivering with fever. "How you doing, Mike?"

"Not great," he croaked.

The flu had hit him overnight. They'd all heard its revenge on his digestive system, but today it made camp in his throat and chest. "Only thing worse than catching a virus is catching it in the wild."

Michael turned his sweaty head and coughed. "I'll do what I have to do."

Trevor looked at Janise, senior counselor and chaperone.

With her wiry hair pulled back with a plain band, Janise looked like a stern African American schoolmarm, but he'd seen her wicked sense of humor. She didn't employ it now, thankfully, merely stated the dilemma. "On the one hand, he needs to rest. On the other, we should get him off the mountain."

They both looked up at the ominous skies. What might just be clouds in town had already been snow at their higher elevation. As more fell, the impact on Michael would be that much worse.

They'd reached the icy mountain lake, their final destination, and he was planning to teach them several vital things tomorrow. But they still had two days hiking back, and the fewer nights the kid was exposed to the elements the better. "All right, look, everyone. We've got a man down. Let's brainstorm our options."

Not surprisingly the girls chose cutting out the final day and getting him home. Janise recommended a litter. Michael balked, but Trevor took the suggestion seriously.

"You're walking fine now, but you haven't eaten or drunk enough and might not be able to. At this elevation your body burns at least twice as much to stay functional and avoid altitude sickness." At first he'd suspected that the culprit, but the raging fever, which only the Tylenol relieved, suggested a virus. Janise had dispensed it twice since the vomiting stopped.

He looked around the worried group. "Let's build a litter."

Michael dropped his head into his hands, but didn't argue. Trevor sent two guys to find four strong poles in fallen wood if they could, cut them if they had to. On softer terrain, two side poles would be adequate. But this was the Rockies. He'd use the tarp from his pack for the base, the sleeping mats from several others to pad it and Michael's sleeping bag for warmth. He'd throw his on too since Michael wouldn't be expending energy.

Two days and one night would get them back. As his industrious group followed his instructions, he cast a glance at Janise. "Let's hope it's not contagious."

Her jaw dropped grimly, as that picture sank in. Worst-case scenario, he'd come prepared with the sheriff's department's satellite phone.

Him, the Almighty Power
Hurled headlong flaming from th' ethereal sky,
With hideous ruin and combustion, down
To bottomless perdition, there to dwell
In adamantine chains and penal fire.

I n the back of a detached garage, behind a half-restored roadster under a tarp, he took out the book, dressing the leather with the oil of his own palms. Into its ancient lore he had probed for hours, days, years, seeking an end, learning the means, fulfilling the command, needing, needing to know!

Before his mind could grasp the words, his finger dragged the yellowed pages, silent lips shaping syllables that had no meaning. Fear instructed him, until at last it all became clear. And in that clarity, a dread affinity. Not mere cognition   recognition.

The book was the key, unlocking not the door he'd hoped, but a door the other never envisioned. Years of servile torment. Anguished hope. Betrayal! All preparing him—for this.

Evil had fallen to earth in writhing desolation, yet did not yield, but rose, unfurling wings of night, lidless eyes, never blinking, never cringing. Into those eyes, he stared, unflinching, armored in his scars.

Thirteen

I n her studio, Natalie pressed the letter to her chest, tears starting in her eyes. Her parents' congratulations on her opening had just arrived, but they meant no less for the delay. Their excitement and joy came through each line, and no wonder. She knew there'd been times they doubted she could make it on her own, but here was the fulfillment of at least one hope.

She couldn't have done it without them shoring her up in so many ways. It brought a fresh pang to think of Trevor in that pub with a man who could procreate but not be a father to his sons. Trevor and his mother and brothers had held it together, sacrificially, but the man's desertion changed them in ways she'd never known. What day had she ever imagined her dad might walk away? Her parents' marriage, their mission, even this letter spoke of faithfulness and devotion. That was her heritage, a blessing she never took for granted.

She slipped the letter into the envelope and opened the box of powdered glazes. On her knees, she organized them in the cabinet, pausing, head tipped at a sound. She drew her head out of the cabinet and looked over her shoulder. Her phone vibrated on the counter.

Trevor.

Pressing a hand to her chest, she answered. "I thought you couldn't call from the high country."

"Can't. Not where we were."

"Were." The word fluttered her stomach. "Are you back?"

"Delivering the adventurers to school as we speak." He hadn't even gone home yet.

"I thought you weren't due until tomorrow."

"Three of the kids came down with flu."

"Oh no."

"Yeah. But even though we had to clip a day, they got better training in some ways than any class before them."

"Ugh. I can imagine."

"I hope not. Let me just say, these guys know each other *really* well now."

"Poor things. What if you'd caught it?"

He groaned. "Don't even go there."

"Seriously, what would you do?"

"Call in the reserves."

She threaded her fingers through her hair. "Was that an option?"

"Yes. But thankfully not exercised."

Once again he'd taken people under his wings and safely harbored them. A person could get used to that. "Can you come to the gallery? I want to show you something."

"I've been six days without a shower. I'll do you the great favor of washing up first."

She laughed. "Okay, but hurry." She didn't care how eager she sounded.

And it obviously showed because when she pushed through into the gallery, Lena said, "Let me guess. The rugged explorer has returned."

A flush burned into her face. "I want to catch him before Jaz does."

"About the drawing? Or the statue?"

She released a slow breath. "Well, that too."

"It's one of the best things you've done." Lena twirled the wide gold bracelet on her wrist. "All those faces should be out here."

"You know I can't do that."

"You think that. I believe seeing oneself unmasked can be life changing."

"How many do you know who want to change?"

Lena shot a look over her glasses. "I know plenty who should."

Natalie smiled. "It's not the same." They might not turn and run as Trevor had, but people hugged their secrets.

Lena lowered her glasses to hang against her chest. "I agree with Fleur. These nature works are lovely, but your gift is covered in damp cloths in the studio."

"Except for one." She looked at the statue standing tall and powerful, avenger and guardian—and mortal. No wings or light rays, and yet the suggestion was there. At least to her and whoever had drawn him.

———

Driving from the high school to his condo, Trevor phoned Whit, but got his voice mail. He left the message that they were back early and he'd be stopping at the gallery, though not for long, he hoped. Too public, too professional.

He called Sara to check in, but her phone went immediately to message. A smile tugged his mouth. It meant something that Nattie was the only one he reached. She hadn't told him to get lost either. She would do that in person, not over the phone. She'd say it kindly and make it her fault.

He slowed for three mule deer crossing the street, then pulled up to the entrance gate and swiped his key, anticipation making the slow swing irksome. "Come on."

He parked in his space and left his gear. He'd deal with it later. Up the elevator, second floor, third. He stretched the kinks out of his neck. His place had a slightly neglected feel, and he opened windows to freshen the air. His shower was long and hot, no skimping there. The knee was in good shape—no soak required.

He dressed in a crew-neck sweater, jeans, and boots. Cologne. Teeth. Teeth again. His phone rang. Sara said, "Did I miss you?"

"Hey. Just letting you know I'm back early."

"Great. Come for dinner."

"Can't tonight."

"What do you mean? Of course you can."

He grabbed his keys and reached the door. "Maybe tomorrow."

"Maybe tomorrow? What, you suddenly have a social calendar?"

"Sara, darling. I was checking in. How's Braden?"

"One week older. A few ounces heavier. Why don't you come see?"

He approached the elevator. "I'm heading to Natalie's. I'll come over tomorrow, okay?"

Silence.

"Sara?"

"Sure. Whatever."

"I'm in the elevator. Got to go."

"Mmhmm." She clicked off.

Had she been this cranky before the baby? Maybe it was postpartum stuff. He'd have to ask Whit.

———

At the sound of Trevor greeting Lena, Natalie hurried from the studio to the gallery, quaking when she realized he stood before the statue of himself on the mountain, holding Cody and the upraised rock, with the lion crouching before him. She had glazed it in hues of bronze, with crushed glass forming the creek around his feet.

"It's not for sale." She reached him. "I finished it for Cody to have when he's old enough. But I hope you don't mind that I displayed it."

The muscles in his throat worked.

"If it bothers you—"

"It's an amazing piece." He turned to her. "It should be seen."

Lena gave her a pointed look.

"I don't want—"

"It's fine." His voice and face softened.

She exhaled. "I missed you."

"I missed you."

The connection she'd felt for the first time on the boulder crackled between them. She half expected a fiery arc. Joy welled up.

He glanced over her head. "How much longer do you have?"

"Take her," Lena said, gazing over her reading lenses. "Before she runneth over."

"My coat's in the studio." She broke free, shooting a chiding look at Lena.

He slid the coffee cashmere coat over her shoulders. "Nice."

"Thanks."

The moment they stepped outside, he gripped her arms. "What is this crazy energy?"

So he felt it too. "Chemistry?"

"More like fusion." He drew her close. "Getting away to the wild is one of my great pleasures. This is the first time I couldn't wait to get back."

"Sick kids—"

"Were a challenge, but not the reason." He slid his hand up around her neck. "I spent every day up there wishing I'd done this before I left."

Her pulse throbbed against his palm, warmth coursing through her as he raised her to her toes and kissed her.

After a moment, he said, "Breathe."

Air rushed out and she gasped it back in. "Sorry."

"Are you kidding?" With a laugh, he kissed her again.

It was no chemical reaction, but a sweet soul-touching.

A throat cleared. Trevor canted Whit a dark look, "Bad timing, dude."

"Maybe. But there's a family here about you training their kids."

"Within view?"

"Close enough."

He let go, but she felt his reluctance. "Come in with me. This won't take long."

"You go ahead. I want to go home and change." She'd been cleaning up the studio on hands and knees, but really she needed to compose herself.

His eyes narrowed slightly, sensing something. "Okay. I'll pick you up at your place, then we're going out."

She shot him a smile over her shoulder and hurried for her car, remembering only when she was halfway home, Jaz's drawing.

———

Trevor shared a look with Whit as they went in, then turned his attention to the two adults and three kids.

"You're the racer, aren't you?" the dad asked. "Gold medals in downhill, slalom, and…" He clicked his fingers. "Anyway." He extended his hand. "Doug Farley. My wife, Julia." He explained how they'd built one of the new homes and wanted to acquire all the skills they'd need to enjoy their mountain living.

Trevor turned to the kids. "How about you guys? You want to climb?"

"Did you really win a gold medal?" the little girl asked.

"He won three. It was super-G, Dad." The taller of the two boys knew his stuff. "I'm Jason. I want to climb, but I'd rather you taught me to ski."

"Oh, Jase. Mr. MacDaniel might not ski anymore." His mom gave an apologetic shrug. She'd obviously witnessed his catastrophic crash.

"I do. Not like before, but I'll do some ski patrol when the new runs open."

"Are you teaching?" Doug's eyes lit.

"No."

"Would you? If the price was right?"

Yeah, he'd pegged this guy. "Sorry." He'd been asked, the Kicking Horse CEO all but begging to have him as their pro, but that wasn't happening, and no rich guy oozing charm would change that.

"I'm Kayla." The little girl beamed. "I want to ski too."

"I want to climb." The middle kid, on his own drumbeat.

"Scotty's been climbing everything since he first pulled up in his crib." Trevor grinned. "Well, maybe we can give you some technique."

Finished with them, he went into the office to get their lessons on the schedule. He leafed through the mail and scowled. Another envelope addressed to him.

"Hey, Whit." He called him into the office. "When did this come?"

Whit's face fell. "Must be today's mail. And that reminds me of something else." He went over and fished around on his desk, picked up a pad, and held it out.

Trevor took the drawing, his chest constricting. "What is this?"

"Natalie's reproduction of something Jaz got in the mail."

"Jaz?"

"Sent to the magazine that ran her piece on you."

"What's with the wings and rays, that fiery sword?" He frowned. "And how did Nattie—"

"She was here when Jaz stormed in."

Trevor laid the pad on his desk and stared again at the envelope. Whit nudged him. "Open it."

He slit it open and drew out the photographs—an infant in a tree. Nestled between the trunk and the upturned, spokelike branches of an evergreen, it was a somewhat secure perch. But the next photo, shot upward from the ground, showed the height of the branches where the baby rested.

Whit's hands fisted as he took in the pictures. "This has gone too far."

The others could have all been accidental situations. This was intentional.

———

Showered and changed, Natalie took Trevor's call with a much clearer head, real affection replacing giddy energy.

He said, "Sorry I got held up."

"That's okay." She smiled. "I have some news."

"Yeah?"

"They're discharging Cody from the clinic. I just got the update from the nurse."

"He got his prosthesis?"

"It's still in production. But he's going home, Trevor."

"That's excellent."

Did she imagine less enthusiasm than she'd expected? "I hope things can be as normal as possible for him."

"Having a robot arm is not normal. That's superhero stuff."

Warmth flushed her. "I wish you could tell him that."

"I'd have spent time with him, if they hadn't shut you out."

"I'm sorry you didn't get to. Hold on, I'm getting a call." She accessed the other line. "Aaron!"

"Nattie, I have a problem."

Her heart thumped. "What's wrong?"

She listened in stark disbelief. "Of course. But, Aaron…are you sure?"

She went back to Trevor, hardly able to breathe. "That was my brother. Paige lost it at the thought of bringing Cody home. She can't do it."

"What?"

"Aaron's bringing him to me."

Silence.

"He's really scared for Paige." Trevor didn't realize the toll it had all taken.

"Can you do that?"

"Keep Cody?"

"I mean, with everything…"

Her heart sank. "I can take care of my nephew."

"I'm talking about the gallery, your work. Taking care of a kid is full time."

And, in his experience, perilous. "I make my own hours. I don't have to go in." True for a while, anyway.

"When's he coming?"

"Aaron's bringing him now."

"Is there anything I can do?"

"No, but I need to childproof the house and—"

"It's fine. You focus there. I'll talk to you soon."

Threading her fingers into her hair, she scanned the rooms of her house for anything that might endanger a curious two—no, three-year-old. He'd had a birthday in the hospital. The time they'd spent before was the interaction of two curious minds and capable bodies. Now Cody was handicapped, and she didn't know how this turmoil had affected his spirit. She did know the fear and confusion of things beyond her control.

Aaron hadn't said how long, but it was a huge sign of trust that he'd ask it and an indication of his deep concern for Paige. How much of that had Cody witnessed? She clenched her jaw, hoping Aaron had the sense to shield him. What mother would not want her baby home?

But that wasn't fair. Paige had no more control over what was happening to her than she'd had over the mountain lion. Given her own dreams, she could only imagine the trauma and guilt assailing her sister-in-law. The personal attacks and rejection could be the desperation of a mother helpless to save her own child.

Natalie baked cupcakes and checked that she had milk. A little while later, Aaron entered on one metal arm crutch. She snatched Cody from him.

"Hey, I told you no more growing. You're too big."

"I have to grow. Bigger and bigger."

"Bigger than me?"

He gave a huge nod.

"Bigger than your daddy?"

Cody looked at Aaron and gave another huge nod, then collapsed in giggles. After too many hugs and kisses for his taste, she put him down to explore and turned to her brother. She had never seen him so hollow.

She hugged him hard. "I'm so sorry."

They stood that way for long beats, then he said, "Are you really okay with this?"

"Of course. I'll do whatever you need."

"I'm not deserting him."

"Not even close."

"Paige is… I'm scared, Nat. I'm so scared she'll hurt herself."

"That's your focus, of course. Will she get help?"

"Top priority. I can't do it unless I know Cody's…" Tears flooded his eyes.

"He'll be fine, Aaron. I promise. And the minute you're ready for him, he'll be there."

"My worst fear used to be getting traded."

She squeezed his arms. "Take care of your wife. Don't even think about me. Whatever she needs to get healthy, that's what we all want."

He gave her a grim smile. "Have you heard from Mom and Dad?"

"They tried to get through the other night, but we couldn't hold a signal. Service is iffy up here and abysmal down there."

"I've talked to them once. They know what's happening."

"They'll be praying."

He nodded, a little of the tightness leaving his mouth. "I'm throwing you a curve."

"You've never thrown anything I can't hit. That's why you're not a pitcher."

He laughed. "I love you, Nat."

"I love you too." Tears blurred her view when he kissed her, then squeezed his son, who clung to him.

"You be good for Aunt Nattie."

Cody started to cry, and it broke her heart.

"As soon as Mommy's better, I'll be back, okay?"

"Get her better now."

"As soon as I can, buddy. I love you." They hugged again. Her brother sent his anguished thanks over his son's head, then handed him over and left.

She spent what was left of the evening reminding herself of Cody's favorite things. Tomorrow she would get him a bed, but tonight, she tucked him in against her and held him until he cried himself to sleep. When she woke in the middle of the night to urine-soaked sheets, she stripped everything, then finished the night with his weight on her chest in the reclining chair by the fireplace.

———

Cody had been potty trained by twenty-one months and out of nighttime Pull-Ups at two and a half, but he'd been diapered in the hospital, and shock and stress could cause relapse. It had for her when things fell apart in her tiny mind.

She dressed him from the designer things in the suitcase Paige had packed for him when they had come to help her move in. He'd been dressing himself pretty well, but struggled with only one arm. The overlapping skin at the other shoulder filled her with sorrow, and not knowing whether it was still painful, she avoided touching the wound, then stopped herself and asked, "Does this hurt, Cody?"

"When I bump it."

"I'll be very careful." She ran her fingers over the red, puffy skin, touching him, studying the broken part, every detail filling her view. Then she pulled his shirt on over his head, drawing one small arm through one sleeve while the other sleeve hung limply down his side.

"Come here, you."

He climbed into her lap. She settled him in the nest made by her crossed legs and pulled on a pair of tennis shoes with zippers. A simple fix to the problem of ties. Not everything would be so simple.

The robotic arm being made specifically for him, a smaller version than they'd fashioned yet, would be a whole new challenge, but his mind was young and eager. She thanked God for the skills he'd given her brother that would pay for such a miracle. For now, she had a little one-armed boy who missed his mommy and his daddy and needed all the hugs he could get.

"Natalie?" The call came from her front door. She'd left it unlocked after bringing in the paper, and she heard Trevor wandering through to the bedroom.

He poked his head inside. "I brought breakfast croissants."

"Don't try denying you're an angel," she said, and that reminded her of Jaz's mail. "Trevor, did Whit—"

"He showed me." His glance said they'd discuss it later. "Hey, Cody." Trevor folded his impressive height into a crouch for the child. "How's it going?"

Cody pressed his head into the hollow beneath her chin and stared at the big man.

"Remember Trevor, Cody? He chased away the lion."

That registered in the little one's eyes, but he said nothing.

Trevor wiggled one little shoe. "Your auntie's hungry. Should we show her what I brought?"

Cody nodded.

She helped him up from her lap. "Don't you have work to do?"

"The outdoor season's winding down. Today's forecast is for snow."

"Down here?"

"We're still eighty-one hundred feet."

"Right." They'd had snow higher up, but only a few flurries in town. Soon the Kicking Horse ski resort would open and bring a fresh flood of wealthy visitors. Good for the gallery, she hoped. Cody tugged her hand, and she said, "Okay, I'm coming."

Trevor raised her the rest of the way, then up to her toes for a hug, nuzzling beneath her ear. "Good morning."

She reached an arm around his neck, and their mouths met. His kiss was strong and confident. She took in the line of his mouth before looking away. "I told myself this is going too fast."

"Mmhmm."

"That I need to catch my breath."

"About that…"

She socked him.

"Don't hit, Auntie Nattie."

"Now see, you got me in trouble."

His eyes were imps of mischief. She slipped away, realizing she was now a role model. She lifted the bag Trevor had dropped on the floor and carried it to the kitchen. "Come on, Cody. Let's share the spoils."

After laying it all out on a platter so Cody and Trevor could dive in, she slipped over to the desk, took a pad of paper, and drew Cody's wound in awful detail. Turning, she saw Trevor watching, but joined them without discussion.

The croissants were buttery clouds of heaven. "How does she do this?"

"She's a magician." He reached over and took her hand. "Okay?"

Nodding, she made a mental note to bring clay home.

"Thank you for bringing breakfast." She repackaged the remainder and set it on the counter beside the crockery canisters she'd thrown and glazed a forest green over speckled tan. "What's your plan for the day?"

"Do I need one?"

"I have to shop. Cody needs some things."

He rose. "We ought to go early, before the snow."

"You want to run errands with us?"

"I'll drive." He scooped Cody up with one arm.

Her breath caught, the images flooding back in a visual barrage hitting her mind like blows. Cody in the lion's mouth, Trevor leaping over the side, wielding the rock, lifting the bleeding child. She gripped the table.

"Nat?"

She had modeled them away. They should be gone, dealt with.

He set Cody on the floor and turned her to face him. "The studio?"

"I don't understand. I moved these out." She'd finished the statue, for heaven's sake.

"There's a lot of emotion here." He cupped her shoulder. "Tell me what you need from the store."

"Some of it I can't get in town." She shook her head.

"Like what?"

"A bed for Cody."

"I can handle that. What else?"

"Pull-Ups. They're diapers that—"

"I know what they are, Nattie. I've spent lots of time with little boys." He wrote down the things she said, then pocketed the pen. "Okay. I'll drop you at the studio and work on this list. When you can see again, call my cell."

"What about Cody?"

"He's coming with me." He held her coat as she slipped her arms into the sleeves, too disoriented to argue. He bundled Cody and got him into the car seat Aaron had left. Whether Cody remembered his champion, or was used to strangers caring for him, she didn't know, but he took to Trevor as naturally as could be.

With fresh clay in the studio, she once again exorcised the terror on the mountain. As she worked, it began to snow. When she'd finished, six powdery inches cloaked the world outside with flakes like airy dumplings plopping down. Looking up to find such beauty filled her with a surprising lightness.

She went to the window and stared. The spring trickled through ruffled icy plates, in curtains of jeweled droplets. Her heart caught in her throat as her eyes captured the image.

Tearing her gaze away, she called Trevor. "How's it going?"

"Just setting things up. You ready to come home?"

Home.

He said, "Cody's napping, but—"

"Don't wake him. There's something else I can do."

"I'll come as soon as he rallies."

"Okay." Staring out again, she breathed in the beauty that so perfectly reflected her joy. This one would be mostly glass.

Satan from hence, now on the lower stair,
That scaled by steps of gold to Heaven-gate,
Looks down with wonder at the sudden view
Of all this world at once.

I t fell from the sky like ash, but white. Feathers and down, floating, swirling. He walked through a cloud, alive with seraphs, darting and dodging and drifting. Hooded he walked but face upraised, spellbound by the icy touch of frozen hands, searching him, finding him, burning him.

How could he breathe the frigid air of angels and still live? He whose breath was smoke and flame, whose fingers scorched the night, whose blood ran black with soot.

Here their paths would cross, their fates align. And he felt dwarfed. Shrunken. His freezing cheeks stung with tears. He was tired. So tired.

He paused at a nearby domicile, the weathered sign announcing it a rental. Moving around to the back, he watched warily for observant eyes, then jimmied the lock and slipped inside the back door, through the oak and linoleum kitchen. Into one corner of the living room, he coiled like a viper, drawing warmth from a radiator set low, but not off, protecting the home's copper veins from aneurism. Though daylight, he could no longer fight sleep or what dreams would come.

He slipped his hand into his cape and took out a roll, then tore from it a section of tape to affix over his own mouth. A necessary precaution. No one lived here, but still someone might hear his screams.

Fourteen

Okay, let me get this straight." Jonah eyed Forney Haines. "You came out last night to have a smoke."

"Put on my boots and walked to the garage. With Mary's emphysema, I go far enough she won't get a whiff and want one herself with the oxygen and all."

Jonah could have told him he carried enough scent to catch a whiff at thirty yards.

"I took my boots off before I came in cuz she doesn't like dirt tromped in." He gave Officer Donnelly a look to make sure she appreciated his consideration.

She gave him a bland stare, no doubt certain a male officer would have been spared that confidence.

"Ten minutes later, I come out for a smoke—"

"You went ten minutes between cigarettes?" Sue asked.

"Well, it was coming on to bedtime…"

Jonah cleared his throat. "You came out and…"

"No boots." Forney spread his hands.

"What do you think happened?"

"Someone took 'em." His tone said that much was clear. "One minute I got boots, ten minutes later, I don't."

Jonah studied the ground around the stoop. All the footprints bore the same boot mark.

Sue said, "Did you hear anything?"

"Not one peep. And Mary's got ears like a bat. Whoever took them was quiet as a ghost."

Jonah nodded. "Well, give us a description of the boots."

"I wrote it all down." Forney handed him a Post-it. "Including what I paid at the Wal-Mart."

Climbing back into the cruiser, Sue said, "Do bats have ears?"

"Sure. Pretty sharp ones they use for echolocation."

"Wonder if that's how Mary knows where he is."

"Could be, Officer Donnelly. Could be." He started the engine.

"So where are his boots?"

"Someone probably took them." He backed the cruiser.

"What are the odds he'll buy himself a new pair?"

"Ninety-nine to one."

"We have one percent chance of finding them?"

"Rubber hunting boots from Wal-Mart. Unless Mary sewed his name inside…"

Sue giggled.

"That's not very officerly."

She straightened. "Who would take somebody's boots?"

"Someone who needs them."

She clicked her tongue. "I hate to think people can't leave something on their own back stoop anymore. What's this town coming to?"

They had a good laugh, considering last year they'd taken down a meth lab.

———

Even though he shoveled, they still kicked powder to the door.

"Come see, Auntie Nattie!" The moment they got inside, Cody took off down the hall, his gait awkward with the body memory still so strong of a balancing appendage.

Knowing the ache of a body changed forever, Trevor followed them to the second bedroom in which he'd taken some liberty. She froze in the doorway.

"We tent dwellers have to stick together."

Near the back corner he'd pitched a small dome tent and outfitted it with air mattress and sleeping bag. The flaps were all open across the top for easy viewing, but it enclosed and corralled the little guy who dove in and rolled. Surrounding the tent were stuffed black bears, moose, mountain goats, and elk. From the Kicking Horse ski shop were size-three winter gear, snow boots, mittens, and a European-style cap with ear flaps and tassels. Against the wall leaned a tiny pair of skis.

He turned. "Hey." He hadn't meant to make her cry.

"I can't believe you did this. It's perfect."

"I'm an outfitter."

"But still…" She held out her hand. "Let me see the damage."

"Nattie."

"You paid for the wolf mountain. And Fleur's painting."

"Fine. I'll figure it out and get back to you."

She sniffed. "Look at him. He's so happy." Cody tackled a moose and rolled with it into the tent. "He might have had such a hard time, but you made his first day awesome."

"This was good for me." Better than she could know.

She slid her hand into his, and that was good too, but, holding it against his side, he said, "You told me we're moving too fast. I don't want that."

"No, it's just…" She moistened her lips.

"You don't want to be Jaz."

She stared at the floor. "I wouldn't hate you. But…you're…"

"Please stop thinking I'm something—"

Cody charged out of the tent and hugged his leg with one tiny arm, wiping out anything he might have said.

"I want da *fash*light."

"It's in the tent. Look under the covers."

Cody burrowed back in.

"Flashlight." She shook her head. "Tell me you didn't get him a pocketknife."

"Swiss Army Ranger—kidding." He hugged her shoulders, laughing. How long since he'd really, really laughed? The release was full and physical. A tiny spider on the window paused as the vibrations reached it, then continued its vertical climb.

———

Laughing with him, Natalie could hardly contain her happiness, but, perversely, it heightened her concern. She turned. "You didn't tell me about the other photos, Trevor."

He cocked his head back. "Where did that come from?"

"I don't want anything to happen to you."

"Don't worry."

"You can't keep me out of it."

"I'm not." But he conceded, "I was leaving. I didn't want to scare you."

"I don't scare as easily as you think. I just want to know what's happening."

He spread his hands. "If I had any answers—"

"Can I play inna snow now?" Cody rolled out, one snow boot on his hand.

Trevor's eyes smiled. "I told him he had to wait for you."

"Well, sure." She scooped him up, but cast a look over her shoulder. "We're not done with this." Then to Cody, "Where could that other boot be?" When she had him all dolled up like a magazine ad, she could hardly keep from hugging him. "Have you ever seen anything so adorable?"

"You forgot his skis."

She sat back on her heels. "They're real?"

"Of course they are."

"He's barely three."

"Two years late." He took the skis from against the wall, the skis and a different pair of boots.

Cody would have been happy to stomp around in the white stuff, but Trevor got him outfitted and hoisted him to one hip.

"Do you think with only one—"

"He's never tried it with two."

"But if he falls…"

"Part of the deal." He nodded toward the door.

She pushed it open reluctantly.

"Relax. We're going on a little hill. And what does he fall, fourteen inches?" The "ski slope" at the end of the block was about a twelve-foot run, but steep. At the top, Trevor set Cody onto his skis, aligned them next to each other, and said, "Slide your feet back and forth."

"Isn't he supposed to snowplow?"

Trevor angled his gaze up at her.

"Sorry."

Watching him work with Cody warmed her. The little guy might have been crying for his mom and dad and wondering what happened to his life, but Trevor had turned this into an adventure. Her heart swelled when, in no time, Trevor had him rocketing straight down the hill into his arms.

"I didn't realize he'd be downhill racing."

"Look at him. He feels the slope." Trevor stood Cody at the top and caught him at the bottom, replaced and caught him again. "Some kids can't help holding back." He glanced up. "*They* learn to snowplow."

She rolled her eyes. Not her one-armed nephew. The few times Cody fell, Trevor lifted him. Once Cody had his mechanical arm, he'd be unstoppable.

As wind dusted her face with snow, Cody dove into her legs. "I'm hungry."

She looked at her watch. "Oh boy. I'd better start dinner."

"Relax." Trevor scooped up her nephew. "We've got it covered."

"Oh?" She tromped behind them to the house. Her house, but Trevor entered as though he paid the mortgage. While she unbundled Cody, Trevor slipped out of his yellow parka and gloves, pulled off the knit beanie, and shook out his hair. The hat had caused a little flip around his ears and neck. Endearing. And more than a little sexy.

She hung her coat and followed Trevor to the kitchen where he opened a cabinet.

"SpaghettiOs?"

"With meatballs." He pulled a can from the half dozen standing side to side like matching soldiers.

Natalie held back, hands hovering, as Cody tried and slipped, then pulled awkwardly into a chair, singing out, "Buskettios!"

Afterward, since he was nearly dropping with fatigue, she brushed his teeth and jammied him, with a Pull-Up just in case, then tucked him into his magical tent with one of each stuffed species. She pressed a finger kiss to his mouth. "Jesus loves you. Aunt Nattie loves you. Daddy and Mommy love you."

Thankfully that didn't trigger tears. He just looked at her to see what came next.

"Trevor loves you," Trevor said from the doorway.

Cody snuggled in, a smile on his lips. She rose from her knees and moved down the hall with the man who'd fit into her life like the glass with the clay—alien in nature yet blending into something new and amazing.

Just before the small living room opened out, he turned and braced her between his arms against the wall. "This has been my best day in a long, long time."

"I can't believe you got him skiing like that."

"Next time we'll build a jump."

"You will not!"

He caught her wrists and laughed, truly happy, it seemed, then brought her fists together and stroked her knuckles with his thumbs. "Sounds weird, but he feels a little bit mine, you know?"

"You breathed him back to life."

Surprisingly, he didn't shrug it off. "It's like this was meant to be—and I don't believe in that."

"I do. Just the fact that you were there. Right there, Trevor. How is that not God?"

Dropping his chin, he said, "If that was God, it was more about you or Cody than anything to do with me."

"I know your dad rejected you, but God—"

"You said you never knew Mad Dog. I'm going to introduce you."

She swallowed. "Okay."

"When I was five, a family friend, Brick Emerson, saw me ski and took on my training. We hit the slopes every day."

"In Colorado?"

"Alaska. There's a little skiing there too."

"You grew up in Alaska?"

"My dad's a wildcatter."

"Oh." A thrill seeker, bored with home and family. Was that the part Trevor saw in himself, the part that drove him toward adventure and risk?

"I was racing competitively at eight, breaking records by ten."

She shook her head. "I didn't know it was such a big part of your life."

"Racing's a drug. Sometimes the need for it still lodges in my solar plexus. I feel the motion, the tension of the start gate, the pump of the countdown. In my sleep I'm shooting out of the gate, feeling the fall line."

"I wish I'd seen you."

He stroked her shoulder. "It's not the skiing I miss most. It's the winning." His voice hoarsened. "The feeling that nothing can stop me."

"Not even a mountain lion."

He gave a slow blink. "I quit racing when my dad left. No time to train, and I wouldn't be anything less than best."

In Fleur's words, *"He didn't like to lose."*

"After Ellis died, Brick all but dragged me back, a foot and a half taller and four years older than the last time I raced."

"Were you scared?"

He shrugged. "Competition was tough. The team I trained with, hung out with, all but lived with were also my opponents. You're a team, but you never forget it's about your time, your finish over theirs."

"The years off didn't hurt?"

"I'd been swift and agile before. I came back with power. And a pretty big chip. Out on the runs, I could forget, I could control the outcome. In two years I was winning gold. I raised the bar on the whole team."

"Pretty amazing."

"It's a grueling, aggressive sport. Mental acuity and toughness make as much difference as conditioning. Digging into the loss and rage made me fierce."

"Mad Dog," she murmured.

He nodded, grimly acknowledging the moniker. "I don't remember who said it first, who called me a mad dog on the slopes, but it caught fire. I think it even found print. And it wasn't only about racing." His brow formed the twist her hands knew so well. "We were wild, the men's and women's ski teams, living hard and fast. I had no limits." He stared at a place behind her head.

She held her breath, feeling it coming like a train in a tunnel.

"The pressure was incredible, everyone wondering if I could sweep gold. I knew I could. I was unbeatable. On the slopes and off—in my own head, anyway. I hooked up with Tanya, both of us medal contenders for that year's Olympics. For two months, we tore up the sheets like we tore up the slopes. She'd covered it and I'd covered it, but she still got pregnant."

Her breath escaped. "You have a child?"

"No." He closed his eyes. "That's the second death I caused, and the reason I never take that chance again."

———

Softly, her voice came out of the silence between them. "You didn't cause Ellis."

"Not as directly as the abortion." Pressure pinched the skin between his brows.

"Wasn't that Tanya's decision?"

"She was racing. She was training. She had everything ahead of her."

"So it was right?"

"You know the answer to that. But I'd have gone on and taken gold and she'd have been having a baby neither of us could raise."

"You never discussed adoption?"

"The baby was gone before the next time trials. That's on me, Natalie." His throat constricted. "So now do you get it? I'm no angel."

"You've done everything since to make up for it."

"Make up for an innocent life?"

"You saved Cody's."

He closed his eyes. "I think the accident was retribution."

"God destroying your career for the life destroyed?"

"Not a fair trade, I know, but it was everything to me."

She rested her hand on his chest. "God doesn't shoot tragedy from heaven like lightning bolts."

"Awfully circumstantial, you have to admit. That race out of all my races. My run out of all the other racers. The banner and me converging in a great cosmic correction." He grimaced. "I knew when I hit it, it was over. And the first thought in my head was I deserved it."

Her fingers touched his jaw. "No."

"That reckless, angry person had to go. As long as I was winning, it wouldn't happen."

"Oh, Trevor."

He clasped her shoulders. "I don't know how far he's gone. Not far enough maybe."

She flicked him a rare full glance. "That might be who you were, but what I saw again this morning reminded me who you are."

Her mouth on his was soft and sweet, his reaction anything but. When he'd first seen her, looking like she saw a ghost—or a god—he'd thought her weak, wistful, even a little weird. No different from anyone else. Yet here she was like a trusted rope, supple, strong, unfailing.

He stroked her silky hair, breathed the scented oil, certain it would smell different on anyone but her. In spite of himself, he found her mouth again, kissing and touching and holding on so hard.

Finally drawing apart, she sighed. "We have to stop."

"I hear you."

"I only slept two hours last night."

She needed time. He needed perspective. This close, he could forget the lessons he'd learned.

He kissed her hairline, brushed her cheek with his thumb, and stepped back, their clasped hands lingering as the distance increased. "I'll talk to you in the morning."

She nodded, okay with that now, but by tomorrow? She might have a whole new point of view.

———

Snow had drifted down all night, and it wouldn't clear itself, so Fleur wedged the storm door open and took down the broom. She shoved against the thickening mass, light and powdery on top but compacted beneath. She expelled an irritated breath.

She used to love the snow. But what made snow wonderful—besides what you could do on it—was how it looked, falling from the sky, fluffing up the ground and trees, the sparkles drifting in the air, a brilliant seabed of dazzle on the ground. It didn't feel wonderful or sound comforting like rain or like anything at all unless there was wind, and no one liked a blizzard. With the cold pinching her nose, she heaved another sigh. She used to be tougher than this.

She jumped when someone said, "Hey, there. Let me get that."

He'd taken the broom before she realized anyone was there, unusual and unsettling.

"Sorry to startle you."

The cloud of her breath condensed below her nose. "Pity parties must dull concentration."

"I don't know about that," he said. "Snow muffles footsteps. Do you have a shovel?"

"I do. It's just big and awkward."

"Let's try it."

She backed inside, running her fingers along the wall of her outer entry until they found the hanging shovel. She took it down.

He told her to stay in where it was warm. "I'll clear the walk."

"I was just going to do around the door."

"It won't take a minute."

"Well, then, thank you. I'll heat some hot chocolate."

The scrape of the shovel and squeaky clumping of the snow told her he was already at it. As she went inside, she heard the storm door close and realized he'd unwedged it to keep the wind out. She removed the gloves and set them on the shelf, hung her coat, brushing the snow dust off. She tugged one and then the other duck boot off and left them by the heater to dry.

In her tidy and organized kitchen, she scooped instant cocoa into a mug and turned on the electric kettle. Outside, he began to whistle. The melody came through in muffled riffs distorted by the wind. She pursed her lips and blew, getting a soft *whoosh* but no more. She'd never been able to capture that tight, high-pitched sound.

Brushing a hand over her hair, she felt the melted flakes. She took a brush from the drawer and drew it through the dampened strands, then replaced the brush and closed the drawer. The water was agitating in the kettle but not yet rolling. By the time she poured and stirred the cocoa, he was tapping on the tempered-glass door. She returned to it, mug in hand.

"Here you go." She handed him the mug and reached for the shovel.

His wet, icy fingertips brushed hers.

"Didn't you wear gloves?"

"Nah."

The wind whirled around them. "Would you like to come in?"

"You shouldn't."

"Shouldn't what?"

"Ask me in."

Her heart made a slow beat, but she smiled. "This is Redford."

"Well, we haven't been introduced. I mean, you're Fleur Destry, right?"

She raised her brows. "You know me?"

"Not yet. I'm Officer Newly. Seth Newly." From the angle and feel of his handshake, he was average height and big boned, his hand callused but fleshy.

"How long have you served in the Redford PD?"

"Couple years. I was injured last fall in the meth bust."

"Shot?"

"Only the chief got shot. The explosion broke my leg. But that was some bust. The chief was like an action hero going through the flames, pulling me out with a bullet hole in his side. I don't even think he knew it."

"You like your job." She could hear it in his voice.

"Oh, the traffic stuff's dull and domestics are a bi——, er, a pain. But yeah. I get to do stuff like shovel your walk."

The corners of her mouth drew up. "I'm pretty sure that's not in the job description."

"The chief's big on citizen assistance. Unlike some forces where the chief only pushes paper, Chief Westfall's out there like the rest of us."

"Shoveling walks."

"Well, that was kind of an analogy. The chief——"

"Wants to make me a detective."

She heard the indrawn breath, but instead of, "You're blind," he said, "You know him?"

"I grew up here. We ran in different circles, though. I was straight As; he was the one mothers warned their daughters about."

Newly laughed hard. "I've heard that. Mostly from him." A long, slurpy sip. "Now he's having a baby. Well, his wife, Tia, is. You know Tia?"

"Yes. But not from school. She was a loner back then. Like Jonah."

"She's really smart. Has a doctorate or something in psychology. She does workshops for the officers, stuff the state mandates, but she makes it cool."

"Her best friend is my roommate."

"Piper?"

"You know everyone."

"Nah." He took another drink. "I had a crush on her."

Fleur laughed. "Who doesn't?"

"Shocked everyone sh—— silly when she picked Miles. Is it the money?"

"No. Piper's not like that."

"Yeah," he said despondently. "I didn't think so." He followed what sounded like a large and maybe final gulp with, "Thanks for the cocoa."

She took the mug. "You're welcome."

"Guess I'll see you around." A rush of cold air accompanied the opening door as he passed through.

She started to close it, then stopped. "Would you mind describing yourself? I like to know what people look like."

He cleared his throat. "Well, I'm basically movie-star handsome."

Her laugh burst out. "Oh. Well."

"Nah. Let's see. Light blond hair, blue eyes—"

"What color blue?"

"Um, well, my mom called them robin's egg."

She pictured that. "Are they still?"

"What do you mean?"

"Sometimes they deepen in hue or fade."

"No, I guess they're still like they were." He scratched, probably his neck, since he hopefully wore a coat and hat.

"You're five ten?"

"Almost."

"Large boned."

"I'm a little stocky, but I work out." He hesitated, then said, "You want to feel my face?"

She shivered. "I usually wait until the second cup of chocolate."

"I don't mind you rushing it." Again the smile in his voice.

Feeling him come close, she set down his empty mug. His skin was hot, probably flushed. Broad forehead; coarse, straight eyebrows; unassuming cheekbones. His nose had a wide bridge, a slight lift. His eyes were set apart, but not too wide, long, probably blond lashes. "How come guys get the long lashes?"

"You're no slouch." His voice sounded husky.

His nostrils were bulbed; the indentation above his lip deeper than some.

"Okay," he said. "Give me a minute." An indrawn and slowly expelled breath. "Go ahead."

A generous mouth, neither lip dominating the other, broad, slightly crowded teeth. His jaw was wide and not particularly chiseled, his jutting chin the width of his unsmiling mouth. His beard was scant, hardly noticeable in the smooth, hot skin. She drew her hands back. "Thank you."

He cleared his throat. "Sure."

"Now I'll know you when I see you." She smiled.

"Is it awful?"

She raised her brows.

"I'm sorry. I didn't mean to say that."

"That's all right. And yes. It is."

And Tumult, and Confusion, all embroiled,
And Discord with a thousand various mouths.

By chance he'd seen them, glimpsed and almost ignored, until her fingers found the officer's face with tender, groping discovery. Breath trapped, he invaded their sentient moment. This one was blind. Rejected. His soul recognized the curse and responded. She too had fallen.

Faultless, perhaps, as he had been, yet scourged. Unjustly. Without compassion. Without mercy. Doomed from inception. Believing oneself like all creatures, deserving of benevolence, but in truth, created for destruction.

Pressed to the window frame across the street, he watched until she went inside. The officer stood as well, staring at the door, but not seeing, not understanding. His world had rules and assurances. He could sleep without wondering what horror might sneak up in the dark.

But she…

She knew the dark. The fear. The unknowing. The knowing! He recognized her helplessness and shuddered. The weak can grow strong. But the memory never fades.

Grimly he left the window, slid the duffel strap over his shoulder, and went out. He might or might not sleep once more in that house, but now he had work to do. He plodded through the snow in rubber boots, an imperfect but not unmanageable fit.

The car started with a wheezing protest. The duffel bag sat silently beside him. The book stayed inside. Today he would watch, learn, and prepare. Today he would come one step closer.

Fifteen

Trevor stepped out his door, disconcerted to find Jaz on the balcony. Keyed gate, keyed garage and elevator. He cocked his head. "How'd you get up here?"

She wiggled a key card she must have snagged at some point from his spares. "You can't make an accusation and not allow rebuttal."

"I wasn't accusing you." He held out his hand for the card, but she retracted it.

"Show me your hate mail." The flaming hair around her face really was a stunning accent to her piercing blue eyes. And such a match to her tone.

"It's not hate mail. It's…" He rubbed the back of his neck. "I don't know what it is, Jaz. A sick joke, maybe."

"You didn't sound amused."

"Yeah, not so much." He turned around and motioned her in. The waft of perfume had a biting essence that could be eau de brimstone. He might have bought it for her, the interaction with her personal chemistry making the difference.

She hitched the purse up on her shoulder. "Did you do something different in here?"

"Rearranged a little."

Her eyes narrowed. "New art."

He cleared his throat. "Would you like coffee? Or something?"

She was on the verge of accepting, then surprised him with, "I'll pass." She pulled out the drawing and laid it on the bar-height counter.

He gave it a brief glance. "I know. I saw it."

"How?"

"Natalie made a copy for Whit." He turned the paper to observe the original, the lines drawn in ink forming the rays almost tore through the paper. Anger? Excitement? Vehemence? He frowned. What was it supposed to say?

Her fingernails struck the counter in quick, sharp clicks. "There's no point withholding yours."

She was already involved, and her hound's nose might sniff out something faster than the FBI—if they took the photos seriously and had the resources to deal with them. These wouldn't be the worst things troubling the US Department of Justice. He went and got the first photo from his desk, the one he'd thought was a gag.

"Think you can you find out what this is?"

Her eyelids opened past the circumference of her irises. "Are those bumps—"

"It looks like it."

Her brow twisted. "Photoshopped?"

"I don't know."

"Kid looks more mad than afraid."

"That's what I thought. Still, it's a bad position he's in."

"If it's real." She frowned. "Is there a note? a threat?"

"Just the photo." And others.

"Can I take it?"

"Let me print a copy." He'd sent Conner the originals, but was keeping his own file. He handed the new print to Jaz.

"You sure you don't know anything?"

He showed her the postmark, which was all he had. Her mouth pulled a lazy grin.

"What?"

"You need my help."

He sucked his breath between his teeth. "'Need' is a strong word."

"Say it."

"Maybe you can uncover a story about a lost or rescued kid."

"You think a searcher snapped this picture and sent it to you for laughs?"

"It feels more like a taunt."

She frowned. "You really do make enemies, don't you?"

He spread his hands. "Honestly, Jaz, besides you, not so much."

"So maybe I overreacted."

He kept his tongue firmly inside his teeth.

She flicked the photo. "I'll see what I can do with this."

"Thanks."

"I get the exclusive."

"Of course." It was a long shot, but as a freelance journalist she had access to databases. It just might pay off.

———

"Oh, honey." Heart breaking, Natalie hugged Cody who woke up asking where Daddy was, where Mommy was, where Trevor was, and the only one she could offer in person was the last. She tried phoning Aaron, but it only upset Cody more. He had to be one confused little child.

She fed him Cheerios and took him to the studio where he explored for about two minutes, then wanted to be next door at Trevor's "a'venture" store.

"Here." She offered him the earthy clay to play with while she worked on the frozen waterfall sculpture. With his one small hand, he squished and smooshed and smeared the brownish gray mass around, then asked again for Trevor.

"We need a television, so he can watch cartoons," Lena said.

Cody rattled off the shows he liked, but Natalie shook her head. Little minds were sponges, even if most didn't clog up in the process. She wanted real wonder in his head, not cars that turned into robots and blasted bigger, badder robots. She didn't know what else was out there, but surely she could do more than plant him in front of a TV.

The moment his chin started to quake with unshed tears, she bundled him up and took him to Trevor. "You've spoiled him. He thinks this is Disney World."

"Hey, buddy." Trevor scooped him up and set him on the counter, then leaned over and kissed her. "Are we okay?"

So okay it hurt. "Yes. Except no one brought croissants."

He smiled. "I got held up. Jaz accosted me with the drawing."

"You appear unscathed."

"As assaults go it was fairly civil."

Jaz was tired of reacting. Good for her, stopping it. "Trevor, would Cody be—"

"Awesome? What else?" He high-fived the tot with an easy rapport, as though Cody also felt the bond. As if part of him still held the breaths puffed into his lungs.

"I mean, is he in the way if I leave him for a bit?" Her phone vibrated with a text from Lena, stating that Carter Granby was at the gallery. "I have an appointment, and—"

"Just try getting him back."

She smiled her thanks and hurried back to meet the person who'd contacted her regarding Fleur. He was a sausage-shaped man in a plum-colored suit, white shoes, black shirt, and the visible light spectrum plus ultraviolet in his tie.

"I don't have to tell you these are wonderful." Carter Granby squeezed his cleft chin, absorbing Fleur's *Whispers in White*. He smelled so pungently of aftershave and mouthwash he must have freshly applied them in the car. "I'm very interested in commissioning her work for our collection, larger than what you have here, mural sized in fact."

"Oh. Well, I'm sure she'll discuss it." But she wondered. "Would she paint on location?"

"Naturally. And we'd film it."

"Film...her?"

"Our center celebrates fine and dramatic arts. Not as static as a gallery—no reflection on yours." He waved a hand. "The video of her creating the mural would play alongside the mural itself."

"Oh."

"My production crew will schedule filming at her convenience."

Caught nearly speechless, Natalie managed, "You know she's blind."

"Of course. That's the point."

While she could picture a video running beside the finished work, she couldn't exactly picture Fleur in it. But that was Fleur's decision. "I'll contact her with your request."

He handed her his card and said, "So she can reach me."

He didn't want her running interference, but it was through this gallery he'd heard of Fleur, and she wasn't about to blindside her friend with something this unusual, and in Fleur's mind possibly invasive. On the other hand, it could be a great opportunity.

She smiled. "We'll let you know."

When the door closed, she turned to Lena. "Something tells me I should discuss this with Fleur in person."

"My thought exactly. Don't forget your nephew."

"I'm on my way there now."

But when she went in, Trevor had Cody clinging to the climbing wall. She didn't dare cry out and distract him, but rushed past an employee and several customers to the man who'd clearly lost his mind.

He slid her a glance. "He's fully harnessed. And he's on the kiddie wall."

"He has one arm," she hissed.

"And two legs."

"Trevor."

"It's good exercise and coordination. I have him fully supported."

Cody pushed with his foot and reached with his only hand for the next grip. His fingers slipped and he swung out. She gasped, but the harness held him.

"Feet on the wall," Trevor said.

Instinctively, Cody's feet went to the wall and stopped his swing. He grabbed a brightly colored hold.

"That's it, big guy."

He was only about four feet off the ground, and Trevor obviously had hold of him, but more people had gathered to watch the one-armed tot on the climbing wall. Cody didn't seem to notice or care that they stared. He wanted to climb the wall.

With her limited childhood, what did she know about a normal child's needs and desires? Okay, so one arm wasn't normal, but Cody didn't know it. He thought he could do anything. And why shouldn't he?

"Almost there," Trevor said. "Grab the blue one."

Instead of the blue one, Cody pushed hard with his opposite foot and clutched the red bar at the top of the kiddie wall. The people watching applauded. Trevor beamed. She didn't know which of them was prouder, tot or teacher.

"Now push off and ride it to the ground," Trevor told him.

Her nephew rappelled with a chest laugh that put tears in everyone's eyes. When Trevor unbuckled him, she swooped him into a hug.

"See me, Aunt Nattie?"

"I saw you. You are absolutely the best I ever saw." She had to stop being afraid for him. His awful thing had happened. Surely, the rest of his life would be blessed.

He squeezed hard, his little arm tight around her neck. People came around, congratulating him, and the looks on Cody's face and each of theirs implanted. She had planned to go right to Fleur's, but when the crowd dissipated, Trevor took Cody and said, "Go work it out."

"You've already kept him."

"Do what you need to do."

She went back to the studio and sculpted Cody, beatific in triumph. Those who'd shared the moment formed the sides of the wall, Trevor prominently—again. Back once more, she found Cody snoozing in a tot-sized sleeping bag on the floor of Trevor's office. "I'm so sorry."

"Why?"

"You've had him for hours."

"Only three."

She was beginning to doubt her ability to care for her nephew. She loved him so much, but she'd never had sole responsibility. Eyes moist, she glimpsed the cherubic sleepyhead, curled like a caterpillar poised to sprout wings.

Trevor followed her gaze. "He looked a little hollow-eyed. How'd he sleep last night?"

"He loves the tent, but…he's restless. He cries out. I probably do too. Nights aren't our best time."

"Nightmares?"

She nodded.

"Why didn't you tell me?"

"He's only been here—"

"About yours."

She raised and dropped her shoulders. "Hard to work into conversation."

"Not that hard."

She could feel him staring. "It's a normal response to trauma. That was a terrifying ordeal."

"Doesn't mean there aren't ways to work through it."

She leaned against the desk. "I would have texted you the last time, but you were out of range."

He took her hand. "Let's take Cody for a hike."

Her mouth parted.

"Revisiting the scene under peaceful conditions can mitigate the fear."

"I'm pretty sure Paige would be horrified."

"With all respect, Nattie, she's not here. And I've worked people through it."

"Three-year-olds?"

"Don't you think that's especially critical?"

She chewed her lip. "What about the snow?"

"Have you looked outside? Most of it's blown off and the sun's making quick work of the rest."

"I have to meet with Fleur now."

"After that, then." He rubbed her fingers with his thumb. "Trust me?"

She nodded, but the thought of seeing the place that kept wrecking her sleep was not a good one.

———

Fleur looked up when Piper stepped into the sun porch even though her sock feet made hardly any sound. The air had shifted.

"Found someone on the doorstep," Piper said.

"Natalie." Fleur laid down her brush.

"How can you possibly know?"

She shrugged. "My superpowers. You have something good to tell me."

Natalie laughed. "I suppose you can tell me what it is?"

"That's beyond my skills. I'm not psychic, you know."

"Well, prepare yourself. Mr. Carter Granby wants to commission a mural for the Granby Fine and Dramatic Art Center."

She shook her head. "A mural. How would I get it in and out of my porch?"

"He wants you to paint on location. And…he'd film it."

Fleur heard but could hardly believe as Natalie rushed on, telling her everything. "Your performance would play alongside the mural continuously."

"The blind artist at work."

Natalie came closer. "Fleur. You're an amazing person. You'd be amazing if you weren't blind. But you are."

Simple, blunt, and true. "I'm sorry. I wish I didn't have to wonder whether they'd notice if I could see like everyone else."

"What difference does it make?" Her friend took her hand. "My defect contributes to my work."

"It's not a defect."

"Oh, but it is." Her grip was cool from being outside. "Your art speaks. And the fact that you can't see it with your eyes makes its message more powerful. You can't fault people for responding to that."

"You're right. I'm sorry."

"Don't be." Natalie covered their clasped hands with her other. "I can't say if this is right for you. Just don't let being blind determine it."

"Would you let him film you sculpting?"

"My nature works, maybe."

Fleur chewed her lip. "I don't know how I look. When I paint. And something so large…"

"It's a big decision. Take your time."

"When I brought you the paintings, I wasn't looking for fame. Just a place for people to see them."

"Excellence shines."

Her friend was dear to think so. "Will you show him your faces?"

"This isn't about me, Fleur. It's your opportunity."

"But a video."

"Unusual, and in my opinion distracting. But it's a changing world. Attention spans are truncated. Many have lost the ability to discern and interpret, to quietly observe."

"So it's performance, not art, they want."

"It's both."

"I find it faintly horrifying."

Amusement filled Natalie's voice. "I thought you might."

They laughed.

"But it might be fun. It'll certainly be different, an experience you won't have here."

Her stool scraped on the ceramic tile as she leaned forward. "I guess I could talk to him."

"That's a good place to start. See how comfortable you'd be working with him."

"But you have to do one thing." She pushed her hair behind her ear.

"What?"

"Show him your model of me."

"It's not even fired."

"Finish it and show him."

Natalie groaned. "Why?"

She truly didn't get it. "Because your faces transcend."

——

He'd half expected Natalie to back out, her reluctance understandable. But this was her community, and that trail one of the most accessible in the area. He didn't want fear to dominate her as much as it might Cody if unchecked. Getting up from a bad fall, going back to the top, and taking the run again made the difference between winning and losing. He'd never have that chance again. But he wanted a win for them.

After disembarking at the trailhead, Trevor hoisted Cody to his back in a pack designed for long-distance trekking with toddlers.

"You're going to carry him?"

"Gives me the chance to test this pack." The contact and containment should also give Cody a greater sense of security. He'd been on his own little legs the last time, no concept of danger. That concept was now alive and real. "Okay, let's do it."

They started up the trail, and where it narrowed to single file, he motioned her in front to focus on the vista ahead instead of her nephew in the pack. More than half the aspen had turned yellow, seemingly overnight. Snow clung to the crevices and shady sections of trail, but the rest was sun drenched in slanting rays.

He doubted the scenery meant anything to the child on his back. His own mind spun between Jaz's warrior-angel drawing, kids in danger, Cody's fear, and Natalie marching staunchly ahead, facing down her own nightmares. Did he know what he was doing? He'd better be completely sure this was right.

He said, "Warm?" when she unzipped her parka. It amazed him how much the weather could shift in such a short time, one extreme to the other, like life.

"You were right about that." Her neck looked taut, her motions jerky. No doubt an onslaught of memories and emotions. She loved mountains, but this trauma could make it a strictly visual experience if she let it. This would help. He knew it would. So why did he feel so uneasy?

Something rustled. She spun.

"Just a magpie." He saw the fear in her face and blocked Cody's view with a shift in position.

"That, um, *threat* is gone, right?"

"It's gone. And they're territorial, the chance of another extremely remote."

"But"—she slid both hands into her hair—"you have your g-u-n?"

"Holstered. Safety engaged."

"Would you use it this time?" Her voice held an edge of doubt and... recrimination?

"No sense having it otherwise. Want me to lead?"

"No." Her brow puckered. "It's only that none of us saw it coming."

"And we're having a good time here, aren't we, Cody?" He jostled the carrier.

Catching his point, she drew herself up. "Of course we are." She pivoted on one heel and pointed. "Look, Cody. That gray bird is called a catbird because it mews."

Cody mewed at the bird.

"My friend Fleur's taught me all about birds and their songs. Want to sing like a blue jay? It's not pretty, let me tell you." She demonstrated that truth, Cody joining in.

Trevor smiled. She was taking a good stab at normal. But as they neared the point of attack, Cody's noises stopped. The arm holding on tightened around his neck.

"I want to go back now." Cody spoke in his ear.

"Don't worry, little guy."

"I want my daddy."

Natalie was far enough ahead she didn't hear and kept walking, even though she was probably suffering too. He should have thought this through better.

"If we do this, Cody, it won't be as scary next time." He gripped the little wrist beneath his chin. "Remember how you climbed the wall? All the way to the top?"

"I want my mommy."

"I know."

"I want my Nattie."

"Okay. Hey, Nat?"

She turned, a false luster in her eyes.

"Cody wants a hug."

While she soothed the tot, he searched the slopes, more affected than he'd expected by revisiting this—or was it something else? Spending time in the wild developed senses more acute than most people's, a sense, for instance, of being watched—or stalked. For the last quarter mile, he'd felt it. If that cub had still been attached to its mother, there could be another cat—unlikely as he'd thought it before.

He carefully reached down and released the safety on his handgun. Time to complete the mission. He motioned Nattie ahead once more. Following, he said, "Cody, I know this is scary because something bad happened. But you were brave, and you're even braver now. You know what brave means?"

Cody pressed his mouth against the back of Trevor's neck. "Means I don't cry."

He felt him quiver. "Means you don't let getting scared stop you." He stroked the child's arm. "We had a hard time here."

"Bad lion."

"That lion was confused. Most are too smart to grab a guy like you." He went a few more paces and a few more. "Now see? We're past it."

"No bad lions," Cody whispered.

"That's right. Just pretty mountains. And birds and squirrels. Your aunt Nattie, who loves you, and me."

The child's eyes went over everything, sober and searching, his brows pressed low. The rapport they'd established helped, but this wasn't easy. Cody's hand gripped his shirt, and the memory came back of wrapping him in his other one, containing the arm they lost anyway, stanching the blood. He couldn't help staring down at the creek far below where blood might still mark the spot.

"It's getting dark," Natalie murmured. "And cold." She zipped her coat. She was smart and tough and brave. So many things he respected and—he'd almost thought loved.

"Okay." He turned around, scanning again. Whatever had them in its sights had moved on or was never there to start with. He clicked the safety back in place. "Let's go."

———

Taking the call in the Bronco with Tia riding beside him, Jonah eased over to the side of the road since any swerving rolled her stomach. "Four new complaints?"

"A regular spree," Officer Moser said over the phone. "All concentrated in the Old Town area."

"What was taken?"

Moser spoke precisely. "Besides Forney's boots, one woolen blanket from a car. One smoked pheasant and towel."

"A towel?"

"Hand towel," Moser said. "You take a hot, greasy bird from a smoke hut, you want some protection for your hands."

"Right."

"Diane Noble said she had a dozen new bar rags outside the smoker. Someone opened the package, took one."

"A thoughtful thief. Sounds like a local. What else?"

"You ready for this?"

He heard the grin in Moser's voice. "Lay it on me."

"Underwear."

"What?"

"Three pairs from a dryer at the Laundromat. Might be a prank, but Wallace says he washed seven briefs, only got four at the end."

Jonah covered the speaker and mouthed, "Stolen underwear" to Tia. Her distended nostril reflected his feelings on that one. "Was Wallace there the whole time?"

"No," Moser said. "Stepped next door to talk fishing at the gas station while his clothes finished up."

He nodded. "We've got a vagrant."

"Sounds like."

Someone cold and hungry who liked clean clothes. "Check around. See who's been laid off or kicked out, who might hang around town hoping for reconciliation."

"All right."

He almost hung up, then said, "Oh, Moser. What's the fourth thing?"

"Wendy Gershwin's bird-watching binoculars."

Such I created all the ethereal Powers
And Spirits, both them who stood, and them who fail'd;
Freely they stood who stood, and fell who fell.

From a distance through magnifying lenses, he watched him—the guardian. On his back, the child. Sweet, tender care piercing. Shaking, he watched them, man and child, his heart punching like a fist in his chest. Rage snapped like a wolf at his heels with equal parts hunger and fury.

Dropping to his knees, he groaned, tortured by this goodness. Rage engulfing. Why? He gripped himself, stifling the cry that ripped through him.

His mission had been small. But this one, nothing he did was small. No inconsequential breath drawn. Better not to have seen, never to have seen. To wonder, even suspect this righteousness, but not *know*. He dropped the binoculars and ground the heels of his hands into his eyes. Then like a junkie he took up the lenses again.

Shivering, he watched them, his unacclimated flesh, his inadequate garb, but, most of all, the sight of this celestial being chilling the marrow in his bones.

Sixteen

Proud of the little guy, Trevor tucked Cody into the SUV, but prevented Natalie from climbing in just yet. Easing her away from the open door, he enclosed her in his arms. "Better?"

She glanced up from just below his chin to somewhere around his mouth. "I guess we'll see tonight."

"You did great." Better than he'd expected, pulling her weight on this adventure for Cody's sake.

She leaned back against the car. "I hope it was the right thing. For Cody, I mean."

"Do you doubt it?" When he'd been such a trooper?

"It's complicated with kids."

"It's complicated." He rubbed her shoulder.

"I remember—" She shook her head. "Never mind."

He looked through the window at Cody, kicking his little boots. "He's been here now with people who care and nothing bad happening. A good experience to counter the bad."

"Or an instant replay."

He tipped her chin up, but she didn't look. "That would require a wild animal attack."

"Or the memory of one."

"Yes, he remembered. But nothing happened. That was the point."

She nodded. "Okay. But the cougar's not always in my dreams. Fear takes other forms, and there are lots of scary things."

"Like?"

"I don't know. Ugly, evil faces. And crowds."

Things that overwhelmed her. "He doesn't have a truck-load of baggage yet. I'm guessing his fears are pretty specific."

"But we don't know. No one understood the impact all that testing had until I almost shut down. I was so cute and amazing, but inside—"

"Nattie." He cradled her face. There was only one other car in the lot and they'd seen no one on the trail, but he suddenly felt watched again. "Let's go home and talk, okay?"

Again the pucker formed between her brows. "I'm not saying this was wrong. I'm just...afraid to make it worse."

He motioned her into the car, glancing around as he walked to his side. It was already twilight, the temperature dropping accordingly. "All I know"—he slid into his seat—"is that facing things is always better. The more you bury it, the more it eats you."

She pulled the seat belt over and buckled. "Did that help you get over Ellis?" She flicked her gaze up to his, then away.

"I'll never get over Ellis." A fallen leaf had stuck in his windshield wiper. "But I'm trying to get over not being there."

"By being there for Cody?"

He stared at the reddish yellow leaf, the brittle veins and capillaries. "A little, maybe."

Tears welled in her eyes. "Thank you."

He started the car. "I know you have more to say. But let's get back." He couldn't remember if that old car had been there when they arrived, and if not, they should have seen someone on the trail. Or the occupants had ignored the instructions and gone off-trail.

Looking over her shoulder, she whispered, "He's asleep."

Trevor glanced in the rearview mirror. "That's normal." Stress and anxiety exhausted. Children instinctually gave in.

He pulled out of the lot, his turn signal flashing and clicking. "You were going to tell me something."

She flicked one short fingernail with another. "I remember being so overwhelmed and having no way to explain it. People kept doing what they thought would help, and I tried and tried and did what they asked and wanted to be happy, but inside I was screaming. I'm afraid inside Cody are screams we can't even imagine."

That hurt to think about. "I hear you, Nattie. We won't push it."

"I know you're right about facing things. He's just too little to resist if he has to."

He reached over and took her hand. "You're wise."

She blinked back tears. "Sometimes love is healing enough."

Something inside broke loose, dissolving in a well of emotion he couldn't spoil with words. He'd thought he was rescuing her, when he'd been the one on the precipice.

———

After spending the day pleading for essential law-enforcement personnel and equipment, Jonah headed home with the mistaken anticipation of peace. Surrounded by woods with his own tributary running through, his cabin wasn't the solitary haven it used to be, but he'd take it.

The coydogs were fractious, probably from being cooped up. He let them out to roam, Scout especially keen on running free, even if Enola hung closer to the house. The pup might one day heed the call of the wild, but Enola had made her choice.

They were the least of his concerns. It appeared Sarge had taken a downturn. Pain tightened his voice like a bark, spit forming a bead at the corner of his mouth as he yelled at his nurse. For a straight-backed military man, the scoliosis seemed especially cruel, robbing him of what proud bearing he might have managed. At least the VA insurance still paid for Lauren, bless her sainted heart.

Her straight brown hair draped Sarge's shoulder as she gently manipulated the spine from that joint to his hip, trying to relax muscles and relieve constricted nerves. Her gray-green eyes slipped from her patient to the doorway where he watched. Her beauty still struck him, though he hadn't pursued her as Tia once thought. That was all Jay.

Her grave expression told him more than words, when she joined him in the hall. "He can't manage the walker any longer, Jonah. The bone deterioration of his lower lumbar is severe, and, I'm sorry, but there are signs of paralysis."

"We use the wheelchair about half the time as it is." He didn't ask about surgery. They turned him down a year ago as too far gone. "What about pain?"

"The points of impingement are excruciating."

"I can see it in his face. And he snaps."

"I'd snap too." She looked over her shoulder. "If we increase his meds, he'll be confined to the bed."

Jonah sighed. "His call, I guess."

"I'm a nurse, Jonah. A doctor might—"

"You think he'd give you up for any doctor?"

She slipped the hair behind her ear. While Sarge would never admit it, he was smitten. Jonah raised his face at movement in his kitchen. Tia must be home.

But it wasn't Tia. As he and Lauren entered the main room, Jay lowered his bottled O'Doul's and took them in, his posture slightly combative. "You cooking?"

"Yeah, but I don't know what. Tia's bringing home whatever looks good to her."

Jay's gaze slid to Lauren and narrowed, one brow crooking. The silent bob of his chin drew hers in return. He had to have seen her car, known she was here when he walked in. Neither spoke as she gathered her things.

She looked up. "I'll talk to a doctor about any treatment that might control pain without incapacitating Sarge. Maybe there's a trial." She started for the door.

"Thanks, Lauren."

Jay said nothing as the door closed behind her. He held out a second O'Doul's. Jonah didn't like the stuff, but took it. Jay had been working his version of the program since his teens with sporadic success. Saving Jonah's life had been pivotal for them both.

"Sarge having a bad time?" He seemed antsy.

"Yeah." Jonah cleared his throat. "What's up?"

He said, "I won the contract for the Snyder house." But Jonah doubted that was it; more likely seeing Lauren or the same agitation he'd felt for a while.

"When do you start?"

"We're waiting for knotty pine. Might take a while since it's scarce."

"Have to grow some?"

Jay pulled a smile. "Once that happens, I'll need crew."

"I guess so."

"Interested?"

He blew his breath through his lips. "Council shot down my new positions in order to pad projects that will 'enhance Redford's image.'" He jammed his fingers into his hair. "Like safe streets won't?"

"Safe isn't tangible."

"Yeah. Well, we were down an officer before annexing Pine Crest. Once the Kicking Horse resort opens, it won't take another meth explosion to compromise effectiveness. I can't keep this town safe without the people and equipment to do it." He spread his hands. "Does anyone get that?"

"Could use a foreman I can trust."

Jonah tucked his chin. "Don't hit me while I'm down. Besides, I'm nowhere close to qualified." What skills he had, Jay taught him when neither believed he'd stay chief. But the town still wanted him after the near-fatal bender that followed his father's suicide. They continuously approved his reappointment, and he hadn't said no yet. Some days it felt like he'd traded one whipping boy position for another. But he knew where he belonged. "Thanks, but I'll keep my job."

As Tia pushed through the door with her marketing bag, they eyed her cautiously.

"What?"

Jonah crooked his mouth. "Tell us it isn't squid or liver you're in the mood for."

She jutted her chin. "It's chicken. But now that I've been to the store, I don't think I can eat that either. Did Lauren leave? I need her to tell me there's an end in sight." She set the bag on the counter, stretched up to kiss his mouth, and left them.

He smiled. "Guess I'll grill chicken and hope she can eat it."

"She's having a girl."

"What?"

"The baby. It's a daughter."

Jonah frowned. "You know this how?"

Jay shrugged.

"Don't give me that wise native stuff."

He grinned, altogether too pleased with himself.

"So if we're getting personal, which one of you broke things off? Lauren?"

Jay drained the fake beer. "Some things aren't meant to be."

"Especially if we're afraid to let them."

Tia came back and circled his waist with her arms. "Mind hurrying that chicken up? I'm starved."

He shot a look over her head. "See what you're missing?"

"I'm not missing it. I'm watching from the safe seats."

———

After SpaghettiOs, Cody started crying. He cried on her shoulder for nearly two hours. He wanted his daddy.

"Should I call him?" she mouthed to Trevor, who stood nursing a glass of wine and waiting to eat the stir-fry he'd prepared while she soothed Cody.

"Can he come?"

She shook her head. He'd flown to Scottsdale with Paige to see a specialist in a very private, very exclusive clinic. "Sh, honey, sh," she murmured. "It's okay."

"Hold me, Auntie Nattie."

"I am, honey. I won't let go." She swayed with him, pressing her cheek to his hair. Finally he calmed down enough to tuck into his tent. He clutched the flashlight as he curled up and slow-blinked to sleep. She backed out of his room and joined Trevor in the kitchen.

"You were right." He handed her a goblet. "It was too much."

"I'm not sure." She took a sip. "I think—I hope—this was cathartic. He finally let it out—some of it anyway."

"You're great with him."

She stared into the faint gold liquid. "It breaks my heart."

"I know." He rubbed her arm.

"I'm not the one he needs."

"You're the one he has right now. And he's lucky to have you." When she leaned into him, he brought his arm around her.

"How ruined is the stir-fry?" She fought a yawn.

"I took it off the heat ages ago. If we fire the flame up high and toss it around a little, it might not be too limp."

"Wonderful." He'd thrown together the abundance of vegetables from her refrigerator and quick-fried them in sesame oil and soy sauce. Cody had not been at all interested, but it smelled good to her.

Smiling, she sat down across from him at her kitchen table. They threaded the fingers of their left hands together, wanting to touch even as they ate. She wished she could look and look and look at him. Maybe then she would believe it.

His phone rang. Letting go to answer, he viewed the caller and grimaced. "I'm dead."

She tipped her head, puzzled, as he answered the phone.

"Sara, I'm sorry. I forgot about tonight."

She worked on her stir-fry, trying not to intrude.

"Yeah, I know. No, I can't. It's not—" Pressing his fingers between his brows, he listened. "I'm really sorry. Something came up. Can we— Sara?" He looked at the phone. "I guess she's gone."

Natalie bit her lip. "What did you forget?"

"Dinner with them."

She checked her watch. After nine. "Should you go?"

"No point now." He leaned back. "But I feel rotten. She always goes out of her way to make it nice."

"Is there anything you can do?"

"I'll talk to her tomorrow." He sounded grim. "It's just a little different with her. For a while, a long time ago, we were…pretty close."

Did he not realize they still were?

"I think she assumed things would go a certain way. I guess we both did. But after Ellis died, she knew I'd never be the same. Before that, I'd been angry with my dad. After Ellis, the anger went inside."

Driven by self-recrimination.

He scratched his jaw. "Once I was for sure a lost cause, she married Whit."

"And you let her."

"It was the right thing for both of them. The right thing for me."

That didn't make it easy. "No regret?"

He shook his head. "She was too close to it. That would have defined everything."

"But you're all still together."

"In a way. Lately it's been strained."

He had to realize why. "If I hadn't brought Cody over—"

"Don't. Everything I did today, I wanted to. It's my fault I forgot Sara. Not yours." He pushed back and stood up, paced to the window, and looked out into her small courtyard.

She joined him there. "Sara will understand your helping Cody. She knows you. And she's a mother."

"That's this snowball's one chance in hell."

They laughed softly.

Then he frowned. "Did you leave your gate open?"

"What gate?"

"Stay here."

"Trevor?" She watched him go out her back door, watched him cross her small yard. There was no moon to temper the darkness, so she could just make him out near the back fence. She didn't think it had a gate, but she hadn't closely examined every inch.

When he came back in, he said, "You have a couple boards down. Maybe the wind."

"The previous owners had the fence for their dogs. I don't need it."

"Don't let Cody out there alone, okay?"

She cocked her head. "Do you think I'd let him anywhere alone?"

"No. But he could crawl through the gap if you got distracted."

Or visually incapacitated?

"No offense, Nattie." He clasped her shoulders. "But things happen that fast."

"Tell me about it."

He searched her face. "Still feel rushed?"

"Don't you think we should?"

"What do I know? I'm way past expiration."

"And what, you've started to spoil?"

He didn't laugh. Catching the warning signal, she pulled back, feeling a potential for pain she'd hardly imagined. "Are you going to leave, Trevor? When Cody's gone?"

He looked away. "I'm not only here for Cody. He wasn't in the picture when I came looking for you. But I don't make promises I can't keep."

His rush home from the mountain survival class, her joyous reception seemed far away and naive. "I should be careful?" She rubbed her arms.

The muscles of his jaw flexed. "You should be careful."

She drew a shaky breath. "Then, can you go now?"

He nodded. "I'll talk to you tomorrow." He paused beside her, searching, but she didn't look up.

She swallowed. "Good night."

When the door closed, she pressed her hands to her face. It was so easy to believe in him, too easy to think he felt what she did. How clearly she understood Jaz—so tired of reacting to that man. "Not going there," she said to the window. "I'm not."

Except she loved him. Probably from the moment he leaped off the trail.

———

Trevor circled her block, checking for anything out of place. There weren't many fences to compare for wind damage; most of the yards opened to the next. The fence looked as old as the house, so probably disrepair. He drove to Whit and Sara's, saw the windows dark, and drove on.

Standing Sara up had clarified just how selfish and inconsiderate he could be. Already feeling like furniture, she'd just been hauled out for the yard sale. He expelled his breath. Not fair. Not fair to anyone.

Yeah, they were still friends—his Teflon people who let his sins slip off them. He expected to grow old with them, but in some ways, they'd never moved past his brother's death. Like an unspoken pact, parts of them stayed exactly as they were. A memorial of arrested development.

He drew up to the gate, scanned his key to activate, waited for it to swing. He checked his rearview as a car passed slowly behind. Frowning, he looked again. That junker from the trailhead?

Too dark. He went through the gate into the garage, took his reserved spot, and noted the car in the guest spot beside him. The moment he entered his place, Whit was on him with a fury.

"Just who do you think you are?"

"I know, Whit. I feel terrible."

"You feel terrible?"

"I got caught up helping Cody and lost sight of things." No excuse, just the truth.

"Cody or Natalie?"

"They're interconnected." He moved into his living room.

"Look." Whit's hands fisted. "I know what's going on, but Sara doesn't. You haven't bothered to tell her."

Trevor shook his head. "I took them out to the trail to work through the trauma. When we got back, Cody decompressed. I couldn't leave them distraught."

"Cut the bull."

"It's true."

"And kissing Natalie in the parking lot? What—" He spread his hands. "Mouth-to-mouth resuscitation?"

Trevor rubbed his face.

"You"—Whit poked his chest—"have an obligation. If this is more than a fleeting episode, Sara needs to know."

"She's *your* wife."

Though shorter by inches, Whit came nearly jaw to jaw with him. "We both know why."

Chest heaving, he looked away. "She chose you, Whit."

"Knowing she'd get the matched pair."

He chewed his lip. "I didn't mean to upset her. I will apologize tomorrow."

"And tell her the truth."

He threw out his hands. "I don't lie."

"So you and 'Nattie' are nothing more than whatever you are with Kirstin or Jaz or..."

He sighed. "I don't know what we are." Not true, or he would have told Sara it was nothing. "But yes, she matters more than Kirstin and Jaz." Or anyone else. After tonight that might be a moot point. He turned. "I forgot, Whit. I simply forgot dinner."

Whit nodded. "Well, make it right. I'm sick of her crying over you."

This my long sufferance, and my day of grace,
They who neglect and scorn, shall never taste;
But hard be harden'd, blind be blinded more.
That they may stumble on, and deeper fall.

Caution. Patience. He must stem the fervor that would lead to haste and haste to mistakes. He left the car in a different place and walked. Wait. Wait. He couldn't act yet. Seeing him once was not enough, not nearly enough to know what he needed to know.

Seed sown must lie still, swelling, splitting, growing. Patience. Caution. Wait. He knew how to wait.

Back in the place he'd slept before, he drew the book from the deep pocket of his cape. He stroked the cover, seeing the room, the tight, bare walls, a piece of foam to lie on, a thick candle on a metal plate upon the cracking concrete floor. The book in the corner.

Closer he crept until he saw. The form on the front sent a shudder through his soul. He looked at it now. Black, pointed wings, rippled muscles, tormented face.

His little hands had reached. Words he'd never seen, never heard. Learn them. Say them. Know them. Know them and leave. He promised. The father of lies.

Seventeen

Sara's eyes were bright as he stood at her door, trying to explain. "I thought revisiting the sight of the trauma under safe conditions would alleviate their fear. Then Cody lost it and I felt responsible. Everything else just went out of my head." He searched her face for softening. "He's been through so much." There it was.

"He's not a man getting back on the horse that threw him. He's a little boy." She pressed the mother's heart beating in her chest.

"I get that. Now." He could still hear Cody crying.

"Come here." She hugged him. "He'll be all right."

He held her, trying to do what Whit wanted, but words wouldn't come. "So, I'm going to work, but I wanted you to know. It wasn't personal."

"Okay." She let go.

How many times had she taken the hurt and moved on? For the first time he considered how unfair it might be.

But her mouth tipped up and her raccoon freckles collected as she said, "Pictionary tonight."

He grinned. "You're on."

"Trevor. If Natalie needs help with Cody, I'm here."

He raised his brows. "That's great. I'll tell her. Or you can."

"Just let her know."

He nodded. Maybe Sara and Natalie could work out their own friendship; then it wouldn't be a big deal to include Nattie in things like Pictionary. Whit was overreacting. Frowning, he got into his SUV. Matched pair. Maybe Whit hadn't noticed he was the one with a family.

———

Because of Fleur's meeting with Mr. Granby, Lena took charge of Cody when they arrived. She hid rolls of Smarties, suckers, and Matchbox cars, and they were playing Huckle Buckle Beanstalk. Natalie's heart warmed. There was surely no shortage of love for her little nephew—or her.

Aaron's concentration was elsewhere, her parents out of reach, but the friends she'd made in this short time were constant and generous. And in spite of the way their conversation ended, in her nightmare last night, Trevor had burst through the crowd and grabbed her off the disintegrating tightrope.

Fleur had come in with her and stood, fidgety, near the podium. Carter Granby would see a lovely, conscientious artist.

"He should be here any minute," Natalie told her.

Hands peaked against her lips, Fleur nodded. "Is your model ready?"

"I've had no time. Carter stayed in town last night, so when I called, he set up this morning for *you*." She turned. "And here he is."

"Tell me quickly what he looks like."

She described a suit similar to yesterday's in flamboyance. "Beige and drapey, with a turquoise shirt and candy apple tie."

"I can't be nervous with a sausage man in gift wrap."

Laughing, Natalie assured her she had no reason to be nervous. After making introductions, she left them to discuss his offer. Lena had Cody upstairs, and Natalie wandered toward the front.

Sunlight shown on Trevor's statue, and someone had stopped to view it through the window. She moved closer to observe the reaction. At first she couldn't make him out and didn't want to be obvious. Then wind cast the hood back from his face, revealing a damaged and tortured mien. With a cry, she staggered back, grasping a platform for support.

No, oh no. Her heart raced. Her throat constricted.

"Natalie?" Lena's voice.

Eyes closed, she saw and hurt. She needed it out. *Oh, please.*

"Help her into the studio," Fleur said.

The pain. The ruin. The excruciating expression. She pressed her fingers to her temples. *Please. Please.*

Lena touched her arm. "I'm going next door for Trevor."

"No, please. Don't." She had to stop dragging him into this.

"Does she need medical help?" said Carter Granby.

"No," Lena told him. "But thank you for your concern."

Gripping the older woman's arm, Natalie entered her sanctuary, needing and dreading a release—then cried, "Cody!"

Lena said, "He's upstairs playing cars. I'll watch."

This was exactly what Trevor meant. Without Lena or someone...

From the dregs of the sludge bucket, she built a mound, gathered herself for long, aching moments, then drove her hands into the clay.

———

"Okay, wait." Trevor clicked the volume up on his phone. "Who is this?"

"Lena. At the gallery."

He frowned. "I can barely hear you."

"Natalie told me not to call, but I thought you'd want to know."

His pulse quickened. "Know what?" He pictured what she described with disturbing clarity.

"I don't know what it was, but she's in the studio—"

"Where's Cody?"

She said, "He's here."

"I'll be right over."

"No, I—"

He didn't wait for her argument. Entering through the front, he scanned only moments before Cody ran to him, clutching a black Firebird. "I huckle-buckled it."

"No, really?" He crouched. No apparent damage from yesterday, but the little guy didn't need any more scariness, and seeing his aunt the way she got would be scary. He looked up at Lena. "Care if I take him next door?"

Cody bounced on the balls of his feet. "A'venture store!"

She gazed over her spectacles. "You think I'll be the meany who says no?"

He scooped Cody up and said, "As soon as she's done—"

"I'll tell her where he is."

Barely back in the door, his cashier, Caitlyn, snatched Cody, whom she had previously dubbed their mascot. "You won't be needing this," she said over her shoulder and tickled Cody's tummy.

"I'll be in the office when you decide to turn him over."

"Not likely." The dimpled blonde swung away.

He considered going to the studio, but if Natalie told Lena not to call, she was probably stinging from last night. He thought of a thousand ways he could have handled the conversation better. He hadn't even said what he meant, just fell back into old patterns. *Don't love me; I'll hurt you. Don't trust me; I'll leave you.*

He rubbed his face, feeling his dad's grip on his shoulder. *"You'll get this someday. You've got me running through you like a gold vein in granite."*

He went out and hit the climbing wall without a rope, lunging up and leaping from grip to grip, breaking their rules a hundred ways. It wasn't gold running through him. It was tar.

"And that, people, is how you get yourself banned from this store and struck from the company insurance." Whit's voice penetrated the dark place in his head.

He stopped moving around the wall and eased himself to the floor. He locked gazes with Whit, then took in the other people watching. He swallowed. "What he said."

The cool breeze hit his sweat-soaked, long-sleeve shirt like a fan, temperate sixties, not withstanding. He'd built up some heat. Moving through the gallery, he ignored Lena's raised hand and went through to the studio.

Natalie stood with clay-smeared hands on her cheeks. A mess of clay on the table, but no model. After a moment he realized she was crying. He turned her around and took the hands she tried to pull away.

"I'm a mess."

"I don't care. Tell me what's wrong."

Her voice was tight. "I tried, but I can't make it. I can't."

"Is it still in your head?"

"I think I blocked it."

He smoothed her hair back. "I thought you couldn't do that."

"I never have." She gulped. "But when I tried to make this"—her whole body shuddered—"I've never felt so destroyed."

He pulled her tight and held her, rubbing her back until some of the tension left.

"I wasn't going to bother you today."

His fault completely. "Can we talk about that?"

She flicked a look up, then away.

Hopefully it was enough to see he meant this. "I wasn't honest last night. I should have said don't be careful. Don't be afraid. I'm not going anywhere."

"Trevor…"

He bent and kissed her, tasting clay and salt and her sweet mouth.

She brought her crusted hands to his face, his neck, his hair. Fingers curled against his jaw, she said, "Take me out of here."

He led her out through the gallery, so Lena would know he had her. She raised her brows, but made no comment. At the last moment, Natalie turned.

"You take care," Lena told her.

The back of her eyes ached. She felt faintly nauseated. But Trevor's arm on her shoulders was hard and firm.

As he opened his door, he said, "Don't be surprised if Whit gets in my face."

She pulled her thoughts in. "About Sara?"

"No, that's cool. I talked to her this morning."

"Then…" She still felt dazed.

"I broke the rules on the climbing wall, working out some tension. Whit's a safety nazi, so we'll snag Cody and make a run for it."

But Whit had Cody. He was walking through the shelves and telling him about the gear and equipment. Anticipating a blowup, she saw only a penetrating look pass between them.

Cody yawned and reached out for her. Taking him, she wanted to weep. What kind of caregiver was she, stunned by something she saw while everyone else had her little guy? She shuddered as the feeling, if not the face, rolled over her again.

"You're dirty." Cody rubbed his finger on her cheek.

She'd forgotten. No wonder Whit held his tongue. She must look like a refugee.

"Everything cool?" Whit said.

"Sure." Trevor smiled. "Thanks for holding on to him."

Whit pocketed his hands. "Sara said you talked."

"I groveled; she let me off light. Pictionary tonight. I'll bring these two." He brought his hand to the small of her back. "Sara said she'd help out with Cody anytime."

Natalie took that in with mixed feelings. "That's…kind."

"She's great with kids. Even before Braden." Then to Whit, "We'll grab dinner and come around eight."

"That's almost Cody's bedtime." She snuggled her nephew.

"We can tuck him in there."

Something was going on that she couldn't quite grasp.

Whit shrugged. "You and Sara covered the details?"

"Just that I'd be there."

Again the undercurrent. The thought of Whit and Sara's, and some kind of turf war made her temples throb. She could beg off later.

———

With Cody down for a nap, she washed in the bathroom, Trevor at the kitchen sink. Coming back together, she pulled a crumb of clay from his hair. "I made a mess of you."

"Mud wrestling would be a mess."

She laughed. "I have a sludge bucket."

"Are you offering?" He cocked his head.

"Absolutely not."

He said, "You believe me, right? What I told you?"

"It's really soon to be making promises. I'm not even sure I can take care of Cody. Real life? The jury's out."

"Everyone needs a hand."

"I need the whole village." She shook her head. "Trevor, what if I'd been alone with him?"

"You'd find a way, Nattie. That's what you do." He looked over her shoulder out the kitchen window.

She turned as the neighbor's tomcat pushed through the bushes at the gap in her fence, his periscope tail dodging in and out.

Trevor cupped her shoulder. "How are you doing?"

Her throat tightened. "It was awful."

"But you handled it. Without even sculpting."

Had she? She wasn't so sure. "Why are you taking me to Sara's?"

"So she can meet Cody in case you need a hand."

She tipped her head, staring at his chin. "Why are you really taking me?"

"So she'll know you matter."

"I'm not sure I'm up for that."

He threaded her fingers with his. "They're my closest friends. I want you there."

"Did you do that with Jaz?"

"They spent some time with her."

"Whit's not a fan."

"Neither is Sara."

She said, "I don't want my business neighbors as enemies." That relationship was more intrinsic than they knew—not something she intended to share, but a real concern.

"That's not going to happen."

The cat jumped onto her wrought-iron love seat, licked a paw, and rubbed it over his notched ear, an old veteran who probably thought all his fights could be won.

She pressed her hands to her eyes, groaning. "Who was it?"

"That you saw?"

She wondered, but she didn't want to see it again. "I was at the window looking out. The face was looking in." Dread penetrated, bruising her. "Why do I feel what I can't see? It's never been this way."

"You said yourself no one knows how it works."

She'd thought she did. Watching Miles have his hair cut was highly emotional—she'd staggered under it—but still held and transferred the image. This...

From the cabinet, she took out the box of PG Tips tea, scooped and clipped the mesh tea ball, and lit the flame under her kettle. She took down one mug and reached for another. "Would you like some?"

Trevor stroked the back of her hair. "Sure."

———

Cody woke up asking for SpaghettiOs, but Trevor scooped him up and said, "How would you like spaghetti in a restaurant?"

Cody blinked. "Long busketti?"

"You know, *Lady and the Tramp*?"

"Yeah! Long busketti."

"I hope you have someplace in mind." Natalie slid Cody's single arm into his coat sleeve, wrapped the rest around, and zipped.

"Of course."

She looked slightly incredulous when he parked at the Tarleton Hotel restaurant. "Are you sure?"

"Sure."

"It's not really for kids."

"Cody's not a kid. He's a rock star."

The cold wind coming off the mountains smelled of snow. Natalie pulled her collar closed. "Isn't it soon and early for another storm?"

"There's no normal to mountain weather." The more snow they got early, the better the base for the ski resort. A hollow formed in his chest. No point indulging it.

He asked for and got a table near the fireplace, a perk of early dining. Natalie rubbed her hands and basked. "Wasn't it warm and balmy an hour ago?"

"Practically tropical."

She smiled. "Well, I know a little monkey who won't mind more snow."

Cody made monkey noises. Trevor looked from one to the other, thinking it could be like this, he and Nattie and a little one or two. He didn't know if it was fear or desire that made his voice husky. "You want something to drink?"

"I'll just have tea."

Cody said, "Cocoa!"

Trevor smiled. "Sounds like a plan."

Spaghetti wasn't on the menu, but Ann, their server, assured them the chef could make it. Cody got chocolate milk instead of cocoa, and Nattie transferred it into a child's cup with a thick bendable straw that he could manage one handed.

"What else do you have in there?" He nodded at her purse.

"Oh, you know, plants, lamp stands."

His mouth quirked. "Mary Poppins."

"Practically perfect in every way but...one." She pulled a self-deprecating smile.

He covered her hand. "That's one's supercalifragilistic."

As Cody tried to repeat it, Trevor noted the scar along his hairline, shiny in the fire's reflection. The inner scars were not that faint, but he hoped being at Whit and Sara's they might avoid another meltdown.

"Cody likes the penguins. Aaron and I took him to a special showing of the movie last spring. He laughed and laughed at the penguins. Didn't you, monkey?"

"I lika penguins. Where's my busketti?"

"They have to cook it, Cody. Here." She pulled out a small pad of paper and pencil. "Why don't you draw pictures?"

"I make a penguin."

"Yes. Lots of penguins." She held the pad still while he moved the pencil.

Trevor watched, curiously, but the circles and lines looked just like his little brothers' drawings. Nothing prodigious there.

Ann came back and offered Cody more milk.

"Where's my busketti?"

"Good question. Want to watch them make it?" With a glance for permission, Ann lifted him from the chair and carried him away.

Trevor leaned toward Natalie who looked a little teary. "Told you he's a rock star."

When Ann brought their salads, Cody wasn't with her. "Chef's got him," she said. "He's having a tour of the kitchen."

Natalie laughed. "I'm beating myself up for being temporarily out of commission and he's getting the grand chef tour."

"Don't beat yourself up, Nat. You're the best he has."

Waiting at Whit and Sara's door, Natalie chewed her lip. "Sara definitely knows I'm coming?"

"Whit's told her." Trevor shifted Cody's weight and knocked.

"That's what all the coded language was in the store? You and Whit?" Trevor smiled.

Covering her ears in the snowy wind, she wondered why he didn't walk in like the last time. Subconsciously separating?

"So." Her breath came out in a cloud. "Will Sara win Pictionary too?"

"Pictionary's anybody's game. You're only as good as your team, you know."

She did. "How do you play it with three?"

"Sara plays for both teams. Guessing and drawing. But tonight we're even."

She shrugged. "Depends how we divide. If it's women against men…"

He cocked his head. "Did you just challenge me?"

"Just saying…"

The door opened.

Trevor turned his head from her to Sara. "Nattie informs me, if you and she take on us guys, you'll be ruling and we'll be drooling."

Sara's face lit. "It would be diabolically unfair." A glimpse showed she clearly loved it.

Natalie drew her first easy breath. Feeding Sara's competitive spirit might just be the evening's saving grace.

Thither full fraught with mischievous revenge,
Accursed, and in a cursed hour, he hies.

Seen! The shock reverberated. She had looked through his scars to the agony and through the agony to the void, recoiling at his dark and terrible power. No one ever had cast eyes on him as she—blind mice the rest, seeing only his affliction. But not this one. Looking deep into the soul, she measured him and left him stripped.

Trembling, he moved in darkness, a milieu he knew and dreaded. More time. He'd wanted more time! But now he must act, in haste and possibly error. A show of power—no handshake but a gauntlet thrown.

He left the car and strode, chilled by wind and spitting snow. No careful choosing of subject or setting—no chance for that! He would take what came, one careless step, one foolish choice. No stage, no camera. No pageant this, but a joust with sharpened lance.

In the shadows he moved, watching, seeking. Hither to and fro…

And there. Her head bowed in baleful retching. Caught unawares. He grabbed and lifted her.

Eighteen

L ying with his wife's head cradled in his arm, his hand resting on her belly, Jonah felt amazingly at one with her and with the life they'd created inside her. He had ached for so long to make right what he'd wrecked, and now it seemed—

His phone rang, and he reached automatically, rolling and shielding his mouth to speak. "Yeah, Moser."

"Sorry to bother you, Chief, but it seems we might have a missing teenager. Might be a mistake, but given the weather, I don't like taking a chance."

If the wind howling off the mountains carried the predicted snow, it meant blizzard conditions. "Hold on."

Tia raised her head as he mouthed, "Sorry." She rested her palm in the warm spot he left and closed her eyes. Out in the darkened room by the fireplace where coals throbbed purplish red, Enola raised her head to study him, Scout, snoozing by her side.

"Talk to me."

"You know Randy Weller's daughter, Michaela?"

That caught him by surprise.

"She was here at the Summit."

"Underage?"

"Lucas served her Coke. Someone else made it flammable."

Still the Summit's responsibility, though less realistic if the place was hopping. Lucas could mostly be counted on there.

"The ladies' was in use, so she went out back to void her stomach."

Anyone but Moser would say vomit.

"Her friends thought it hilarious, until she didn't come back in. They went looking, but she was nowhere to be found. They called home, thinking her parents came and picked her up, but the folks haven't seen or heard a word. They're here now, but no one seems to know anything."

"Michaela's not wild or foolish. I don't think she'd upset everyone for fun."

"Could have gotten a ride from someone else."

"Or she's wandered off and lost her bearings, maybe passed out somewhere in the storm. What's it doing over there?"

"Blowing."

True to its name, the Summit perched at the top of the street and backed onto open mountainside. Having spewed out there himself, back in the day, Jonah pictured it all with clarity. "Get someone calling all her friends. Don't let her parents go off and get themselves lost. I'll call the sheriff to organize a search."

"I hope it's for nothing."

They could always hope.

———

Trevor had to smile. Natalie had instinctively served to Sara's sweet spot, and Cody tugged her heartstrings to the point of tears, before sweetly dropping off to sleep. From a couple of comments, he guessed Sara still nursed some denial, but she'd get it eventually. As for Pictionary, he and Whit gave as good as they got and if there was little gloating as Natalie bundled Cody—

He and Whit locked eyes when their phones vibrated simultaneously.

Whit reached his first and read the text. "Search team. That's us. Staging: Summit Saloon."

Trevor frowned. "Not a good night to be lost."

"Not a good night to search," Whit added, rising.

Natalie and Sara stood up with them, concerned, but this was what they did.

He said, "Nattie, I'll run you home. It's on the way."

"Okay." She hurried to gather Cody.

Whit kissed his wife and went on ahead.

Climbing into his vehicle, Natalie heaved a sigh. "Thank you for not leaving me there."

He laughed. "You did great."

"You don't know how intimidating it is."

"No, I get it." He squeezed her hand, then focused on driving. The roads were mostly dry, but visibility terrible, gusts creating ground blizzards from the dusty snow.

When they reached her house, she said, "I can get Cody." She climbed out quickly and removed the child, calling, "Go ahead."

The minute they were inside, he took off. Always prepared with gear in the SUV, he still took longer than he liked to reach the Summit. Anyone out in this would be all but blinded.

"Teenage girl," Whit told him when he arrived.

Trevor's stomach sank.

Collars pulled up, the police chief and Sheriff Gilmore had their heads together over a map. Trevor scanned, but didn't see Tia among the SAR personnel. She was the best they had for trails, but this was shaping up differently. Jonah looked out at them, lights from the fire engine flashing over his face. "Our missing girl is sixteen, small build, brown hair, wearing a Redford High hooded sweatshirt, blue jeans. Her name's Michaela. Presumed intoxicated. Might be the first time. She may have lost her way, fallen, or passed out."

The sheriff took over. "Chief, you and your people search the streets and buildings through town. SAR, we'll form a grid search out from the parking lot up the slopes. Be careful. We've had one cougar attack, and, in spite of the snow, it's autumn, not winter. Beware of bears."

Any bear with half a brain would have booked, but some had less than half.

"Also Michaela was sick in the lot. Her stomach could revolt again."

Trevor turned to Whit. "At the scent of vomit, send up a flare."

"My vomit sensors are shot. Common occurrence at my house."

The sheriff said, "Keep your line as well as the terrain allows. All right, let's go."

They aimed the flashlights low to minimize glare off the blowing snow. Trevor blinked it from his eyes as they searched for places a girl might lie unconscious. There'd be no tracks.

He told Whit, "I can't believe she'd take to the woods in this. If she's staggering drunk, wouldn't she move downhill?"

"The stuff available now, she might be following UFOs."

The wind jammed the breath back down his throat. "It would take some hallucination to draw me out in this." He looked over his shoulder where the Summit's two parking-lot lights marked the upper edge of town.

Noreen Malmquist, the firefighter directly to his right on the grid search line, had been in the saloon when the girl vanished. He turned to her. "Did anyone notice a vehicle leaving the lot while Michaela was out?"

"The smokers on the porch said no."

The only access to the tiny back lot, on wheels, was past that porch. But the sheriff and chief had to consider foul play. Small, elite community or not, she was a teenage girl in a compromised condition.

At a blast of snow, Trevor pulled the face protector up over his mouth and nose. The higher they climbed, the colder and darker it got.

Beside him Noreen cried out, angling her flashlight about thirty feet up a stony promontory to the girl swaying on a ledge. His chest seized. The ledge was hardly wider than her feet. Even if she realized her danger, she couldn't seem to stop swaying. That would be the booze.

Trevor shot his light up the stone. No way she got there without equipment. Several searchers headed around, but that would take too long. He spoke into his radio. "Situation's precarious. Subject extremely unsteady. I'm climbing."

"Go ahead, MacDaniel. Do your stuff."

With time they'd come at it from the top and lower a rope, or in this case a team member. But she looked ready to pass out. He had rope, but he'd have to free climb to set it. With his headlamp lighting the way, he reached up.

Just today he'd done this on the climbing wall—without the storm. His fingers dug into the frigid rock, his feet found purchase. *Hold on,* he willed her. If he could reach the ledge and secure her, others could hoist her up. Wind choked. Snow flew in his eyes like talcum powder.

Someone spoke to her from below, urging her to hold still, help was coming. He stretched and pulled, three or four flashlights lighting the rock face from below, careful, he hoped, not to blind her. He propelled himself up to one frosty hold after another, balancing caution and haste. It would do her no good if he fell. Just a little more.

Before he could find the next grip, cries preceded the sickening sound of her fall. Clinging like a lizard, he pressed his face to the stone, sick inside. It was a survivable distance. They might have softened her landing, but he couldn't bring himself to look.

As searchers rushed to the fallen girl, he moved stiffly down the rock. In five more minutes, he'd have had her. His feet hit the ground. Throat tight, he circled the promontory.

Noreen hollered, "Get a stretcher up here!"

———

Outside the Pastimes Book and Media Center, Jonah released the radio button and prayed. With the gusting wind and lousy visibility, they couldn't bring the chopper in to transport her to the hospital. Firefighters were on the mountain with a stretcher, and the ambulance stood by in the Summit parking lot. It would have to be enough.

He'd spoken to Michaela in assemblies, worked beside her in fundraising drives. She was not one he'd have ever picked for this. Officer Donnelly came up beside him, silent and stoic. She'd lost her husband in jail last fall and given birth to their second child a few months later. She'd been tempered by that, a solid officer, but none of them took this stuff easily.

He said, "Let's get up to the Summit. I want to talk to Michaela's parents."

Moser swung over in one of the cruisers, and he and Sue climbed in. It felt like an avalanche had landed inside the car, and they were all trying to decide which direction was up. Jonah reached the sheriff by phone and got the details. What was she doing up there?

He entered the saloon, where the parents paced. He knew Randy, a small, weathered man, but not the wife. "Randy, Mrs. Weller. Michaela's had a fall on the mountain. I don't know how serious her injuries are, but we're working to get her down right now."

They were rightfully stunned. "Who's she with? Why was she up there?"

"I don't know. Did she have a boyfriend or someone she might sneak out to see?"

They looked at each other, confused. Her mother said, "She's dated a little casually. She's only sixteen."

At sixteen he'd been anything but casual. "A friend you don't like? Someone older?"

"She's friends with good kids. She doesn't have secrets."

Everyone had secrets. But Michaela's were probably not dark and dangerous. "Was she acting strange, depressed…"

Randy's face twisted. "You think she jumped?"

"We know she didn't. Either she lost consciousness or her balance. The fall was accidental, but that doesn't explain why she was on a rock ledge in this weather."

The wife began to cry. Randy bent his head to hers. "She's going to be okay." His eyes pleaded.

Jonah gave what assurance he could. "We're doing everything we can."

He went out the back, reaching the staging area as Trevor MacDaniel came off the mountain. The man looked shell-shocked. In things like this, getting close hurt the same as not even.

The back door pushed open and Jazmyn Dufoe charged out. "Trevor!"

Dread drained the man's face. There wasn't anything Jonah could do for Michaela, but he could save the one who'd tried to help from this particular assault. "Go home," Jonah told him and turned to face the reporter.

Seeing her main target escape, Jazmyn demanded, "Chief Westfall, can I have a minute?"

He planted himself. "I have about one."

———

At first she thought it must be Cody. But peeking in, she heard nothing but his slightly nasal breathing and the whisper-soft humidifier issuing a fine, thin fog. Back out in the hall, she heard it again, the knocking. Groggily, she went to the door. "Yes?"

Trevor said, "I know it's late."

It was almost three. She opened the door. His skin was wind chapped, his lips tinged blue. His gloved hands shook.

He looked at them. "Adrenaline."

"Come here." She pulled him inside, the night chill entering with him, or maybe it was anguish. She could only glance and look away, but their search must not have gone well. "What happened?"

He pressed the back of his hand to his nose, sniffing from the inclement weather. "A teenage girl got lost and fell."

"From what?"

"A crag behind the Summit Saloon. I can't imagine how—" His face contorted. "It doesn't make sense."

She knew what was going on in his head. *It's the ones that if we'd found them sooner...*

He sighed. "I got you up."

"Well, yes, but I slept the other half of the night."

He smiled grimly as she pulled him toward the couch. "You don't need this."

She tugged his coat sleeve, and he shrugged out of his parka, shed the gloves and hat as well.

"How badly is she hurt?"

"Bad."

"I'm so sorry." She rubbed his arm.

"I almost reached her. If she'd held on five more minutes..." He dropped to the couch and lowered his face to his hands.

She sank in beside him. He smelled of wet pine. Fragments of needles stuck in his hair.

"I don't know what I'm doing here."

She rested her hand on his back, touched and encouraged to finally give him comfort. "I'm glad you are."

"I keep thinking I could have climbed faster, gone a different way, let her know I was coming. Others were talking, but why didn't I holler out to her so she knew?"

He wasn't looking for an answer. She closed her hand around the back of his neck and rubbed the ropy tendons.

"If I could see the rock like you do..."

"Mine was a single boulder on a sunny afternoon. You were out there in the dark, in the storm."

"I know. But that doesn't stop it."

She slid her fingers into his hair. "What does?"

"I don't know. Answers maybe."

Or prayers. This wounded guardian deserved a dose of mercy. As if feeling her lifting him up, he turned his face, and she took it in. Regret. Failure. Shock and confusion. His weathered cheekbones, his bristled jaw, his raw and haunted eyes.

"Aw, Nattie."

"No. Please. I want to see it."

"I didn't mean to show you."

She touched her fingers to his face. "There's a plastic-wrapped block of clay in the garage. Can you bring it to the kitchen, with the board it's on?"

He went and got the clay. Standing at the counter, she worked until the gray hues of dawn infused the room. Eyes gritty with fatigue, hands cramping, she let go, and Trevor was there, before and behind her.

He gripped her shoulders and kissed the side of her neck. She leaned back, and he held her for long, silent moments, his prickly jaw pressed into her cheek.

———

With a borrowed cup filled with coffee, Trevor left Natalie's, but not for home. Something didn't sit right. Heading back to the Summit, he replayed the night before. A young girl gets sick and staggers off, loses her way, and gets disoriented. Did she want a high place to see where she was?

Not if she was plastered. That would take work to get up there, and she'd stay at the top, not climb down to the ledge. It didn't make sense.

He parked and surveyed the wind-swept lot, strewn with aspen leaves and detritus, but almost free of snow. He stared up the direction they'd gone and made out the tip of the promontory. For all he knew, it was a place kids hung out.

Clearing his mind, he came at it from a different angle. This was a teenager. What would make her climb the mountain instead of going back inside, or, if the door had locked, working around to the front where people might help her?

Embarrassment? She might be horrified at having puked. Maybe she had it in her hair or on her clothes. Maybe she wanted snow or pine needles to wipe it clean. With the ground blizzards, going even a little way could have disoriented her. He tried to make that fit and failed. Striding out, he searched for answers. Nothing along the way illuminated.

The promontory was closer than it seemed in the dark, but no less daunting. Last night, he climbed the face, but now he moved up the slope through the trees around the rocky protrusion. It was blown dry of snow at the top. He looked down, something sour in his mouth. Had she meant to jump? Was the booze to fortify her suicide?

He tied a rope to a trunk and lowered himself. Certainty made a fist in his stomach as he measured the distance by his own reach to the crest of the promontory. Now he knew what had bothered him last night.

He pulled back up to the top and went down the other way. It was less steep and drier on the windward side. He drove to the police station and was directed to a small office by the fluffy woman whose name tag read RUTH MASON.

Trevor knocked on the chief's open door. "Can I talk to you?"

Pushing away from the desk, Jonah said, "It's a little cramped, but…" He motioned to a folding chair.

Trevor remained standing. "I think there's something you need to consider about Michaela's accident."

"I'm listening."

"I was just up there, and there's no way she got onto that ledge herself."

Jonah leaned forward. "What do you mean?"

"You know she couldn't climb the face. But the distance from the top is enough that dropping down would have carried her over, even sober."

Jonah frowned. "If she didn't climb up or drop down…"

"Someone lowered her."

He slow-blinked. "Someone helped her down and left her there?"

"I don't know if 'help' is the word. I just know she didn't do it herself." An examination of the scene would prove it.

The chief rubbed his jaw, holding his thoughts in the dark eyes.

"I left my rope on the pinnacle, if you want to check this out."

"I will." He stood up. "How are you doing?"

He gave a half shrug.

"You almost reached her."

"You know how it is with almost."

"I do." He tapped his fingers on the back of his chair. "You know, Tia's a trauma counselor. She debriefs my officers…"

"I talked to someone last night." Well, not talked as much as watched her pull the pain out of him into the clay. "Any word on Michaela?"

"Concussion. Broken bones. Trevor, it could have been worse."

"It could have not happened."

Jonah nodded once. "We'll get to the bottom of it."

"Okay." Leaving the station, he nearly walked into Jaz and stopped as if hitting a force field.

"Trevor."

"I can't tell you anything you haven't heard already."

"You were there. You almost reached her."

He was starting to hate that word.

She blocked his sideways maneuver. "What were you doing at the station? Giving a statement?"

"I was checking on Michaela's condition."

She narrowed her eyes. "There's something else. You know something."

He studied her, then released a hard breath. "I don't know anything, Jaz. I wish I did."

———

From the top of the promontory, Jonah eyed the situation as Trevor had described it.

Moser shifted beside him. "We're up here why?"

"Checking it out." Ignoring the rope, he swung over the edge.

"Careful." Moser said.

His feet touched only when he released his hold and slid, catching himself with the dangling rope. Trevor was right that Michaela's momentum would have carried her over. How hard would it be for someone to lower her? Not difficult with her slight build. Looking down to the place she fell, he wished it could have been an accident. The thought of someone leaving her burned him up.

He started up the rope, Moser reaching down and pulling him over. "We have a crime scene, Moser. Gather a team and search the woods both sides of this promontory."

"For what?"

"Evidence of another person."

"You think someone took her, dragged her up here, and didn't finish it?"

"Rescuing Michaela took all our attention and resources. If he left her dead, we'd have searched for him." A daunting thought, looking at the forested slopes. "Interview everyone at the Summit last night. Someone might have seen her go out and taken advantage."

"That means people we know, people she knew."

Jonah said, "Yeah, and there may have been someone we don't know. Have Lucas generate a list of people he served, even if it's only a description."

"Did they get"—Moser cleared his throat—"a rape kit?"

It sickened him to say, "That's my next call."

He dropped Moser off and headed home. Tia met him at the door, her face tight. Sliding an arm around her shoulders, he went in. "I can't fight with you right now."

"Fight. Why would I fight?"

"Never mind."

"Jonah." She gripped his hand. "Is it Michaela?"

"I don't think her fall was an accident."

"You think she meant to jump?"

He shook his head.

She paled. "Someone pushed her?"

"No one pushed her." He explained. Nothing about last night had fit what he knew about Michaela. Of all the scenarios, abduction made the most sense. And though people thought Redford a safe and wholesome place to raise kids, he knew better. His own father had taught him.

Looking past her at Sarge, he said, "I'm going to be pulling some long hours. I need you to be vigilant." To Tia he added, "You and Sarge are tucked away up here, and if there's someone around with evil intentions…"

"We have the dogs."

Though she called them dogs, they were as much coyote. They'd be alert to trouble. "Still have your handgun, Sarge?" The man was so badly bent, no one would guess him a threat. They'd be wrong. He may have been a cook in the corps, but he wouldn't hesitate to shoot.

The old man nodded. "I'll keep your bride safe."

Jonah threaded his fingers into Tia's crazy auburn hair. "You guys stay close. Call if you need something."

"We're under house arrest?" She crooked a brow.

He kissed her temple, breathing in whatever scent blend she'd used, and whispered, "Just don't leave Sarge if you can help it."

"We'll be fine." Tia's tone softened. "Don't do this alone."

"I'll use everything I have." Enola pressed her head into his hand and Scout pushed her aside to do the same. He rubbed both dogs. "Take care of each other."

"Take care of yourself. No bullets this time."

This was a wholly different situation than last fall, but he still had the strange sense of going into battle.

Man falls, deceiv'd
by the other first: Man therefore shall find grace,
the other none.

First blood! But not the champion's, unless the wound were to his pride. No fawning press, no victor's parade. Failed! Unhorsed. Disgraced. And yet, no mortal wound delivered. The gentle hand of fate, extending mercy to her own.

Succored at that breast, this woeful warrior drank sparingly the loser's draft. Excused and commended—well met, valiant lord—this field of loss a passing sorrow. For who was she to him?

A careless blow, precipitous. Fear-driven haste. Error.

For the tool, he mourned, broken and dismayed. The helpless paying the mighty one's debt. For her, he wept, and for himself—another censure to his score. But he, no hope of mercy having, must complete the mandate given.

Nineteen

Exhausted, yet disturbed by something, Trevor rolled to his back and cracked open his eyelids. "Jaz?"

"I need to talk to you."

He blinked. "You are not in my bedroom."

"It's not like anything's going to happen. Besides, it's after twelve."

And he'd been awake all night. "Out." He rubbed his face. "I'll get dressed and join you." More than irritated, he threw on jeans and T-shirt and went into his kitchen where she was rummaging in his cabinets. "Want something?" He opened the fridge and drank from a carton of orange juice.

"I'd just love that OJ, now that you slobbered the carton." She sounded snotty, but her eyes were bright. She was enjoying this—of course.

Hunger hit with the double punch of sleep deprivation and physical exertion. "Have you had lunch?"

"No."

"I'll make sandwiches."

"What kind?"

"Tuna salad on ciabatta. It's your only choice; take it or leave it."

"That actually sounds good."

He ran a knife through Piper's homemade ciabatta rolls and peeled them open, then combined white albacore tuna, boiled eggs, some mayonnaise, chopped onion, and cilantro. "You want greens?"

"Sure."

He laid fresh field greens over the tuna, closed the rolls, and handed over her plate.

"Thanks." She looked slightly askance.

"You're welcome."

She took a bite. "That's good."

"I've perfected the recipe."

She chewed and swallowed. "Why didn't you tell me someone pushed that girl off?"

He frowned. "Where'd you hear that?"

"I don't reveal sources."

"Your source is wonky. No one pushed her."

"Mmm. This is really good." She dabbed mayonnaise from the corner of her mouth. "So why were you talking to the chief?"

"I told you."

"But that's not true. You'd have talked to the hospital for news on Michaela."

"They can't tell me. All that HIPAA stuff."

"No. You know something."

"I know lots of things." He bit into his sandwich and made the most of the mouthful.

"Why do you always make me pry it out?"

"Jaz, if I knew something you should run with, I'd tell you. Talk to Chief Westfall."

"Chief Westfall's a vault. It takes dynamite to get anything out of him."

He pulled a glass from the cabinet, ran it under the faucet, and drank. "Want some water?"

"You told him something. I know you, Trevor. You went out there and figured it out."

Sometimes she was scary. He ate the last of his sandwich and washed it down with water, then tucked the glass and plate into the dishwasher.

"Where were you last night?"

He looked over his shoulder. "On the mountain."

"After. I waited for you here."

"You know, Jaz, I'd like my key back."

She finished her sandwich and licked her finger. "That's not the point."

"It's my point. You have no boundaries." He held out his hand.

Glaring, she took it out and slapped it in his hand, but didn't let go.

Fine. She wanted to know? "I was with Natalie."

Her eyes widened. "It takes an idol?"

He leaned his head. "The statue is for Cody."

"Whatever." She released the key card. "I want to know if we have something to worry about in Redford."

"Yes, Jaz. I think we do."

Her face lit. "Tell me what you know."

He did. "But you can't say anything until the chief allows it."

"Who else knows?"

"Just you and the police."

Giddy, she clasped her hands. "I hate you less today."

"Good. Did you find anything on that photo?"

She slumped. "I'm still looking."

"What about a baby in a tree?"

Her jaw fell slack.

From the office drawer, he took the rest of the photos. She tucked her chin to her shoulder, an instinctive recoil that proved she was human.

"Sorry."

"Have you shown the chief?"

"I meant to." Then Cody had come and Natalie needed him. "Now his hands are full with Michaela."

"He has other officers."

"Can you really see them doing something with this? I've sent the photos to the FBI. They know about this incident." He pointed to the car accident. "If you can learn anything on the others…"

"You mean whether they lived?"

That, above and beyond anything else.

She frowned. "Why are *you* getting the pictures?"

"The six-million-dollar question."

Pacing, Jaz tapped her chin. "The editor thought your photo in my article suggested a dark side. It's why he chose it."

"To match your eloquent tone."

"But this guy made you an angel."

"You think angels have no dark side? All that smiting? Don't forget the fiery sword."

She brightened. "Maybe he saw you on TV."

"And what?"

"I have no idea." She handed back the photos. "Make me copies. I can work on this if Chief Westfall won't include me in Michaela."

"Okay, Jaz." Seeing the spark that had intrigued him, he allowed a faint smile. He hated her a little less today too.

———

Natalie watched Cody running the Matchbox car over the table and the objects she'd arranged to make roads and ramps. It was hard for him to play cars on the floor without another arm to brace as he moved it along. Kneeling at the table, he kept his balance pretty well, but she ached thinking of all the adjustments he'd have to make.

At least the robot arm would lend balance and support. She supposed it would grip. Maybe it would be the marvel they claimed. But right now, her little nephew was dealing with impairment.

Moving toward the dining room, Natalie called her brother, hoping for good news, but he sounded ragged.

"I'm in a walking cast and the physical therapy's going great, but I can't say that much for Paige. She's separated emotionally from Cody and me."

"What about the special clinic? Those highly qualified doctors?"

"I don't know, Nat. The doctor calls it dissociation, but talking to her, she sounds like she's on a spa getaway. I guess in a way she is."

She tried not to say anything Cody might catch.

"I don't know what I'd do if you weren't loving my little boy for me. Until I'm freed up from rehab, I'd need to hire care."

"I'll do everything I can, Aaron."

"I know. Should I... Does he want to talk to me?"

"Of course he does." She looked over her shoulder.

"Does it help?"

She hesitated. "It's hard to tell. I think it makes the separation immediate. He cried for more than an hour last time."

"Then I won't." His voice choked. "But hug him for me."

"Every day."

"And, Nattie? Pray."

Already, Cody had helped her pray for Michaela. Now she asked him to pray for his mommy. Pretending he didn't think about her would be silly, but he didn't seem to miss her as he missed Aaron. At least this gave him some part to play. A plea to God for healing—especially from this precious child—had to be powerful stuff.

She'd keep him safe and happy even if they had to stay inside her little house—except he was too rambunctious. He wanted adventure. He wanted the rough and tumble fun Trevor provided. He wanted Trevor.

She sighed when he asked for the fourteenth time to go "clima wall." Trevor wouldn't be there, but others could harness and help him. She sighed. "Okay, we'll go."

The day had warmed considerably, the fall splendor bringing people out en masse. Traffic clogged the highway, but her mind felt clear. No nightmares last night, no recurring face. She'd been there for Trevor, not the other way around. It felt so good.

She unstrapped Cody and followed him into High Country Outfitters. Whit had a preteen girl on the climbing wall. She lifted Cody to watch.

"I wanna climb."

"Have to wait your turn, honey."

"Clima big wall."

"You'll climb the kiddie wall."

He squeezed her neck, pressing his lips to her cheek. "Climb now."

She laughed. "Oh, are you going to have your way. Come see something." She walked him over to an oversize poster of Trevor at an impossible angle on an impossible ski run. Fleur was right about his form. Maybe he'd let Cody and her watch the recordings of his races.

"I wanna ski," Cody said.

She laughed. "There's no snow left."

"Trevor will have him on a wakeboard in the river by next summer." Whit came up beside her.

"No doubt." Except she wouldn't have Cody that long. She gave him a squeeze. "He wants to climb the kiddie wall."

"We can do that." Whit got him harnessed, let him pat his hand in the chalk, then got him started with a grip on his back and a taut rope.

When Cody was halfway up the wall, Sara came in with Braden curled against her chest—two perfect little knees drawn up, two perfect little arms. Tearing up a little, Natalie said, "Cody thinks he's a monkey."

"Of course he does. With Whit and Trevor, Braden will be scaling this freestyle before he can walk."

Trevor entered the store, looking better than she'd expected. He squeezed Sara's shoulder and kissed Braden. Then he came to her and kissed her softly on the mouth, his hand warming the small of her back. "Sorry I kept you up last night."

"I'm fine."

"See me, Trevor," called Cody, the subtle one.

"I see you, sport. Show us how it's done." His hand stayed on her back.

"I thought you'd get some rest."

"Jaz spoiled that."

"Jaz?"

They all turned.

"Someone told her Michaela was pushed."

Working the rope, Whit frowned. "That woman's a menace."

Trevor shrugged. "She's doing her best."

Cody shouted, "I clima wall!" Sensing their shifted attention, his volume had increased each time he spoke.

"You're the champ," Trevor called. "Lean back and rappel."

From the corner of her eye, she saw Sara watching—not Cody, but her. And Trevor.

As Whit lowered her nephew to the floor, Trevor unharnessed and lifted Cody into his arms. "Gimme five." He and Cody slapped. Again tears burned. Her heart swelled. One hand to share a victory was still a blessing.

As Cody squirmed loose and took off down the aisles of camping gear, Trevor said, "I need to talk to you."

Sounded serious. She called, "Cody, slow down."

He kept running, jarring a stack of packaged duffel bags. They slipped down and spread across the floor. Cody rounded the corner and ran right into them. She watched him fall as though in slow motion, his one hand hitting the floor, then his opposite shoulder, then his face. She cried out.

"It's all right, Nattie. He's all right."

He wasn't all right. His mouth was bleeding. His nose was bleeding. She dropped to her knees and pulled him into her chest, the sight of his pain and injury imprinting as his crying pierced her.

Trevor crouched beside them. "Let me see."

Cody raised his head, still wailing.

"Yeah, pretty good face plant. That's the unfortunate result of not listening."

Cody buried his face, but the crying diminished as he kept peeking at Trevor.

Sara came up from behind with a damp cloth. "Dab it with this."

Natalie applied the cloth. There wasn't as much blood as she'd thought. Why had it looked like so much?

Sara said, "Check his teeth."

Cody shuddered with spent sobs.

"Let's see your injuries." Trevor peered closer. "Well, I've seen worse." He winked. "He'll be fine."

She cradled him. "Okay, honey?"

Cody whimpered, but it was for effect. He pulled free.

"All right, but no running in here."

"'Kay." He sniffed.

She wiped the floor and held up the bloody cloth. "I should wash this out."

"I'll do it." Sara squeezed Trevor's shoulder. "Taking care of you and Whit, I'm so prepared for calamity, it's not funny." There seemed a thin desperation in the words, Sara reestablishing the status quo.

Natalie said, "Sorry about that," as Trevor restacked the duffel bags.

"No harm, no foul."

Cody reached for a hydration pack hanging in the end cap.

"I need to get him out of here."

"He's just curious. I showed him how those worked the last time." Trevor crouched. "Listen up, Cody."

Cody turned.

"You pay attention to Aunt Nattie. She knows what's what."

Cody nodded with mirrored sobriety.

Trevor rose. "I'll walk you out."

In the lot, she sighed. "It happened so fast."

"One of thousands of falls he's going to have."

"But he can't catch himself."

"This was a step in realizing that." He lifted Cody to the large hewn log with slots for bicycles. "Ride this bronc for a minute, okay?"

Cody grinned. "Broncosaurus."

Trevor turned her away. "Before you sculpt Cody's crash—"

She groaned.

"I need to tell you something."

"What?"

"The girl that fell last night didn't get on that ledge by herself. She was put there."

She had to glance up. He was dead serious. "Why?"

"I don't know. But you need to be careful."

"Me? Why—"

He caught her face between his hands. "Just pay attention to anything unusual. And if you remember what you saw, call me."

It hit her like a stone. "You think I saw the person who attacked Michaela."

"You don't just see a face. You see everything inside it."

Her breath made a slow escape. Had she seen a sadistic predator?

———

A flash caught his eye as Natalie and Cody went inside. He turned, but couldn't tell what the sun had glanced off.

Inside the store, Sara was waiting, Braden against her chest like a breastplate. She cornered him between the fingerboards and chalk bags. "You kissed her."

"I did."

Her brow puckered. "You said it was a rescue."

"You said it."

She clasped his arm. "Trevor, she's falling in love with you."

He watched reality dawn, wishing things could just be easy. In a perfect world, dads didn't walk out, five-year-olds didn't die, and friends could be happy for friends. In this world, young girls fell when help was yards away and love could hurt as much as hate.

"Why Natalie?"

"Why not?"

"She's—you're—you don't even know her."

"Like I know you? You're right. I didn't grow up with her."

She cupped Braden's head for solidarity. "But you were with her last night. You kept her up."

"In her kitchen. While she worked."

"On what?"

"Sculpting, Sara. She's a sculptor."

"In the middle of the night?"

"Is that different from Monopoly?" Only in the players, he realized. "Why are you being judgmental? That's not the person I know."

Hurt watered her eyes. "And I don't even know you." She took her baby to the office, all but slamming the door.

He turned to Whit with cocked jaw. "I thought you guys were taking time together."

"What am I supposed to tell her? You can't see Trevor anymore?"

"I haven't done anything different or been anything but myself."

"Exactly." His eyes darkened.

"Look, I'm sorry. She's obviously struggling with Natalie."

"It wouldn't matter who it is."

Trevor gripped the back of his neck. This wouldn't get them any-where. He pushed out through both doors simultaneously. The daylight had a brittle quality as if it might shatter and reveal storms and darkness behind the peaceful calm.

His friendship with Whit and Sara was the brightness in his life, his warmth, his safety. They could be close because they were close before it all broke apart. Whit sat with him the day his dad left, when his boyhood bones turned to steel. Sara wept with him over Ellis. These were not light-weight friends.

He drove back to the city building.

Jonah turned from the computer. "Think of something else?"

"I'm not sure, but there might be an eyewitness."

Jonah straightened. "Who saw Michaela?"

He shook his head. "Earlier that day, Natalie Reeve saw someone who scared her pretty badly."

"Can she give a description?"

Hands spread, Trevor cocked his head. "Normally, no problem." He explained as noninvasively of Natalie's privacy as he could.

"And you think she saw, but doesn't remember."

"I think fear's blocking what she saw. Could Tia talk her through it?"

Jonah leaned back in the chair. "She works with a licensed counselor, but..." He tapped his lips with his pointer fingers. "I'll talk to her. It could be the break we need."

———

Fleur made her way down the sidewalk from the bakery toward the corner, tap-tapping with her stick. While she knew the way, there was always the chance of impediments, dogs leashed to poles, debris, sale tables moved outside of stores. People greeted her as she went, even strangers. That's what kind of town Redford was. Until last night.

No one understood why one of their own teens would go off like that. Did she mean to hurt herself? There'd been no suicide in Redford since the former chief of police, Jonah's father. Fleur shuddered. What a dark time that had been. But if anyone could figure out—

"Fleur."

She paused, turned her head a little to the side. "Officer Newly?"

"Wait there. Let me park the cruiser."

She moved to the edge of the sidewalk and leaned against a brick storefront. It had absorbed the sunlight and radiated heat to her back. After a short while, Officer Newly approached.

"Sorry to hold you up."

"I'm in no hurry. The sun is out. The wind has stopped. No snow to shovel."

"That's all true. But I need you to know something," he said. "It's sensitive to the investigation—last night's incident? I'm guessing you heard."

"You mean Michaela's accident?"

"Yeah." He leaned closer. "Thing is, we don't think it was an accident. There's reason to believe someone took her from the parking lot and left her on that ledge."

"An abduction?"

"It's looking that way. I'm telling you because, well, she was vulnerable and you're…"

"A blind woman."

"You're amazingly capable and self-sufficient. But if there's a predator…"

Fear engulfed her.

"Until we can talk to Michaela and find out for sure, I don't know how safe it is for you to walk alone. I hope that's not insensitive."

"Of course not." The fear trickled into her limbs, dissolving their strength. "I appreciate your concern."

"Can I give you a ride?" He sounded so earnest.

"As long as it's not in the backseat with handcuffs and Miranda rights."

"No ma'am." He laughed and took her elbow. "This way."

Sun! to tell thee how I hate thy beams,
That bring to my remembrance from what state
I fell, how glorious once above thy sphere;
Till pride and worse ambition threw me down.

Staring at the monument, he had felt the ache, that longing, which so pitiably denied, he would reject, lest it lead once more to misery. Gazing, stricken, at his foe immortalized, he'd seen the depths to which he'd sunk, all hint of glory shriveled, all transcendence turned to dust. What remained in desolation? To strike and destroy that which he would love and cherish, which he would worship had he the capacity.

Strike, tear down, destroy. It must be done, the idol cast down. The noble visage shattered, fulsome form wrecked and broken. Seraphic guardian unmade.

In that commission would come relief, if only for a breath. He had no expectation of peace. He knew well the Final Act, the coup de grâce, but must before that make his message known.

No longer daunted, but renewed in purpose, he stepped into the sunny world.

Twenty

Natalie couldn't remember, didn't want to remember. But then she thought of the girl Trevor and the others had gone out in the storm hoping to help and save, while someone else intended such great harm. Whatever she could do mattered, no matter how horrifying.

The knot in her stomach loosened when she saw the grassy meadow enclosed by fir and spruce with a creek along one edge and a cozy cabin she could sink into like a deep warm comforter.

Bars of light broke through the tree branches, liquid gold on the foliage below. Sumac flamed. Sky blue spruce dangled long papery cones like honeycombs. Patches of snow clung to the dark recesses under the trees, but sunlight warmed the pungent grasses. Great mountain swells rose up all around.

"Wow."

"Pretty nice," Trevor agreed.

Not at all on par with the new mansions, but so much richer in its way.

Tia admitted them, greeting Trevor, then said, "Thank you for coming to the cabin, Natalie. Jonah's worried about leaving Sarge alone." Tia had exotic beauty without the conceit that often accompanied it.

"It was worth it to see this setting."

She ushered them in and introduced a woman standing in the kitchen. "This is Carolyn. She's overseeing my internship. We'll be working together, if that's all right."

Natalie glanced over briefly with a smile, then let her gaze roam. The last thing she needed was new faces. "Trevor thinks what I saw might help. I'm not even sure it was real."

"Do you see things that aren't?" Carolyn's tone was calm, nonjudgmental.

"I never have. My visual memory is precise and acute, but it's not mystical. I need real input to process."

"Why do you think this might not have been real?"

"Because it's gone. There's no eidetic image. Every time I tried to model it...nothing."

Tia poured and offered her a cup of tea.

"Thank you."

Carolyn went on gently probing. "So what do you think it was?"

"I hope a hallucination."

"Any medication that might cause hallucinations?"

"No." She sipped her tea. "I don't take anything."

"Why don't you want it to be real?"

She stared into her cup. "He..." She swallowed a sudden hard pain.

Trevor said, "When it happened, you said you felt destroyed."

"I did?" She took a drink, not wanting to feel it again.

"They've been real emotions you saw—mine, Sara's, Paige's, and Aaron's. The people at the opening."

"I know."

Tia said, "Any reason to think this is different?"

"I didn't hold it." They'd come full circle.

"Let's sit down." Carolyn motioned.

They moved into the main room by the fireplace.

"Hypnosis can help witnesses recall details and events. Like every tool, it's imperfect, but in this case, worth a try?"

Natalie shrugged. "I've never done it."

"With something like this especially, I'd like to start with prayer, unless anyone objects."

Her prayer was simple and brief, but Natalie felt the peace and solemnity.

"Tia, why don't you begin with a relaxation exercise? Would you prefer we did this alone, Natalie?"

"Trevor can stay." She wanted him to. Sinking into Tia's voice, she felt herself relax. As awful as it might be, she wanted to help.

In a rich tone, Tia said, "Bring yourself to that morning, Natalie. What did you feel?"

"Excited for Fleur." She explained Carter Granby's interview.

"And then what did you do?"

She saw herself walking toward the windows where the sunlight shone on Trevor's statue, how he seemed to glow like the archangel she'd imagined. In the glare of the window, she saw someone else staring at the statue. Everything went black. She gripped the arms of the chair. "Trevor?"

Groping for his hand, she sat up.

Tia tipped her head. "What happened?"

"It all went black."

"Are you all right?"

Natalie shook her head. "I've never had a block."

"Well," Carolyn said, "let's try something else. I'll name something, and you just say what comes to mind."

She nodded.

"You might still want to close your eyes."

She did.

"A window."

Instantly she was back at the front of the gallery. Her throat tightened. "A spiral."

"One of your sculptures?" Tia asked softly.

"No." Tears burned up and slid from the corners of her eyes. "It's red. Painful."

"How does painful look?'

She opened her eyes. "It reminds me of something, but I can't place it."

"Something you've seen somewhere else?"

Her head throbbed.

The door opened and Chief Westfall came in. He looked like a scrappy Hugh Jackman, and since she'd only interacted with him a few times, his image imprinted as he crouched down in front of her. "Hey, Natalie. How's it going?"

She shrugged. "Not good."

Tia said, "Natalie's doing great. It's just a process."

"What do we have?"

"Something about a red spiral. It had a painful connotation."

He fixed his stunning eyes back on her. "Could it be a tattoo?"

She frowned. "Maybe."

"Anything you can give us helps."

Like Trevor, this man carried the weight of others, yet the warmth in his eyes encouraged her.

"I'll try again. I just can't promise results."

"Whatever you can do." He smiled.

Another imprint.

———

Looking on, Trevor experienced something he'd never felt before—jealousy that the chief's features were now fixed in her mind. It bugged him to think of her hands modeling Jonah Westfall's face. As Natalie sat back in the recliner and closed her eyes, Trevor covered her hand with his, comfort and appropriation. Had he lost his mind?

The man was married, having a kid. His wife was in the room. Across their little group, he caught Carolyn watching, and shifted focus. This was about what Natalie saw, what might catch a predator. This was about Michaela.

"Where were you when you saw him?" Jonah's voice was low.

"At the gallery. He was outside the window, looking at Trevor's statue, and the look on his face—"

A collective gasp. She was remembering.

"Go on," Jonah urged.

"It was like worship. Only...it hurt. His face—" She bolted up, shaking.

Jonah locked her in a stare. "What about his face?"

"Scarred. An angry, raised coil over half his face like an old-fashioned stove burner." She ground the heels of her hands into her eyes. "And the other side had long, straight cuts."

"Fresh cuts? Scratches?"

"No. Old, deep scars." Her voice sounded raw.

Trevor squeezed her hand. "Can you model it?"

"I'll try." She was blind to anything else, he knew.

"I'll take her to the studio. But, Chief, if she saw him, he probably saw her."

Jonah rose. "I don't have the manpower to guard her while we solve this." He cursed the city council.

"I'll do it."

"What about Cody?" Natalie gripped his wrist. "If I'm a target, he's in danger."

That and something else she'd said sent dread straight through him. "Chief, there's more to this. Can you meet us at the gallery?"

"I'll follow you over." He paused. "Tia, Carolyn, thank you."

"As if we had anything to do with it." Tia smiled crookedly. He started to speak, but she raised her hands. "You are what you are, Jonah."

———

Natalie's stomach clenched like a fist, her whole body clammy as Trevor drove to the studio. Forming the image in clay would make it real. Holding that face in her palms could hurt more than anything she'd done. But holding it in her head was worse.

Trevor's hand closed over her knee, warm and heavy. "Almost there."

She nodded. For her sake and Cody's, for Michaela and any others, she had to do this. She'd give Chief Westfall what she could—if she could.

"Nattie?" Trevor pulled open the car door.

"Thanks."

He used her key to let them in. "Alarm code?"

She told him.

She groped her way to the table and found the clay she'd beaten the day before. Damp. Cold. Grainy. She began to gather the edges in, pulling the clay toward her and into the center in a mound. On the table, her phone rang.

"That's Piper," she said. "Can you press Speaker?"

He did.

"Hi, Piper. Is Cody okay?"

Piper said, "Yes, but, Natalie, someone broke into the bakery."

"Oh, I'm so sorry." Her head throbbed.

"The police called. I have to go over there."

But that would leave Cody with Fleur. She turned. "I've got this, Trevor. Go get Cody."

He shook his head. "I'm not leaving you. We'll go together."

"No, please. I have to do this. I can't keep it in any longer."

Clearly uncertain, he looked from the phone to her, then told Piper, "I'm on my way."

Relief came out in a rush. "Thank you."

"The chief will be here in a minute."

"I'll be fine. Get Cody. Keep him safe. I couldn't bear anything else hurting him."

"Lock the door behind me."

"It locks automatically." A moment later, she heard him test it from the other side. Grimly determined, she reached for the clay.

———

On his way to the gallery, Jonah picked up the call. "What is it, Newly?"

"B and E at the bakery, Chief. Description from the witness sounds a little hinky."

"Hinky how?"

"I think you ought to talk to him. It's Bob Betters."

Jonah scowled, picturing the auto sales manager, sleek blond hair, shiny face.

After what he pulled on their "date," Bob Betters had no business anywhere near Piper's bakery. He said, "I'm working something, but I'll swing by there first and hear him out."

Bob stood up from the bumper of the PT Cruiser and hung his thumbs in the pockets of his Dockers as Jonah approached.

"Bob. Officer Newly." He nodded to them.

Newly spoke first. "Back door's unlocked. Piper's pretty sure she didn't leave it that way, but can't say for sure she set the alarm. She's coming over to see what's missing. Meanwhile, Bob says he saw someone exit that was in no way Piper."

"One of her employees?"

"He looked like a bat."

Jonah turned. "Come again?"

"He was wearing a hood and something gray or black with...wings."

"Wings."

"They were wrapped around, but yeah, looked like wings."

"Some kind of cape?"

"Attached at the wrists maybe. You want my guess, it's that freak, Miles."

"He look six-seven?"

Bob scowled. "No, I guess not."

One thing he knew, Bob Betters lacked the imagination to make this up. "Any reason you were right around here?"

"You mean the main street, in the city where I live?"

"All right. Just tell Officer Newly what you were doing so it goes in the report."

"Sure, Chief." A sneer touched his nose and mouth.

Jonah turned to his officer. "Piper okay?"

"Yeah. She'd left for the day."

It was probably one more in their string of burglaries, but he didn't like that the thief broke in. "Find out how much cash she had on hand."

Newly nodded. "Will do."

———

Natalie pulled the head and neck out of the clay like a primordial birthing. Groaning, she shaped the features, eyes, forehead, nose, and mouth. Tears streamed as she prepared to make the scars.

A noise broke her concentration. The chief at the front door?

Swallowing hard, she wiped her hands and went through to the gallery. She was halfway to the locked front door when it opened. Carolyn had asked her if she saw things that weren't real. Now she believed she might. In the dusky shadows, a winged man pushed inside, hooded and cloaked. He headed for the statue of Trevor and Cody, the way he moved and the crowbar he'd used to pry open the door conveying his intention.

She changed course between two sculptures, rushing toward him as he raised the crowbar. "Stop. What are you doing?"

He jerked around. She froze. The scars. The desolation. The rage.

She spun back toward the studio, his trapped image filling her vision as he rushed up from behind. Running, she gripped one sculpture platform, then another, when something hard and sharp struck the top of her head. Pieces of her waterfall fell about her as she collapsed, the whimsical spiral being the last thing to fade.

———

Jonah jolted as a batlike figure thrust up from the gallery floor and fled toward the studio in the back. After wrenching the damaged door open, Jonah rushed in and dropped to Natalie, bleeding on the floor. He found a thready pulse and called for emergency assistance.

He searched for something to stanch the blood and found a cloth on the podium shelf. He grabbed it and held it to the laceration on her scalp, applying pressure until EMTs Scott and Noreen arrived, lights whirling, sirens crying. It was much too late, but Jonah pushed out through the studio and scoured the surrounding area for the assailant. From the left side of the lot, Trevor MacDaniel approached with a toddler in his arms and a stunned and darkening expression.

"What happened?" His voice was harsh.

"Someone struck her. He fled when I got here."

"Is she—"

"EMTs are with her."

The toddler clung to Trevor's neck with one arm, the other sleeve empty. The child he rescued from the mountain lion must be Natalie's nephew.

Trevor's jaw rippled. He clearly wanted to go inside, but the little guy was not letting go. "Chopper?"

"That's my guess."

Trevor cupped his hand around the nape of the boy's neck and told him, "Auntie Nattie's okay." He looked over and said, "We need to talk."

———

With everything in him, Trevor controlled his shock and fear. Seeing the fire truck as he pulled in had pumped him with adrenaline. He'd have charged inside, if not for Cody. He sucked a deep breath and carried the child into his office.

He'd been gone less than an hour. The chief was supposed to have been there. Instead, Natalie was alone, and she'd been hurt, critically, if the man's face told him anything. The stone in his stomach grew. He set Cody down.

"Auntie Nattie?"

"Some people are helping her, Cody. But guess what? Your dad's coming." He had called Aaron when he left the studio, and given the urgency, Aaron chartered a plane. That urgency had now multiplied. Trevor took out his phone and texted him. Aaron might not get it until he landed, but he wouldn't come in blind.

Whit came in through the back. "What's going on? Chopper's coming in."

Trevor crouched beside Cody. "Remember that helicopter that flew you to the hospital? It's going to give your auntie a ride." He looked over his shoulder at Whit's stunned face. "Can you wait with Cody while I—" But Cody dove at him. He wasn't settling for someone else. "Okay. All right. I'll stay."

He lifted him back into his arms. "Hey. No crying. Everything's okay." It was so far from okay the words almost strangled him. "It's going to be okay."

Whit eyed him. "Want me to go next door?"

"Yes. Absolutely." At least he'd know.

"Two attacks in two days, Trevor."

"It's worse than that. But we'll talk later."

When the door slammed behind Whit, Cody pressed into his chest. Holding the sweaty little boy brought back painful memories. Ellis had been a sober kind of baby. When he did laugh, it was better than coming in first.

Cody raised his face. "Daddy's coming?"

"Yep." He squeezed Cody's arm.

"Mommy's coming?"

"I don't know. Have to wait and see." He had a real tenderness for this kid, but not being there with Natalie felt like claws sunk deep.

Cody stuck his fingers into the weave of Trevor's sweater. "I'm hungry."

He had intended to take them out to dinner. That opened a fresh wound. "How about some gorp?"

Cody had laughed at the funny name the first time he heard it, but now he just stuck his little fingers into the sweater, sinking and tugging, wringing comfort from the texture.

Tucking Cody's head tighter into the crook of his shoulder, he went into the darkened store. He stroked the fine, soft curls. Until Aaron came, he was all Cody had.

He poured the trail mix onto the desk and settled Cody in the chair.

"That bad lion hurt Aunt Nattie?"

"No, Cody. That lion's gone." Another predator took its place.

"Will her arm fall off?"

"She's going to be fine."

Cody stayed focused on the trail mix when Whit came in, a good thing, as Whit's expression wasn't.

"She's in and out," he said under his breath. "They're concerned about pressure and bleeding in her brain."

A surge of guilt and sorrow. "I was gone forty-eight minutes. How could he get to her—"

"Who? What's going on?"

"Natalie saw someone. He was fixated on the statue."

"Wait, wait, wait." Whit frowned. "Are you saying it's your stalker?"

He frowned. "I don't know about stalker, but Natalie said she saw worship and agony."

Whit's face twisted. "Worship? That's psychopathic."

"Could be." His gut twisted. "It scared her so much, she blocked it, but I made her remember. I thought it was Michaela's abductor. I didn't realize…"

Whit's shoulders slumped. "They're connected?"

"I don't know." He cocked his head at the helicopter blades lifting. He could almost feel the air pumping, bearing her away.

"It's Charlie in there," Whit said. "You know he's good."

He did know. It was the best comfort he had right now.

"Aunt Nattie inna 'copter."

That little boy had good ears. He also had tears pooling. He raised his arm, and Trevor lifted him. Chest to chest, he rubbed the little back and murmured, "It's okay. You gotta trust me on this."

Trust? He felt utterly powerless. "Go on home, Whit. As soon as Aaron comes, I'm going to the hospital."

"Okay. Let me know what we can do."

It was up to Natalie now. She either had the fight or didn't. Whit squeezed his shoulder and went out, pausing as the chief stepped in.

Jonah said, "You wanted to tell me something?"

"Show you." He unlocked the drawer and handed Jonah the photos. "I've been getting these in the mail. No explanation."

The chief flipped through them, muscles rippling along his jaw.

"My brother's a cop. He put me in contact with the FBI. They have the originals." He handed over Natalie's reproduction of him as warrior angel. "Jazmyn Dufoe received this drawing through the magazine that ran her article. The editor thought she'd laugh her head off, but even she found it creepy."

Jonah frowned. "Why didn't you show me before?"

"I didn't put it together until Natalie described how the guy looked at the statue. I don't know if this has anything to do with Michaela, but this one's twisted enough to do what we suspect."

Jonah pocketed the pictures. "Come take a look at her model—what's left of it."

"Okay." Trevor bent and scooped Cody up. They went in through the gallery where one officer was securing the scene with tape, another taking pictures. Trevor shielded Cody from the hideous amount of blood soaked into the carpet, a crowbar lying a short distance away. "Did he use that—"

"Don't touch anything. We're processing the scene."

His stomach plunged. "How bad—" He caught himself. His need to know what that fiend had done didn't mean Cody should hear it.

Jonah pushed open the door to the studio with his shoulder. "Again, don't touch."

Seeing what she'd done after he left, he knew how painful it must have been. But especially awful were the deep, crusting claw marks ripped through the face and graying at the edges.

Jonah said, "Recognize him?"

Trevor kept Cody tight to his chest, his little fingers once again sinking and pulling, sinking and pulling. The head or hair wasn't finished, points at the top looking almost like horns. The ears were mostly undamaged, but the face... "She was just beginning. There's nowhere near the detail she would have given it."

Jonah pointed to the gouges. "Did she do this?"

"I can't imagine. It's...personal, ripping through the face like that."

Jonah said, "I'll try to get some state techs out here. In the meantime, keep your eyes open. He's dressed like a bat."

Trevor opened and shut his mouth. "How..."

"He broke into the bakery and a witness described him."

"This guy robbed Piper?"

"Looks that way. And I saw him flee from here."

Trevor shook his head. "What are we dealing with?"

Jonah stared at the gouged model. "I can't even guess."

They both turned abruptly when Aaron pushed through the studio door, ignoring the crime tape, his face pale with shock. "Was that Nattie's—"

"Daddy!" With a wail, Cody all but dove into his arms.

Trevor felt more than the child's weight lifted.

———

It was as though she'd been injected with nanobots, lights flashing, bright lines shooting across and dying away. There was pain and confusion, and then she was sitting on a rock in the middle of a burbling creek. It sparkled in sunlight. Gold flecks in the gravel dazzled her eyes.

There must be banks and land on either side, but everything beyond the rippling water blurred. She heard the gurgling flow, felt the warmth of the flat, chalky rock. She couldn't see, but sensed someone beside her. Everything moved around her, but she sat still and silent beside her still and silent companion.

It seemed a waiting place. A pause in the flow of time—of life? Her thoughts reached out and touched her companion's. As the peaceful water coursed around them, she sighed. His name was Death.

Above them all th' Archangel: but his face
Deep scars of thunder had intrenched, and care
Sat on his faded cheek.

H e shuddered. He cringed. There'd been so much blood. He would
have stopped the blood if he could. Stopped the pain of the one
who saw, forming him with wondrous, traitorous hands.

For what strange purpose had she made him as he might have been?
Seeing his likeness in the clay, unmarred, had crushed and wounded
him. His fingers gouged with violence, not ordered by his thoughts but
by some dark and primal urge to strike from sight even the impression of
wholesome life, for in truth he had no past not sullied by fear and misery.

And yet her gift convicted him, that she would see past waste and
ruin, to a finer soul than ever inhabited his wretched shell. For that
kindness, he mourned her suffering, dread upon him like ravening jaws,
ripping him with guilt.

No blame belonged, though he bore it still. That had always been
the way, and were it not, some other woe would take its place. He had
perfected agony.

Twenty-One

Approaching the paramedic team in the hospital hallway, Trevor must have shown everything he was feeling.

Charlie held his hands up and said, "You'll hear it anyway, so I'm telling you myself. We lost her in the chopper, got her back in two."

For two minutes she'd been dead.

"She came to for a while. That's the good news. A ten on the GCS."

He needed better news than her not being comatose. The shaking started inside his chest as he breathed the hospital smells of fear and antiseptic.

"We've been hanging around to hear, since it got sort of personal up there."

And as a favor to him, Trevor knew.

"At this point, they'll have to tell you anything else."

"They won't tell me anything unless her brother includes me in the family loop."

"Yeah, all that HIPAA stuff. Good luck, man. Hope she pulls through."

Pulls through. As though this were just a tight space, a crevice she would work her way out of with the right technical maneuver.

He pressed his palms to the sides of his head as the flight emergency team walked away. He sank into a chair in the surgical waiting room. He felt utterly helpless, as terrified and confused as the day his dad left. A cavity opened inside too primitive for words.

Aaron came in and sat down beside him. Staring at the wall, he said, "So, I know what you did for Cody and for me, but how are you involved with my sister—besides landlord and tenant?"

"Nattie's my—" ANR Inc. Aaron and Natalie Reeve? They'd been paying rent to her without a clue. The thought made him want to laugh and cry.

"You didn't know she owns the building?"

"We don't talk that much about our businesses. We just…" He swallowed. How could he make it believable? "She's special." A stupid word like *unique* that applied to everyone. "She's important to me." It hadn't taken this to realize it.

Aaron rubbed a hand over his face. "What happened?"

"She saw a guy."

"And modeled him?"

"Not at first. It paralyzed her process, formed a block."

Aaron looked confused.

"I know. Not at all normal—for her. Working with the police chief and a couple counselors, she retrieved it. While she was making the model, he broke in and attacked her."

Again, the wall took Aaron's focus, tricolor forest in a copper frame, a posted STAFF ONLY sign, an exit light over the doors. "She never hurt anyone." His voice broke.

There was no correlation between goodness and safety, or five-year-old boys wouldn't snap their necks looking for kittens.

Aaron cleared the emotion from his throat. "How bad is it? You saw her?"

"No. I had Cody. I didn't want to traumatize him again."

"Thank you for that." His face twisted. "I never should have asked her…"

"She loves him. She appreciated your trust." Even if she couldn't do it alone.

After what might have been a few notches or a few rotations on the clock, Aaron raised his head. "She had her heart broken in college. Some schlep who led her on, then couldn't take it."

Trevor nodded. "I don't intend to hurt her."

They sat in silence as it all sank deeper.

Again, Aaron broke it. "I've always thought she's one of those souls who wouldn't take long on earth to get perfect."

"I'm not letting go." He pictured her wrist clamped in his grip as she dangled off a cliff. An experienced climber could maintain that grip longer than they showed it in the movies, but eventually the muscles seized and cramped and failed.

Aaron teared up, then soldiered through the emotion. "Do you believe in God?"

He swallowed. "I'm ambivalent."

"Nattie would want us to pray."

He stared at his hands, reposing uselessly on his thighs. Either God was moved to action by their pleas, or events followed a course determined by cause and effect. He had begged God for Ellis, then watched his mother put her baby in the ground. It had rained, a kind of sleeting rain, while his small body hovered over the curtained hole in a casket too big, as though he'd grow into it.

The shaking took his chest again. Since there was nothing else his hands could do, he brought them together and lowered his head. Maybe he'd used the wrong words that time, or the anger and self-loathing had clogged the channel. This time he kept it simple.

When the diminutive neurosurgeon came in, both men towered over him, yet he held the power over the immediate direction of their lives.

"I'm Dr. Derozier." The nasal cast to his voice was probably a northeastern seaboard accent. "You're here for Ms. Reeve?"

"How is she?" Aaron asked in a steadier voice than it appeared he could manage.

"The patient presented with an epidural hematoma, resulting from contact force. In debriding the wound, we discovered fracturing of the skull, though surgical evacuation of the hematoma revealed no disruption of the dura mater."

"Doctor, please," Aaron said. "Speak plainly."

Between himself and his son, his wife, and now this, he must be weary to death of jargon.

Dr. Derozier's nostrils drew in. "Neither the fracture nor the shards of glass in her scalp penetrated the brain; however, the tissue may have sustained trauma from the blow. There's no sign at this time of spinal cord compression or brain stem involvement."

"That's good, right?" Aaron probed.

"It's good. She had a period of lucidity after resuscitation—" The doctor caught himself, rose onto the balls of his feet and drew a breath through his nose. "She was conscious for a time prior to surgery, which...ups her odds."

Trevor swallowed hard. "Will this affect her ability?"

"You mean cognition, memory—"

"She's a prodigy. An artist with eidetic memory."

Aaron looked surprised that he knew about it. He didn't fully grasp their relationship.

Dr. Derozier paused, clearly skeptical. "We know very little about that, and frankly it's the least of my concerns. Traumatic brain injury can cause personality shifts, memory loss, cognitive difficulties."

Aaron closed his eyes.

Trevor pressed, "Are you saying that's what she has? TBI?" He'd dealt with enough fall victims to be familiar with not only the term but the symptoms.

"Too soon to tell. But you should prepare yourselves." The doctor started each sequence as though unsticking his tongue from the roof of his mouth. "Head injuries are complicated."

"But she's okay," Trevor said.

"She's holding on."

"Can we see her?"

"Maybe tomorrow. We got her through the golden hour, but we'll be watching closely overnight. She's not out of this yet." He gave them a nod and walked away.

Aaron lowered his chin when the surgeon left. *"My God."*

"She's not a quitter."

"I know that." The man's throat worked as tears welled. "My baby sister is a pit bull all wrapped up in such a soft touch you'd think her a kitten."

The Natalie they knew. TBI changed things. Like a belligerent stranger taking residence inside a loved one's head.

Aaron looked up. "You want to see her when we can?"

"If you don't mind."

"As long as she wants it too."

The crime-scene tape drew a larger crowd the next morning than Natalie's grand opening. Squinting in the overbright sunlight, Jonah frowned at the locals and visitors pressing in. Word had spread and more were arriving as he stood there. He might as well sell tickets and hot dogs.

Jazmyn Dufoe hollered to him, and he raised the tape to give her his obligatory statement. Yes, Natalie had been assaulted. He didn't know her condition. He had no suspect, but he'd seen someone fleeing the scene. He withheld the description of the costume—if that's what it was. "We're processing evidence. The state authorities are assisting."

"Is Natalie all right?" The concern in Jazmyn's face seemed authentic.

"I don't know."

She chewed her cuticle. "Is she alive?"

He hesitated. "She was when we flew her out. That's all I know."

"Is it the same one who abducted Michaela?"

"I can't speculate."

"Is there anything to connect the two? Should the women in town do things to protect themselves?"

"People should always be aware." Too many times it wasn't enough. "I understand you received some odd mail."

She looked startled. "What about it?"

"You wouldn't have the original envelope and art, would you?"

"Of course I do. I told Trevor he ought to show all that to you."

"He has."

"Is this about that?" Her face formed a hawkish sharpness.

"I don't know if it is or not, but I'd like that evidence for testing, if you can get it to me."

"I'll get it now if you tell any other print reporters, 'No comment.'"

She always gave it her best try. "Hurry back."

She opened her mouth to push her point, then closed it. He was already turning to the next thing.

"Jonah?"

Fleur's voice reached him from the crowd. He changed course and allowed her under the tape just far enough that they could speak with relative privacy. He didn't want to alarm her, but if Natalie had been targeted, Fleur might also.

"Please tell me she's okay."

"I don't know. She has a head injury. It could be severe."

"What happened?"

"Someone struck her."

She moaned softly. "Why?"

Jonah shook his head, then realized she couldn't see him. "I don't know, Fleur. But stay away from the gallery, okay? It won't be accessible until it's processed and released, but I'd rather you kept some distance."

"What about the faces?"

"What faces?"

"Natalie's sculptures."

"Her art—"

"Not the nature pieces in front," she said, "but the models in back. She didn't want them seen."

"Everything in there is evidence, Fleur. And I need to get back to it." He jutted his chin to Newly, who was watching from his post on crowd control.

"Yeah, Chief?"

"Can you take Fleur home?" Then to her he added, "Will you let the other gal know, the older woman?"

"Lena," Fleur said.

"That's the one."

Seeing she was in good hands, Jonah joined Moser inside. He had secured the scene last night, awaiting the state investigators who'd arrived an hour ago. No doubt they knew their job, but he did not intend to miss one detail himself. Slipping on his gloves, he passed through the gallery that still smelled of iron-rich blood, replaying what he'd seen the day before.

The subject had fled, but not before defacing—literally—the model of himself. Jonah passed into the studio and found two of the techs murmuring. No wonder. They'd pulled the coverings off several of the busts. It was like an old-fashioned waxworks with likenesses of people more real and revealing than their personas.

Jonah looked from one to the next. People he knew, people he didn't, and according to Trevor MacDaniel, people Natalie may have seen only once. With insight like that, she could have threatened any one of them. He tapped his fingers on the huge slab of Corian that formed her work surface. This search might not be as narrow as he'd thought.

———

In the crush of curiosity, Fleur touched Seth Newly's arm, hoping what she'd sensed in him before would help her now. "Seth, will you do something for me?"

"Sure."

"One of the sculptures in the studio is mine."

"You mean the gallery?"

"No. In the back where she works. There are busts."

"She made one of you?"

"Next to the one Natalie sculpted of me is my own version. Will you get it for me?"

"Everything in there is evidence."

"Please. It's extremely personal." It was trivial for her to think of, but the idea of anyone seeing it didn't feel trivial. She heard him scratching his head, felt his doubt.

"I'm pretty sure I can't remove anything from a crime scene."

"It has nothing to do with her attack. Please, Seth. Natalie keeps it covered on the board with hers. Where you see her version, take the covered one beside it."

His hesitation hung over them like a fog, his feet sinking slowly in quicksand. She had felt something more than his face that last time, but could it rival his allegiance to his leader, the chief who'd carried him through the flames?

He sighed. "I'll see what I can do. Don't leave this spot."

She stood arm in arm with palsied Mary Carson whom she'd called when she couldn't reach Natalie on her home or cell phone. Retired and widowed, Mary regularly drove her where she needed to go, and they'd come to the gallery, never guessing this.

"Redford used to be such a safe place. Our little haven tucked away from the troubles of the world." Not receiving an answer, Mary asked, "Are you all right, Fleur?"

She told Mary yes, but she wasn't. Only two things would help. For Natalie to be all right, and Officer Newly to come through for her.

———

"Um, Chief?"

Jonah turned to Newly, whom he'd instructed to get Fleur out of there.

"I need a word."

"Quickly."

Newly lowered his voice. "Fleur needs one of these heads. She made it and it's personal."

Jonah frowned. "It's part of evidence now."

"Can't we make an exception?"

"If Natalie doesn't survive, this is a homicide. I'm not compromising the crime scene."

"But, Chief. Just look, okay?"

Jonah went with him to a beautiful likeness of Fleur that captured an exquisite longing, anticipation, and courage.

"That's the one Natalie made. It's this one Fleur needs." He reached for the covered shape beside it.

"Newly, I'm warning you."

When Newly lifted the cloth, they both stared. Jonah shot a quick look at his officer, understanding immediately why Fleur wouldn't want it seen. The hollows where her eyes should be gaped at them like dark pits of pain. He glanced over his shoulder. The techs were photographing and logging the busts. He'd called them in himself, knowing this case as big as anything Redford had seen.

"There needs to be a chain of evidence."

"Sure, I know."

"You will take personal responsibility for this piece."

"Right, Chief."

"Go out the back." He shot him a look that conveyed more than his words. Newly would see to its safety—or pay the consequences.

———

"I'll take you home now, Ms. Destry."

She smelled the sweat working through his cologne. She had stressed him out. "Thank you, Officer."

The sleeve of his jacket felt stiff under her fingers. Then his hand directed her into the seat of his cruiser. As soon as both doors closed them in, she said, "Seth?"

"Nothing can happen to it. I still have to log it in as belonging to the scene."

"I'll keep it safe."

"It technically should be me."

"Please. I don't want anyone to see it."

She heard him swallow.

"You already did."

"I had to convince the chief."

"He saw it too?"

"But no one else. It would have gone to the state lab and been photographed and recorded."

She drew a ragged breath. "I never should have made it."

"Please don't be upset."

She couldn't help it. As Natalie said, the model reflected the wound in her soul.

"It was the only way to convince him."

"I understand." But it didn't help.

"It just shows how it is being blind. And it's a whole lot better than any sculpting I did."

She laughed grimly. "I wasn't going for an award. I was expressing..." *How I see myself.* "It was Natalie's idea. Because I feel faces, she thought maybe I could form them."

"If I let you take it home, you have to leave it alone. The chief'll have my hide if anything happens."

"I'll leave it. Thank you."

"The chief's a good guy. I guess he understood."

Probably more than Officer Newly.

He parked and said, "I'll carry it in to where you want and put the location in my notes." He cleared his throat. "It's not protocol, but as close as I can get."

She heard his concern. "You're very kind."

"The chief's more about taking care of people than going by the book, so he might not chew me out too bad."

"I appreciate your sacrifice." She smiled, realizing how much she did. They passed through the kitchen to the sun porch where even the autumn rays had increased the temperature. She'd be able to spray the covering cloth when she misted the ferns. "Is there space on the shelf here?"

"Sure. I can fit it between these ferns."

She heard him slide it into place and said, "I made a lot of fuss."

"Don't worry about it."

"You must think I'm self-absorbed."

"Who isn't?"

Again she smiled. He could have denied it, but went for honesty instead.

"So, I guess I'd better get back."

"Thank you." She touched his arm.

"I'll let myself out."

She heard the door close, then lifted the cloth and slowly stretched her fingers to the clay, seeing through them what Jonah and Seth had seen.

Art thou that traitor angel? Art thou he,
Who first broke peace in Heaven and faith, till then
Unbroken, and in proud rebellious arms
Drew after him the third part of Heaven's sons.

hirst drew him out from hiding. Next came hunger, and then fear.
Everywhere they looked for him, and he'd almost been caught. A
female cop had stopped just short of searching deeper shadow, the
shade that held him ill-concealed if she pursued it further.

The injured girl awakened in this hushed, complacent vale a sense
of indignation that such a one as he could contemplate an interruption
of their peace.

Hounded, hunted, cringing, cowed, he hid and waited, shamed
by fear. Where now the confidence that thought to challenge heaven's
choice? Where the strength, the will? From what could he find power?
Yet he must! Or leave the dare unmet. Could he depart in silence, as so
many times before?

No. In this, his closing act, he must illuminate the darkness before
its last embrace.

Twenty-Two

Trevor joined the crowd outside the gallery that all but blocked off commerce to his place—not irrelevant, but so far down the list of concerns that it hardly registered. While Aaron sat with Natalie, he'd hurried home to shower and pack what he needed for the long haul, stopping here to get answers before driving back to the hospital.

Ready to talk his way through to the chief, he paused when Jaz called out his name. Of all the hassles he didn't need, all the irritations he had no energy for... He glared. "Not now."

She lasered him with her eyes. "Now." Her red hair ignited in a streak of autumn sunlight. She swore the color was real, and there was nothing to indicate otherwise in her peaked, rust-colored eyebrows and the coppery freckles over all the skin he'd seen, which was less than she'd wanted to show him.

He said, "I need to see the chief," but went along when she tugged his arm. "Okay, what?"

"I gave him the original drawing. He thinks it's connected."

He doubted Jonah told her that, but Jaz made her own assumptions and pawned them off as truth.

"You're at the center of this, aren't you?" She studied his face, but she couldn't read him as Natalie did—as she had.

"What do you want, Jaz?"

He'd asked it gently, but she glared. "What do *I* want? I thought *you* might want to know while there's nothing on swamp-boy, I found the baby in the tree."

That caught him. "You did?"

"It was Podunk, Missouri, so it never made national news. The couple claims someone took the baby from his crib and put him in a fir in their backyard. They heard him crying and got him down. He's alive, Trevor."

The pulse throbbed in his neck. "Any suspects?"

"They questioned an old boyfriend, but no arrest."

He drew a slow breath through his nose. The baby was alive. "Jaz…"

"I know. You owe me big."

"Maybe it's the same with the others. Found with no incident, no criminal report. Not even a story."

"It's a story now. Don't forget you promised me exclusive rights." She pressed in so close he smelled her fruity lip gloss. "And I want updates on Natalie."

He furrowed his brow.

"Don't pretend you weren't just there, wherever they've taken her. You look like you slept in a chair."

He'd spent the night in the surgical waiting room, hoping fruitlessly to see her this morning.

"I want to know everything you know."

"She's alive."

"What about her stuff?"

"Stuff?"

"The savant thing."

"You know about that?"

"She told me." At his incredulous expression, she cocked her head. "What, you don't want your girlfriends talking?"

"If she told you, you'd know she's not a savant."

"Whatever." She waved a hand. "Is her gift at risk?"

"Everything's at risk with TBI, Jaz." His voice thickened. "It's not good."

She took a step back, gaping. "You're in love."

He jammed his fingers into his hair. "Can we avoid a scene?"

"Scene?" She held up a hand. "I'm so over you."

Please, God.

"But I'm sitting on Natalie's story. And it's mine. Entirely."

"Well, that's between you girls." He pulled a wry smile.

She said, "I really hate you," but the sting was gone.

He nodded. "I know. Now I need to see the chief and get back."

Something moved over her face, passing into something else. Natalie would have captured and understood both expressions. Not his concern.

He needed answers, but Chief Westfall had left the crime scene.

———

The rock was empty, neither warm nor cold, the water flowing, though dimly as beneath overcast skies. The gold-flecked bed looked muddy as the water dragged over the rocks. She lay down on the chalky gray surface, lethargy cleaving her flesh to the stone. It was clay, cracked and powdered by the sun, the water dissolving the edges and washing it away. What would happen when it was gone?

"Nattie." The voice was barely a whisper. The creek or the breeze.

"Listen to me, Nattie."

She breathed the scent of clay, drew it into her lungs. She was more clay than flesh now.

"You have to come back. You can't let go."

Let go? She wasn't letting go. Just…

"I love you. Are you listening?"

Her hands were gray—gray as the clay. She used to make the clay into what she wanted. Now it was taking her into itself.

"Don't you leave, Nattie. We're not done here. Do you hear me? We're not done."

She heard him. She knew him, but how?

"We have too much ahead of us to quit now."

Her hand felt strange. Warm. Held. Color infused the gray. The breeze moved her hair. No, a touch. Fingers through the strands.

"I won't let go, and you can't either."

Her hair turned brown, deepened. The skin of her neck warmed. Her lips, her mouth warmed.

"I don't care if you don't kiss me back. I know you want to."

Hands cradled her face. The water seemed far away. The stone softened, the clay dissolving. Breath fled her lungs, then rushed back in. Her eyes fluttered. She moaned, hurting and reveling as her body awakened.

"There you are."

The face was suntanned and strong, his eyes the color of deep, shady moss. The edges crinkled with a smile that creased his sandpaper cheeks. He was spectacular—whoever he was. She startled when he tipped her face and kissed her, stroking her hair, her neck.

"I'm so sorry, Nattie. I shouldn't have left you alone."

She breathed his scent as he kissed her again, then held his forehead to hers.

"Are you okay?"

She held his eyes. She must know him. Love him?

"Nattie"—his voice broke and he changed course—"Aaron had a rehab session with his trainer. He said he'd come tomorrow."

Aaron.

"And Cody's fine. He wanted you to know."

Why did thoughts of Cody resonate with this man? Something scary. Danger.

She gripped his wrist. Where was she?

"It's okay. Calm down."

She groped the bandage on her head, pleading with her eyes. What happened?

"Someone attacked you, hit you over the head. You've been unconscious two days. But you're going to be all right, okay? You're going to be all right."

She moaned.

He reached over and pressed the Call button. "That'll bring the nurse. Can you stay awake another minute, so they believe me?"

She didn't know. A minute was so long.

———

His heart pumped like a piston. Wherever she'd been, she was back. Confused, but conscious. No long-term vegetative state, no suspended coma sleep, year after year after year.

She closed her eyes. He wanted to shout her name, but forced his mouth to stay shut. Let her be. Let her take it as slowly as she needed to. Each waking would be better. Wouldn't it?

His throat felt like someone had drilled a new tunnel through it by the time not only the nurse but the doctor came in. Please let her wake again.

When the nurse rubbed her hand, Natalie opened her eyes and looked from one of them to the others. The tendons in her throat worked. Her lips parted. No words came.

"Ms. Reeve, you suffered an acute head trauma, including skull fracture and hematoma." Dr. Derozier checked her eyes with a light. "Blink if you understand me."

She did.

"Squeeze my hand."

A squeeze. Trevor's hands clenched in solidarity.

"Blink if you know who you are."

She blinked.

"Taylor Swift, pop star?"

Her brows puckered slightly. She stared.

"Good. No one should have that delusion."

Taylor Swift was a fine young singer—if not in the doctor's opinion—but Natalie's reaction to the ploy had been genuine. She was in there.

"You have swelling in your brain that's affecting your speech center. As that swelling decreases, functionality may return."

The doctor turned to him and said, "Waking up was the first hurdle. Now we'll see." Then he was gone.

The nurse completed her tasks, asked if he needed anything, then left. Natalie slept.

After three hours, nurse and doctor returned. They ran through the same basic routine. Natalie wasn't Sandra Bullock.

Dr. Derozier left for the night. The day-shift nurses turned into night-shift nurses. Trevor had another cup of coffee, another unidentifiable meal from the cafeteria. Aaron called to say he had to fly to Scottsdale to meet with Paige's doctor. Trevor reclined the chair that didn't fit him even sitting and tried to sleep.

Buried in her covers, with hardly enough air to breathe, Fleur trembled. The down and cotton shield offered no defense, but she couldn't pull them off. The world had been safe, and now it wasn't.

She buried her face under the pillow. How could she begin a day in which the structure of her life, the belief in goodness, was torn away?

The phone on her nightstand buzzed. Groaning, she unearthed a hand, found the phone, and pulled it under. "Hello?"

"Um, hi. This is Seth."

Officer Newly. One tiny light ray. "Good morning."

"So, I know you and Natalie walk to the bakery, mornings, and since you can't go out alone—well, you can but I warned you not to—um..."

She pushed the covers off her head.

"I'm at your door and I'll walk you there, if um..."

"Just a minute, Seth." She sat up and slid her legs over. Pulling a robe over her fleece pajamas, she went to the door. The morning felt cold, but dry, so it would warm up as the day went on. A nice day for walking, but still...

"Did I wake you?"

"From the morass."

"Huh?"

"Come in. Piper brought home a bag of loot. Let's see what's in it."

"Does that offer come with cocoa?"

"Of course." The bands on her chest snapped, and she drew a deep full breath. Goodness—she believed.

———

Bagel in one hand, coffee in the other, Trevor entered the room of hope and fear. Natalie turned and took him in, her eyes reflecting those same emotions. He set down the irrelevant food, bent down, and kissed her. Her gaze followed him up.

"How's your head?"

She rasped, "Hurts."

His breath exploded. "That's great!"

Confusion in her face.

"Not the pain. You talked. Nattie, you talked!"

She swallowed. "What happened?"

"He attacked you, hit you in the head. You've been in and out of consciousness."

She swallowed. "In the creek?"

"Here. In the hospital." What did she mean "creek"?

She closed her eyes. "My head hurts."

"I believe it, but the swelling must be gone, or going." He pressed the Call button on the controller and the nurse responded.

The doctor must be on rounds, because he came quickly—in hospital terms. He checked the monitors, then turned to his patient. "I understand you're talking. Can you tell me your name?"

"Natalie." A little weak, but no hesitation.

"And his?"

She searched him with her large brown eyes. The tendons in her throat stood out. "I knew it."

Trevor said, "Don't worry," but his mind took it and ran.

"Trevor," she said. "You saved Cody."

He forced a smile. "That's right."

"Did you rescue me?"

"No."

He could almost hear the questions in her mind. *Why are you here? Why did you kiss me?* When she'd opened her eyes, he'd assumed...

"I'm glad you're okay."

"Thank you. For Cody. I wish there was something...I could do."

The ache spiraled up. Another forced smile. "We'll talk later."

As he moved toward the door, she asked the doctor, "What happened?"

Repetitious questions were symptomatic of concussion. And TBI.

In the hall, he paused, clamping the back of his neck. He looked up when Jonah approached. "You're not going to get anything useful. She's a month or so shy of current time."

Jonah sighed. "Other than that?"

"Drowsy. Confused. Concussed. Her answers are slow and confused, and I'm getting the sense her motor skills and reflexes aren't what they should be." All that would improve with time, he had to believe. "Have you found the guy?"

Jonah shook his head. "He's invisible."

"You saw him."

"He hasn't been spotted since. He's either gone—"

"Or holed up. He has to stay somewhere."

"Redford's twice the population, five times the area we were policing before. All the rentals and time-shares, summer homes, ski cabins…"

"What about the gallery? Fingerprints?"

The chief shook his head. "We did get a fingernail chip from the model. Could be Natalie's but the state'll run DNA. Eventually. Since this is assault—not homicide, thank God—it'll be farther down the queue."

Trevor scowled. "We have nothing?"

"We have a working theory."

"How does that catch him?"

Jonah braced his hips. "Have you been home?"

He shook his head. "I'm not leaving Natalie unprotected. When Aaron can't be here, I am."

"Okay. But…"

"But what?"

"If this is about you, he might not act again until you're back."

Dread moved through him. If Natalie's attacker was some psycho fixated on him, then he'd led the beast to her. "Is it?"

"I'm still trying to piece things together on Michaela. Possibly that will yield a whole different avenue."

But he didn't think so, Trevor could tell.

———

Michaela lay supine in her room surrounded by teen technological apparatus. Cell phone at hand for texting, laptop for school work and social networking, an iPod feeding tunes to her ear canals.

Jonah tapped the door frame and smiled. "Hi, Michaela."

"Chief!" She removed the earphones and turned off the music.

She wore a white foam neck brace and halo, a fiberglass cast from one shoulder to her wrist, wrappings around broken ribs that thickened her torso under a baggy men's softball jersey. She had another cast from her waist to her left foot.

"How are you feeling?"

"Like a robot. Can you hand me that?"

He put the plastic cup with bendy straw into her hand and waited while she took a drink.

"I can do it, but it means I have to move."

"I completely understand." He'd suffered enough bruised and cracked ribs—not to mention a gunshot—to empathize. "May I sit?"

"Well, yeah. It'll take me from like the six-hundredth battle Napoleon fought."

Again he smiled. This kid had heart. "So you know why I'm here."

She sighed.

"Anything?"

She looked toward her window and chewed her nail. "I mean, it's like I said, too mixed up."

"Mixed up or scary?"

She frowned. "I'm not remembering right."

"There's no right or wrong here."

"But there is." She looked back. "I mean, it can't be what I think."

"Try me."

"It's too weird."

"Let me tell you something, Michaela. I saw some crazy stuff on my benders back in the day. How much was real?" He shrugged. "Maybe more than I knew."

She closed her eyes, then dragged her gaze back up. "You believe in God, right? I mean, I see you in church."

He encouraged her with a dip of his chin. God gave him what it took to make it through the day and do some good inside it.

"So, like, what about demons?"

His brows rose.

"I know, I know. It's stupid."

"Stupid was letting your friends doctor your Coke. Not what happened afterward."

Her face flushed. "I'm never drinking again."

"Good. At least until you're legal and responsible—like about a hundred and two."

She groaned.

"Why demons?"

"Well, I was, you know, yakking in the lot, and I saw one."

"Can you describe it?"

"First it had this big hood, then the wind blew it back and there were horns."

"What kind of horns?"

"Just two points, kind of straight up."

Had Bob Betters mistaken horns for bat ears? Jonah thought back. Bat or devil, what he himself had glimpsed could go either way.

"His cape was like dragon wings. And his face—I mean, it was dark, so maybe—"

"Don't rationalize. Just say what you saw."

"It was all craggy and scarred, but he wasn't old. I think he wore a mask."

"Maybe, maybe not. Could you work with an artist?"

"I really don't think so. I must have passed out, because the next thing I was on that ledge."

"You didn't see him again?"

"No." She shuddered. "And I never want to."

"Okay."

"I imagined it, didn't I?"

"I don't think so. No way you got where you were without help."

"Some help." She was shaking.

"I'm just glad you're recovering. You have a lot ahead of you."

"A lot of work." She pulled a face.

"You're up to it."

"Thanks, Chief."

Jonah gave her a smile as she replugged her ears. Her description matched. Some freak had dark aspirations.

Which way I fly is Hell; myself am Hell;
And in the lowest deep, a lower deep
Still threatening to devour me opens wide,
To which the Hell I suffer seems a Heaven.

Curled, he rocked, hands gripping horns on a skintight, skull-tight hood. In this garb, he'd haunted fairs and festivals, as brazen and defiant as pretenders in medieval dress, touting his perfection. Why not? For him it was no act, no skit, but rather truth unveiled.

The master of studies had taught him well the nature of his soul. How apt a student he had been! How clever and astute. He took the lessons deep inside until he knew full well the hollows and caverns and pits. But not all!

For in him there remained that part that saw and cherished goodness, that recognized and cauterized the threat and danger to it. And if, despairing, he gave in, what champion would there be?

The one he'd come here to engage? A challenge still unmet.

Or was there something more—some intention not unveiled, but taking root and growing?

Twenty-Three

Trevor sat, fingers threaded in his lap, watching Natalie sleep. Since she first awoke, they'd gotten her up walking, done basic physical therapy and batteries of tests. Some sessions she was clearer, others muddled. She still didn't look at him with full recognition, but seemed to accept his presence.

He thought he'd willed her to come back, but he was simply the one talking when she did. His throat constricted. He rescued people, pulled them out of danger, saved them from harm, but he hadn't kept Natalie safe.

He couldn't undo that. He could only make sure no one got past him now. Whatever this freak might want from him, it would not hurt Nattie again.

"I promise you," he murmured.

Her eyes fluttered open. She searched around the room, breathing sparsely. He took her hand before recalling the gesture might not be familiar to her.

She turned. "Trevor?"

"I'm here." He pressed her hand between the two of his.

"Something happened, didn't it?"

"You were injured."

She touched the bandage. "Is it bad?"

"You're better now than yesterday, much better than the day before." He stroked her fingers with his thumb.

"It's been that long?"

"Over two weeks."

"Two…" She blinked, taking that in.

He leaned forward. "What do you remember?"

Her brows formed a tiny V between them. "I was in the studio. You went to get Cody." She gasped.

"It's okay. He's back with his dad."

She released the breath with clear relief.

"I left you in the studio, Nattie. Why were you out in the gallery?"

"The chief." No delay this time. "I heard something and thought the chief must be at the front door."

"Honey, next time you hear something, will you go the other way?"

A spark of amusement found her eyes. "I'd be leaving a lot of people on doorsteps."

His heart warmed and ached at once. "Nattie." His voice thickened. "Do you know me?"

"Know you?"

"The last few days you haven't remembered…everything."

"I'm sorry." Her face softened.

He canted his head. "Sorry."

"I can imagine how that felt." Her eyes were purple wells, her skin translucent—and she worried how he felt.

"I just want you back."

Something flickered over her face. Pain? Fear?

She said, "Can I go home? Will you please see if I can go home now?"

———

When Trevor went out, Natalie studied the IV port connecting her to this place for the past *two weeks*. She stared at the amber walls, the monitors, the poster art, the black female nurse who came in with Trevor. She held the thickly lashed eyes as the woman introduced herself and said Dr. Derozier had signed her discharge that morning.

They must not realize she was broken.

She'd lain on the rock, becoming clay. Trevor called her back, but she'd left part of herself behind—the part he'd found courageous. What was there now for someone like him? No glitz like his supermodels, no fire like Jaz. Who was she?

"Just because you're out of here, don't expect smooth sailing," the nurse said. "You might experience headaches, dizziness, an inability to concentrate, and fatigue."

No kidding?

"Don't be surprised if you're restless and irritable, but if the symptoms increase or intensify, call your doctor."

Restless and irritable, right.

"Posttraumatic seizures can develop a month to three months after the injury. Frequent, heavy use of alcohol increases that risk."

"So I shouldn't get bombed tonight?"

The woman arched a brow. "Honey, after what you survived, I'd be pampering my brain. Lay off the caffeine and take a vacation. You've got healing to do."

Her hand felt awkward as she signed the forms. A simple thing, writing her name, but she had to focus on each letter, biting her lip to concentrate. If the nurse noticed the difficulty, they might not let her go.

As Trevor got her things packed, Aaron arrived. The hug he gave her went on and on. Oh, how she loved him. "You're out of your cast." She beamed. "Good as new?"

"Getting there. But forget about me." He leaned his head back. "How are you?"

"I'm going to be fine." She had no choice. The Lord gives and the Lord takes away and whoever hides her gift loses it. But what should she have done, show the faces? Let people see themselves as God saw them? Everything inside displayed for all the world?

"I finally reached our folks, and here you are going home."

"Are they worried?"

"Of course they are. But your news was better than mine." His shoulders slumped. "Paige is leaving."

Natalie searched his face. "She's… How…" Words were too hard.

"They've canned the dissociation theory and decided that, in her right mind, she doesn't want to raise a disabled child. It's not what she signed on for." His voice was bleak and angry.

"Oh, Aaron. Will she see him at least?"

"She's not requesting custody. Or visitation."

Poor little Cody. How could she!

"The truth is, she mostly had him with a nanny. With my traveling so much, I could hardly blame her, but now I wish… Anyway…"

No wonder he hadn't cried for his mommy. He'd hardly had one.

Aaron turned to Trevor. "I have my hands full right now. Can you look after my sister?"

She said, "I don't need that."

Trevor slid her a look. "The guy who did this—"

"I can't remember him. I don't know anything that happened after hearing Chief—what I thought was Chief Westfall." She put a hand to the bandage.

"Your assailant doesn't know that."

At this point she didn't care. "I just need to go home."

"Until they get him, you're coming home with me."

"That's not your decision." A flash of fury must be the emotional volatility they kept talking about.

"I have gated access, keyed elevator and doors. As secure as it's going to get."

Aaron stared at her, puzzled. "Do it, Nat. Don't take chances."

They were right. But she felt like crawling out of her skin. "I wish everyone would leave me alone."

Trevor's stare penetrated. Whatever he was thinking, she couldn't tell. He said, "You'll have your own space."

Clenching her jaw, she ground out, "Okay, fine. Until they catch him."

They were both so relieved she ought to feel good. She felt fractious. Combative. More hugs from Aaron, then the wheelchair the nurse had gone to fetch. Not sound enough to walk, she guessed, but good enough to leave, thank God.

Trevor pulled his SUV to the curb. She transferred herself into the vehicle, and they started the long trek home. Hordes of sightseers ogling the last glorious display of aspen turned the road into a bloated snake. Why couldn't they all go home? She tapped her fingers on the armrest and stared out.

Finally they reached the exit. "Can you take me to the gallery?"

With his wrist tucked over the wheel, Trevor turned. "It hasn't been cleaned up from the crime techs and…blood."

"Oh." Sorrow and fear overwhelmed her. The dream felt broken. She felt broken. Would she even sculpt again?

———

Trevor let her into his condo and took the bags they'd packed at her place into the guest room. "How are you feeling?"

She looked around her. "Weird."

"You're not trapping images, are you?"

She should have known he'd realize it. "Everything's just there. Solid."

"Is that a bad thing?"

"I don't know. What I had was crazy hard, but God made me different for a reason." She looked him square in the face. "I couldn't change the world, but I could see. I saw with *his* eyes." Those she'd shown had been impacted. Even Jaz. "Now it's gone, and I can't help thinking I wasted it."

"You're far from healed."

She pressed her fingers to her temples remembering the lights inside her head. Had the blow, the damage to the top of brain where more happened than anyone knew, destroyed the nerve connections that made her different? People got hit by lightning and woke up with synesthesia, amnesia, and who knew what else. Strokes and aneurisms—

"I'm not making light of it, Nattie, but we were preparing for worse. When you spoke that first time…" His voice hoarsened.

"You're right. I should be grateful. I am grateful. For so much. I just don't…know who to be."

He took her hands and brought them to his lips. "Then just be."

———

Fleur hurried into the sun porch, biting her lip. "Tell me I'm not crazy."

"Saner than sane," Piper assured her.

"Okay, because I invited Seth Newly to dinner."

Piper's paperback snapped closed. "Our own Officer Newly, Redford PD?"

She nodded. "How else can we find out what's happening on Natalie's case?"

"I know, right? Jonah won't even discuss it with Tia—believe me, I've tried that source."

Fleur wrung her hands. "Want to cook? We could invite Miles and make it four. That might not be as obvious."

"Why not?" Piper laughed. "Start cleaning."

For Natalie's sake and her own peace of mind, she had to know progress was being made. But the nerves that gave her work a frantic edge were also about Seth Newly, about freeing hopes and feelings she had bottled up since the blindness, about daring to feel like a woman.

Three hours later, the house smelled of lemon-scented Lysol, coq au vin with raspberries, roasted baby potatoes with wild mountain sage, and an arugula salad from herbs in the sunroom.

Piper said, "As suppressed as Miles is in other areas, he has an adventurous palate. I can count on his honest opinion too."

Fleur smiled. One day, maybe, her hands would know how Miles looked, but for now she had only the impression of his size and the awkward way he moved through space. "He's not inhibited by tact."

They laughed.

"And he's so cute with his new haircut. I wish you could see."

Something she only experienced every hour of every day.

"That old helmet head spoiled the effect of the expensive clothes he never wears out and used to throw away until I convinced him to let me launder and pass them on."

"Good for you."

"He shuddered at the thought, but my teddy's agreeable any way he can be."

That was true.

"He's just a sweet, beautiful man who got mixed up too early. Unmixing him is proving a long process. But one thing I learned growing up in my family is that I'm not looking for the easy road."

"He's very lucky to have you."

"Speaking of that—Officer Newly just climbed out, all scrubbed and eager with his hair standing out at odd angles. I could fix that, but it would spoil the effect."

Fleur's pulse quickened. "Tell me everything before he gets to the door."

"He's cute in a squeezable way, and he brought you white spider mums. I think he's already blushing."

Fleur elbowed her.

"And here's Miles with wine. It was probably bottled by monks in the fifth century."

Admitting both men, she heard Miles whisper to Piper, *"In vino veritas."* He was obviously in on the plan.

Seth said, "I know you have that whole room of plants and flowers, so I brought these potted ones. They don't smell great, but—"

"Thank you, Seth. I love spider mums." No harm cheating a little.

Seth proved a loquacious guest. Primed with vine and vittles—or maybe the company?—he creaked back in his chair and said, "While I can't say it's safe in Redford yet, there won't be much to worry about soon. Pretty sure we'll be seeing some FBI around."

"FBI?" Fleur paused with her cup raised. "Doesn't there have to be kidnapping or crimes in other states or something?"

"Between you and me"—she felt him lean in—"there might be both. Look what happened to Michaela. And the other stuff? This guy's not normal."

"What stuff could be worse than leaving Michaela on that ledge?" Piper teased for details.

"Leaving toddlers in streets and babies in trees. Oh, and one kid for the alligators."

"You can't be serious." Fleur expected him to burst out with, *"Just teasing the blind chick."* He must realize what they were up to and be fooling them back.

"No, really. And the kicker is, he's got devil horns and bat wings and a face straight from hell."

Now she was insulted. "If you didn't want to tell us, you should just say so."

"I'm not kidding." He sounded defensive. "That's all in the case file. I guess you'd say the guy's a demon bat."

When had the room gotten so cold, the air so heavy?

"So he's in disguise." Concern and doubt threaded Piper's voice.

"It's a game," Miles said. "Hurting people. Hurting people's a game."

Fleur shook her head. "It can't be a game. There must be something deeply disturbed in him." She had wanted this information, but now she wished she'd never asked.

"Makes no difference," Seth said. "When we get him, he's toast."

———

Just be, Trevor said, but how? She'd always believed God was in control. So had he intended—even used—the person who struck her to accomplish his will? Because she'd hidden the gift—or the part Fleur and Lena told her should be shown—had he taken it away?

The first time Trevor offered, she'd resisted the pleasure of his Jacuzzi, sitting outside while he nursed his sore knee. Now it was her turn for therapy. Wearing her own yellow and white tankini, she slipped into the steaming water. Heat crawled up her legs, her back and stomach. Her arms stung, but only for a moment. Her shoulders and neck sank into the enveloping warmth, muscles and tendons releasing. The throbbing in her head diminished.

Trevor came and stood beside the Jacuzzi in jeans and T-shirt.

"You're not getting in?"

"I'll set the jets."

He'd suggested but wouldn't share the spa. Why would he? She stared at her reflection in the still water. Nothing special. Just a girl.

"Nat?"

She brought her arm across her chest to press the crook of her neck and shoulder where tension had returned.

"Hey." He knelt beside the spa. "What's wrong?"

She stared out the windows, unable, unwilling to give the sadness words. It was a private grief, a selfish one.

"I see you're not looking at me anymore. What's that about?"

She turned. "Please stop pretending nothing's changed."

He searched her face. Instead of answering, he went into the dressing room and came back in his trunks. She watched him step into the water, submerge in the center, and come up soaking beside her. "I wasn't out there because I didn't want to be with you."

"Then why?"

"For starters, the first time we did this, you sat out."

"I hardly knew you."

"In the hospital you didn't know me at all. Now maybe you do, but—"

"You don't know *me*." Tears stung. "This me."

He shook his head. "Only one thing's changed."

"The way I was and what I did and how I lived my life. I feel like I've been knocked off the shelf, and instead of the only unicorn in the glass menagerie, I'm a horse like all the others. I don't even know if I can sculpt anymore."

He stroked her arm. "No point assuming that."

"If I can't, what about the gallery?"

"Oh, my rent'll carry you awhile."

She groaned. "Aaron told you?"

"ANR. Clever."

She pressed her hands to her face.

"Whit and I would have bought the building if it had been for sale."

She lowered her fingers. "Aaron's offer included use of his discretionary tickets as long as he plays in Denver."

"I like him more and more."

In the steamy solitude, with misty droplets on the windows and Joshua Radin playing low, she softened against him. "Trevor, I'm starting over now. You were hurt that I didn't know you. But I don't know myself."

"You're smart, you're tough, you're sweet, forgiving, funny. You don't expect things."

"What would I expect?"

"Right there is what makes you special. Maybe celebrity jaded me, but someone who doesn't even think of what's in it for her is amazing."

"I have hopes and desires."

He stared hard. "I hope so."

"But—"

"I spent the last weeks knowing I could lose you. I'm not willing to do that."

She brought her fingers to his face, feeling the skin, the bone, the form of him. She'd made him in clay, but this was the original. "You're not disappointed that the part of me that attracted you is gone?"

"You mean that you can look at me without needing clay to wipe me out?"

"I wasn't wiping you out."

"Come here." He pulled her across his lap and tucked her shoulder under his arm. "This is where I want you. Today, tomorrow, whether you see like the rest of us or like God. Right here, where you fit like nobody else."

———

Jonah stared at Mayor Buckley in his doorway. "You realize I'm having dinner with my family? For the first time all week."

"I wouldn't be standing here if this wasn't crucial to Redford."

"Mayor—"

"Hear me out, Jonah. It's in your best interest."

He knew whose interest it was in, if the self-important man came all this way in person. Jonah expelled his breath and ushered Buckley into the main room, in earshot of the dining room where Tia and Sarge ate, although Tia's fork had frozen halfway to her mouth. Jonah spoke before Buckley could start working the room. "What can't wait until tomorrow?"

"I understand you're thinking of inviting the FBI to join the investigation."

They'd parleyed it around, but he doubted they'd get anywhere. "The feds have resources, personnel, a budget."

"Well, I want you to know, I have personally spoken with Dave, and our city manager agrees that in light of these new events, your requests are reasonable."

Jonah absorbed that without emotion. "You're approving three new positions and the equipment I asked for." All of which had been shot down.

"We want you to do the job we appointed you to. I know the state's got techs and labs it's sensible to make use of. But there's no need to bring in the feds. The endangerment of a local teen and an assault on a local woman, that's our business, and we take care of it."

"You think word'll get out that Redford isn't the Utopian Camelot you want people to believe?"

"I think our citizens need to know they're in good hands right here. Yours."

Their stares sparred.

"I made you chief and kept you there when others doubted. I fought for you when your daddy put the shotgun to his head and some wondered who pulled the trigger."

Jonah stiffened.

"I told them your dalliance with the bottle wouldn't keep you from becoming the best chief of police Redford has ever known."

He imagined a shot of Kentucky bourbon burning down his throat like sweet nectar of the gods. There were entire days he never thought of it, but Buckley made him want to drink.

"Some fought me, but you're in this position because I believe you can do the job."

And he'd give him what it took to do it. "If this is connected to crimes in other states—"

"Your concern is Redford and the people of our city. You find this clown and take him down."

"He's no clown. He's a demon out of hell."

Buckley eyed him up and down. "Well, you know that terrain."

Jonah swallowed the retort that came to mind, not out of respect for the man but his own self-respect. And it was true. A real demon might wear his father's face.

"Good night, Mayor."

"Good night, Chief."

He watched the man leave, then rejoined his family.

Tia said, "Why doesn't our august mayor want the FBI to help?"

He looked at her. "I don't know."

Sarge harrumphed. "He wants no one poking around in his business."

"Which again begs the question, why?" Tia said. "It isn't as though they'd investigate anything besides the attacks."

Sarge waved his fork. "There's no controlling what they poke into."

"What else do you know?" She narrowed her gaze.

"What man in power hasn't done things to get there? Your mother called him a mystery."

Jonah shook his head. "The FBI doesn't care about infidelity. What else is there?"

"He's a deal-maker."

"Like the one he just made with me."

"If there's something in it for you, there's more in it for him."

The man had gone to see his mother, probably reminding her secrets should be kept. "If it's important enough to fill and outfit three positions, I'll take it."

"Are you sure you're not dealing with the devil?" Tia said.

He reached over and took her hand. "Well, with more boots on the ground, I might have time to look into other things."

Her smile spread. "That's the man I love."

His phone vibrated. Frowning, Jonah answered. "Yeah, Moser."

"If you're looking to fill new positions, I'd like you to consider my nephew."

Jonah's jaw fell slack. "Did you bug my kitchen?"

"Beg pardon?"

"How did you know about the positions?"

"From Ruth."

"How did she—never mind. If your nephew's anything like you, bring him in to see me."

He hung up and stared at his phone. Buckley must have been confident enough in the outcome to spread it through Ruth to the rest of Redford. One of these days he was going to stand up to the man. But not when it meant getting what he needed to keep his people safe, to catch the demon preying on his town.

Up and down unseen
Wing silently the buxom air, embalmed
With odours. There ye shall be fed and filled
Immeasurably; all things shall be your prey.

S ounds of strife recalled to him the mission he'd abandoned. He
had thought this town a perfect place, but no such place exists.
"Give it back!" The small voice wailed.
"Crybaby-crybaby-crybaby-cry."
Taunt and crying, taunt and squealing.
"Shut up before I break your heads." A low and growling bellow.
"Shut them up before I break yours too."

Glass shattered. A woman screeched, laying her voice atop the others.

Two scrappy urchins banged out through the door into the masking dark. Heedless as rabbits they scurried, returning him to days before the darker days replaced one nightmare with a worse.

He saw his poxy hands delving, delving for something to fill his mouth, not knowing who it was that saw his garbage plundered. How much better to have starved!

Through the fog he followed, having seen at once the roles they played, one the bruising bully bigger than his sobbing sibling. In the mist he loomed and found the cringing one he sought. Staring down, himself the cautionary tale, he looked into the weepy eyes and spread his leathered wings.

Twenty-Four

Wearing warmups, Birkenstock Boston clogs, and a handgun, Trevor slipped out to his balcony to take the call. The morning was gray and blustery, but he hoped he could avoid disturbing Natalie, sleeping in the guest room.

"Bro." Conner's voice broke up with the signal. "Got your message, but I'm not sure what I can tell you."

Trevor adjusted his position on the balcony to get another bar on the cell phone. "Help me understand police procedure." He had spoken to the chief last night, as frustratingly vague and noncommittal a conversation as he'd ever had. "It seems to me, something like this, they'd bring in the FBI."

"That's not as easily done as you think. Contrary to TV, agents aren't loaded and waiting for hostile takeovers of everyone's cases."

"What if the suspect's responsible for crimes in other states, then brings it here."

"If it's a case the feds are running, they'll come to you," Conner said. "That's where you might get some jurisdictional posturing."

"Okay, but in this case, the photos—"

"The photos you already sent Agent Lamont…"

"The photos I got for a period of time right before an abduction here in town."

"What abduction?"

Trevor pinched the bridge of his nose. "An intoxicated teenage girl."

"A teenage girl. Imagine that. Any connection to you?"

"She was left on a stone promontory. Like a kid on a water tower or in a skiff or a tree." The cloud swirled in like gray fingers searching him.

"Dead?"

"Not dead, endangered." He snapped the collar up under his chin.

"That's still thin."

Trevor cleared his throat. "He attacked my girlfriend."

"Come again?"

"I said—"

"You're in a relationship?"

"Focus, Conner." He shifted the phone to his other ear. "She saw him staring at a statue of me."

"They made you a statue? I'm gagging."

Trevor dropped his head back. "Natalie made it. She's a sculptor. It was her nephew I rescued. That story on the news."

"Is she sane?"

"Come meet her yourself."

"Whoa. Warn me to sit down, Bro."

Trevor gripped the rail. "Are we through with that? I'm worried here. This guy's obsessed."

"All right. I hear you."

But he didn't. Not really. "He fractured her skull."

Silence. Then softly, "Yeah, I'm a schmuck."

"You didn't know. But, Conner, he's playing for the king. And pawns are expendable."

———

Fleur sighed. She had arranged a ride to the art center to get a sense of the place and make a final decision regarding the mural. This morning she had cancelled it. Dinner with Officer Newly had not put her mind at ease, but tortured it.

She paced her home like a cornered cat, only this impaired kitty could not leap past a threat she couldn't see. A demon bat. She shuddered, then jumped when her phone rang. "Hello?"

Mary Carson's palsied voice invited her to the church ladies' knitathon. "Your touch is so delicate, everyone still talks about the scarves you made last year."

"That's kind," Fleur said, about to refuse. How could she go out in a place where babies were left in trees? A knot of anger clenched her hand, defiance springing up. How dare this scumbag throw her back into that place of helplessness and fear? Who was he to make her feel blind?

"Sounds great," she told Mary. "Mind giving me a ride?"

"Oh, honey, that was my next question. Want to host us?"

The laugh came with no effort. "I'd love to."

Turning, Trevor saw Natalie, heart-wrenchingly rumpled and vulnerable, at the sliding door. How much of the conversation had she heard?

She stepped into the misty morning, pulling the nubby robe closer at the neck. "Who was that?"

"Conner." He curled her into the bend of his arm. "Did you sleep?"

"Some. You?"

"Some." He nuzzled her hair with his cheek, then looked up, tensing. "I hear something at the door." He pulled her inside behind him. He reached around to the small of his back and closed his hand around the Colt's grip. Instead of moving to the peephole, he called, "Who is it?"

"Me. Whit."

With a hard exhalation, he released the gun and admitted him.

Whit looked from him to Natalie to the holster and frowned. "Something wrong?"

"Just being careful." Whit should have called before coming. "What's up?"

"Well, this is probably the farthest thing from your mind, but you have the Farley kids' climbing lesson this morning."

He'd come in person to say that?

"You were supposed to take them to Wither Point, but with the weather, we could keep it in house."

"You want to do it?"

He wiggled his hand back and forth. "Doug's...all about you."

"Then cancel it." Whit was every bit the instructor on the wall, only without the cachet. If that wasn't good enough, there were hot sulfurous places Doug could visit. He reached around and drew Natalie to his side.

"I can," Whit said, "of course. But I got thinking, if you stay holed up, it prolongs this whole thing."

"What do you mean?"

"The weeks you've spent at the hospital, there's been nothing. No photos, no attacks."

"That's bad?"

"If they're trying to catch him."

The chief had said something to that effect. It had seemed ludicrous, but what if they were right?

Natalie said, "If Trevor teaches, someone else will get hurt?"

"If he knows Trevor's back, he might come out of hiding. At any rate, we should get back to normal."

"There's nothing normal about this." Dark circles of fatigue bruised her eyes.

Trevor circled her shoulders. "I'm not leaving Natalie alone."

Whit crossed his arms. "I could stay with her."

Trevor narrowed his eyes. What else was going on here?

"People are talking. Michaela's rescue went south. Your girlfriend was attacked. You virtually disappear."

"And what, I'm supposed to apologize?"

"Your halo's slipping."

"That's not funny."

Whit shrugged. "Small-town dynamics. We trade on your cachet."

"You think I care what Doug Farley and others think?"

"I care. Our bottom line cares. Without you, we're sporting goods."

He closed his mouth and heard Whit. Their margins were narrow. He might downplay his fame, but it had an impact. His reputation and personality energized the business. And he'd left Whit stranded without rope. "Sorry."

"Look, I get it." Whit glanced at Natalie. "But it doesn't have to be all or nothing."

He hated leaving her physically and emotionally fragile. But this was Whit. "You'll stay?"

She turned, surprised.

"Don't worry," he told her. "Whit can handle things."

"It's you I'm worried about."

"He's right." Trevor tightened his jaw. "We shouldn't let this affect our lives."

"Not—"

He drew her up and kissed the corner of her mouth. "Trust me here, okay?"

"I don't want you to go." Her lips hardly moved.

"I know." He clasped her shoulders. "But it's the right move."

He glanced over her to Whit, conveying with a look the sacrifice and the expectation. No more ambiguity regarding Natalie's importance. Whit nodded, getting it.

———

Natalie fought the panic as Trevor went down the hall to shower. He was all but announcing his return to the field, inviting a new challenge, a fresh attack. Did he realize this adversary was no wild creature? Throwing rocks wouldn't help.

She slid her hand into her hair and encountered the bandage still covering her wound. She wanted to demand Whit take his stupid concerns and leave. But their business was no smaller concern than her own. She sighed.

How long before she could return to her gallery, try to find her way in the clay? How long before she felt safe there and whole anywhere? She dropped her chin and saw the robe she'd pulled over her pajamas—and looked at Whit.

"You're fine."

Anything but. "Do you think he's still here?"

Whit didn't ask who. "He came all the way across the country. He's not finished with Trevor."

She nodded, chewing her lip.

He narrowed his eyes. "So, how are you? Really?"

She shrugged. The time on the rock had been strange and surreal, but she felt more vulnerable now.

Whit pressed his palm to the counter, his wedding ring making a faint click. "This can't be easy."

"I don't expect easy." She'd been coping one way or another her whole life. "Are you hungry?"

Whit looked surprised. "I could eat."

She opened the refrigerator to find a dozen plastic-wrapped dishes. "What's all this?"

"Sara feeding Trevor."

"She makes his meals?"

"While you were in the hospital."

"He was there too."

"Thus the packed-to-capacity fridge." He smiled. "That pie plate's a quiche."

She slid it out, fumbling with the plastic. Her hands were slow, her fingers clumsy. She was still striving for normal. Fighting another wave of panic, she microwaved the quiche and, when it finished, slid a steaming slice to Whit.

When Trevor joined them, she said, "I heated a piece for you." As though he were merely going to work.

"Thanks." He took the plate and wolfed the food down, eager to be off.

She played with hers, not as hungry as she'd thought. When he leaned down to kiss her, she said, "Please be careful."

"Always." He brushed her cheek. "Listen to Whit. He's got good instincts."

He didn't get clobbered defending a statue. Her heart caught at that sudden fragment of memory. A crowbar. Destructive intentions. Her heart raced, but she didn't show Trevor. If she could remember...

"Don't worry," Whit said. "Nothing will happen at the store."

She looked over, unconvinced. "He knows where Trevor works. He sent the photos there."

"It's too public. If he's watching the place, he'll realize Trevor's back. But he's been too secretive to risk interference from bystanders."

"What then? What's he going to do, Whit?"

He sighed. "No clue."

Loading their dishes in the dishwasher, she said, "Do you mind if I shower?"

"Knock yourself out. Not…literally." He crooked a smile.

The levity eased a little of the strain. She hated this endangered-witness role. Whit should be at work or with his own family, not baby-sitting her. With an even longer sigh, she locked the door and undressed. Except for a few punctured veins, the rest of her was unscathed. Only the part that mattered had broken.

She painstakingly shampooed the hair around her shaved and sutured scalp—a grizzly reminder of the attack if not the attacker. As she stuck her face in the water, a flash shot behind her eyes. Pain. Scars. Yearning.

She braced herself, palms splayed against the tiled walls. Water spilled around her like the creek around the stone. Her breath came hoarsely as another powerful fragment returned. She groped for the door, pressed it open. Steam billowed out as she grabbed her towel, too impatient to do it right.

Holding the towel against her chest, she rushed into her room, took her phone off the charging cord, and punched the contact. "Chief Westfall?"

"Natalie. What is it?"

"I remember something."

"Tell me."

She swallowed. "He had horns. I know it's crazy—"

"Don't worry about that. Just tell me what you remember."

She frowned. "It's just a fragment. But he had a crowbar. He was going to strike Trevor's statue. Does that prove it's the person sending photos?"

"Proof is for courtrooms. All I need are clues." He cleared his throat. "Back to the horns. Was it a mask? a costume?"

She sighed. "I can't see… Maybe if I try the clay. Do you have the model I started? If I could see it…"

"It's at the state lab, but the gouges did a job on it."

"Gouges?" She racked her brain for gouges.

"Not you, I take it."

He had gouged himself? Like Fleur boring holes in her eyes. "No, not me."

"If you think of anything else, please don't hesitate."

"Okay." She pulled on jeans and sweater, laced her leather walking boots, and zipped her fleece-lined jacket, then jumped when she opened to Whit outside her door.

"I heard you talking. Everything okay?"

"I need clay."

"The gallery's a mess."

"I have some at my house."

He squinted. "Probably not a good idea."

"I told the chief I'd try." She moved past him.

"Natalie, Trevor wants you here. For security."

She reached the door with him right behind. "If I can remember and they catch him, that's Trevor's security."

Whit searched her face. "Just wait for him. Let me call."

"No, Whit. I need to do this." She had to try while it was there… almost there. The clay could draw it out, bring it back, make her who she was again. She opened the door and stepped outside. "Will you give me a ride, or do I need to find someone else?"

Expelling his breath, he motioned her out.

Marauding clouds faded everything outside the windows, hiding the mountains as though a giant eraser had rubbed them out, leaving only a dirty, gray smudge. Like the inside of her brain. When Whit pulled up to her house, she started to climb out.

"Stop!" His speed showed his athleticism. "Stay behind me."

When he had secured the premises, she carried the model of Trevor from the mud room to the kitchen. She removed the cloth and studied what she'd made the night Michaela fell. Would she ever do it again? A soft, bitter scoff filled her throat. Didn't she want to be normal?

Gently, apologetically, she pressed Trevor's features into a mound. She stared at it, wondering, did she have a gift, or had sculpting been an exorcism, driving visions from her brain into the clay like demons into pigs?

━━━━

Jonah pulled out of the station that was starting to feel like a jail cell. The case was taking a toll, eloquently expressed by Tia this morning with, *"You need help."*

Natalie's description corroborated Michaela's. Someone role-playing a dark fantasy?

"Chief." Sue's voice came over the radio.

"Officer Donnelly."

"I'm following up on last night's domestic, thought you might want a heads-up."

"Go ahead."

"Beatty and McCarthy responded, neutralized the situation. But come to find out, one of the kids didn't come back after flying the coop. Rolanda Pitman called in this morning wondering if the officers had her son."

"Age?"

"Four."

"Took her all night to miss him?"

"I'm thinking a two-by-four to the head."

"Make sure there are no witnesses." Too late he recalled they were on the radio.

Sue laughed grimly. "I'm en route. He's probably hiding out, but with this other stuff, I thought you'd want to know."

"I'll back you up." He knew the address. Turk and Rolanda Pitman were regular combatants. Their sons were hellions. Go figure.

———

Sue brushed her hands down her uniform top and straightened her belt as he got out of the Bronco. She had waited outside without specific instructions to do so. Getting him shot when they took down that meth lab had made her a maniacally attentive officer.

"Let's do this."

The house smelled of stale pizza boxes. Rolanda smelled of gin, and Jonah was twisted enough to want a hit from her bottle. Turk had passed out with an ice pack that was now a water-filled baggie on his cheek. He'd tended his bruised face, but not realized his child was missing? Jonah's hands clenched.

He'd be calling Connie Wong, the county's overburdened social worker, but he didn't mention that to Sue. Connie had removed Sue's son from her home before the family realized he had a mild form of fragile bone syndrome. Even catching him from falling could have caused the hairline fractures on her little boy's arms. These Pitman boys were sturdy. But one of them was lost.

Sue conducted the interview. They'd run out the back when their fighting put Turk in a rage. He and Rolanda pounded it out until the neighbors called the cops. The older boy came back. Rolanda must have been seeing double because she could have sworn it was both of them.

"No sign of him this morning?" Jonah cut to the chase.

"He'd be trashing the kitchen."

"Yeah, kids like to eat." With his ears on fire and his jaw a vise, Jonah moved through to the backyard. It opened onto a greenbelt that dipped down in the middle to a runoff. Swathed in thin gray cloud, it was tree lined and waist high with brushy growth. This time of year no water flowed, except in flash-flood conditions.

He pressed into the brush. Good place for a four-year-old to hide, but why not come back when the coast was clear, when the night got cold, when everything got dark and scary? Maybe it was scarier inside. He'd known by that age.

Sue stayed in the house to get the kid's statistics, search the home, talk to the family. He moved down into the undergrowth. The fog had moved in with the dawn, the temperature dropping even as he searched. He braced himself with all he had when he saw the child hanging like a bat—right side up, thank God—from a cottonwood tree.

He took in the child's location, close enough to the house that responsible parents would have found him. Nor was he in extreme or imminent danger, though his lips were blue, his face a little dewy. The sleeves of the batlike cape had swaddled him, a cord suspending him over the gully. A frantic child could have broken loose. This one hadn't tried too hard.

"Hi there, Brody."

"Devil's gonna get you."

"I'm not worried." He caught the bundle with one arm and loosened the knotted cord. A good tug pulled it free. He could have unwrapped and set the boy on his feet, but carried him up the gully through the tangled stems and branches.

"Devil's gonna drink your blood."

"Devil tell you that?"

"Gordy."

"Your brother tied you up there?"

"He watched. Told me if I didn't stay, Devil come back and drink my blood."

Jonah stepped into the yard. "Devil tied you up?"

"Tied me up in his wings."

Jonah swallowed. "Did he hurt you?"

Brody shook his head.

"Touch you?"

Another shake.

"Do you know what I mean?"

A nod.

"You sure?"

"He said he'd put me where my dad wouldn't look."

Jonah considered that. "Then went away?"

"And Gordy said I had to stay."

"Did Gordy see the devil?"

A nod. "He ran, then he came back. Then ran off again."

All night the older boy had known his brother hung from a tree. That apple wasn't falling far—or else he was terrified.

Controlling the rage, Jonah called for EMTs to come check Brody out, then carried him into the kitchen, unwrapped him from the batlike cape, and set him down. "I'll keep these wings." He wadded the thick cape that had a sort of piping, which gave it a scalloped edge.

Brody looked disappointed, but didn't argue. He was more shaken than he'd pretended with all his tough talk.

Rolanda rushed her son, feeling his face and cursing. "What happened to you? Why'd you stay out in the cold? Turk! Get in here and see what happened to your boy."

They heard the sound of sliding furniture, then Turk lumbered in. "Whatchu bellowing?"

He ought to arrest them for criminal negligence, but his own officers had failed to account for the kids during the incident last night. A defense attorney could muddy the waters with that—and should. He'd write them up himself.

Looking from one parent to the other, Brody clammed up. From across the table, Gordy stared with sullen eyes over his cereal bowl. Sue shook her head to indicate the amount of information she'd gotten from him.

Jonah fixed his stare on Gordy. "Want to tell me what you saw?"

Gordy shook his head.

Rolanda cuffed him. "If you know something, say it."

"Nuh-uh."

Jonah narrowed his eyes. "Devil tell you not to?"

Gordy scowled. "Didn't have to."

"How come?"

"His face did."

Bingo.

Meanwhile the Adversary of God and Man,
Satan, with thoughts inflamed of highest design,
Puts on swift wings, and toward the gates of Hell
Explores his solitary flight.

Sacrifice engenders loss. Loss begets the offspring grief. Grief
vomits bitterness. Bitterness spews rage. Each one ravaged him
as he watched through lenses from far off through the window
of her home.

For there, amid irrelevant ones, this blind one stirred desire, a tender
yearning he had long forgone—that blessed solace love.

Foreign, it found a barren berth, no nurturing warmth in which to
grow. Death had dwelt there far too long to yield an inch of room. And
yet he watched with aching heart, the fair and fallen maid, his own
Persephone?

Pitiful to think it, even worse imagining. He knew what he had
come for, and in it was no place for nursing starved emotions that never
would be filled. It would rather drain from him in parasitic drafts the
will to see his mission through.

Alone he'd come and single-minded. So he must remain. Yet he
bathed his dry and desolate eyes in this sweet and stolen sight of her.

Twenty-Five

Jonah left Sue's cruiser at the station, but kept her. From his Bronco, he called Trevor. This latest episode strengthened the link between his photos and the events here in Redford, yet it hadn't directly involved MacDaniel—that he knew of. Reaching Trevor's, he said, "We need to talk."

"Okay. Come by the store."

Surprised that he wasn't with Natalie, Jonah switched the turn signal and headed for the business next to his former crime scene. He didn't know that much about either guy. Tia had interacted with them and didn't consider Trevor an egotist, despite his former celebrity. In her opinion, he'd been knocked down a few times. She called Paul Whitman a regular guy who might stand out apart from Trevor.

So they were two active guys, whose business model fit the community, who gave back by helping people who got lost or in trouble in this rugged place. How did that make one of them a target? Jonah looked at the folder wedged between the seat and console. Having been a battered kid himself, those pictures incensed him. But he still had no context.

"So what are we doing?" Sue finally said.

"Retracing our steps. You haven't talked to Trevor MacDaniel. I want your impressions. Anything that strikes you."

She'd keep to the background, watch, listen. Her cynical eye didn't miss much. They went in and saw Trevor, belaying a kid on the climbing wall. At the same time, he instructed the boy beside him on the proper technique to lower what looked like a younger sister. A man who might be their dad hollered encouragement, moving his arms as though he were the instructor.

"I'll need a minute to finish here," Trevor said.

As Sue stayed to watch, Jonah walked around their operation, trying to see what might have drawn a predator's attention to Trevor MacDaniel.

Fame? Olympic medals, the publicized rescue of a toddler from a cougar? He didn't blend well into the background, but was that enough?

Trevor joined him beneath the wall-sized poster of a gold medal run. "Thanks for waiting. We can talk in my office."

Jonah glanced at the young female employee checking him out. Married, over thirty, with a kid on the way, didn't seem to dampen the enthusiasm.

Trevor's office was large enough for two desks, files, the usual computer, fax, printer setup. When Sue joined them, he introduced her. "Or maybe you've met?"

"I don't think so." Trevor extended his hand.

Sue took it silently, observing, measuring.

"How's Natalie?" Jonah said.

Trevor sighed. "It'll take a while."

He hated to pile on but had to ask, "Have you received any new photos?"

Trevor tensed. "Why?"

"Found a little boy hanging from a tree—"

The blood drained from Trevor's face.

"He's fine. Sorry. Didn't realize how that sounded." Or maybe he'd needed to see a reaction. "The child hung there all night, could have frozen if this storm had moved in sooner."

"Who was it?"

"Brody Pitman. Parents are Turk and Rolanda. Know them?"

"No."

"Both their boys think they've seen the devil."

"They have."

Jonah ran a hand through his hair. "Michaela thought he might be wearing a mask. The boys said maybe."

Shaking his head, Trevor sat against one of the two desks. "Nattie would have realized. No way her eye missed that."

"Through a window with the sun glaring? She told Tia she thought she'd hallucinated."

"It was no hallucination that fractured her skull." Trevor's tone darkened.

At the beeping Jonah reached down and silenced his page. "Let's go back to the photos. The first arrived…"

"Shortly after Cody's rescue. The others over a few weeks. Somewhere in there, Jazmyn Dufoe's article ran."

"What's her connection, do you think?"

"Are you asking if she's part of it?"

Jonah shrugged.

"I showed her the photos. Believe me, she had nothing to do with them. But she did learn something about the baby in the tree. The incident happened somewhere in Missouri, and he was recovered safely. Never made the news. Just a local story. Like this morning, I guess."

"And the others?" Sue said. "The boy in the swamp, the water tower?"

"She's still digging. That's one thing about Jaz. She never quits."

Uncomfortably true. "So we have disturbing photos, a bizarre drawing, and an extreme reaction to your statue."

"The way he looked at it?"

"The way he wanted to destroy it." That seemed like news to him. "Natalie used the words *worship* and *destruction*. Tia got the sense he might not know what he wants from you. But we know he'll use people to get it. Vulnerable people. Innocents."

"What can I do?" Trevor spread his hands, frustrated. "Lure him out? Make him come for me?"

He meant it, but that wasn't their first course. "The sheriff has deputies combing the land behind the Pitman place. Maybe the scene will give us something. In the meantime, stay close to Natalie, now that she's remembering."

"Remembering." Trevor's arms fell slack. "Him?"

"I thought you knew. She called me this morning."

"I need to go." He grabbed wallet and keys from his drawer. "You know how to reach me."

When the door shut behind him, Jonah turned to Sue, brows arched.

"If I was lost, I'd take his help."

"Tall, strong, and handsome?"

"I was thinking 'good.'" She flushed. "He reminds me of you."

Jonah answered the page as they walked out. The cape he took from Brody was a break, but Beatty and McCarthy redeemed themselves finding the vehicle parked behind the Laundromat. It came up stolen.

"There was only one thing in the duffel bag besides spare clothes," Beatty said. "An old book called *Paradise Lost.*"

———

Whit's text saved him the shock of not finding them at home, but the objective was to have Natalie in a secure location. Had Whit missed the finer points? Trevor forced himself to chill out as he drove. Coming in like a bad dream wouldn't help. But what else was this?

He passed the bakery and touched the brake, saw a parking space and took it. Laden with stuffed croissants, he rang Natalie's doorbell. Every other time he'd knocked or let himself in. But today he used the bell.

Whit admitted him with a muttered, "Sara's got nothing on her in stubbornness."

He hadn't thought Natalie stubborn, but that was because she did it so considerately. He walked into the kitchen, and his heart broke all over again, watching her try to find her way with the clay. She seemed as clumsy as a novice, and impatient, slamming her hands down in the closest thing to temper she'd ever shown.

He hugged her from behind, kissing her hair behind the bandage. Heat came off her head as though she was literally burning wood. How did the brain work? He'd never studied anatomy, never went to college at all. While Whit got an MBA, he'd been carving the slopes, then conceiving a business using what skills he had left. What was he even doing with a brilliant woman like Natalie?

He gave her neck a rub. "Don't force it."

"I need to show Jonah." She sounded slow and thick, her speech degraded from before. Probably fatigue. Maybe pain or the pain relief, if she'd taken it.

"Come have something to eat. Whit?"

"I'm going, but thanks anyway."

After eating, she went back to work. Clay filled the creviced web between her thumb and hand. Her nails were caked with gray brown that streaked her fingers. A smear darkened her cheek where she'd wiped sweat or a tear, but she still had no more than a vague head shape with rudimentary features.

"I...I can feel it, but I can't make it happen."

He wanted to tell her to stop trying, but he knew how it felt when only cutting the gates sharper and hugging a line that left no room for error would beat a competitor's time. He knew how it felt to cross the line with hundredths of seconds ticking off and hear the screams of applause. "Tell me what you feel."

She closed her eyes. "The first time I saw him, there was this pit of despair, a hunger that was famine and fury. There was destruction, but not toward me. Not even toward you except..." She sighed. "Then he saw me and pulled up his hood as though to shield me from his wounds."

"So you remember, but you don't see him."

"I remember it happening. But because I *saw* him, I don't remember the features."

"And the second time? When he hit you?"

She shook her head. "I hardly saw him. He was going for the statue. I tried to keep him from damaging it."

"You what?"

"I told him to stop."

She couldn't be serious, but she was. His chest felt hollow. "It's a statue, Nattie. If you'd let him have at it, you might have gotten away."

———

Having taken part in the church ladies' mission to the scarf- and gloveless, Fleur answered Piper's call with a lighter heart than she'd started the day with. She ran hot water into the sink. "You'll be happy to know I'm once again a productive member of society."

"Were you not?"

"Sadly, no. But the chance came up to do for others and—wait for it—I forgot about myself."

"Isn't that a funny thing?" Piper said. "Just like Miles when someone's in trouble."

Fleur squirted soap into the sink. "So what's up?"

"I thought you'd like to know, Natalie's out of the hospital."

Fleur shut the water off. "When?" It didn't surprise her that Piper knew first. Her bakery was the heart of town.

"Yesterday afternoon—except, are you ready for this? She's staying with Trevor MacDaniel."

"No way."

"Way," Piper said. "For protection. He said they can't spare any officers since they're all looking for the demon bat."

"He said demon bat?"

"No, sorry. Just quoting your Officer Newly."

So Natalie was with Trevor. Fleur slid a plate into the sudsy water. "I hope she keeps a clear head. I hope she *can*. Piper, how is she?"

"Trevor said okay. But really there's only one way to know."

"Reconnaissance mission?" Fleur bit her lip. "I don't know where he lives."

"We don't have to. She's at her house trying to model the guy who hit her."

"That's only a couple streets." Fleur straightened. "I accept this mission."

"Are you sure?"

"As soon as I finish the dishes. Neither sleet nor hail nor dark of night nor whatever will hold me back."

Piper laughed. "Yeah, all that. Call me, okay?"

Fleur made quick work of the cups and saucers the knitters had used. She packed breads and a quart of soup into a basket she carried over one arm, like Little Red Riding Hood off to Grandma's, then took her stick and stepped outside. Moisture settled on her face. More mist than snow, and the sidewalks seemed merely wet. Not cold enough to ice, she hoped, but walked with care, letting the cane tell her what might cause trouble.

From their morning walks, she knew the way as well from Natalie's description as when she could see. But she had no one seeing for her now. Her world was not utter darkness, but a vague twilight, a land of gloom and shadow.

This late in the day, she passed no one else on the residential street until the corner, where she heard quick, furtive steps. She paused. People always announced their presence with a greeting, a courtesy she deeply appreciated.

She could easily be marginalized, ignored, and avoided, but not in Redford, one of the reasons she stayed when her parents and younger siblings moved to Grand Junction. This was her place, her people. But whoever was there now made no effort.

"Hello?"

Nothing. An animal maybe. *No Big Bad Wolf,* she prayed. A deer, pausing to study her, though she caught no gamey scent. Tension found the muscles along her spine. Seth didn't want her walking alone. In her concern for Natalie, she'd forgotten. But it was only two blocks, and she would not be afraid.

———

Natalie turned when her doorbell rang, but Trevor caught her arm. "Please."

He seemed a little exasperated, but she didn't think the bad guy would ring her bell. Trevor opened the door, blocking with his body, then moved aside.

Her heart rushed. "Fleur!"

"You're not in bed?"

"She should be," Trevor muttered.

She hugged her friend. "You remember Trevor?"

"Why don't you two sit?" He clasped Fleur's elbow and led her to the couch.

Natalie sighed. "I'll fall asleep."

"Then I'll talk to Trevor," Fleur said.

Natalie felt a guilty relief when he moved into the kitchen with his phone. She'd seen his pity as she worked, accomplishing nothing over and over. It hurt him to see her like this. It hurt her.

Fleur squeezed her hand. "How are you?"

"You'd know, if you could see me. I'm looking right at you."

"No eidetic images?"

"And I've tried and tried to sculpt, but it's useless. I thought I had a gift, but all I did was paint by number."

"No," Fleur said. "I felt what you did."

"But not anymore. The clay is nothing but dirt and water."

"Have you tried it with your eyes closed?"

Natalie sank back in the couch. "Oh, Fleur."

"I'm serious."

"I'm too tired to think about it." But even as she said it, the thought took hold. If she stopped trying to see the way she used to, would her hands remember? Maybe her talent wasn't all centered on one anomaly. But then, her hands were clumsy as well, and her balance wasn't great, and talking took work. And so much energy. She was not herself, not at all herself.

Hearing Fleur and Trevor, she realized she had fallen asleep. With a soft moan, she opened her eyes.

"Feel better?" Trevor's mouth crooked up, a shade beneath smug.

"Sorry, Fleur."

"Don't be. At the risk of sounding giddy, I just spent forty minutes with gold medalist Trevor MacDaniel. And guess what—once the new slopes open, he's taking me out."

"A one-armed child and a blind woman. Trevor, you have a new vocation."

He seemed to seriously consider it. "I've resisted teaching people's privileged offspring. But this… You could be right."

The warmth in his eyes melted her. She was falling harder and deeper for this man every day.

They shared fruit, crusty rolls, and the quart of Piper's butternut soup that Fleur had brought. Then she said, "I'd better go before the snow gets serious."

Natalie hugged her tight. "Thank you for coming. I missed you." And to Trevor, "Will you take her home?"

"Yeah, but you're coming too."

"I think I'll just lie down."

He raised her to her feet. "I'll bed you down at my place."

Her mouth and Fleur's made matching hollows.

"You know what I mean."

But that didn't keep her heart from doing a giant slalom of its own.

Jonah studied the cape. The inside was sewn with large flat pockets, one holding cord like that used to suspend Brody Pitman, a used strip of duct tape in another. Common tools for abduction, although Michaela had not been bound. No bruising or residue to indicate it anyway.

With a frown between his brows, Jonah turned to the book. Along with the cape and horns, *Paradise Lost* might indicate an obsession with Lucifer, although most of the selected passages were of lamentation. He regretted what he did? Wanted to think he had a conscience?

Jonah frowned. He'd never actually read it, but he guessed the story didn't work out great for the protagonist. Did his share of damage, though. Was that what this was, an attempt to cause as much ruin as he could before they got him? That would be sooner rather than later, if he made even one mistake. Actually, the car, the cape, and Natalie were a start. The book... Well, they'd see about that.

He went home and found Jay on the porch of his cabin, as still as Enola standing beside him. His fingers barely touched the coydog's head, but they seemed to be in communion. Jay's black hair was pulled into a short tail at the nape of his neck, his coffee complexion warming in the sunset streaks breaking through the cloud-cluttered sky. They were looking for Scout.

Sometime, day before yesterday, the yearling pup had gone. Jay claimed he'd seen it coming. More coyote than his half-dog mother, Scout felt the wild. Maybe when it really got cold, he might come back, but the drive to breed and run and hunt with his own kind had proved stronger than human bonds.

Jonah climbed the porch steps. He hadn't asked Jay to keep watch on his family, but with his construction project stalled, Jay had spent a fair amount of time there. They went inside without speaking.

Sarge dozed by the fire, a shell of the man he'd been even the year before. Tia sat at the table studying. She would never have accepted this imprisonment if she wasn't imposing it on herself to complete the course work for her license.

He bent and kissed her. "Good news. I hired Moser's nephew."

"Does Moser's nephew have a name?"

"Yeah, but we'll never use it. He's a spitting image, so we're calling him Fax."

Her dark eyes were amused and relieved. "And the other two positions?"

"Working through résumés. Don't worry. I'll hold your dear dad to his promise."

Tia darted her brows up with a tip of her head toward Jay.

"Oh." Jonah grinned. "Sorry."

She sighed. "You may as well tell him."

Jay wore a perplexed expression when they filled him in. "Does that make you mayorette?"

She rolled her eyes. "It makes me annoyed we're talking about it. Besides, I only have Sarge's word. It's not like mommy dearest or Owen Buckley filled me in."

"Might come in handy." Jonah chucked her chin. "Never know."

She put a hand to her belly. "I swear this baby kicks every time you talk, Jonah."

"She's a daddy's girl," Jay said.

Tia looked from Jay to him. Since they'd learned the gender but decided not to tell, she obviously thought he'd cheated.

Tia pinned Jay with a stare and said, "How do you know it's a girl?"

"The way you move."

"You're watching me move?"

Jay pulled apple cider from the refrigerator. "Little things register."

"What things?"

"A softer step. A sway." He shrugged. "It's your face too."

"My face?"

"If it was a boy, you'd have a warrior face."

Jonah didn't say she had a killer warrior face whenever she wanted to.

Tia cocked a brow. "And what will you say if it's a boy?"

"Congratulations."

Sarge stirred and opened his eyes. "Chief."

"Hey, old man," Jay said—their joke, giving him Jonah's title.

Sarge pointed a finger. "That nurse Lauren isn't through with you."

"Oh, she's very through."

Tia tipped her head. "Are you ever going to say what happened?"

Jay's stoic face was all the answer they'd get.

Tia turned to Sarge. "Piper came by with muffins."

"By herself?" Jonah asked.

"Oh, she's immune. Don't you know lightning won't strike twice?"

"The guy broke into her bakery. That's twice in my book."

"She carries pepper spray."

"I know. I got her law-enforcement strength."

"There, see?"

He set Milton among Tia's strewn textbooks. "We think this belongs to our guy. Could you scrutinize the underlined passages and give me some insight? Looks like there are notes in the margins, but I can't make sense of them."

Tia took the book, her face curious. *"Paradise Lost."*

"It's the only personal item we found in the car, besides clothes."

"It's old." She studied the winged accuser on the cover. "Maybe a special edition. The cover usually has Adam and Eve, being forced out of Eden."

"That looks like Lucifer, and he's pretty grim."

She looked up. "In that drawing, didn't you say he made Trevor an angel?"

Jonah met her eyes. "If he sees Trevor as a warrior angel and himself as this, it could be a showdown, a clash of good and evil."

She flipped open the cover. "Let me see what aspects of Satan he identifies with. I guess you need it right away?"

He spread his hands. "Before anyone else gets hurt."

More destroyed than thus,
We should be quite abolished, and expire.
What fear we then? What doubt we to incense
His utmost ire?

He crept back and stopped, frozen. Confused, he searched, back and forth with his eyes then himself. Here. He'd left it here. He scanned the back of the Laundromat. The car was parked here. But it wasn't.

His hands clenched as the realization sank in. No no—No! A scream rose up. He choked on it, eyes watering. They might be watching. If they found the car, they'd be watching, waiting for him.

He saw no one, but crept into a shadow deeper than the night. The car meant nothing. The clothes were nothing. One cape he'd given the boy; the other covered him now. The rest was worthless.

Except the book. Only the book. Always the book mattered. He tossed back his head, unable to stop the cry.

Hastily, he had scrambled out of his shelter this morning—almost discovered—leaving all in the car until he found a new place to hide. And now...

Gone. It was gone. Weeping in rage, he paced the cage around the commercial trash bin. The words were his, learned and memorized, but still he needed it, would not be without it. How could they take his only solace?

They would pay. He would make them pay. He would take what they treasured, what *the chosen* treasured. He had never struck in vengeance, but now, for this, there could be no recourse but retribution. For this loss, they would pay!

Twenty-Six

Natalie gasped. No breath would come, as out of the smoke the face appeared. In the face—pain, rage, violence. The face she couldn't remember. Ruined flesh, gaping mouth. Wider and wider it opened, sucking her into the mud, the slag gargling in its throat. She thrashed, trying, but unable to form him as the clay swallowed her.

"Nattie. Honey. Stop thrashing."

Groaning, she dragged up to the surface, consciousness returning with a dull throb across her head. Night draped the bedroom in black, Trevor all but invisible. She winced when he turned on the lamp.

"Bad one?"

She sat up, rubbing her eyes. "At least Cody wasn't in it."

"You know he's safe. Not so sure I've got you covered."

"No, Trevor."

"Hey." He took her hands down. "It's natural. I screwed up."

"Please don't say that." She pulled the covers to her chin, chilled and sweaty from the dream. "It was a nightmare, not a condemnation."

"Want to tell me about it?"

She blew out her breath. "His face."

"You saw it?"

"I saw what it was in my dream. Right before the slag sucked me in like quicksand."

"No wonder you thrashed." He sat on the bed and rubbed her knee.

"I'm sorry I woke you."

"I wasn't asleep."

The clock read 1:00 a.m. "Worried?"

"Frustrated." The mattress creaked when he slid over beside her, tucking an arm around her shoulders. "I keep trying to get why he targeted me. What triggered his fixation?"

She rested her head in the hollow where shoulder met chest. He felt warm and smelled musky. "You're larger than life. I doubt too many nor-mal Joes get stalked."

"I'm just a guy."

"Sorry, Trevor. You're not just a guy. You make miracles. Do you really think that goes unnoticed?"

"Miracles." He shook his head. "I stopped looking for miracles when Ellis died."

"That doesn't mean they stopped happening. I see them in beauty, in goodness, even in the pain and suffering that give souls depth and nobility."

"In what happened to you?" He stabbed the heart of it.

"It's a storm now, but I'm watching for the rainbow."

Something tender creased his brow. "You make me want to believe."

"Then believe."

"Maybe I do." He braced her face, pressing his forehead to hers. "Aaron told me to pray in the hospital. I half expected a crack to open up and swallow me."

"Yet here you are."

His eyes crinkled. "Not even a whiff of sulfur."

"I could have told you that."

He sobered. "I prayed for this."

"Nuh-uh."

He stroked her arm. "I wanted you back in my life, and..."

Her eyes teared.

"Now I'm making you cry."

She laughed. "Stop it."

"Can we do this, Nattie? Would you want to marry me, knowing everything you know?"

He rendered her speechless.

"That's the other reason I'm awake. I keep wondering if it's fair. Can you see us together? Kids and battles and wrinkles?"

She pulled her feet up under her. "Don't you think it's a little soon?"

"To imagine?" He cocked his brow. "I thought every woman—"

"I don't race down mountains, Trevor. I don't rappel in blizzards or chase mountain lions. I snowplow."

His mouth pulled. "Can't feel the slope?"

"I don't like being out of control, and I *don't* like falling."

He said, "You know what it feels like."

"Of course I do."

He took her hand. "Because that guy broke your heart."

Her jaw fell slack. "Aaron has a big mouth."

"He was making sure it didn't happen again."

Aaron of all people should know there were no guarantees. "Well, it doesn't matter, so forget it."

"Are you kidding me? My life's an autopsied corpse."

"Nice image."

"But true. What haven't I told you?"

She sighed. "I was amazingly naive. No, not naive, infantile. He—"

"What's his name?"

"Gage Valerian."

"Be serious."

"I am. Gage Remington Valerian. I should have known right there," she said ruefully. "He's some minor politician now."

"A slick talker with a ready handshake and a dagger in his belt. What happened?"

"My brain happened."

"Shallow chump. I hate politicians."

"He had big aspirations. I was hardly able to handle people at all. Too weird, too freaky, too impaired. I was still trying to be like everyone else, but I couldn't."

He stroked her fingers with his thumb. "His loss, big time."

At the time it felt like hers. "I believed he wanted a life with me. I imagined every minute of it. Then I didn't have to imagine, because we made it real. Only it wasn't real. Not for him."

The muscles in his throat worked. "I won't take advantage of you."

"I know. But I still…"

"Need to be sure."

She sighed.

"Don't. It's perfectly reasonable." He rubbed his face. "Think you can sleep now?"

She yawned. "We both need to."

Rising, he leaned over and kissed her. "I won't be far."

Watching him go, she wished she'd said what her heart knew. *You're everything I want.*

———

Swilling the barely palatable coffee, Jonah looked up from his desk when Moser filled the doorway, his uniform impeccable. Sue pressed in beside him, rumpled and flushed. *Laurel and Hardy.* She'd kick him to Kansas if she could read that thought. Besides, she hadn't retained that much after the baby.

Setting down his cup, he said, "What?"

"State called," Moser started.

Sue ran over him, saying, "They found a DNA match to that fingernail."

Jonah raised his eyes to Moser.

"Evan Zachary McCabe. Came up in the missing and exploited children database."

That took the wind out. With the printer clacking behind him, jerking and spitting pages into the tray, he wished he could press rewind and back them out of the room before anything more was said. "What's the story?"

Moser passed the baton to Sue, who said, "He's from Jackson, Mississippi. Went missing when he was six years old. Parents ran the local pharmacy—the nonlegal kind."

He waited.

"They claimed someone took the kid out of his bed, but he'd been known to go out scrounging for food whenever they were not in the mood to cook edible stuff. Like every day." She hardly contained her disgust.

A six-year-old wandering the streets, going through the trash, maybe knocking on doors. A regular pattern, most likely. Until the wrong door opened. Jonah clenched his jaw. "Anything else?"

Moser said, "I asked the detective on the case to fax everything they have. Evan's still officially missing."

Of course he was. Jonah's stomach collapsed like the target of a wrecking ball. They'd identified him. But it didn't feel good.

———

Trevor gave the code over the intercom to admit Tia and Carolyn when they came to check on Natalie. He met them at the elevator and brought them up. Sensing they wanted time alone with her, he said, "Let me know when you're getting ready to leave. I need to go to work, but I'll come right back when you're done."

Natalie followed him to the door. "If you have things to do, I'll be fine. I'm in a fortress."

Hardly impenetrable, but his address wasn't in the directory, so his twisted admirer might not realize where he lived or that she was here. Might not. "Let me know before you're all done."

She said, "Okay."

He held her eyes, then he left. She wouldn't be alone, and this was important. Whit had called him in for a state-of-the-business conference, but he found the whole family in the office.

Sara flushed. "Trevor, how are you?" She pulled his cheek down for a kiss.

"I'm okay, thanks." He squeezed her shoulder and took the baby. "Did you put more sand in this sandbag? He could hold up a dike."

"Are you calling my baby fat?"

"He's solid. Sturdy." He kissed the soft head. "Why do babies smell so good?"

"Product. Hate to break it to you, but he'd smell like mustard and spit-up milk if it weren't for baby shampoo and diaper cream." Her eyes had a hint of tears. She was trying hard, but their last encounter hadn't gone well. It seemed like years ago. He should have called.

Caitlyn poked her head in. "Um, Trevor..."

Leaning around her, Jonah said, "Can I have a minute?" By his expression, the news wasn't good.

"Come in."

Jonah opened a folder, took out the angel drawing, and laid it on the desk. Trevor shifted Braden to see the paper he set down next. A copy of...a book cover? It looked like Satan on it. Trevor looked from one picture to the other, realizing they were chillingly similar.

"What is it?"

"Paradise Lost."

That told him nothing.

Sara said, "It's an epic poem about the fall of man."

Jonah glanced at her, Whit, and the baby. "Maybe we should—"

"These are my friends, Chief, and considering what happened to Natalie, I'm not keeping them in the dark."

"Okay." Jonah tapped the picture. "Does that book mean anything to you?"

"I've never heard of it."

"Well, Tia thinks he's identifying with the fallen angel and sees you as his nemesis, perhaps Michael the archangel who threw him down from heaven."

"What, is he nuts?"

"Possibly. The DNA we found in Natalie's studio matches a child abducted eleven years ago. Evan McCabe."

Dread stiffened his back.

"The abductor was a professor of medieval studies, specializing in the Dark Ages." Jonah gave the last words the sinister tone they deserved.

For the first time, he imagined a worse fate for Ellis than falling to his death. The memory came back so hard he smelled the summer air, trees and grass, and sweaty bodies. He saw Ellis, tall for five, unwieldy like a colt, his eyes begging him to stay. The team waiting, needing their star. Whit's eyes burning. *"Come on, Trevor. Let's go."*

Little brothers were always there; this basketball game would establish their dominance once and for all. He remembered the stretch and agility of his body, basketball his main outlet in the years off skiing as his muscles came into their man strength. He'd felt like Superman, leaping tall buildings in a single bound.

"The kid is wanted for questioning in the professor's murder."

Whit said, "He killed him?"

Jonah shrugged. "He would have been twelve years old."

"And now he's what?" Trevor asked.

"Seventeen."

"So it's kidnapping. You can bring in the FBI?"

"As far as we can tell, he's acting on his own, Trevor. There's no coercion."

"There was."

"It ended five years ago."

Trevor tipped his head back, frustrated. "So, what then?"

Jonah said, "I need to show Natalie a photo, see if she can confirm that the person who struck her—"

"Fine. Follow me over." He turned to Whit. "Can we do this later?"

"I'll wait." Whit, always magnanimous.

Borne on the shoulders of his teammates, he'd gotten Conner's message. Then the desperate search, begging God, bargaining. Give him Ellis and take anything. The rusty railing over the drainage ditch. The broken little body.

Pain, sorrow. Guilt, the awful crushing guilt.

"Trevor?" Sara's voice penetrated.

He loosened his grip on Braden.

"I'm leaving now too," she said. "Walk me out?"

"Okay." Bearing Braden, he walked her to the car. The day was crisp and clear, no hint of summer anywhere. There were things to say, so he shoved the past back to the shadows and said, "Thank you for the meals."

She unlocked and opened the door. "I hope they helped."

"They still are."

"That's right. Natalie's there." She tossed a blanket out of the car seat. "For protection."

This couldn't go on. "I've never lied to you, Sara. I'm not starting now."

Tears sparkled in her eyes as she gave him one more chance at denial. "You love her."

"I guess the things that made it impossible before are breaking down. I want you to be happy with Whit, and I want to be happy too."

She sniffed. "I know. I just...don't want to lose you."

"Nothing will stop our friendship. You matter. You always have."

"I love you."

"I love you too."

She reached for the baby. "I'm sorry I said the things I did. Natalie's..."

"It's okay." He transferred Braden's wobbly weight. "When you get to know her, you can share your honest opinion."

As she bent to load Braden, Trevor looked around at the denuded aspen branches, their trunks rubbed by mule deer antlers, the creek as low as it would be until snowmelt. Everything was winding down.

She drew her head out and spread her arms. "Hug?"

"Of course." He held her an extra beat, remembering the stiffening grief of Ellis's death they'd shared, the soul-breaking sobs. He could not have made a life with her, so intimately tied to that pain, but still he cared. "No one knows me the way you do. Not even Whit."

The other women had been placeholders, aborted attempts to move past this relationship into something that could work.

"Is it Ellis?" Her voice trembled.

"Yes." Natalie knew about but hadn't been in it. "I have to let go."

Sara nodded tearfully, understanding, he hoped. After one more squeeze, she got in. He watched her drive away, then realized Jonah had pulled around and was waiting, watching. Fine. He had nothing to hide.

———

Relieved that they hadn't come to help her see something she couldn't, Natalie enjoyed Tia and Carolyn. The respect and affection between the older and younger woman was beautiful, and it embraced her.

"That scent is perfect for you," Tia said, smelling the essential oil she had created. "I'm always amazed how people choose the right ones."

"It's the one I liked best."

"I brought something else, though. For the headache."

She said, "How did you know…"

"A fractured skull?" Tia raised her eyebrow. "I'm guessing there's a headache."

"I thought it would be gone by now. But I'm still not right. Simple things are hard." That was more than she'd told anyone, but these women were healers. She could feel it.

Tia took a bottle of oil from her purse. "May I rub this on your wrists and temples?"

"Of course."

Tia came around behind the couch. She must have opened it, because the aroma filled the air. Her hands were astonishing. "Carolyn would like to intercede for your continued healing, if that's all right."

"More than all right." As one prayed and one ministered, she felt the dull, underlying headache ease. Tired and dizzy, thick and slow after so many days, she'd been frustrated and frightened, but a sense of well-being overcame it all. She wasn't forsaken.

Weeping may tarry for the night, but joy comes with the morning. She didn't know if Tia said it or that line from the psalm just came to her. Whatever happened would still be God's plan.

Vaguely she realized other voices had joined the women's. She must have dozed, but tuned into the discussion in progress.

"It's not great timing, Jonah."

"Can't be helped. I need this."

She opened her eyes. Trevor and Jonah were both there. She straightened. "What is it?"

The chief said, "Sorry to interrupt, but I have a six-pack of headshots I'd like you to look at. For identification."

"I'll try." Doubtful it would do any good, she studied each one, still amazed, though less dismayed, that nothing happened. She could live with it. That unicorn horn had gotten in the way.

Almost through the six photos, sadness lodged in her chest. She touched the middle photo on the bottom row. "This one. Except his face was scarred."

"Are you sure?"

"Well, it's only memory…"

The chief's eyes softened. He returned the folder to his jacket. "Can you remember anything else?"

And suddenly, she did. She gripped the edge of the couch. "He didn't strike me."

"What?"

"It wasn't an attack. I ran into the pedestal. The sculpture fell." The weight. The sharp, searing pain. Him bending over. *Blood. Too much blood.* His fear…for her.

Trevor said, "He had a crowbar."

"It tested negative for blood," Jonah told him.

"He didn't hurt me." She looked from one to the other. "I think he tried to help."

———

In the darkness, Tia held him. The case file, the photos found at the abductor's home told a story too wretched to express. What he'd seen and learned about Evan McCabe drove him to his knees, but he found no peace.

"How can we do this? How can we bring a child into this world?"

"Our baby will have us, Jonah." She ran her hand down his side, brushing the bullet hole.

His skin shied from her touch. "It's not possible to watch every minute."

"We'll watch all the possible minutes." She caught his hand and brought it to her belly. "She knows you'll do anything for her."

Thinking of his tiny daughter struck terror inside. "If I had a cop on every corner, they'd still find a way. My father *was* a cop. *Oh, Tia.* Am I walking in his footsteps?"

"He only wanted power. You want people safe and justice done."

He rolled to his back. "I want a drink." It seized him with a mind grip like a claw on his brain, in his throat and chest.

"But you won't." Tia stroked his face. "Because it can't help. It never will."

His hands clenched. "I'm hunting a victim. A child hurt worse than I ever—"

"He's not a child anymore."

"Where were we when he was? Where were all the others?" How could they fail so many and let the cycles go on and on and on? Sins of the fathers. Mothers. Neighbors. Sins of humanity upon the innocent.

"You'll do the right thing." Her touch soothed him, healed him, drew him. He turned and loved her until the driving ache had dulled. "Don't ever excuse me," he rasped. "If I hurt you, hurt her—"

"You won't." Her eyes flamed. "If I thought there was even the chance, I wouldn't be here."

Now conscience wakes despair,
That slumbered; wakes the bitter memory
Of what he was, what is, and what must be...

S till distraught, but having begun the process of revenge, he freed
the flimsy latch on the sliding door into the darkening porch.
Tomorrow would bring him one step closer, but now he must hide,
hide and rest if it were possible. Sharp white moonlight through tattered
clouds illuminated the overburdened shelves. He found ferns and vines,
and flower boxes—and one cloth-covered mound.

Surely not useful, he moved past it, then, strangely apprehensive,
returned. He raised the drape and staggered back. Gaping holes stared
accusingly, a death mask probing him. Terror turned his limbs to water.
He sank down and drew his knees tightly to his chin. His legs would not
hold him if he tried. Groping, he crawled to a corner of the porch behind
the shelves and huddled, shaking while the empty eyes stared, pitiless.

By some queer twist, he slept, unconcerned that the one who left
before dawn would notice him. He had seen her going other days before
the sun rose in the sky. Hidden by the plants, even if she ventured into the
room, he'd be safe.

Mist awakened him, a chill breath on his cheek. The light was dull.
The air damp with foliage and soaked earth. She stood over him with a
spray bottle, touching ferns with sensitive fingers and issuing mist to the
greedy fronds. On the shelf behind her, the model gaped, but he saw now
it was her face. Her mien with hollowed eyes.

She turned and carried the bottle to the opposite shelf, pausing when
her hand encountered clay instead of cloth. Her head tipped as she

pondered. Reaching down, she groped and found the covering. Paused again, wondering. "Hello?"

He could be silent, so silent. No breath, no motion, not even a twitch.

She lifted the cloth, draped the head and sprayed. *Fwit. Fwit. Fwit.*

Gray light filtered over her features. She placed the misting bottle in the corner, turned her head once to listen over her shoulder, then went into the house.

She came again, soon after, hovering in the doorway between kitchen and porch, sensing him? Finally, she entered, set a fresh canvas on the easel at one end and rolled a cart over from the wall. The cart held paints. The chemical smell rose up as she opened and squeezed dabs of certain ones onto a palette.

He ached from sitting, but made no move. His body was under his control, and pain had no power. He would watch. A shadow, nothing more. And yet his presence troubled her, a tightening between her shoulder blades. A pause between brush strokes. She knew, but didn't know. Didn't want to know.

Twenty-Seven

Fleur pushed the grays over the canvas, matching the drizzle she'd felt in the morning. The air pressure lent this storm substance, or maybe it was something else that raised the tiny hairs at the back of her neck. Her brush faltered from drawing a pewter swath through the white beside it, and she said, "Who are you? What do you want?"

Her heart stopped when he said, "To watch."

Fear clogged her throat like the stopper in a drain. "Because I'm blind?"

"Yes."

"How long have you been hiding?" The thought of him there…

"My whole life."

The swelling in her airway let a ragged breath through. "How did you get in?"

"Your inadequate lock." His voice sounded thin and reedy as from disuse or nervous tension.

Trembling, she turned back to the canvas and said, "Do I have the colors right for the coming storm?"

He shifted behind the shelf at her back. A ridge of nerves tightened down her spine.

"Just right."

She felt the edge of the canvas, gauged where she'd left off, and dragged the brush, top to bottom. He waited silently as each successive stroke depleted the paint in the fibers, then she added more white and pulled it into the preceding strokes. She worked a flurry of it into the top right quadrant.

It wouldn't do any good to scream. Her neighbors were at work. Run? She'd flail helplessly until he seized her. And there was something pleading in his tone. It might be hunger, she thought, since he'd broken into the bakery. "Would you like something to eat?"

He waited a long moment before answering. "Hunger is nothing."

"But if you had something, you'd eat?" After more silence, she shrugged. "I might make something."

She put her brush in turpentine and wiped her hands on a cloth, damp with the same. She pulled the painting smock over her head and laid it across the quilt rack. Carefully she made her way to the kitchen and washed with soap and water. She could dial 911, but she'd heard him follow and guessed he was watching.

Piper had brought home blue cheese and sausage croissants. Fleur liked them, and they were easy to warm in the toaster oven. She brewed a pot of hot water. "Tea or cocoa?"

His voice sounded strained when he said, "Cocoa."

With shaking hands, she scooped the cocoa into a mug. "Is it snowing?"

"It's wet."

The air felt ponderous. She put mugs of chocolate and crockery plates at two places, then brought the croissants from the oven to the trivet on the table. She sat but didn't hear the scrape of another chair. She did hear the sip of lips drawing hot chocolate.

Taking a croissant, she bit into the warm rich pastry, then set it on her plate. "My roommate makes these."

"I know."

He knew Piper lived there and ran the bakery? She forced herself to calm. "You should eat."

A shuffle, then the sounds of frantic chewing and swallowing.

"Please take more. They can only be warmed once before they get tough."

She bit into her own, blessing Piper for friendship and joy. She hoped Miles would one day break through his fears and become the person Piper saw. She hoped Natalie would recover her ability or find peace with its loss. That she and Trevor would make it. And for herself? She prayed Jonah and Seth would find her in time.

She licked her buttery fingers, then dabbed them on the napkin and drank her hot chocolate, now warm and silky. "Would you like some more?"

No answer.

"The water's hot. It's no trouble."

Nothing.

She sat frozen. Was he staring at her? The moisture left her mouth. Her limbs felt as brittle as dry sticks. The skin rose on her arms like a rash. If he grabbed her, she'd scream. There'd be no stopping it. She felt the scream building.

She reached for her cane, moved it through the air, touching nothing. Rising, she heard the door in the porch slide open, slide closed. Cold air drifted in.

Her heart pumped against her ribs. It didn't mean he was gone. He could be luring her. She knew she shouldn't, but couldn't stop herself.

Moving into the chilled space, she breathed for a scent of him, but the plants in their soil and the oil paints masked other odors. She pressed her cane behind one tiered shelf and then the other. Nothing. Shaking, she flipped the lock and felt the air grow still.

———

Followed by officers Donnelly and Newly, Jonah approached Fleur's home. He'd brought Sue to take the statement if it got delicate. Newly had picked up the radio correspondence and come over on his own. Jonah warned him not to make this personal, but Newly's color was up.

Fleur was clearly shaken as she admitted them, but nowhere near hysterical. No signs of physical trauma—bruising or bleeding. And no signs of a struggle—bumped furniture or anything spilled or broken. His gut told him the violation was to the premises, not herself, but he said, "Are you all right?"

"I think so."

"I have Officer Donnelly and Officer—"

"Did you let him in?" Newly blurted. "I warned you about—"

"He let himself in," she said and showed them into the sun porch. "Through here."

Jonah surveyed the space, dim with the incoming storm, but she hardly needed light to work by. Sue went over and checked the door, indicating Fleur had relocked it. Couldn't blame her for that.

Her hand shook when she pointed. "He was behind the shelf."

"Just standing there?" Newly stalked over.

"Sitting, I think, to start with. He spoke from down low."

"Can you describe his voice?" Jonah asked.

"Not really high or low, but thin."

"Young?"

"I'd say yes, except it also sounded old, or weary. I asked what he wanted and he said to watch me."

"Watch you what?" Newly demanded.

Jonah sent him a look to amp it down.

"He watched me paint. And then I got some food."

"You fed him?" Newly all but came out of his skin.

"Newly," Jonah murmured. One more outburst and he'd boot him. "Did he ask for food?"

"No. I just thought he seemed hungry. He had a croissant and cocoa. And then he left."

"Did you wash up the dishes?"

"No."

Sue moved into the kitchen to collect them.

Jonah asked, "Did he say anything else?"

"He said he's been hiding his whole life."

Tears pooled and fell, whether a release of tension or sympathy he couldn't tell. "That's good recall, Fleur. Anything else?"

"Not re—"

"Where's your head!"

Jonah turned, furious. But Newly wasn't looking at Fleur. He was looking at the shelves.

"Your sculpture, Fleur. Did you move it?"

She grew still. "No. But I found it uncovered this morning." She slipped a lock of hair behind her ear. Her voice tightened. "Did he take it?"

Jonah said, "Newly, search the house. Sue, take a look around outside." He put a hand on Fleur's shoulder. "I'm going to find him. In the meantime, can you stay with someone?"

She frowned. "Natalie's with Trevor, and Piper—"

Newly strode back in. "It's not here, Chief."

No telling why the wretch took the model, but Newly had caught what the rest of them missed. "Good work, Newly. Now get out of here. You're off duty."

He said, "Put me on security for Fleur."

That was not a bad option, if she was up for it. He looked from one to the other. "I guess it's up to her."

———

Fleur shivered to think her home had been invaded. Pathetic as he'd seemed, he had intruded into her personal space, making light of her "inadequate lock." She had flipped it every night, with the obligatory tug to feel the door catch, turned her back to walk inside. Had he been watching? Had others? The back of her neck felt clammy. The porch was all windows, her favorite place. Even though she couldn't see more than a specter of light, she could feel it.

Seth said, "You okay staying here? If not, you can wait at my place until Piper gets off. Good thing you won't see it, though."

"You're sweet, Seth. But I know how hard you've all been working. You need a day off."

"To do what? Laundry?"

She tipped her head. "Do you need to?"

"Well, yeah."

"We'll go there then." She felt bitter relief in that thought. "And Seth?" She clutched the arm he offered. "Please don't tell people about my self-portrait. I'm horrified that he has it." She could feel Seth's stare.

"That guy broke in and terrorized you, and you're horrified he has your statue?"

She didn't expect him to understand. "Please."

"Well, you know I won't tell. I'm on the hook for it anyway."

She smiled sympathetically.

"Chief's too busy to realize just yet."

She said, "Maybe he'll forget altogether."

"Yeah." He sounded doubtful. "You ready?"

Sadly, too ready.

———

Driving in for a day of in-house survival training, Trevor phoned Jonah and asked, "Anything?"

"Nothing you're hoping to hear." The man sounded harried.

"He can't just vanish."

"Think about it," Jonah said. "He breaks in and holes up in any of the vacant or temporarily empty places. Even though we're still trying to reach people and find ways to check them out, he might be back in one we already searched."

"How's he getting around? I thought you found his car."

"There've been three stolen in the past two days. All recovered in city limits and no sign of him."

"What's he living on?"

"Whatever he gets. Some of the time-shares and cabins have canned and dry goods."

He gripped the wheel, frustrated. "What about the FBI?"

"He hasn't committed a felony or—"

"Natalie's assault—"

"Was an accident. According to Natalie herself."

He hadn't been able to shake that conviction. True or not, she believed it. "Michaela was no accident. Wreckless endangerment at least."

"We'll question the suspect when we find him."

"If."

Jonah blew out his breath. "Trevor, I know how dangerous he might be. But until he does something—"

"Like murder?"

"A Mississippi detective wanting to question a twelve-year-old victim six years after the fact doesn't make him guilty. I know it sounds like I'm making excuses, but this is reality. The mayor wants us to handle it, but even without that I still have nothing to take to any other agency."

Trevor frowned. "So we wait until he strikes? Someone as vulnerable as Fleur again?"

"He didn't hurt her. Never touched her. I don't mean that as callously as it sounds. I know it scared her. And sure, there's unlawful entry, but there's no criminal code for observing a painter."

The weight of it settled on him.

"All we have is fear he might do something, based on pictures of events no one can verify. For all we know, he was trying to prove himself to you."

"As what? My dark side?"

A beat, then, "Maybe so."

Trevor pulled his SUV into the lot and said, "Just so you know, Chief, I'm not waiting for a crime. If I have something to go on, I'm acting."

"Don't make me come after you instead of the one we want."

"Got it." He parked and strode to the door, unlocked it and looked down.

An envelope lay on the wet stoop, snow collecting on its edges. Snatching it up, he tore it open and took out the photo. He had a moment of disconnect before realizing it was of him—holding Braden.

No. No no no no no!

He rushed back to his car and squealed out of the lot. He didn't see Whit's, but Sara's car was in their driveway. He charged the door and found it locked.

"Sara!" He hammered with his palm, his pulse hammering in his neck.

She pulled it open, eyes wide. "What?"

"Where's Braden?" He gripped her shoulders. "Where is he?"

Whit came up behind with his son against his chest. Trevor thrust the photo at him. "This was at the door." His throat felt like someone had run blades through it.

The color left Whit's swarthy cheeks. His hand tightened around his son's head. "What—"

"You need to get out of here. Take your family out of here."

"We're not leaving you alone." Sara's voice shook.

Whatever debt they thought they owed was long paid. He said, "Sara, you have to. I can take care of myself, but not all the rest of you."

"You don't know. He might be..." She read his determination and raised her chin. "All right. I'll take Braden and go stay with my mother." She turned. "Whit—"

"I've got his back."

While I to Hell am thrust,
Where neither joy nor love, but fierce desire,
Among our other torments not the least.

Cradling her face, he slipped through storm and cold to a new refuge, moving, moving constantly, carrying her now into a half-formed mansion sitting idle. Like a king in space so vast, chamber upon empty chamber, he held her gently, bearing her secret like his own. Not death eyes, but loss, deep and hollow. Pits of loss and longing that drove inside him like stakes.

For his loss, the consuming insult and injury, he wanted to strike back! He'd found the object, the tool to exact pain and suffering, and yet her eyes...

Setting her tenderly in the corner, the cavities watching with pity, her blindness, blessed blindness that, not seeing, had not recoiled. To follow his vengeful course, to betray the mission that lifted him from ashes would now betray her also. Agony and indecision.

He had come to challenge, to force the hand, even destroy! But... not an innocent. Not one like himself. As he was. Once.

He felt it crumble, all his grand delusion. What lies, what figments he'd woven. What was he that even hell would deign receive him? Weeping, he rocked. Rocked and rocked. Then, tears deserting, arid heaves and sobs. Nothing. He was nothing. And now he knew his course.

He had left one message one place, another in the other. The guardian must choose.

From the door, along the base of the mountain, in borrowed boots and winged cape, he plodded. In a hut, the metal door yielded, the lever pulled. Engine whirring, he climbed aboard and rose.

At the right moment, he leapt, sliding, skidding, rolling. Gaining his feet, he trudged through snow like heaps of ash. The time was now, and he must come, heaven's chosen. He had thought to carry, captive, one cherished babe. But in truth, the child was already lost and crying to be found.

Twenty-Eight

Leaving Whit and Sara, Trevor answered Natalie's call. He'd left her only an hour ago, trying once more with clay, this time in his kitchen. "What's up, Nat?"

"I think you'd better come home."

Again his neck muscles tightened. "Is something wrong?"

"You got mail."

What? There? "Did it come to the door?"

"Urgent. I signed for it, but there's no return address."

"Don't open it." He wheeled out of Whit's and tore down the wooded lane and onto the highway. Jonah had a point about the impossibility of finding someone hiding in this terrain with the nature of the community. The locals were tight, but half the population transient.

Natalie met him at the door. Except for his name and *home* address, the envelope was blank. Maybe that car the other night, before Natalie was attacked…

If the guy knew where to find him, why hurt her? Trevor scowled. He still couldn't believe it had gone down the way she claimed.

The purple hollows had paled, the crease between her brows smoothed. Her eyes were brighter and her speech had almost no lag until she got tired, though her motor skills and balance had a ways to go. The blow still seemed to have destroyed whatever anomaly caused her eidetic memory.

She said, "Open it, Trevor."

He didn't want to. Braden was safe, but reluctance dragged at him. Two missives in one day? What was this guy trying to say?

"It's not going away."

He tore open the envelope and stared at the photo, a closeup of a young boy's face, haunted eyes mutely pleading. Eerily close to that last expression of Ellis's, it clamped his heart like a vise. This had to stop. He had to stop it. He turned over the photo and, for the first time, found words: *angel falls.*

Angel. This innocent child? Or him? Was he calling the archangel, challenging his nemesis? Falls. Falls from grace, falls to hell, falls to his death? Whichever one of them it was, he had to know where the angel would fall, and why.

"Trevor?" Natalie's voice hardly registered.

Angel falls. Why did that strike a chord? Something... He recalled a conversation—with Tia? He took out his phone and found her in the contacts. "Tia, this is Trevor. Does 'angel falls' sound familiar to you?"

She paused a beat, then asked, "Why?"

"It's bumping around in my head."

"Isn't it one of the new ski runs at Kicking Horse? In the basin maybe?"

The black double-diamond that would follow the ridge and plunge down the clifflike hollow. "Is Jonah in his office?"

"No," she said. "County court. It's a grand jury. They drag on forever."

"Can he take a call?"

"Not when he's testifying. Officer Moser—"

"If you talk to him, tell him 'Angel Falls.'" The chief would come if he could, but this was obviously personal, something between him and a young man—a monster?—he'd never met. He hung up and told Nattie, "I need to go."

"Please don't."

He looked at the photo, heart kicking. "This kid's in danger. Just like Cody. It's what I do." He hugged her hard. "Don't worry. I'm coming back." Adrenaline charged him. No more waiting and worrying. Race day.

He called Whit. Their dialogue was short, no time wasted in argument. Whit would organize a search. Trevor was going on ahead.

He loaded ski gear and drove to the resort parking lot closest to the hardest runs. They hadn't opened, but the snow base was building, and once they started operating the snow machines, the slopes would fill with an elite clientele. Today's snow came hard enough to limit visibility, but he could still see that, strangely—or maybe not—the lift to the basin was running.

He put on the pack that held things he'd need—rope, ice picks, and first-aid supplies—then got his skis and poles. He clipped into his boots, stomping the heels into his skis. He poled to the base of the lift and boarded.

Snow wiped out the landscape as he rose into the cloud, barely seeing the lift-control shed at the top. He launched seamlessly, schussing down the slope to the narrow trail that led to the Angel Falls sign. The double-diamond symbol warned all but the most skilled to keep off.

There were tracks in the snow. Not from blades, footprints.

Heart hammering, Trevor paused. He took out his phone, grateful for the cell tower atop the mountain. He reached Jonah's chief officer and told him where he was and what he saw. They had reached the chief, but as with everything, timing was all.

He blinked through the falling snow, then followed the tracks, not into the basin, but along the ridge. Sidestepping up a rise, he negotiated the narrow spine where no trees grew. One misstep could be death.

As the sky brightened, he blinked through the clumps of falling snow. He had nearly navigated the entire crest. This end terrain was treacherous. Had Evan McCabe left a child where one gust of wind could send him onto rocky pinnacles below?

Trevor raised his face once more, and there, through the storm, a shape, huddled and dark. Wind swirled the snow, then it settled, drifting more lightly than before. A bluer tint came to the sky. Smaller flakes began to sparkle. The figure raised its head, transfixed by the sky.

Trevor moved to talking distance. "Where's the child, Evan?"

The young man turned from the sky to him, his ravaged face a testament to his torment.

"Where have you put him?"

"He is before you."

"Stop playing games."

Evan cocked his horned head. "You think this a game?"

"I want the child."

"You're too late. His candle has burned."

Trevor said, "You can stop this now. You hurt the others, but—"

"I hurt no one."

"You dropped that toddler in the street."

"Negligence put him there!" He gripped his head.

"You took pictures."

"To prove. To convict." A breeze billowed the cape.

"And Michaela?"

"You were supposed to save her."

"You put her in mortal danger."

"You should have taken to the air and borne her to earth."

Trevor shook his head. "I'm not an angel."

"I've seen you in my dreams."

"Your dreams are dark and twisted. An infant in a tree?"

"His needs were nothing to them. Careless custodians. How precarious the fates of their charges."

Trevor frowned. "So, you what, instructed them?"

"Yes! But there are so many. And I'm weary."

"Of making people suffer as you suffered?"

He hung his head. "You have ears but don't hear."

"Tell me where the child is."

He slowly spread his wings. "He is before you."

The realization sank in. The boy in the photo. "Evan…"

Eyes closed, he tipped off the edge, cape fluttering.

Trevor saw him hit the slope, roll and catch in a crook of the stone, then begin to slide. This was no intentional terrain, no groomed slope, but he aligned his skis and plunged down the white and rocky edge of the basin.

Stopping took every fiber of strength and skill, and even so, he crushed his hip against a stone. After throwing himself onto his chest, he grabbed Evan's wrist with a death grip.

The kid's eyes opened, torches of despair. "Let go."

"I'm not letting go."

"It's over."

It would be, if he fell.

"Stay with me, Evan." He stretched one arm back and tugged the zipper of his pack enough to grab rope. In the seconds he let go and looped the rope around Evan's head and shoulders, they both slid a foot. Trevor dug the splayed edges of his skis into the snow and tightened his grip.

"If what you said is true, you helped other kids. You woke people up."

Evan gave a slow blink. "Too many. Can't find them all." He groaned. "Ribs."

His adrenaline was spent, pain awakening. Shock would follow. Trevor couldn't reach his phone without letting go again. The pitch was too steep. He'd have to trust them to find him, not on the ski run as he'd said, but over the cliff.

Natalie said he made miracles, but he was only human. An ache opened up. God hadn't had the best from him for a long time. But only he had power over life and death. Trevor made his appeal.

Cold crept into him from the ground, sank bitter fingers from the air. The snow stopped falling, but as the sky cleared, the temperature dropped. Locked together, he held Evan's dulling eyes and demanded, "Stay with me."

"Hurts."

He said, "What happened to the boy in the swamp?"

"His mother heard him screaming."

"That's good. That was smart."

Evan's lids sank.

"Who else?"

They fluttered open.

"How many others?"

"So many. Everywhere. No one sees the danger."

"But you showed them."

His voice rasped. "I showed them."

Trevor started to speak, but his words were lost to the beat of helicopter blades. He jerked a look over his shoulder as it came close and hovered, and then he saw Whit descending with a stretcher on a cable.

Together they secured Evan McCabe into the stretcher. Looking up, he could see Jonah in the chopper, assisting the waiting paramedic as the cable drew the injured youth into the air. The cable returned to draw Whit up, and that would be capacity.

Whit's hollering was lost to the blades and engine, but he was obviously saying to wait for the helicopter to return. Yeah, not happening. Trevor gripped Whit's arm and grinned, then let go and leaned into the slope.

———

In the copter, Jonah shook his head as Trevor took off down the mountain. Well, if anyone knew how to do it…

"Chief?"

He turned to paramedic Charlie Boyer and noticed the kid trying to talk.

"For just a moment," Charlie said and lifted the oxygen mask.

Evan gasped. "Where is he?"

"You mean Trevor? He's taking his own route."

The kid's chest heaved. "He flew?"

Jonah half smiled. "You could say that."

Evan's eyes closed, his face settling. "I knew it."

Charlie replaced the mask. He and Jonah shared a look. As angels went, they could do worse than Trevor MacDaniel.

———

Trying to keep her mind off what Trevor might be doing, Natalie watched the archived footage she found hidden away. All the races, the interviews, the personal interest stories, and run after run after run. So much of his life on those slopes. Trevor was every bit the star Fleur described.

But that wasn't the man she knew. His confidence had been arrogance. His determination, cutthroat contention. The passion and commitment he now used to help people had been channeled into beating his competition and winning, winning, winning. It made a champion. But not a hero.

She had to wonder who he'd be if that banner hadn't torn free and ruined his knee. He'd called winning a drug, and, curled into the smushy leather recliner, she'd just observed the junkie. Maybe the family friend had done right to pull a shattered teenage Trevor back to the slopes.

Without a channel, the ferocity she saw might have been self-destructive. In a wholly different way, it still had.

Only in losing it all, had he found his core, his conscience, his capacity for good. Dominance did not become him. Deprivation tempered and refined, gave him beauty, nobility, the qualities a confused mind—and hers—had rendered angelic.

Smelling his cologne and his own musky sweat, she twisted around. "You're back!"

He pressed his hands on her shoulders, jutting his chin at the screen. "What are you doing?"

"Watching you."

"That's enough! Meet me in the Jacuzzi." His hands and face looked chapped. He limped badly.

Heart rushing, she pulled on a suit and went into the place he let himself be vulnerable. Moments later, bracing with his arms, he lowered himself into the opposite end. She prepared herself for awful news, another Michaela—or worse.

"Trevor?"

Eyes closed tight with pain, he leaned his head back and adjusted his leg.

"Please. Tell me."

"We got him."

"You found the child?"

His eyelids raised half mast. "Eleven years late."

"Evan?" She leaned into the churning water. "You got Evan?"

He spoke slowly, deemphasizing what she knew had taken heroic effort.

Looking into his face, the strongly hewn jaw, thick-lashed mossy eyes, tender mouth, pain-creased forehead, she said, "He could have gone to the authorities. When he got away, he could have gotten help from dozens, hundreds of people. But he stayed lost—until he found the one he trusted to bring him home."

Trevor swallowed. "I wish you hadn't watched that footage."

"Do you think I can't tell the difference between then and now?"

His lips parted, but he held the thought.

"You know what I see?"

He winced as though it might be painful.

"I see children who know their dad will never walk away. People who live because someone risks his life for them. Aches and injuries and wrinkles. Probably a replacement knee."

He had fixed on her as though she were the one with his wrist in a death grip on a snowy pitch. He shuddered as she pushed throught the water to him, took his face in her hands and kissed his eyes, between his brows, one defined cheekbone, and his mouth. "I imagine our life, Trevor." She rested her hand on his heart. "And I want it."

———

Charging after Cody, he'd though of nothing but snatching the child from a formidable foe, cheating death of one more victim. His need to protect pitted against the animal's primal instincts. If Ellis entered his mind, he wasn't aware of it. None of Nattie's family on the trail registered, not even she. He'd been put there for one thing—to save Cody's life.

Evan sought him out—God only knew why. His thought stalled. God *knew* why.

Maybe he was the besieged hero standing between darkness and innocence. Was that so bad? Maybe there were miracles, and mere men could participate. That he could love was a miracle. That Natalie loved him, even greater. Maybe what seemed unredeemable could be forgiven, if he forgave himself.

She'd been telling him that one way or another since they met.

Water dripped from his hands as he pulled her into his arms. "Well, if that's what you want..."

She snuggled in, reading as much, he was sure, from the rasp in his voice and the throb of his pulse as his face would have told her. "But let's be clear. If there's an angel here, it's you, Nat."

"Keep telling yourself," she murmured. Then laughed.

Readers Guide

1. With her gift, Natalie is able to transfer the faces and emotions of people she sees to a sculpture with uncanny accuracy and insight. How do these sculptures affect the people who see them? Natalie says she sees people as God sees them. Do you agree with her? What would Natalie see if she looked at you?

2. Throughout the book, Trevor is referred to as a hero by everyone but himself. How does Trevor see himself? What aspects of his personality and lifestyle are unherolike? How do these aspects affect his heroism?

3. Natalie has spent much of her life set apart from other people because of her eidetic memory. How does that change when she moves to Redford? How do the events of *Indelible* change Natalie and her outlook on life?

4. Each of Evan's sections begins with lines from *Paradise Lost,* and his copy of the book is his only possession. Why do you think Evan identifies with this story? Who is he identifying with? What part does Trevor play in Evan's personal *Paradise Lost*? Do Evan and Trevor fulfill their roles? How does the story of *Paradise Lost* fit with the book's overall themes?

5. Natalie loses her eidetic memory after a head injury. Despite being almost a handicap throughout her life, she mourns its loss. Why? How does she cope with this change? Do you think her memory comes back, or do you think its absence is permanent? If the latter, how will this affect the other aspects of her life, such as her art?

6. For most of the book, Evan's motivations are shrouded in mystery. What did he intend to achieve by endangering those children? What were his plans for Trevor? How do you think Evan's story will end?

7. What effect does Fleur's friendship have on Natalie? What effect does she have on Evan? How much of this stems from her blindness, and how much simply from who she is?

8. What part does Trevor's past—specifically, his brother's death—play in his current life? What part does it play in the lives of Sara and Whit? How does that one event color the decisions Trevor makes today? Similarly, how does Jonah's past influence the choices he makes?

9. Trevor's relationship with Whit and Sara is complicated. How would you describe it? How did you feel about Sara's part in the relationship in particular? What would you do in Trevor's place? In Sara's? In Whit's?

10. Because of his past as an abused child and an alcoholic, Jonah is terrified of becoming a father. Is his fear legitimate? How do you think he can overcome these fears in fatherhood?

Acknowledgments

Thanks to those who made this book better than I could have alone: Jim and Jessica Heitzmann, David Ladd, Jane Francis, and Kelly McMullen. Thanks to Karen Mohler for prayers. And thanks to my stellar agent, Frank Weimann, and the editorial and production staff at WaterBrook Multnomah / Random House.

About the Author

Kristen is the best-selling author of two historical series and ten contemporary romantic and psychological suspense novels including *The Still of Night*, nominated for the Colorado Book Award; *The Tender Vine*, a Christy Award finalist; and Christy Award–winning *Secrets*. She lives in Colorado with her husband, Jim, and sundry family members and pets.

A suspenseful tale of separation, longing, and unity.

KRISTEN HEITZMANN

INDIVISIBLE

A NOVEL

Police chief Jonah Westfall can't penetrate every Redford secret.
He has no idea of the pain that has entered his quiet town, a pain
fueled by love and a guilt teetering on the edge of madness.